FINAL RECKONING

By Derek Blount

For information, contact Happy Prince Media, LLC at info@happyprincemedia.com.

Visit us on the Web:
happyprincemedia.com
derekblount.com

FIRST EDITION

Print ISBN 978-0-9967006-5-8

E-book ASIN B08NLCPZLZ

For Bethany.

Always.

PROLOGUE

THE CAR HAD BARELY COME TO A STOP when Stephanie Espinosa opened her door and touched high heel to parking lot pavement.

"Excited, honey?"

Stephanie paused, took a calming breath and smiled at her mother.

"I really am."

The smile was fake, but the sentiment was honest. There was some sense of irony to Stephanie that she was fulfilling a childhood dream at an age she no longer associated with childhood, but the incongruity was overshadowed by an intense feeling of serendipity. At nineteen-going-on-eternity, her new dream would be realized in tandem with the old one. It was going to be perfect.

She grabbed her oversized purse from the floorboard, grunting only a little at the weight, and closed the passenger door. Her mother walked around the vehicle and pressed the button on the small remote before dropping it into her own purse. The blinkers flashed twice in response. It was a nice car. And new.

The pair walked toward the escalator away from the sedan whose classic emblem allowed them to park on the exclusive top level of the underground parking garage instead of descending to its depths. It was a luxury to which Stephanie would never become accustomed. Her father had lived the hard working, hand-to-mouth existence of a struggling small business owner for her entire youth, but the construction boom in Dallas changed all that. He had signed three significant contracts the year before and five this year. Big business, more employees, and finally some real money as a reward and a nice car for his wife to show it.

Stephanie might have wished the money had come sooner—perhaps when she was actually living at home—but the timing worked well in a more important way. She was attending Texas State College without having to take out student loans, and she wasn't having to work while there.

She didn't care about the loans, but she was grateful for the freedom from work. If she hadn't had the time to broaden her studies, to expand her mind, then she would have remained trapped in her former meaningless existence.

The two ladies reached the top of the escalator and emerged into the elegant park in front of the massive structure. Stephanie took it in. The lush green of the manicured lawns surrounding the entrance. The marble fountains. The immense walls of glass housing the deep red interior of the Dallas Opera House. It was breathtaking.

"It's really something, huh?" her mom enquired.

"Yep. It really is."

They strode to the front doors and merged with the small crowd attempting to enter. It took only a moment. This wasn't like going to a basketball or baseball game. No single file cattle lines. No metal detectors. This was classy.

Stephanie shrugged the weight of her oversized purse higher onto her shoulder. The motion produced only minor clinking sounds.

Once inside the building, she immediately noticed her little girl dream was not restricted to her own generation. In the very grown-up lobby of the very adult and serious building bounded girls of all ages, a high percentage outfitted in the bright yellow ball gowns of the princess whose story they had come to see. They waited in line with their parents—mostly moms—to purchase merchandise or a red rose of their very own.

They had all seen the movie, the animated classic or the reimagined film with live actors, and now you could sense the anticipation of these little princesses anxious to witness the stage version and perhaps even sing along to the songs whose lyrics had been inscribed to memory.

That had been Stephanie from her earliest recollection. But there had never been the money for tickets. Not then.

But this was now, and she had a ticket in her hand. Level five. The Grand Tier.

She glanced at her watch then pulled her mother by the arm toward the elevator. When her mom had called to surprise her and ask if she could come home for a couple of days to see a performance of the touring musical while it was in town, everything had clicked into place for Stephanie. No more waiting. This was it.

She had accepted and asked if she could pick the tickets herself. Her mom had been fine with it. Stephanie found the perfect seats available for a Wednesday evening performance.

Serendipity.

They rode the elevator to the top with two princesses, an eager mother, a bored-looking father and a couple who appeared to be on a date based on the casual arm-touching and look-then-look-away eye gazing. The doors opened and the princesses led the pack to the Grand Tier entrance guarded by a friendly usher checking tickets and offering direction.

As she entered the theatre and headed toward the front row, Stephanie fought a brief wave of vertigo. Walking down the steps in the aisle, with gravity pulling you toward a sheer drop-off of vast proportions, was unnatural. It reminded her of going to the Grand Canyon, the rare childhood family vacation, and walking to the edge. Scary. Exciting.

Reaching the base of the short stairway, she extended her fingers to the railing and trailed them along the dark walnut board. The railing was wide and flat, at least eight inches across. It gave a nice sense of separation and safety from the cavern of empty space beyond.

It was perfect.

She didn't allow herself to look at the stage. Not yet. She walked to their assigned seats, the fingertips of one hand dragging along the railing while her other arm kept her purse secure against her side so she wouldn't bump into the theatergoers already seated.

Finally reaching her seat, she turned and faced the stage. It was beautiful. The curtain was down but a gossamer screen in front had an image projected on it. A single rose.

In the immense space between her seat and the stage, the opera house chandelier shone brightly. Three hundred individual glowing LED rods of various lengths cascaded vertically from the ceiling like the world's most anorexic and technologically advanced stalactite formation. The colors within the rods of the chandelier shifted hues in a hypnotic fashion.

The first notes of a wistful refrain emanated from the orchestra pit and reverberated through the performance hall as the chandelier rods began to ascend into the ceiling.

Stephanie took the opportunity to peer over the railing. It was a long way down. The Grand Tier was akin to watching a performance from the roof of a five-story building. It wrapped like a horseshoe around the performance hall. Below it were three more tiered horseshoe seating arrangements followed by the ground floor Orchestra Level where rows upon rows of seats were uniform with the stage. Those seats were more expensive than the nosebleed section, but Stephanie didn't care. She had picked this exact spot for a reason.

She was relieved to confirm there were no spotlights affixed below her railing. She had noticed them when they were walking in and had chastised herself for not having thought about it. You never realize how big a performance hall spotlight is until you're standing within a couple of feet of one. They're huge. They wouldn't affect your view of the performance since they sit below the railing, but she was still grateful the center portion of the Grand Tier was free from them. Good fortune.

She placed her bag on the floor with some relief, eased into her seat and felt her mother's hand on her arm. She was trying to make small talk. Ask her questions. Stephanie ignored her and watched the chandelier complete its ascension into the ceiling as the orchestra played louder and the lights dimmed. Only the tip of each chandelier rod was now visible. The effect was a starry night sky twinkling above the darkened performance hall. Her mother sank back into her own seat and tucked her hands into her lap.

The music shifted to the dreamy movement that introduced the fantasy world about to inhabit the stage. As the narrator's deep voice began to tell the story, Stephanie heard soft crying nearby. Joy and sadness and sentimentality all around her, and the performance had yet to truly begin. It had been months since Stephanie had shed a tear—something that would have seemed remarkable if she had thought about it—but right then, for just a moment, when the music swelled, she too felt something. A twinge in her stomach. She saw a petal fall from the projected rose on the screen. She shifted in her seat and her heel kicked her purse. A clink.

The moment passed.

The narrator continued his tale of sadness. The prince's fate was tied to the rose, and that fate was all but certain, for who could ever learn to love a beast?

A smile almost touched Stephanie's lips. *Who indeed?*

She lifted her purse from the floor and placed it in her lap. It was almost time. Destiny.

Stephanie unzipped the bag. Another fruit of her father's labor, her mother had been able to purchase new cutlery for her kitchen. The fancy kind of knives from Germany that aren't available at Walmart. Butcher knife. Carving knife. Boning knife. Paring knife. Bread knife. Cleaver. And a full complement of steak knives. Stephanie's purse was heavy for a reason.

She set the bag on top of the railing and held it with both hands. Not yet.

She wondered who was sitting in the orchestra seats five levels below. She hadn't paid attention when she glanced down earlier. Any princesses?

The screen lifted from the stage. Curtain wide open. The lights turned bright. A bustling village with bustling villagers sprang to life in time with uplifting music. They were bidding each other good morning. The happiest song of Stephanie's childhood.

She lowered her hands to the base of the purse, gripped it tightly and flipped it over, emptying the contents as she leaned forward and swung it back and forth over the railing. When the last knife had fallen, she let the purse drop as well.

The screaming erupted from below as Stephanie rose from her seat and climbed onto the railing. The wide walnut board was perfect. She had no problems balancing as she stood erect and faced the seats of the Grand Tier, her back to the stage where the music still played. For now.

Stephanie's mother reached for her. Even in the dark, she could see the whites of her mother's wide eyes.

"Steph! What are you—"

Stephanie extended her arms straight to either side. Her mother wouldn't understand. Not yet. But she would soon. At the Reckoning.

The hysteria below reached the orchestra. The music wavered into an uneven termination. Notes of joy overpowered by screams of terror.

Stephanie looked at her mother—beyond her mother—and spoke her last words.

"I am the first."

She didn't jump, merely allowed herself to fall backward, arms still extended.

The descent was quick. Just before impact, Stephanie's lips parted in a genuine smile.

CHAPTER 1

TRISH O'BRIEN SAT CROSS-LEGGED on her bed. Her laptop lay closed on the pillow. Her textbooks sat unopened on the desk. The television was off. No music played. Sunlight streaming through the narrow window provided the only illumination.

She listened to the silence and stared at the unoccupied bed on the other side of the dorm room. It was still made. Sheets. Bedspread. One teddy bear. Two brightly colored decorative pillows plus a specialty throw pillow upon which a photo had been printed of a smiling couple, one half of which was now dead.

Stephanie's clothes were still in the closet. Her pajamas were still in the built-in drawers under the bed. Her toothbrush was still in the cup by the bathroom sink.

Trish pulled on the gold chain around her neck until the cross emerged from her shirt. It was flat, gold and three inches long. She rubbed it between her thumb and forefinger, alternating top-to-bottom then side-to-side, what she always did in times of stress.

There were too many questions.

Little questions like what would happen to Stephanie's stuff? The clothes and bedspread and toothbrush? Would Stephanie's parents come to collect it all or would it be ignored in their grief?

Trish knew them but not well. It was her second year to room with Stephanie. The prior year, when she and Stephanie were both freshmen, the Espinosas had visited twice. Both times they were kind enough to invite Trish to join them for dinner. They seemed like nice people.

What were they thinking now? How could they possibly deal with the coming days?

Trish hadn't seen them this year. They were only six weeks into TSC's fall semester. It had been Stephanie's first time to go home to Dallas since the prior spring. She had stayed at school over the summer to take additional courses. Trish had returned to New York to spend time with her mom.

Had something happened with Steph over the summer?

Leading to another nagging question—had Stephanie seemed different this semester than their freshman year?

Yeah. When Trish thought about it, she did seem different.

But different how? And well beyond how, different *why*?

That was the biggest question of all. Why? That word plagued Trish. She and Stephanie were friends. She knew her. You don't live with a girl that long, see her study, see her put on her makeup, console her as she cries about a boy or a poor midterm score, shop for groceries with her, listen to her make out in the dark with her boyfriend while you pretend to be asleep, or walk halfway across campus to deliver an emergency tampon to the ladies room of the student union without *knowing* her. Without being real friends.

What happened at the Dallas Opera House...that wasn't Stephanie. Not the Stephanie she knew.

So *why*?

Someone doesn't just wake up one day and decide to kill herself, much less drop an arsenal of kitchen cutlery onto innocent people attending a musical. *That doesn't happen.*

Something changed Stephanie. Something happened that created a poisonous spore in her mind, and that spore germinated into some kind of mental cancer that overtook her friend.

Could it have been actual cancer? A brain tumor? Would they do an autopsy on Stephanie? Cut her friend open on a cold metal table? Would her parents want that?

Trish sniffed absentmindedly and only then realized she was crying again. She wiped her eyes, surprised there were any tears left.

She tucked the cross back into her shirt then put her hand on the laptop. She didn't open it. She had had enough. No more.

Trish recognized the incongruity. Honesty with herself was second nature. You couldn't pursue journalism if you weren't willing to look objectively at everything and everyone, including yourself, so she understood shunning the screen was the opposite of what she should want to do. She was part of the permanently connected generation. She didn't get the news about Stephanie last night from a friend or a classmate or even from Stephanie's parents reaching out to her. She learned about the "Dallas Opera House Massacre" through a news-alert. Then she saw footage. Within an hour after the deaths had taken place, YouTube had more than twenty different uploads from audience members in attendance that night whose first reaction to the horror was to whip out their phones and start recording.

Trish didn't want to see any more of those videos. She could hear Stephanie's mother screaming her daughter's name in one. Another had managed a shaky close-up of Stephanie's body. That was when Trish closed the laptop.

She didn't want to look at any of her social media sites. Zero desire to read what comments and posts the campus cadre felt were clever enough or heartfelt enough to share with the universe.

She had left her phone turned on. If anyone actually called to talk to her, she would answer. Not a single person had. Her phone had dinged a steady stream of message alerts, but no voice calls.

Trish understood. Text was easy. Social media was easy. You posted something meaningful but avoided the uncomfortable prospect of having to speak with someone in the midst of loss. Perhaps it was being polite, trying to avoid interrupting whatever things might be happening the day after a roommate traverses the murder-suicide path. Maybe. But excuses of any type are universal when people want to avoid the distasteful.

The more likely scenario was that Trish didn't have any phone-level friends. Certainly no knock-on-the-door-to-see-you-in-person-level friends. Just text-level.

Once upon a time, she had lots of friends—many in the phone-tier—but that was when she lived in New York. And before the bad stuff. This wasn't the first time Trish's life had been upended by death. But Texas had seemed so far removed from New York. An escape. When Trish arrived at college in Abramsville last year, she had been just friendly enough. No more. And the lack of anything beyond text-level friends proved it.

No phone call from Andrew was a surprise though.

Trish again turned her gaze to the picture on Stephanie's throw pillow. The couple was cheek-to-cheek, and Andrew's smile was as big as Stephanie's. What was he thinking now?

Trish uncoiled her legs and put her feet on the floor. She walked to the door but stopped in front of the full-length mirror affixed to the back of it. Her green eyes were bloodshot. No makeup. Her hair was tangled in a red and auburn mess that hung to her shoulders.

So what? She thought as she opened the door.

She grabbed a rubber band from the catch-all basket Stephanie had hung below the light switch. Ponytail would do. She needed answers.

CHAPTER 2

TRISH FOUND HIM IN THE QUAD. Andrew Kraft was sitting on a bench under the shade of a massive oak tree, a spot Trish knew he and Stephanie had frequented for studying together when the weather was nice. He was alone, something Trish would have thought strange given the circumstances but wasn't she alone, too? He had a textbook open on his lap but glanced up on her approach.

"Hey," Trish said as she covered the final distance between them.

"Hey," he replied. His eyes were glassy but not dull. He made no motion to get up. There was no evidence of a forthcoming hug or any other form of mutual consolation. Trish guessed all people reacted differently in times of grief and stress.

"Mind if I sit?"

"Help yourself," he said as he moved his backpack from the bench and placed it on the ground.

"How're you doing?" Trish asked, lowering herself to the painted wood.

"I dunno. Weird day," he ran his hand through disheveled brown hair. "I have a headache."

"Yeah. Weird and awful. How could..." she let the thought die on her lips. "Andrew, are you sitting out here studying?"

"Yep."

"How can you study right now?"

Andrew snapped the book shut. The noise made Trish jump.

"What am I supposed to be doing, Trish? I still have exams, and bio-chem is going to kick my ass if I don't study. They're not going to call off the test, are they? They're not going to pat me on the head and give me an 'A' because Steph killed herself."

Trish put her hand on his shoulder. "I'm sorry, Andrew. I didn't mean...look, I don't know what to do either. It just doesn't make sense. For Steph to do that. How could she? *Why* would she?"

"I don't know, Trish. She sure as hell didn't tell me ahead of time."

"Did she say anything or do anything leading up to it? Did you notice anything weird about her?"

"Besides the knife-dumping swan dive?"

Trish bit her tongue against an immediate retaliation. Bit it hard enough to hurt. *People react differently,* she reminded herself. *Give him room.*

"What she did was terrible. I know that. But she couldn't have wanted to do it. It was Stephanie. She would never..."

"But she did. And you don't do something like that without planning it. She wanted to do it, exactly like that."

"Why?!" Trish raised her voice more than she intended. Two students on the sidewalk stopped their conversation to glance over, but they continued walking.

Trish took a calming breath. "We need to know why."

"Really? If you figure it out, is that going to change what happened?"

"No. It won't."

"I've been dating Steph for almost nine months. It's the longest relationship with a girl I've ever had. And you know what? I don't think I care why she did it because in the end, it's not going to matter. It's done. All we have now is the aftermath and moving on."

"That's cold, Andrew." Tears formed in Trish's eyes, but she blinked them back. "We owe it to her."

"Owe her what? Listen to me. Somebody didn't do this to Steph. She did it to herself, and to those people at the musical, and to me and to you. Nothing is owed to her. Nothing."

Trish stood. She couldn't believe what she was hearing.

"I'm going to walk away now. I don't know who you are."

Andrew dropped the textbook onto the bench and rose to face her.

"Wait," he blinked twice, his eyes less glassy then before. "I'm sorry, Trish. I'm pissed off, I guess, I don't know what I am, but I don't mean to take it out on you."

Different people react in different ways, she reminded herself again. *Don't meet anger with anger.*

"It's okay. I get it. Maybe we can talk another time."

"Sure," Andrew nodded. "Are you going to the service tonight?"

"Huh?"

"The special service. Candlelight vigil sort of thing the church is doing. Everyone is meeting at the bonfire field. Pastor Berry is going to lead us."

"You know I don't do church, Andrew."

"Yeah, Steph told me you'd always turn her down, but church meant something to *her*. The best thing you can do for Steph now is to pray for her." He paused. "It's the only thing at this point."

"I'll think about it," Trish sighed as she turned from Andrew. In only a few steps, the coolness of the oak's shade shifted to warm sunlight on her shoulders. She squinted at the brightness as she continued down the sidewalk and out of the quad.

She *was* going to think about it, and those thoughts would turn to action with rippling consequences in only a few hours.

CHAPTER 3

TRISH PUSHED HER HANDS into the pockets of her jacket as she walked. The brisk wind made the fall evening chillier than she had expected. Despite having experienced it last year, she had not yet grown accustomed to the indecisive weather in Texas. Fall and spring were particularly notorious with temperatures often undulating by more than thirty degrees in a given week.

Then again, she had spent the day ruminating on her roommate's death. *Unexpected* had defined her life the past twenty-four hours. Screw the weather.

Walking across campus to attend a church service certainly fit the unexpected theme. Even if it was a candlelight vigil and not a traditional service, church was church and here she was, marching right into it.

A sour air bubble rose from her esophagus and exited her mouth in an audible burp. Not very ladylike. Screw that, too. She didn't break stride.

Trish didn't consider herself to be much of a drinker, but today was just a "screw that" day all around. She and Stephanie had a bottle of peach schnapps tucked into the back of Stephanie's pajama drawer. They had bought it last year—technically had given the money to a legal-aged classmate who had made the purchase on their behalf—and had celebrated the completion of spring midterms with a couple of Sprite-mixers.

When Steph became more involved in the church, the drinking ended, but the bottle stayed, and Trish had helped herself to the remainder of it this afternoon. Only one can of Sprite in the tiny refrigerator. That worked okay for her first two drinks. The next four went down just fine without the soda.

A follow-up bubble chipmunked Trish's cheeks till she puckered her lips and blew the air out slowly. The aftermath left an acidic peach taste that was fifty shades of unpleasant. She needed gum. She had none. Screw this whole mess.

She rounded the administration building and the glow of the bonfire field appeared just beyond the faculty parking lot.

The glow wasn't from the bonfire itself. In fact, even if the church had lit a fire for this special event, that wouldn't be the bonfire anyway. The bonfire, after all, was *The Bonfire*. Mandatory capitalization. A Texas State College tradition since the dawn of time—along with about a hundred other traditions that Trish sometimes lost track of—and the bonfire wouldn't take place for another eight days when the TSC Pioneers football team played the annual homecoming game against the hated Woodson State University Bulldogs. The outcome of that game could be added to the list of things Trish now didn't give a rip about.

The bonfire field's present glow was from the commercial-grade light clusters set at each corner of the field, reminiscent of what you'd find illuminating a night game at an outdoor sports arena except these lights were portable and only lived on the bonfire field a month out of the year, providing ample lighting for students if they needed to work on constructing the tower of logs into the wee hours of the night.

Right now, the bonfire site was devoid of any construction activity. The tower itself was just beginning to take shape. At this stage, the field was still largely a repository for dead trees great and small, largely stripped of their branches and stacked in neat rows along the perimeter according to size. The largest of the logs had already been utilized to form the base level of the bonfire, a massive number of logs standing upright and bound tightly together. With that base level in place, the final construction phase was set to begin. Starting tomorrow, the student crew would go full-bore, working day and night for the final week until the stacked logs would resemble a tiered wedding cake taller than several of the buildings on campus. On the final day, a big doghouse with "WSU Bulldogs" spray-painted on the side would be lifted by a crane to the very top of the bonfire.

Hooray, sports.

As she neared the field, the wind shifted and blew directly into her face. Trish caught the rich aroma of burning wood. She had been wrong. There must be a fire after all. She just couldn't see it yet due to the mass of people, a crowd much larger than she had expected.

Given the circumstances of Stephanie's death—that she hadn't been tragically killed in a car accident or violent crime but that she had been the perpetrator of such violence—Trish anticipated only a handful of attendees at the candlelight vigil. To her surprise, there were at least fifty students on the field. Perhaps twice that number since she couldn't tell how deep the crowd went. As the individuals making up the congregation shifted or swayed in the cool air, she began to see flames in the cracks between their silhouettes.

The moment she stepped up the curb and her feet hit the grass of the field, she heard his voice. The preacher. He wasn't using a microphone, but his voice boomed loud and strong.

"Brothers and sisters, I say it every week. Bad things happen! The world is a bad place and bad things are going to happen."

Trish was taken aback at how clear his voice was. She hadn't heard a word approaching from the parking lot. It was almost as if his voice carried perfectly with no diminishment right to the edge of the bonfire field and then just stopped at the curb.

Now that she was on the grass, she could hear every word.

"This world is going to keep being a bad place. It's full of sin. Greed. Malice. Selfishness. Only sin doesn't go by those words out in the world, does it?"

The murmur of the crowd seemed to indicate that no, it does not.

Trish began making her way through the outer circle, pushing toward the flames. She met no resistance. The congregation was accommodating. She glanced at faces but saw no friends. An echoed reminder of her lack of social network. She saw no uncontrollable tears or raw emotion, but the faces all seemed to be attuned to the preacher's voice.

"No! It's not greed. It's *achievement* to get all those material possessions that Madison Avenue convinces you that you need. It's not malice. It's *justice* when you mete out punishment to someone who's coming between you and what you want."

Trish pushed her way further to the center and saw him for the first time.

The preacher was tall and describing him as thin would be an understatement. He'd need a year's worth of double-cheeseburgers and power lifting to attain the bulky physique of a scarecrow. Shadow and light from the bonfire played over his angular face. Probably in his early thirties, he was neither handsome nor ugly, but that in no way made him forgettable. Not with that voice.

"It's not selfishness. No, it's *empowerment*. Knowing what you deserve and having no qualms about taking it. That's not sin. It's strength!"

The preacher's name was Christian Berry. Trish knew because she had heard it a thousand times from Stephanie. Pastor Berry had changed her life. Opened her mind. Attending his church had saved Stephanie from herself.

"That's what the world wants you to believe, brothers and sisters. Don't listen! There is such a thing as sin, and there is only one way to save yourselves from it. To forsake the world and to belong to something greater. That is your calling. That is your redemption!"

As Trish neared the center of the crowd, she saw another light. This one was mounted above a video camera. Trish could see the top of the news van parked in the field just beyond the mass of people. A satellite dish rested on a pole that rose ten feet from the roof of the van. The cameraman maintained a half-lunge, trying to capture the perfect angle of Pastor Berry. Probably keeping the bonfire flames just inside the camera frame for dramatic effect.

If Pastor Berry noticed the camera, you couldn't tell. He never looked at it. He was speaking to the people who were present, not those tuning in on television.

"What happened to our dear sister is the result of the evil in this world. She lost her way."

Trish sidestepped between two more students. The scent of smoke was stronger. She was nearing the center. Closer to the preacher. She saw Andrew. He was standing to one side of Pastor Berry, a solemn look on his face as he nodded his head in time with the preacher's words.

Standing to the other side of the pastor was another student, taller than the preacher with a build that suggested he did nothing *but* eat protein and lift weights. Trish recognized him, too. Slade Stone. Everyone on campus knew Slade, or at least knew of him. He had been a national story the past spring. The kind of story that becomes a cautionary tale for gifted athletes who coaches want to scare straight. He wore the same solemn expression as Andrew though Slade's face somehow gave the solemnity a sense of menace as well. His eyes appeared black in the darkness. They were set a little too far apart on either side of his flat nose. When viewed in combination with the overly large muscles flaring from his neck, Slade had the appearance of a cobra.

"Stephanie did something terrible," the preacher continued. "She let the devil inside! She became one with the world and forsook a greater belonging."

The students closest to the bonfire were less accommodating. Trish had to push with her elbow and shoulder to squeeze past them. She didn't bother saying "excuse me."

Once she was through, she saw there was a reporter next to the cameraman. She wore a beige trench coat clearly intended to make her appear professional. She held a wireless microphone at waist level, it bobbed up and down. Trish could tell the reporter's patience with the sermon was waning. She was ready for her own camera time.

"Our sister is no longer with us," the preacher's eyes shifted down. He was no longer looking into the eyes of the assembly. He was staring into the flames. "She has gone where we cannot help her."

Trish understood the implication. She glanced to Andrew, wondering what his reaction would be. His eyebrows knit and his expression hardened. No tears. He said earlier that he was pissed off. The feeling clearly hadn't passed.

"I don't know why Stephanie did what she did," Pastor Berry spoke in a softer voice. It no longer boomed. The cameraman took a step forward, capturing the dramatic monologue. "But I do know we must use her actions as a lesson. We must learn from her failings, brothers and sisters."

Smoke wafted up and stung Trish's eyes. Heat radiating from the bonfire bathed her cheeks. The preacher was directly across from her, on the other side of the flames.

"There is only one hope, my friends. One hope and that hope can be described in one word. Do you know what that word is?"

"Bullshit."

Trish didn't shout it, but she gave the word plenty of oomph. Enough so everyone in the circle heard it. Enough to elicit a gasp from the girl standing next to her. Enough to turn the head of the reporter. Enough for the cameraman to pivot her direction, camera rolling.

And enough to make the preacher pause.

"That is *not* the word the good book uses."

CHAPTER 4

"**I** DON'T GIVE A DAMN about your good book."

Trish recognized the sound of her own voice but was surprised to hear it. She hadn't meant to speak. Public confrontation—public speaking period—was not in her comfort zone. And yet, the words continued to come.

"I don't give a damn what it says, and I don't give a damn what you say. Total lack of damns."

As the last word passed her lips, it was accompanied by another foul-tasting burp. She tried to bite it back with compressed lips, but that just made the acrid after-schnapps fumes move into her nose.

"You are upset, sister," Pastor Berry said. His voice maintained the same calm as before. He was unperturbed. He raised his hands—palms facing her in a placating manner—and offered a gentle smile. "Of course, you're upset. We all are. This has been a terrible, terrible tragedy. That's why we must come together. It's why we are here now."

"More bullshit." Trish took a step toward the preacher, fully feeling the heat generated by the small bonfire. The flames danced between them. The cameraman kept focus on her. The reporter was holding her breath. Trish again surprised herself with her screw-it-all mentality.

"Endless bullshit. That's what you're serving. You're not here for Steph. She's dead. There's nothing you can say that will change that. You're not here for her." Trish poked her finger toward the preacher. A flame licked the bottom of her hand. "You're here for *you*."

The cameraman swiveled to capture the preacher's reaction. This was gold.

The soft smile was frozen on Pastor Berry's lips, his expression remained unchanged, but for just a moment, something flashed in his eyes. Rage. Trish swallowed and took a slight step backward, away from the flames, but she kept her hand raised toward him. She was still pointing. She tensed the muscles in her arm so her finger wouldn't shake.

"That's not it at all, sister," he said. His eyes returned to the equilibrium of a stoic gaze. "In times like these, the best we can do is come together to support one another, to pray and to worship. It's what Stephanie would have wanted."

"Don't you dare!" Spittle flew from Trish's lips. "Don't you dare say what she would have wanted! You don't have the right!"

Though the pastor was maintaining his calm, the same was not true of Slade. His lips screwed up in anger. The nostrils flared under his flat nose. His dark eyes were intense. He took a step toward the fire, but Pastor Berry subtly placed his hand on Slade's forearm. Gentle restraint. Slade retracted his step, but the anger remained on his face.

"Perhaps now is not the best time, young lady." Pastor Berry sounded reasonable. Understanding. It pissed Trish off more.

"I'm sorry. Is this not convenient for you?"

Andrew moved from the pastor's side and began making his way around the bonfire toward Trish. Unlike Slade, there was no anger in his eyes. Pastor Berry did nothing to restrain him.

"I'm merely trying to think of all our brothers and sisters gathered here. They, too, are upset. I must minister to the needs of the many at present, but I can feel your suffering, child. Let's meet together, you and I, and find our way to a better place."

"Are you fucking kidding me? Stop pretending! If you cared about Steph, you wouldn't be out here in this...kumbaya...circle jerk! You'd be asking yourself why. You'd be trying to get to the bottom of why she's dead. But that doesn't sell tickets to your church, does it?"

Andrew reached Trish and placed his arm around her shoulders. He put his other hand on top of Trish's forearm, gently pushing her trembling hand down to her waist.

"Our church has no tickets. The price of admission is an open heart. Stephanie was one of us. None of us will ever understand why she did what she did, why she fell away. To dwell on that question is to only invite more pain into your heart."

Trish felt Andrew's arm squeeze her closer. He took a step back, leading her along with him. Leading her away. Trish realized she had started to cry, but she didn't know when.

She let herself take two steps with him, but just as he began to rotate her shoulders, to point her away from the bonfire and back to her dorm, Trish planted her feet and turned to face the preacher.

"You may not care, but I do, and my heart isn't going to hurt any worse. Bring that shit on. I will find out what happened because she was my friend. I will find out the truth because I loved her."

Trish staggered back a step. Andrew's firm arm helped her regain balance. Her head was swimming. Screw the peach schnapps.

"You can all go to hell," she mumbled the words and put one foot in front of the other toward her dorm room. Andrew remained with her each step of the way.

Behind her, she could hear the strong voice of the pastor begin again. "Do not judge her, friends. We must pray for her just as we pray for each other."

Trish wondered if she could make it to her dorm bathroom before throwing up.

CHAPTER 5

THE ROOM WAS DARK when Trish awoke. She was lying on her side, curled into a fetal position. Her head was still swimming. She reached toward the nightstand, feeling for her cell phone to check the time. Her hand encountered only a pen and an empty Sprite can that dropped to the floor when her fingers brushed against it.

A low rumble of distant thunder accompanied the sound of rain pattering her window. When did that start?

Trish tried to recount the past few hours, but the events blurred. It definitely wasn't raining when she and Andrew got back to her dorm. He had helped her all the way into her room. He hadn't been happy with her actions at the church thing.

Oh yeah, the church thing.

Shit.

Trish closed her eyes at the fuzzy memory. She remembered being mad. At the preacher guy. At everyone who was there. At herself.

And Andrew was mad at her. She remembered that. But she had fallen asleep.

Another roll of thunder. Deep and long.

Sleep was good. She needed sleep. She also needed to take four Advil and drink a quart of water or tomorrow morning would be very bad, but doing those things would take so much effort. She needed sleep more. She needed to stay right here in bed. Maybe forever. At least until her head felt the right size again.

She gradually abandoned the fetal position and extended her legs. Sleep was the right thing.

Her feet pushed into something hard and heavy on her bed. She pushed harder, trying to knock it to the floor so she could stretch all the way out. No luck.

"You're awake."

Trish's eyes snapped all the way open.

"Andrew?"

"No."

Trish pulled her feet up, away from the man sitting on her bed.

A flash of lightning illuminated the room for a split second. Long enough for her to see a massive, shadowed form.

Thunder cracked as her bleary mind—clearing much faster than she would have thought possible—recognized the unmistakable silhouette.

"Slade?"

"Don't say my name. Don't say anything. You'll just make it worse."

"What are you doing in here? Get out of my room."

"You don't listen, do you?" He remained motionless. In the darkness, Trish couldn't tell if he was even looking at her. "That means you're either stupid or deaf. I know you're not deaf, so I guess you're just stupid, Trish."

He knew her name. They had never even spoken before. But he was here. *Here.* A coldness rippled through Trish's body. This was bad.

"Get out of my room, Slade."

She felt his body shift. She couldn't see him, but she knew he was facing her now.

"You didn't listen before, but you will listen now. You will not move. You will not scream. If you do, things will be much, much worse for you."

Trish wanted to cry out for help. Tried to calculate how long she could scream before he choked her. A second? Two? Would that be long enough for someone to hear? For someone to rescue her? Where was her damn phone?

"You don't want to do this, Slade."

"I told you not to say my name. I told you not to talk. You are so stupid."

Slade sighed. The bed moved with him. She could smell his faint, sour body odor.

"What you did tonight. Coming out to the service and saying those things. You embarrassed him. And he was trying to do something good."

"I didn't mean to…"

"Shut up. Just shut up. Pastor Berry is a great man. He didn't have to arrange a service for that whore, but he did it anyway. Because he wants to help. And you show up and ruin everything."

Trish bristled at the word "whore" but said nothing.

"You don't believe in what we do. I don't care. I don't want to save your soul. Hell is where you deserve to be after what you did tonight." He paused, choking down rage. "There were TV cameras there, Trish. You embarrassed him on fucking television."

Trish tried to push herself away from him, one quiet inch at a time, but the mattress betrayed her.

"I told you not to move," Slade's voice brimmed with anger. "You don't listen. Maybe you should be punished. That would help you to listen. Do you want to be punished, Trish?"

"No," Trish shook her head. She tried to think of a way out. Something nearby she could use as a weapon. Could she reach anything before he was on top of her?

"People think of punishment as pain. A spanking for a child. A punch in the mouth for an adult. But that's not real punishment. If you want someone to really learn a lesson, you have to take something precious away from them. Something they can't get back."

Another shiver ran through Trish's body.

"Are you a virgin, Trish? Probably not. You probably gave it up in middle school. But you were always in control. You never had it taken from you, did you?"

"Slade, you don't want to..."

"What I want, you stupid bitch, is for you to understand."

He leaned toward her, placing his hands on either side of her supine body, and lowered his face within inches of hers. Trish felt the mattress compress around her under his weight. She wanted to scream but no sound emerged.

"You're going to understand. Right now."

His breath was hot against her face. It smelled of meat.

"You're going to drop this, Trish. Drop it cold. You're going to leave Pastor Berry alone. Leave school if you want. Get away from here. I don't give a shit. But you are going to drop it. Do you understand?"

Trish nodded. Then, remembering the darkness, she spoke. "Yes."

"This is a warning. If you wake up tomorrow morning and change your mind, if you decide to be brave and girl-powered and that shit, you will not be safe. Not from me. I will make your nightmares come true. Do you understand?"

"Yes."

"I'll be watching you." He leaned closer, Trish turned her head, pushing the side of her face into the pillow, afraid he was going to try to kiss her. His mouth stopped an inch from her ear. The heat from his breath touched her eardrum as he spoke two syllables. "Closely."

He pushed himself up and rose from the bed. When he opened the door, light from the hallway flooded the room.

"Goodnight, Trish." The words came out as a sing-song hiss and the door closed behind him.

Trish leaped from the bed, locked the door, turned on the light, grabbed the chair from her desk and slammed it underneath the doorknob, bracing the door.

She dropped to the floor, her head splitting with pain from the flurry of activity. A sob racked her body. She looked around for her phone. It wasn't on the floor. She couldn't get up. She clasped her knees to her chest. Her hand found the gold cross on the chain around her neck. She rubbed it between her thumb and forefinger.

A flash of lightning again illuminated the room. Trish reflexively counted. She made it to five before the thunder growled. The storm was passing already.

She rocked herself and suppressed a shiver. She didn't know if sleep would ever come again.

CHAPTER 6

THE BREEZE SWEPT OVER THE DESERT FLOOR and blew through his hair. It swirled the rising smoke from the ebbing bonfire. The wind should have cooled his skin. The smoke should have stung his eyes. But John Michaels felt neither of those things. He was too overwhelmed with terror.

He was back in New Mexico. In the compound in the godforsaken desert. The place had haunted his dreams for four years, ever since he and Sarah had escaped—narrowly—with their lives. Not all of their fellow program participants had been so fortunate.

John's nightmares tended to resemble a playlist featuring Hell's greatest hits, highlighting various special moments of atrocity that occurred during the program. Sometimes the raw horror of a specific occurrence, and sometimes the more subtle dread of losing his humanity without a tinge of regret. The descent to darkness he had so miraculously avoided.

Whatever the nightmare, there was one constant, the chilling presence of the leader of the program. Marcus Kane. The apex predator.

Most often, as tonight, the intrusion into John's unconscious took the form of the nightly bonfire that had accompanied the ritual spiritual awakenings. The mammoth form of Kane stood on the other side of the flames. Powerful. Intimidating. The chanting started, the participants of the program intoning in rhythm, "Kane, Kane, Kane." Voices growing in volume and intensity. All except John, who was silent in his realization that everything that mattered to him was no longer his. And from across the bonfire, after Kane had affixed his gaze on each of his flock, he turned to face John.

The fire dancing in his eyes, Marcus Kane smiled.

John bolted upright with a gasp.

Just a dream.

He glanced to his left. Sarah lay still, her hair strewn over her pillow. Steady breathing. He hadn't wakened her this time.

Always just a dream. But always so real. Those eyes...

John's stomach hurt. His ulcer was new. Still in the get-to-know-you phase of the relationship. John thought it was certain types of food that reacted poorly with ulcers, but he had been meticulous in his diet since the diagnosis. If dreams could have the same effect, this did not bode well for his future gastric peace.

He lifted the sheet—damp from his sweat—and eased out of bed. Sarah continued to sleep. He stared at her for a moment, envying her slumber but not begrudging it. She deserved every minute.

John was a firm believer that people rarely changed. Despite countless motion pictures where the main character changes and grows, and despite a plethora of self-help books where the various authors assure you a better life if you're willing to change, John knew that reality almost always proved that people are who they are. Their behavior might change for a time, but with unfailing regularity, they would eventually return to their natural path.

Sarah had proven the exception to the rule. If anything can change a person, it's a traumatic life experience, and "trauma" would be a humorous categorization of what John and Sarah had survived in the desert of New Mexico.

Like iron forged in fire, Sarah had emerged from the experience stronger. She no longer obsessed over past failures. Now each day dawned with a fresh perspective for her. She dealt with whatever life threw at her on an hour by hour basis. No looking back. No wistful longing of the many ways in which life could be different. Better. The desert had cleansed her.

John left the bedroom and padded down the hall, mindful of his footsteps. It was the middle of the night. He paused at the pink door for only a moment, just to listen, then proceeded to the kitchen.

He selected a glass from the cabinet then opened the fridge door. Once upon a time, a cold beer or a room temp scotch would have been just right to accompany his insomnia, but there was no alcohol in the house. It wasn't the ulcer—though he knew alcohol wouldn't play well with his new gastric companion—John hadn't indulged in a drop since New Mexico. That was his old life. He could no longer afford for his senses to be diminished in any capacity.

He extracted the pitcher of tea from the top shelf and filled his glass. Closing the fridge door, he drained the top half of the glass in two big swallows. It was cold and semi-sweet, a sort of compromise to their Southern surroundings. He still couldn't handle the kind of sweet tea in which the locals indulged. Two sips of that sludge and John's teeth felt fuzzy. He didn't miss Boston—there were things in life more important than where you lived—but he hadn't yet adapted to the latest iteration of his new life.

The small town in Oklahoma marked his and Sarah's seventh home in the four years since the nightmare in New Mexico. On the advice of the Texas Ranger who had saved John's life in the desert, the couple had agreed to enter federal protection. Earl Valentine—"Cutter" to John and most others but always "Earl" to Sarah—had soft-played the idea at first. While John convalesced in an El Paso hospital from the near-fatal wounds he had sustained from Marcus Kane, Cutter had tempered his warnings with a guarded optimism that protection may not be necessary.

It was all about the odds.

John and Sarah had beaten the odds once. Following a tragedy that had planted the seeds of depression and a gradual unraveling of their marriage, they had grabbed a lifeline and enrolled in the exclusive life recuperation program in New Mexico. The program took place at a compound isolated in the desert. The perfect scenario, as it turned out, for a cunning psychopath to conduct secret chemical and behavioral experiments on the unaware members of the program.

As charismatic as he was physically intimidating, Marcus Kane had used the program to brainwash its members, whittling away their humanity until there was only their leader and his promises, and finally, death. With each iteration of the experiments—and each new crop of unsuspecting program members—Kane marched further toward his mysterious goal.

Until John and Sarah Michaels entered the picture.

Ultimately, John had orchestrated a hostile takeover of the program, saving the lives of its members and ending the brutal machinations of Marcus Kane. John knew that he and Sarah should have died in the desert. Only through events John could only describe as beyond coincidental had he and Sarah survived. That and the well-timed appearance of a Texas Ranger quite far from Texas. Yet they *had* survived. They had beaten the odds.

Or so they had believed.

In the aftermath, while the FBI was still in the initial stages of investigation, Cutter had arrived at the hospital in El Paso to lay out the facts for John and Sarah. At its core was one terrifying truth:

Marcus Kane was not the mastermind of the program. More than a hundred people had met their demise at his hands in the desert of New Mexico, but Marcus was simply executing someone else's vision. The vision of his father, Hiram Kane.

As Cutter explained, Hiram Kane was a ghost. An almost-forgotten Keyser Söze legend within the law enforcement community. After committing horrific acts of violence decades prior, he had simply vanished along with his three young sons, of which Marcus had been the oldest. And Hiram was still out there.

Cutter had balanced this news with the pragmatic estimation that the FBI's profile of Hiram Kane was that of a man focused solely on his own goals. As such, veering from those goals—and possibly risking their successful completion—to pursue an agenda of vengeance against John or Sarah was unlikely.

In other words, the odds were in their favor this time. But, as Cutter emphasized, with a new investigation into the Kane family underway, the window was open for John and Sarah to be supplied federal protection, and Cutter felt it prudent to take that opportunity.

John had agreed. He wasn't about to trust his and Sarah's lives to the reliability of some government employee's psychological assessment of Hiram Kane. He was finished with trusting other people any more than absolutely necessary, so he and Sarah had entered the protection program with one significant requirement by John—that Cutter Valentine remain his primary contact.

The FBI did not care much for that request. Cutter was a Texas Ranger, not a federal agent. Plus, the protection agency emphasized that the whole point of the program was secrecy. Every additional link in the chain represented heightened exposure. John didn't care. The agency relented, and Cutter became the handler for the Michaels. John never regretted the decision.

They were only four months into WITSEC when the arrangement paid off. It was Cutter's groundwork—not the FBI's investigation—that uncovered a man named Fisher Knox probing agency contacts as to the whereabouts of John and Sarah. They were living in St. Louis at the time under the last name alias of "Puckett." At that point, there wasn't enough evidence to apprehend Knox. He hadn't done anything illegal. He'd just been asking questions. Cutter chased it anyway. What he discovered was equal parts encouraging and disturbing.

Knox was a low-level networker in New York and from what Cutter could discern, he wasn't acting on behalf of Hiram Kane at all. That was good. The bad news was that Knox had apparently learned of a past connection between a high-ranking member of a local crime organization and Hiram Kane. By that point, most of America had read details of the sensational story from New Mexico. Hiram Kane's name was out there as the possible unseen mastermind behind the nightmare. People were talking. Once Knox learned of the connection, he figured he could gain the favor of the boss if he located John and Sarah so that the boss could in turn eliminate this couple and possibly be owed a favor by Hiram Kane.

That was bad news indeed. When John had accepted federal protection, he assumed it was to protect him and Sarah from a possible act of vengeance by Hiram Kane. If random criminals were now entering the game, that changed the odds. Cutter didn't like this development either.

Though it didn't appear that Knox had learned anything concrete about their location, Cutter requested a new placement for the couple through the protection agency. Five days later, John and Sarah were in Salt Lake City under the new alias of "Sweezey" and John's insomnia had returned in full force. Relying on others was never something he had been good at and depending on unseen faces to safeguard his and Sarah's lives did not sit well with him.

Two months into Salt Lake City, further complications arose. Cutter uncovered a possible connection between an agent at the FBI and Hiram Kane. As with everything else related to Kane, nothing concrete could be proven, and the agent denied Cutter's suggestion as nothing more than coincidence and desperation. But it was the straw that broke the camel's back.

To his credit, Cutter had been completely open with John and Sarah about this development, as he had all aspects of the Hiram Kane investigation. When John then informed Cutter that he felt they were no longer safe under federal protection, Cutter didn't argue.

Options were discussed, and John's life of crime began.

CHAPTER 7

JOHN PLACED HIS GLASS OF TEA on the coaster beside the keyboard and eased into the chair behind his desk. As he sank into the leather, he glanced around the room. A line of small windows ran the length of one end of the study, placed high on the wall so the top of the windows edged the ceiling. You would have to stand on a stool to be able to peek through them and see the outside world. That also meant no one from the outside world could see inside the study.

With the exception of the front den, the entire house sported these high-placement windows, an obscene holdover from an unfortunate architectural trend of the 1970s. The house was ugly, but when John had found it on the internet, he knew it was perfect. He paid cash for it the following week under what would become his current alias.

The exterior of the house was a dated eyesore, but the interior was much better. Before they moved in, Sarah had tackled a refurbishment. Knowing how rarely they would venture beyond the safety of the walls, she ensured the interior was comfortable.

The only aspect John handled was the security system.

He used a remote to awaken the wall-mounted monitor screen. It was one of two eighty-inch televisions hanging on the wall opposite his desk. As the screen on the left came to life, twenty squared pictures showed the individual views of various security cameras discreetly placed around the home's exterior, trees, and yard. Four more cameras monitored neighborhood access points to their street. The fact that those cameras were not mounted on John's property and that they recorded public zones violated not only HOA restrictions but also several privacy laws. John, however, lost no sleep over that pittance. He had plenty of other reasons for sleep to avoid him.

Besides a foraging rabbit in the back yard, the night appeared quiet. It always did. It was a quiet neighborhood. Safe. But that was no excuse for a lack of vigilance.

The security system had been installed by a specialized firm during the general renovation (with the exception of the street cameras, which were installed in the very darkest hours of night and for an undeclared private fee to the crew). John had paid in cash, a valuable motivator for the workers to develop selective amnesia about this specific project.

Sarah believed it to be overkill, or so she told John, but he didn't care. Let it be a thousand times overkill rather than the alternative of a single degree less security than required. As long as Hiram Kane was out there—and all he represented—John's family was not safe.

He turned on the desktop computer, entered his password, then used the remote to link the other eighty-inch television as an extension of his desktop monitor. The middle of the night was the perfect time to start the day.

The desktop monitor displayed the foreign market indexes. It would be hours before the exchange in New York opened, but plenty of activity was occurring in parts of the world where it was daylight. There was money to be made at all hours, and in John's new reality, money was the difference between life and death.

John and Sarah had been on their own for over three years now. When Cutter had agreed to move them out of federal protection, it had cost the Ranger dearly from a professional standpoint, but he had saved their lives. John truly believed that. The equation had been simple in John's mind. If the Feds couldn't guaranty their safety, then John and Sarah would hide themselves. Criminals of all types and levels regularly evaded the detection of law enforcement and the media. John saw no reason that he and Sarah couldn't do the same thing.

Of course, when learning to behave and live like a criminal, one must start somewhere. Cutter proved invaluable in this regard. As a Texas Ranger, Cutter was never tied down to a single specialty within law enforcement. His field was not narrow. In his decades wearing the star, Cutter had studied an incredible variety of criminal activity. To effectively combat the crime, Cutter learned how it was being perpetrated—and by whom—and instinctively knew whom to arrest and who to allow leeway to conduct their business in exchange for information and a shot at much bigger fish.

When John and Sarah broke from federal protection, Cutter had arranged their new identities through the same channels an international drug kingpin might utilize. New identities. New housing. New jobs. Everything they needed to start a new life.

But John did not rest easy. Somewhere in his mind, he equated a lack of movement with complacency. And complacency could ultimately result in death. So he asked Cutter to teach him, to introduce him to his contacts, to show him what he needed. John wondered if he was requesting too much. He was, after all, asking a lawman not only for permission but for help in learning to become a law breaker. Cutter didn't bat an eye. His own sense of justice overrode the law book. If giving John the tools to succeed in keeping him and Sarah safe also meant that John would be breaking certain laws in the process, it wasn't worth fretting over.

Once the initial introductions were made, John took things further. He never told Cutter all he was doing, though John often wondered if Cutter suspected. He may look like an old cowboy and sound "Texan" straight from stereotype casting, but Cutter was one of the sharpest men John had ever known. He probably ascertained that John had gone far beyond simply establishing new identities, but Cutter never said a word to him about his extracurricular activities.

John logged into the dynamic chain browser—an offshoot of the dark web's Tor network—and began checking the brokerage accounts of his various offshore entities.

Got my mind on my money and my money on my mind.

The reality had been simple for John. The most successful criminals could evade capture because they could afford it. They could buy their anonymity. The underground system wasn't free. And where Cutter had been able to launch that first set of independent identities by calling in favors, it wouldn't work the same for John. He would need cold, hard cash to buy such accommodations in the future. In that world, the adage that "money talks and bullshit walks" had never gone out of style.

John not only needed the ability to relocate every few months— still operating under the assumption that remaining static for too long was an invitation to discovery—he also needed contingency plans. Multiple contingency plans. And every one of them would cost money. But the price of *not* having those options was far greater. The searing eyes of Marcus Kane watching John through the flames of the bonfire reminded him of that fact every night.

So John set to work creating their safety net. He did the math. Each new identity, each new life, each contingency plan for escape would require hundreds of thousands of dollars. He had to earn that in short order. Every day presented danger. Every contingency plan provided a potential avenue of safety. The sooner he had the money, the safer his family would be. Following the rules wouldn't be an option. It would take too much time and bring the possible notice of the IRS or other agencies which he would prefer to stay away from.

In his prior life—before his transformation in the desert—John would never have dreamed of breaking the law. He used his intelligence and skill to work for others. He made them a lot of money and was well compensated in return, but he was honest. He never even cheated on his taxes. The irony was not lost on John that his reward for stopping one of the most heinous murderers of modern times was to compromise his own integrity and become a criminal himself. But when it came to weighing the value of his integrity against the safety of his family, John decided integrity was no more than a luxury, and an overrated one at that.

After reviewing the last of his recent transaction activity, John took a sip of tea and opened one of his forty email accounts. The key to being a successful criminal was proper organization.

He opened the top drawer of his desk and extracted a pen and legal pad. As he reviewed the contents of his various in-boxes, he jotted notes. He would later organize these notes into his database and begin the process of determining what action, if any, today would require.

A dull pain hit John's midsection, just enough to make him hold his breath for a moment and let it out in a long, slow exhalation. First burn of the day. John silently cursed the ulcer as he opened his news retrieval feed. The information on his legal pad could only be put to use when referenced against what was happening in the world today.

He scrolled through variations of the usual headlines, bypassing business reports for the moment. That would always be reviewed after the real news of the day. Even small stories mattered. He stopped his scroll on one such small item. The headline hadn't caught his attention but the still-frame from the video gave him pause. It was the flames that did it. He clicked and began watching the video. It was a snippet from a local evening news broadcast in Texas.

The anchorwoman set the stage for the pending clip. A vigil of sorts at a university for the young woman who had committed the atrocity at the Dallas Opera House the prior day. The anchorwoman raised one eyebrow as she threw to the clip, indicating the viewer was about to see something shocking...or at least intriguing. John only half-watched as he looked over the notes on his legal pad. He heard a preacher giving a speech only to be interrupted by a young woman saying something that was bleeped in the newscast. He looked up in time to catch the back-and-forth. John took another drink of tea as the camera panned from the preacher to the girl, the flames of the small bonfire between them. The girl continued her verbal attack and pointed an accusatory finger at the preacher. The screen swung back, capturing the preacher's reaction, a close-up of his face above the flames.

The glass of tea fell from John's hand and shattered on the floor next to him.

CHAPTER 8

THE SOUND OF THE GLASS BREAKING didn't register with John. He paused the video, reset it to a frame from a moment before, then dragged the image from the desktop monitor to the eighty-inch television on the wall. He pushed his chair back from the desk and walked to the large screen, his bare feet missing the shards of broken glass only by luck. His eyes never strayed from the image.

He stared at the screen, mouth agape.

"Is everything okay?" Sarah stepped into the room, eyes bleary from sleep. John didn't turn toward her. He was transfixed. The burn in his stomach was gone. Ice had replaced it, permeating his gut and gripping his heart. He was cold.

Sarah looked from the broken glass on the floor—the source of what had awakened her—to her husband. He was in a different world.

"John, what is it? You look like you've seen a ghost."

He tilted his head toward her and spoke softly. "I think I have."

She crossed the room to join him in front of the television, following his eyes to the image of the thin, taut-faced man staring past the camera. The frozen words at the bottom of the footage identified the man as "Pastor Christian Berry."

John glanced toward her. "Do you see it?"

Sarah shook her head slowly. "He looks kind of angry, but...what am I supposed to be seeing?"

John grunted and returned to the desk, this time watching where he stepped. He played the video. The preacher's face transformed from anger to benevolence in an instant. The interchange between him and the girl continued. Another student, a young man, made his way around the bonfire and led the girl away. The on-scene reporter stepped into the picture and offered muted commentary while Pastor Berry continued to speak in the background. The video stopped. John sat, dropping hard into the chair. His legs would no longer support him.

He moved the video back to the earlier image, paused it again and enlarged it. The preacher's gaunt face took up the entirety of the television. That one moment. Right after the female student had charged him with "you're not here for her, you're here for you," and levelled an accusatory finger at him. The close-up shot. Over the flames.

His eyes.

John would know those eyes anywhere. He could never forget them. He saw them in every nightmare.

The cold he felt turned into a fluttering queasiness and began to spread. He realized he was shaking. Not much. Tremors. But real, nonetheless.

"Daddy? Is it morning time?"

John spun at the sound of his daughter's voice. DJ stood in the doorway of the study in her pink footed pajamas, her stuffed tiger dangling from one hand while her other hand rubbed her squinting eyes. Sarah was already in motion.

"Oh, honey, it's not morning yet. Did we wake you?" She scooped DJ into her arms and planted a gentle kiss on top of her head.

"It's okay, Mommy. Hobbes was awake. Tigers are mocnurnal."

John inhaled a great breath and released it, fighting against the adrenal surge. The complexities and dangers of his life faded into obscurity as the only two things that mattered shared a moment in the doorway.

DJ was only a month shy of her second birthday, but she had a vocabulary and attitude that far exceeded her age. All the best qualities of her mother and father—and the worst—were imbued in the little girl, and she somehow magnified them. She in turn amazed and delighted and horrified John and Sarah every day. Denise Jennifer Michaels was their miracle.

She also didn't exist. She was birthed by a midwife at their home in Wichita, Kansas. John and Sarah had lived there for the last trimester of Sarah's pregnancy under the last name alias of "Hancock." Two weeks after DJ's birth, the family of three moved to a new home—and a new identity—in Crestview, Florida. No birth certificate was applied for in either location. No government agency knew of DJ's existence. John had even debated whether to inform Cutter, but Sarah had resolved that question with very little discussion beyond smacking John in the forehead.

John rose from the chair and skirted the broken glass as he joined his ladies in the doorway.

"Tigers are *nocturnal*, sweetheart."

"Just like your daddy," Sarah chimed.

John wrapped them both in his arms. "DJ sandwich," he said as he and Sarah squeezed their daughter between them. Her hair smelled of baby shampoo.

"Back to bed," he whispered to his daughter as he released the hug. He glanced to Sarah. "I'll clean up. Sorry about that."

Sarah took two steps down the hall, DJ already falling asleep on her shoulder, when she glanced back toward her husband. "After I lie down with her, I'll be back. You need to tell me what's going on."

"Of course," he nodded.

After Sarah disappeared around the corner, John turned back to the television screen. The adrenaline still pulsed in his bloodstream, but the fight or flight instinct had been given decisive direction by the appearance of his wife and daughter.

He made no move to clean the glass from the floor. He put his hands on his hips and began to think. Of all the contingencies he had envisioned, this was the most unexpected.

CHAPTER 9

"THE TIME DRAWS NEAR, brothers and sisters, and when that time arrives, we will face a choice." Christian Berry's tone was soft as he addressed the others in the room. He had turned his chair so that he sat straddling the back of it, his long legs protruding from either side. "We can shrink from that choice. We can be like those poor souls in Revelation and cry out to the mountains and the rocks to fall on us and hide us. Many people—most people—will do exactly that."

He looked around the room, meeting the eyes of each person seated in the circle of chairs. Forty-four young men and women.

"But that will not be me. I will not shrink. I will not hide. And I do not believe you will either." He lowered his gaze toward his clasped hands then lifted his eyes toward his flock with steel intensity.

"I shall rise. And you shall rise with me."

Heads nodded. Forty-four sets of eyes returned his gaze with equal intensity. Berry nodded with satisfaction. The hour was late but there were no yawns or bleary eyes. The group was wired. Just as they should be.

"It has been a long night, but I do not apologize for keeping you out so late. The sun will still rise at its appointed hour, but you will not feel tired. For you know there are things far more important than sleep."

They had stayed at the bonfire site until eleven o'clock, at which point the larger assembly dispersed and the inner circle had returned to the church. There was no advance discussion, and no one outside the circle had attempted to join them. Slade had been the last to enter the church but now occupied the chair at Berry's right hand. The gears were turning smoothly. Just as they should.

"There is something I must tell you. Something...sacred. It is not to be repeated outside of this group. Not even in a whisper."

Almost as one, the forty-four leaned forward, eyes wide.

"When I say that the day is coming, I no longer mean that in ambiguous, future terms. The day is coming *soon*. It is almost upon us. Stephanie's death, tragic as it was, embodies the sign. Her passing serves as an esoteric marker, to be witnessed by many but understood by few. I speak of end times."

A sharp intake of breath from one of the young ladies punctuated the dramatic statement. Berry paused, letting the words sink in. He settled his gaze on Andrew, searching for signs of question or defiance. He saw neither. Only stillness. As it should be. Berry surveyed the rest of the group with his eyes as he continued.

"I do not yet know the exact day, but I have a strong suspicion. I shall be dedicating myself to prayer and study. It will be revealed in time. Our path will be made clear. Until then, brothers and sisters..." Berry rose from his chair but gestured with both hands for the others to remain seated. "Until then, it falls on me to ensure you are prepared. And it falls on you to make yourself ready. We can have no doubt. No fear. Only devotion."

Berry stepped through a side door. On a table in the hallway, communion trays had been placed by an unseen figure. The trays were aluminum but painted gold. Two were large dishes that held small wafers. Twenty-two wafers in each dish. The other two were larger trays which contained tiny clear plastic cups, each cup roughly the size of a thumb. The disposable cups were nested into holes in the top of the tray. Twenty-two cups were in each container, each cup filled almost to the brim with communion wine. Berry knew that the deep purple liquid would still be cold. The timing of the tray placement had been impeccable. Of course.

Berry set the trays one on top of the other—they were designed to be securely stacked and carried down the rows of a congregation—and returned to the large room to address those seated there.

"We must center ourselves. We must focus." He set the trays down on his empty chair, then lifted the top two which contained the wafers. He handed one to Slade on his right and the other to the young woman on his left.

"Communion accomplishes that. It focuses our minds and makes our spirits ready."

The trays were passed around the circle, each person selecting a wafer and passing the tray to his neighbor until the circle was complete and all had a wafer in hand.

"Be silent," Berry intoned. The room was quiet as a tomb. "Eat."

Forty-four heads bowed and solemnly ate the wafers.

Berry repeated the process with the trays of communion wine. Each person selecting a tiny plastic cup and passing the tray along. When the trays met at the far end of the circle, Berry allowed several moments to pass before he spoke.

"Be silent." Berry controlled his breathing. Deep inhalations and quiet exhalations. Five of them. "Drink."

Forty-four cups rose to the lips of the congregation members and the wine was gone. Berry nodded in satisfaction.

"This is the beginning. Our church will continue regular services, but the family in this room now—for that is what we are, a family—will meet together each night going forward. We will prepare ourselves each night. We will partake in communion each night. And we will be ready."

Heads nodded. A couple of "amens" could be heard.

"Return home. Sleep will not come easy for you tonight. Nor tomorrow or the next. You may feel anxious. Perhaps energized. This is your soul. Your soul will not rest with the end times upon us." Another pause. "Nor should it."

Berry walked around the outside of the circle as the group began to stand. Andrew remained seated. Berry placed one bony hand on Andrew's shoulder as he passed. His slender fingers first gripping then patting him gently. Only a moment's touch but perhaps enough. Andrew rose and joined the crowd filing toward the door.

Berry stood by the church door and acknowledged each of the forty-four as they departed. There were no umbrellas opened. The storm had been brief. The rain had stopped. It was a quiet exodus. Minds were preoccupied. And rightly so.

Slade was the last to leave. "You need me?"

Berry placed his hand on one of Slade's hulking shoulders and shook his head. "Go home. Rest. You will have much to do in the coming days."

Slade nodded and walked down the pathway, soon fading into the darkness beyond the streetlight.

Berry stepped inside the church, closed the door and locked it. He didn't have to turn around to know he was being watched.

CHAPTER 10

THE MAN STOOD IN THE DOORWAY on the far side of the room, his considerable mass filling the doorframe. He watched as the pastor locked the door to the church. His gray hair was cropped short. Despite his age, the man wore neither glasses nor contacts. His eyesight was perfect. He folded his meaty arms across his sizeable chest and leaned against the doorframe. Over the years, his physique had changed. His upper torso was barrel-like, his waist the same size as his chest, but there was no denying the muscle corded under the fat.

Hiram Kane waited until the door was locked before uttering his first words.

"Your clusterfuck at the bonfire is all over the news."

Christian Berry sighed as he bent to pick up the empty communion trays. "I'm sorry, Father. I didn't think there would be a public confrontation. I'll deal with it."

Hiram made no move to help as his son tidied up the fellowship room. The chairs could remain set in a circle. They would be used again in this fashion each night for the foreseeable future. He had listened to every word of the gathering. At least that part went according to plan.

"Any reaction from the boyfriend during the enlightenment?"

Berry continued around the circle, straightening the chairs with precision. "Virtually none, a strong indicator of success. We're well on our way."

Hiram offered a noncommittal grunt. There were still a great many moving pieces to consider. His plans had been meticulous, designed to control virtually all possible variables, but that adverb plagued him. *Virtually*. It conveyed the reality that not every factor could be controlled. Hiram Kane abhorred this fact. Particularly when they were, indeed, growing close to the ultimate goal.

"Tell me about the girl at the bonfire."

Berry sighed again. "Stephanie's roommate. She told me about her. Tried to convince her to come to services, but she refused. Nonstarter. Doesn't believe in God. She's from New York. She's a loner. A nobody."

"A nobody that just put your face on the news," Hiram growled. His son paused his chair-straightening. Hiram had to admit that Jonas Kane played the role of Christian Berry remarkably well. His youngest son had not taken after Hiram physically, but he had inherited his father's intelligence, and Jonas was undeniably gifted in the art of persuasion. He made a great preacher. But that did not make the Christian Berry persona bulletproof. It had only been three years since the identity had first been established. The risk of someone recognizing him was low, but those odds increased dramatically if his face was splashed across the news.

"It was dark at the bonfire. I didn't allow myself to be interviewed on camera. We should be fine."

Another grunt from Hiram. He wasn't going to speculate.

"It was a mistake regardless. You should have reached out to that girl earlier in the day. Gauged the situation. Dealt with it in private if necessary."

"You're right. I didn't think about it. My focus was elsewhere."

"Your focus is beginning to concern me, Jonas. None of this would be an issue if your Mexican whore hadn't created the circus that she did. She was supposed to kill herself. Simple. Neat. Instead we end up with *las cuchillas locos* making news all over the globe."

"What Stephanie did was unexpected," Berry said as he finished straightening the chairs, "but it also offered proof positive of her commitment."

"That proof came with a price. We don't need the public eye on us. Not now."

"Yes, I'm aware."

Hiram left the doorway, taking two steps into the room. "You walked a dangerous line with that girl."

Berry closed the gap between the two and stood in front of Hiram, not quite eye-to-eye as the son had never attained the stature of the father.

"I had to push boundaries with Stephanie. It was important for us to make a full assessment. She was the perfect subject for it."

Hiram detected no belligerence in his tone. That was good.

"Horse is out of the barn now. We'll work with what we've got. Any chance the roommate knows about your boundary-pushing relationship?"

"None."

"Good. Keep an eye on her. If she starts to push things, we'll deal with her as necessary."

"Progress has already been made on that front." Berry sidestepped his father and proceeded through the door with the empty trays in his hands. "If you need me, I'll be in the lab."

Hiram watched his son disappear around the corner, then nodded with satisfaction. Variables still existed, but nothing that could stop them.

CHAPTER 11

T HE CUP NESTLED BETWEEN TRISH O'BRIEN'S HANDS was no longer warm, rendering the cardboard sleeve around it unnecessary. The heavily-creamed coffee had been served piping hot, but Trish had been able to manage only intermittent sips for the past half hour. Her head ached. Her stomach gurgled. Her mouth was dry. She had washed her face but had forgotten to brush her teeth, and the sips of coffee did little to camouflage the nastiness that coated her tongue. She had put on fresh clothes but hadn't pulled her hair back, random auburn strands fell into her eyes. She blew them back with sharp, projected huffs from her lips rather than remove her hands from the cup to brush them away.

The night's storm had cleared. The sun was up now. The parking lot was bright. Cars came and went as customers serviced their morning addiction. It was a safe environment. No one even looked her way as she occupied the short table farthest from the door, but that didn't make her feel better, just more alone.

She had made her way to the coffee shop a couple of blocks off campus at dawn's first light. She hadn't been able stay in the dorm room any longer. Even with the morning sun, leaving the room had been hard. She made herself do it anyway, steeling herself at her door for ten minutes before she could will away the overwhelming desire to curl back up in the corner. In the end, she had managed it. She left her room, exited the dormitory and controlled her speed as she made her way across campus. Her legs wanted to sprint. She didn't. She stayed on the sidewalks, kept her head on a swivel and chewed her lip until it bled a little, but she soon reached the coffee shop, its interior well-lit and secure with a handful of employees beginning the day's activities.

Sitting at the little table hadn't succeeded in making her feel particularly safe, but it had managed to calm her mind, enough to start thinking more clearly at least. Enough to know that her sense of not feeling safe was irrational. It was residual anxiety from her encounter with Slade. An aftershock. But she was doing better now. Logic had edged into her thoughts to accompany—and often counter—the deep currents of emotion. As she sat slouched into the right angle made between the back of the chair and the wall, she inhaled the aroma of fresh pastry and ground beans. Better. She set the cup on the table and absent-mindedly pulled the gold cross from her shirt. The necklace stretched tight from the back of her neck to her hand as she rubbed it between her thumb and forefinger.

"Okay," she muttered to herself. "One thing at a time."

She assessed the situation. Physically, she was fine. Hungover, true, but not hurt. She had been threatened but not assaulted.

Options. Black and white. She could go to the police, or she could choose not to report the incident. Everyone knew Slade had a history, but it would still be her word against his, and she was the one who had showed up drunk and threatening at a memorial for her friend. That wouldn't exactly work to her advantage.

But that was really beside the point. She wasn't going to report it regardless. She already knew that. If she was going to, she would have done it already. She would have walked straight to the police station instead of the coffee shop. Even if her conscious brain had been overcome by adrenaline and residual fear, her subconscious had been working just fine.

She wasn't going to report this to the police because doing so would undermine her goal. Last night, she had told that scarecrow preacher that she was going to find out what happened with Stephanie, that she would uncover the truth about why her friend killed herself at the opera house. Nothing had changed that imperative. If anything, it had been reinforced.

In yesterday's dazed numbness, Trish had felt confused, betrayed, frustrated and angry. She had lost her best friend in a terrible and tragic way. She wanted answers but had none. Andrew might be able to accept that, but Trish obviously had very little in common with Steph's boyfriend. She needed answers. It ran in her blood.

There was a reason Trish was majoring in journalism. It sure wasn't the money. She knew better than to hope for riches from the profession. And it wasn't the possibility of fame that danced around a world of instant news. It was, in fact, the most old-fashioned of reasons—Trish wanted the truth. She wanted not just to write or expose, she wanted to investigate. She wanted the *why* at the heart of the story.

There had to be a why when it came to Steph's actions. Trish had felt it in her gut, and not just because they were friends. It simply didn't make sense, and Trish wouldn't accept that. Their friendship only added emphasis for her. It gave her insight that no one else in the world possessed and underpinned the reason it had to be Trish to deny the easy explanation and uncover the truth.

Confronting Christian Berry hadn't been part of a grand plan. Trish had no illusions about the facts. She went to the memorial at the bonfire site because she was angry and inebriated. But things happen for a reason, or so some believed. And Trish's brash actions undeniably had an impact. Her confrontation with Pastor Berry had led to the visit from Slade.

She weighed those events on a mental scale. A verbal confrontation by a drunk girl with a mature adult was met by breaking and entering coupled with the threat of assault. That was not an equal response. That was not normal.

Of course, she couldn't objectively place that outcome at the feet of the preacher. It was Slade in her bedroom. It was Slade leaning over her, pinning her to the bed. But while it wasn't Christian Berry doing those things, Slade's actions did strengthen Trish's notion. His overreaction and violence echoed Stephanie's behavior in Dallas. They were both members of Berry's church. A connection? Her mind said, "conjecture," but her gut said, "no question."

If she went to the police, they would question Slade. And while there would be a report, she saw very little possibility Slade would end up behind bars. What would happen, though, is even more of a spotlight would be placed on Trish. She didn't need that. In hindsight, going to the memorial and confronting Berry had not been smart. It may have furthered her conviction that something was amiss, but it also presented her as a threat to Berry. He now knew who she was. That would make things more difficult for her.

So what to do next?

She needed to learn everything she could about Berry and his church. She had a possible inlet through Andrew, but based on his behavior and attitude yesterday, that might not be a simple process. Plus, there was Slade. He had warned her. That had been the whole point of his frightening visit, to tell her to drop it, to stay away from Pastor Berry.

"Get used to disappointment, Slade."

It was easy to whisper it to herself in the coffee shop, but she was only hours removed from the stark terror she had felt when dealing with him in person. She could remember the heat from his breath. And the smell of it. Real life bravery was a whole different proposition than coffee shop bravery.

But she wasn't going to let it stop her.

Moving on. Options. How to move from Point A to Point B, and how to deal with a genuine threat like Slade. If he decided Trish needed to be taught a lesson, she would be hurt. Or worse. She could press charges afterward but ask any victim if they'd prefer to see their predator serving time or to have the whole thing never happen in the first place, and Trish guessed the latter would be a unanimous answer. She too would prefer to avoid an assault completely.

Trish tasted salt and realized she had been chewing on her lip and reopened the cut. It was bleeding again. She stopped rubbing the cross, tucked it back into her shirt and dabbed at her mouth with a napkin. She wasn't equipped for this. Not yet. She needed help.

She again thought back to yesterday. Her best friend had died, yet no one had called to check on her. If she didn't have a friend close enough to spark a phone conversation in that circumstance, she probably didn't have one close enough to allow for a request like: "Hey, would you mind helping me out on a little project? Of course, helping me might mean you get beaten up, raped and murdered by a steroid-beast, but I'd really appreciate it."

Yeah, she didn't have any friends with whom she could have that conversation.

She needed someone brave. She needed someone who cared about her. In a perfect world, she needed someone who knew something about investigation.

She sat up straight in the chair as the obvious answer hit her. She made to grab her phone off the table only to remember she no longer had a phone. Slade was in possession of that, unless he had just thrown it in the trash somewhere.

She stood and tossed her half-full cup into the trash on her way out the door. The student union had payphones, and she needed to use one.

CHAPTER 12

JOHN MICHAELS TURNED OFF THE DIRT ROAD at the red mailbox he recognized from the only other time he'd been here. He drove slowly toward the house. At some point in the past, it had been painted white but had settled into an aged gray over the years. The windows of his sedan were open. The gravel crunching beneath his tires was the only sound. Everything else was quiet. No dog barking. That must mean Cutter wasn't home.

John hadn't called ahead.

He stopped in front of the house and stepped out of the vehicle, leaving the windows open. The sky was clear. The trees surrounding the house weren't dense, but they were plentiful. Country living. It was a nice afternoon. The drive to this little patch of nowhere from John's home in suburban Tulsa—located just north of nowhere—had been good. He'd needed time to think about what he would say to Cutter. The four hours behind the wheel had provided him that. It had also given him an opportunity to reset.

It had been an intense day. The conversation with Sarah had proven an undulating mix of heat and emotion and anger and support, which pretty much encapsulated their relationship since they began life on the run. Living in fear of every "what if" scenario.

It had taken John some time to convince her that the preacher on the video had to be the third Kane brother—Jonas Kane—particularly since the only argument he had was a gut feeling based on the man's eyes—what Sarah largely dismissed as nothing more than a hunch.

John had a difficult time conveying how far beyond "hunch" this feeling went.

Eventually, the conversation reached the point of accepting the possibility of this particular "what if" and graduated to the "what next" options of action. Sarah was not supportive of John's plan to pursue an investigation of the man on the video. If Christian Berry was, in fact, somehow a member of the Kane family, then Sarah's opinion was that they should anonymously tip off the proper authorities and then keep as much distance as possible, perhaps move to Oregon or North Dakota or even Alaska if necessary.

John felt differently. It was DJ that had turned him. In the darkest hours of the night, with the iron clutch of fear in his belly at seeing the eyes from his nightmares despite being fully awake, his daughter's appearance had triggered a profound protective response in John. He and Sarah had been running, but if he could end it, if he could save his daughter from a life of fear of which she wasn't even yet aware, then he would do it. Whatever it might take to allow DJ to grow up as a normal little girl.

For John, that meant not relying on a faceless agency to solve the problem. Hiram Kane had resources, connections, some of them in government agencies. That much had been made clear from Cutter's investigations. John wasn't going to take the chance of someone warning Kane that he had been spotted and allowing the monster to slip into the ether again, or worse yet, possibly linking the anonymous tip to its source. Solving the problem—keeping DJ safe—meant aiming for the root. He needed incontrovertible evidence that Christian Berry was Jonas Kane. If Hiram Kane was with him, then two birds with one stone. With evidence in hand, John would then take the next steps in eliminating the threat. He hadn't yet worked out what those steps would be, but one thing at a time.

Whatever the plan might be, John knew he needed Cutter. John could scoff at the competence of government agencies, but he knew that being critical of them didn't imbue him with any practical experience or ability to tackle a clandestine investigation. It would do him no good to pursue this on his own and commit some rookie blunder that would alert Kane (either one of them) to his presence and most likely get him killed. He'd prefer DJ to grow up with a father.

He needed Cutter.

The front door to the house opened, startling John out of his reverie. A woman emerged, wiping her hands on a well-worn apron, her hair the same color as the house.

"John?" She took two steps onto the front porch. "My word, it is you."

"Hi, Maggie," John said as he went to meet her. "I didn't know if anyone was home. Sorry for showing up unannounced."

Maggie hugged him before he reached the top step of the front porch then extended her arms as she gripped his shoulders, taking a good look at him.

"Still not used to the south, are you? Unannounced are the best kind of visits." Her face turned serious. "Is everything okay? Sarah and DJ—"

"Are just fine. They're at home. I needed to visit with your husband about something and thought it would be best face-to-face."

"I see. Well, Earl is in the back pasture. Not sure how long he'll be, but I do know how long it will be until the teacakes I have in the oven are ready. In five minutes, you're going to try one," she paused and looked him up and down. "Maybe try three or four. You're skin and bones."

She pulled him toward the door with no resistance on his part.

"These are incredible, Maggie. Thank you."

John swallowed his bite of teacake. The treat resembled a puffy sugar cookie but was not as sweet. It was still warm from the oven. He chased it with a gulp of iced tea.

"So glad you like them, dear. They're Earl's favorite though I don't bake them as often as I should. Making the dough is a very hands-on project, and my hands aren't what they used to be." She flexed her fingers and appraised them with an accusing eye. "Now, dare I ask what brings you to our humble home?"

Maggie picked up her mug and sipped her coffee with an inscrutable expression on her face. Perhaps not mistrust, but not far from it. John offered a half smile. Her instincts were on point. "I'd rather talk to Cutter first if that's all right. Is he doing okay?"

Her eyes narrowed. "Depends on the day and may depend on what you're planning to talk about. Retirement hasn't been entirely easy on him, John. We bought this place, moved far from the city, got away from it all, but there are some things you just can't get away from."

John nodded. He knew that truth all too well.

"Maybe I can help with that," he began.

Maggie's visage changed to one of consternation. "I thought so," she sighed. "John, if this is to keep your family safe, there is nothing that Earl or I wouldn't do, but if you're planning to ask him to go hunting, then please reconsider. Don't put that on him. Don't put it on me."

"But what if it worked? What if he could solve that final case? Closure. Wouldn't that make a difference?"

"No, it wouldn't. He might think it would—he hated retiring without having caught that man—but it's never been about that Hiram Kane." She set her coffee mug on the table, stood and walked to the kitchen window. "What haunts Earl isn't the criminals he didn't catch, it's the people he couldn't save. Did he ever tell you why he went to New Mexico that time?"

John shook his head. "He never really talked about it, but I know it had to do with the aftermath of when he shot that child killer, the Baptist. The trial. All that."

"That's where you're wrong. Earl killed that monster, and he was right to do it. That man deserved to die. The mess afterward—the trial and the newspapers—Earl thinks that's why he went to New Mexico. To get away. To come to terms with what he did. But that was never it. If it was, then killing Marcus Kane and stopping that madness in the desert would have been enough. It wasn't. Because when it came right down to it, none of those things could bring that girl back."

"What girl?"

"The one who survived the Baptist. The one who killed herself anyway." She stared out the window. Her eyes distant. "Earl blamed himself, you see. He saved her body, but he couldn't save that poor girl's mind. She was too far gone. Nothing is ever going to bring her back, and nothing he did in New Mexico or in the years after that can change it." She turned to face John. "Catching Hiram Kane won't change it either. Earl needs to move on."

"I'm sorry, Maggie. I didn't realize."

"He's a damned old fool, John." Her eyes were full and threatened tears, but her voice was strong. "Earl spent his life doing the right thing. This world is a better place because of him. But still...that one girl." She snatched a dishtowel from the counter and dabbed her eyes with it. "I have to believe that time heals, and if we just have the time, it will get better. But that won't happen if he gets dragged back into it."

John stood and walked to her, but he didn't touch her or attempt to comfort her. No sense pretending. "I understand what you're saying, Maggie, and I truly am sorry, but I'm going to protect my family. The best way I can do that is with your husband's help. I'll give him the facts and let him make up his own mind. If he says no, I swear I won't push it. I'll do it on my own. But I need him."

Maggie looked at the ceiling and sniffed loudly. "I suppose I'm not surprised." She turned away from him, steadied her gaze out the window and spoke in a voice devoid of warmth. "He's out in the back pasture. Just walk along the fence until you find him."

"Okay." John took his first steps toward the door.

"You can take your tea with you if you'd like."

"Thank you, Maggie."

John left the glass of tea on the table and walked out.

CHAPTER 13

CUTTER VALENTINE PINCHED THE BASE OF THE GLOVE and tugged it upward on his wrist, ensuring it was snug on his hand. The tan leather was supple from frequent use. He gripped the long handle of the come-along and pulled until he heard two more clicks from the ratchet arm. He grabbed the line of barbed wire strung along the top of the fence. It was held taut by the hand-winch.

Stringing the wire was as much art as science. It needed to be taut to peg it into place. Time loosens all fencing and stringing the barb wire—particularly the top strand—with any slack would result in a substandard fence in a matter of weeks. Best to do it right the first time. The greater danger for Cutter was winching it too tight. One click too many and the wire would snap, recoiling quicker than a person can react and leaving some nasty cuts in the process. Cutter had his share of scars, but he was a fair hand at fence repair by this point.

He strummed the top wire. One more click would do. No more. No less.

A short bark from the tall grass on the other side of his pickup turned his head. Walker came bounding around the open tailgate, tongue out and tail wagging. He stopped at Cutter's feet and looked into the distance.

Cutter's eyes followed the mutt's line of sight until he spied movement—someone walking along the fence. Cutter lifted his cowboy hat and wiped his brow with his forearm. His shirtsleeve came away only slightly damp. The fall weather was kind to working outdoors. His blue-gray eyes were still sharp, and the stranger only took a few more steps before Cutter recognized him and a smile spread beneath his thick gray mustache.

Cutter kneeled next to Walker, and the dog looked at him expectantly.

"Yeah, go get him," he whispered.

Walker took off and covered the distance to the man in moments. Cutter could hear soft laughter as the mutt greeted John Michaels with a wagging tail and a slobbery lick. John used both hands to scratch the dog's ears and pat his head. Cutter had always suspected that John wasn't much of an animal person, but he hid it well when it came to Walker. That particular mutt had played an important role in a chain of miracles four years ago. Walker had saved Cutter's life, which enabled Cutter to save the life of John, who had been busy saving the lives of the other victims of Marcus Kane's program.

To some people, a dog is just a dog. To Cutter, Walker was a friend to whom he'd be forever indebted. John seemed to appreciate that and showed respect for Walker as well. As for the mutt, he simply liked John, and he had proven an astute judge of character over the years.

Cutter liked John as well, though he recognized him as an acquired taste. He wondered what John had been like before they had met, when John was bleeding out from stab wounds in the Sonoran desert. He knew John's past career on Wall Street meant he had to be exceedingly good with people as well as numbers to be successful, but after almost dying in New Mexico, John seemed to expend very little effort with people.

Of course, the exception to this rule was John's family. Cutter had never seen someone with such singular purpose as John Michaels. He intended to protect those closest to him no matter what. Cutter respected that. He also respected John's intelligence and survival instincts. In the old proverb of giving a man a fish versus teaching him to fish, when John had asked Cutter to provide him with the tools necessary to live life as a ghost, Cutter hadn't balked, and John had taken to it like a born fisherman.

As he watched John stroll along the fence line, Walker bounding alongside him, that fact caused him concern. John had been on his own for a while now. For him to be making a house call, something was amiss. Cutter removed the gloves from his hands and tossed them onto the tailgate.

"Howdy, stranger," Cutter called out. "What brings you to this neck of the woods?"

"Teacakes, apparently," John said as he closed the distance between them. "Never had them before, but they may be my new favorite food."

"Not many make 'em like Maggie. She's a keeper." Cutter extended his hand, and John gave it a firm shake.

"No question there, but I'm afraid she's not very happy with me right now."

Cutter raised his eyebrows. "That so? That's normally territory I occupy. I spend more time in the doghouse than Walker. What's the story? Your ladies okay?"

John walked to the tailgate and sat on its edge. "Sarah and DJ are fine, but something unexpected has come up. We need to talk."

Something in John's eyes told Cutter that whatever had surfaced was serious indeed.

"I want to show you something on my phone and then tell you what I think," John continued.

"Fair enough," Cutter nodded. "Let's take a look at what you've got, then you can put on that extra pair of gloves and help me pin this barb wire while you tell me about it."

Cutter leaned on the tailgate next to John. Walker sat on the grass between the feet of the men, looking up at them with his canine grin. John held up his phone and started the video.

CHAPTER 14

MAGGIE WATCHED AS HER HUSBAND CLOSED THE DRESSER DRAWER and dropped a stack of underwear into the old leather duffel bag on their bed. She made no move to help him. She wasn't crying. She was too angry for that.

"You don't need to do this, Earl."

Cutter opened the drawer that contained his socks, then stopped before reaching inside. He instead turned and walked to her, put his hands on her shoulders and squeezed.

"Yes, I do, Mag. And you know it."

"I don't know it. What I do know is that you made me a promise. Do you remember that promise?"

Cutter sighed and returned to packing. His silence didn't surprise Maggie. It didn't sit well with her either.

"When you helped John Michaels go on his own, when the FBI cut you out of their investigation afterward, you promised me it would be one more year. You knew that without the FBI it would be next to impossible for you to find Kane on your own—you were honest with me about that—but you wanted to try anyway so I agreed to one more year, and then I gave you another year after that. That was two years beyond when you should have retired for good."

Her hands were on her hips in her angry stance, but her voice broke on the last word. Maggie knew waterworks might be due any minute. It was ridiculous. She was no child bride upset that her husband's sense of duty was calling him away from home. She was too old for that nonsense, but the tears were coming anyway.

"Two more years of watching you come home frustrated. Two more years of feeling you toss and turn in our bed. Two more years of hoping you'd find that man so you could be finished, yet still praying every day that you wouldn't find him because what if this was the day there was a knock on my door with someone on the porch telling me you weren't ever going to come home again."

The tears came. Cutter folded three pairs of starched jeans and placed them in the duffel.

"I didn't want to browbeat you into retirement, Earl. I wanted to be a supportive wife, but when the day finally came and we had that talk, and when you agreed it was time to hang up your spurs, it was one of the happiest moments of my life. You were finally mine. I didn't have to share you anymore. I didn't have to worry whether you'd be coming home. And now you're right back into it. Why, Earl?"

She finally abandoned her angry stance and sat on the edge of the bed. Hands clasped in front of her. Her knuckles ached.

Cutter stopped packing. He sat next to her and put one arm around her shoulders. She had fit perfectly under that arm for decades. He used his other hand to brush a tear from her cheek, the finger calloused and rough but the motion gentle.

"Because Maggie. Because what if John is right? He's probably not. This is most likely a wild goose chase. But what if that man really is Jonas Kane? And what if this is our only shot at catching him and his father?"

"Then let someone else do the catching. It doesn't have to be you."

"No, that's one thing I know John is right about. If this is the Kane family, then we can't afford to draw any attention to an investigation. We have the advantage of surprise. That doesn't happen often."

"Don't go, Earl."

"What if I don't go? What if this *is* Hiram Kane and his son? We know they're up to something. How many people will suffer—how many will die—if they have their way? And if I turn my back on it and just let it happen, what does that make me?"

He stood from the bed and zipped up the big leather bag.

"I have to go, Mag. It's probably nothing, but I have to see. And you know me well enough to recognize that, whether you want to admit it or not."

Maggie sniffed. She turned to look her husband in the eyes. Like his hands, those eyes were hard as steel yet as gentle as could be.

"Damn your sense of responsibility, Earl. And damn John Michaels for dragging you into this."

"You don't mean that, Darlin'. Everything is going to be fine."

She stood and placed her palm against his chest, the empty place on his shirt where the silver star hung for so many years.

"Promise me," she said. "Promise me this is the last time. Promise me you'll come home and stay home."

He put his own hand on top of hers and smiled, the corners of his bushy mustache rising.

"I solemnly swear."

"Okay then." She sniffed again and strode for the door. "I'll put the teacakes in a sack for you. No sense in letting them get stale here."

Her voice didn't betray the fresh tears that welled into her eyes.

CHAPTER 15

TRISH SAT ON THE BENCH outside the Physical Sciences building, keeping one eye on the front door while she pretended to study the tablet in her lap. Her screen showed curriculum notes from her modern literature class, an elective that had sounded more interesting than it had proven to be.

She wasn't paying attention to the notes anyway. Her real work had taken place earlier in the day, after she had made her phone call at the student union. Dialing a "212" area code had felt good. It occurred to her as she was dialing that after growing up with a smart phone that retained all her contacts, she knew only two phone numbers by heart—her mother's cell phone and the number she was punching into the Jurassic communication device. Of those two numbers, the former was known from childhood, and the latter she had been persuaded to memorize before she ever left for college, just in case she needed to reach him but didn't have her own phone. Who knew?

The student union had semi-private booths set up with pay phones that were almost never in use. All the booths were empty when Trish had made her phone call. She was grateful. That conversation had been intense. She had tried to stick to the facts, but her voice had seized up when she relayed the experience with Slade in her dorm room. The call had ended within a minute after that. "I'll be there in twelve hours" were the last words spoken.

A restroom visit for some cold water on the face ended her time at the student union. The next stop was the library. A section on the second floor held long tables with desktop computers available for

student use, almost as empty as the pay phones since every student at
the university had at least one computer of his or her own, but Trish
needed one today. She had research to do.

She felt ridiculously paranoid for not wanting to use her own
laptop or tablet to begin looking into the life of Christian Berry, but she
could live with being paranoid. As the old saying went, better to be safe
than beaten, raped or murdered.

Unfortunately, the research had not taken long. The search engine
results generated for "Christian Berry" were almost entirely about
other people with that name. Other than one mention in a local
newspaper about his participation mentoring student athletes and his
name on his own church's website—though no picture was included on
the very basic webpage—there was no other information about the
Christian Berry whom she was seeking. No social media pages. Not
even old stories from participation in high school athletics or other
extra-curricular activities. His digital footprint was minimal almost to
the point of nonexistence.

What she needed to do was real research. She needed to talk to
members of the church. People who would know Stephanie from her
involvement with that group. People who had spent time with Pastor
Berry. Trish needed to dig. To scratch. To learn. But she had promised
on the phone that she wouldn't do anything to draw attention to
herself. She wouldn't even be returning to her dorm room.

So here she sat outside the Physical Sciences building. It was one
of the taller buildings on campus at four stories high, and it sat
adjacent to the bonfire field. There was plenty of activity happening on
the field with the final week to complete bonfire construction. And
there was now activity at the Physical Sciences building as well. She
watched the faces of students exiting the front door. Class had just let
out, and any minute...bingo.

Trish watched as Andrew Kraft left the building, backpack slung
over one shoulder. Less than forty-eight hours after his girlfriend made
national news, Andrew was back in the swing of things. Resilient. And
not right.

She slid the tablet into her bag, rose from the bench and fast-
walked toward Andrew, fully intending to perhaps not break the
promise she had made on the phone earlier but to definitely bend it.

CHAPTER 16

TRISH APPROACHED ANDREW from behind and put her hand on his shoulder.

"We need to talk," she said as he swiveled his head to see who was touching him. Andrew kept walking at the same pace.

"About what?"

"About last night," she replied, withdrawing her hand as she fell into step next to him.

"What about it?" His tone wasn't rude. Not friendly either.

"I wanted to thank you for walking me home. It was a crazy night."

"You thanked me last night, right before you passed out." He slid his arm through the other backpack strap so the pack rode evenly on both shoulders.

"Yeah, sorry about that."

"Are you sorry about showing up at the memorial and acting the way you did?" Again, despite the nature of the words, Andrew's tone wasn't harsh. That seemed to be a positive sign.

"I may have made some poor life choices yesterday," she conceded. She needed a meaningful conversation with Andrew, but she had no intention of apologizing. "I was upset. I'm sure you understand. The day was rough. The night was horrible. It didn't get better after you left me in my dorm room."

She watched his face closely, searching for reaction. She didn't believe Andrew had anything to do with Slade being in her room, but Andrew did have a key thanks to Stephanie, and Slade hadn't just phased through a wall. She could read no reaction in Andrew's face whatsoever, which proved nothing either way but made her feel better. There was no guilt in his eyes.

"So what do we need to talk about?"

"Steph. I'd really like to talk about Stephanie."

"Why?"

Seriously? She wanted to scream, to argue, to slap him, but they had already been down this road yesterday. Instead, Trish gently clutched his arm and pulled him to a stop.

"Andrew, look at me." He turned to face her. Their eyes met. Other students filed by on either side, but no one jostled them. "I know we haven't spent much time together—Stephanie is our only link—and I know you probably have plenty of other people that you can confide in, but I don't, and I need to talk to someone. You don't need me, but I need you, Andrew."

She looked at the ground then raised her gaze again to his.

"Please..."

The word hung in the air between them. She maintained an earnest expression while watching him carefully. And there it was. Something. Maybe not much but something in his eyes. A crack in the veneer of apathy.

He sighed.

"Okay, let's talk. It's the right thing to do. Come on."

He walked toward the annex of the English and Literature building. It held an abundance of tables of varying size and was a popular place for group study. They could talk there.

Andrew stayed three paces in front of Trish. She watched his backpack bob up and down in rhythm with his gait. Step one accomplished. He was willing to talk. Step two would be more challenging. She needed him to open up, and for that, she might have to do the same. That was a risk she hadn't taken with anyone in a long time. Certainly no one at the university. Not even Stephanie.

She readied herself as they walked into the building. She was so focused on the conversation about to take place, she took no notice of the hulking figure observing her from the shade of a nearby oak tree.

CHAPTER 17

CHRISTIAN BERRY SAT AT HIS DESK in his office at the church. The computer screen in front of him contained a rough draft of talking points for his next sermon. He wasn't looking at the notes. He was staring out the window.

The office sat at the back of the building with windows open to the slight greenspace which consisted of mostly grass, a few trees and some sparse playground equipment which was rarely used given the equally sparse number of children in Berry's congregation.

At the edge of the church's property sat two buildings: a modest house occupied by Berry as the resident pastor and a considerably more modest combination of work shed and living quarters occupied by the church's rarely seen custodian-slash-groundskeeper. Hiram Kane was walking across the grass toward that structure now. He had been using the tunnel less frequently the past few weeks. With the goal now within sight, was the old man growing overconfident, or did he just desire fresh air?

Hiram never complained about his living conditions. Maintaining appearances was important, but even beyond that, Berry believed he genuinely liked the shed. He suspected his father felt the spartan conditions cleansed his mind and sharpened his focus.

A soft chime from his cell phone made Berry glance down. A message from Slade. The troublesome girl from the bonfire was talking to Andrew Kraft. Berry thumbed a quick reply.

"Monitor only."

He wasn't concerned that the girl was talking to Andrew. They knew each other. He was her dead roommate's boyfriend after all. She could be talking to him out of grief and not necessarily trying to cause further trouble for Berry, but the situation did bear watching. Besides, he needed to have something to keep Slade occupied.

Since being disgraced and abandoned by the TSC football program in the spring, Slade had developed into a useful field lieutenant, an important cog in the machine. It was exactly what Berry had foreseen, and precisely what Berry had intended when he orchestrated the events that led to Slade's dismissal from the university's athletics program. Things truly had been falling into place.

His father had long assured him this would be the case. In answer to his son's litany of questions and objections, Hiram would provide a direct answer on occasion and simply say "it will come" on others. He had been right on every count thus far.

It will come.

Berry returned his attention to the computer screen and typed out "God will provide" followed by "if God is for us, who can be against us?"

He smiled. Berry wasn't certain if God was still out there, but if so, he most certainly would not be for them.

He looked out the window in time to see his father reach the door to the custodian's quarters. Hiram paused long enough for a surreptitious glance in all directions. Ever watchful. Ever subtle. No one would suspect he was paranoid. He entered the building and closed the door behind him.

Berry returned his attention to the screen. Even while alone, he thought of himself as Christian Berry at times like this. He believed it to be a rare mind that could reidentify itself, effectively creating its own multiple personality disorder but regulate it such that the disorder was, in fact, completely controlled and in order. The only time he returned to being Jonas Kane was in the lab in the basement of the church. Or in the secret place. At all other times, he was Christian Berry.

And Christian Berry needed to wrap up planning for the sermon. His congregation had grown tremendously, as he had known it would. When he had first reopened the old church, only a smattering attended. That number had since expanded to almost three hundred. Every available seat would be taken for the Sunday morning service. He didn't really care about the masses, but the forty-four would also be present in that service. He needed to make certain the sermon had the right message for them.

He had already prepared the contents of each of his planned nightly sessions with the forty-four. That wasn't the sort of thing he would leave until the last minute. Those messages had to be well-crafted and build upon one another in a specific way. He could improvise as necessary, but the backbone of each spiritual awakening would remain the same.

The Sunday morning service, while reaching a greater number of ears, paled in importance to the awakenings. But appearances must be maintained, particularly for a charismatic preacher on a Sunday morning.

Berry interlaced his slender fingers and pushed his hands—palms out—toward the screen until his bony knuckles cracked with the sounds of eight small caliber rifles. He returned his fingertips to the keyboard and began to type the last sermon he ever planned to deliver.

CHAPTER 18

TRISH FOLLOWED ANDREW to the back of the sizeable main room of the English and Literature Annex. The area was full of tables with groups of students occupying most of them, studying or making a half-hearted effort to do so while they visited with friends. It was loud but not so much as to deter conversation. It would be a good place to talk.

Andrew found a small table along the back wall and took a seat. As Trish covered the final steps to her own chair, she mentally prepared herself for the conversation about to take place. She needed insight into Christian Berry's church group. She needed to understand how—or if—what was happening at the church had influenced Stephanie's horrifying actions. Andrew represented the best possibility of that. He was the only person Trish knew that was part of that group, and he was also the person who should be the most invested in understanding Stephanie's death. But *should* does not always equate to *is*, and Andrew's callousness was inexplicable to Trish. She had to find her way beyond it. She had to crack whatever comprised that protective shell.

As she pulled out her chair, she flashed back a decade. Sitting down at the kitchen table with her father. She had been pestering him with questions about his work—a common occurrence—and he had one of his less common "honest moments" where, exasperated, he would say, "fine, ask me anything and I'll tell you" and he would live up to it, often revealing things more mature than appropriate for a girl her age. She cherished those times. It was like she had a secret pass that gave her access to the adult world for a brief window. She never knew if her father allowed it solely out of exasperation or if he trusted her and felt she was more mature than her age and could therefore handle the truth. She had always hoped the latter.

That day the questions had revolved around how he got information from bad guys that would help him solve crimes. They had been watching detective shows (also probably too mature for her age) and the last episode had taken place almost entirely in the interrogation rooms of the police department where the main character—a tough-as-nails female detective—was questioning three different suspects in succession in an attempt to drill down to the truth. Her partner—who was not a police officer but rather a writer of mystery novels—kept inserting himself into the process and somehow the two had woven an intricate web that led to a confession by the real killer, who seemed quite surprised that he had stumbled into confessing his crimes.

Trish's father frequently groaned while watching the series due to the lack of realism. Trish didn't care. She liked the show and was pretty certain the detective and the writer would eventually fall in love, a development she found almost as compelling as the weekly triumph of bringing a criminal to justice. That particular episode had sparked Trish's curiosity about how crimes were solved in real life.

"In real life," her father explained, "about two percent of crime solving is done in the interrogation room. The real action happens on the street. That's where the information is, and most of the time, it's just confirming what you already know. Most criminals are not complicated."

While disappointed to learn her favorite show was somewhat less than realistic, Trish was nevertheless fascinated with this glimpse into how cops gathered the intelligence necessary to bring criminals to justice. She had one follow up question after another. Her father went on to explain that information was collected under one of two circumstances: "gotta-have-it-now" or "gradually." The first category was as simple as it gets. If you needed something immediately, you had two options—the carrot or the stick. You either bribed the guy with something he wanted (or needed) or you threatened him. Either way, it helped to know the person well enough to have an idea of what bribe or threat would be most effective—people were all built differently when it came to that kind of thing—but that knowledge wasn't always a luxury you had on the street. That was also why the gotta-have-it-now intel was frequently the least reliable.

On the other end of that spectrum was the gradual collection of information. That was her father's preferred method and what he believed himself to be best at. Getting to know people on a deeper level. Collecting facts and details a little at a time, here and there, until you progressively built a network of information that could help in a number of different ways when it came to solving crimes.

Those relationships were give-and-take. Sometimes you had to be willing to open yourself up to build trust, even when it was with someone you didn't trust at all. Give them something, a little of what they need, even if they don't know they need it. Over time, the relationship will solidify into something of value to the other person. And then, when *you* need something, you'll have cultivated that person into a position where they *want* to give you something of value.

As Andrew sat across from Trish, an unreadable expression on his face, she tried to apply the lessons from that day into her present situation. Based on her encounter with him the day before, Trish believed Andrew was either in denial of his emotions related to Steph's death, or he had no emotions about it whatsoever. The latter was unfathomable to Trish.

For months, she had heard Steph relate stories of this special boy who really "got her" and of her plans for their future together. Those stories had slowed over the summer and stopped completely by the time the fall semester began so Trish had to consider the possibility that the heat had eventually worn off of the relationship between Stephanie and Andrew (and clearly any thoughts about a life together were no longer present in Steph's mind when she elected to erase every possible future of her own by leaping from that balcony). Still, they hadn't broken up, so some level of feeling had to have remained. And even if you only kinda-sorta cared about someone, wouldn't you be upset if that person had died? The jury was still out on Andrew, but Trish clung to hope that under the surface, he was gripped by unacknowledged grief or anger or bewilderment or any sort of feeling that would allow her to convince him to help her. But how best to draw that out?

Andrew looked at his watch. "We're here. Let's talk."

"Okay but promise me something."

"What?"

"Promise me we're really going to talk, that you're not just going to make a half-hearted effort to humor me then dismiss the conversation."

"I'm here, aren't I?"

"That wasn't a promise. I mean it. This is serious. Swear to me we're going to have a real conversation."

"Above all, my brothers and sisters, do not swear—not by heaven or by earth or by anything else. All you need to say is a simple 'Yes' or 'No.' Otherwise you will be condemned."

"I see." Trish clenched her jaw around the words. "That's very helpful."

"I'm sorry, Trish. I didn't mean that to be condescending."

"It wasn't condescending. Only a bit rude." She sank back in her chair. "Just so I can prepare myself, will you be quoting a lot of scripture during this conversation? I assume that was from the Bible."

"Yes, it was from the Bible—fifth chapter of James—but no, you don't need to worry about too much scripture being quoted to you. I don't know it well enough. Nothing like Chris...Pastor Berry. I happen know that chapter because we were studying it last week. And I only recited it because I don't plan on swearing to anything and wanted you to know why. But for what you're asking, my yes is yes. I'm here, Trish. I'm ready to talk. It's the right thing to do."

That was the second time he'd used that phrase in the last five minutes.

"Why is talking to me the right thing?"

"Because you're lost. What Steph did...I don't understand it, but that doesn't matter. What's done is done. My understanding or my lack of understanding has no bearing on it. But I do know my place in this world and in the next. That's what really matters. You don't have that."

"I don't have a place in the next world?"

"No, you don't, but that's not what I meant. I was saying you don't have an appreciation for those things. You're living in the here and now. This world means something to you. That's why what happened with Steph is making you feel the way you do. So I'm here to talk because maybe, just possibly, it's not too late for you. Maybe you can be saved. Ignoring that possibility would be wrong on my part—a dereliction—so having this conversation is the right thing to do."

Under the table, Trish pinched the skin behind her knee, just above the calf, hard enough to feel like a wasp was stinging her. *Don't argue. Don't fight. This is an opening. Use it.*

But what college student uses a word like freaking "dereliction" anyway?

"Thank you, Andrew. I appreciate your concern. Really." She hoped her words sounded sincere even though they tasted quite the opposite. "You said you were studying James. What was that about? Was Steph studying the same thing? Were you two together in the class?"

"Not a class, Trish, a Bible study. Why are you interested in this?"

"Because I want to know what was going on with Steph before she...died. Your Bible studies had become a big part of her life. What was James about?"

"That chapter was about patience in suffering."

"Like what you're enduring right now talking with me?"

Almost a crack of a smile. Almost. She couldn't see it on his face, but she sensed it beneath the surface.

"Here's the thing, Trish. I need to know where you're coming from. If you feel lost, if you're looking for hope—for purpose—we can talk all you'd like. But what you said last night, when you told Chris that you were going to get to the bottom of what happened to Steph, that leads me to believe that this conversation isn't directed toward saving your soul but is instead about you looking for dirt on Chris or the church. I think you've already done enough damage as it is. I don't want to contribute to any additional harm."

Damn. Why did he have to be so perceptive? Or perhaps her attempts that she believed to be subtle and clever were in fact something less than that. Either way, she was faced with a choice. Press forward or employ a different tack. She thought of the conversation with her father. *Give and take.* She had to be willing to give in order to take.

"Look," she sighed. "You're not completely wrong, but please see this from my side. I'm not out to get your preacher, and I'm not trying to tear down your church or your religion or anything else. I loved Steph. I want to know the truth about what happened. It may not have anything to do with the Bible studies or anything along those lines, but I'll never know if I don't ask the questions. Don't you see? This hurts me here." She placed her hand over her heart. "What happened with Steph is wrong. I can't live with it. I need to know the truth. My soul will never be satisfied until I do."

"Do you believe you have a soul?"

The question was frank. She was taken aback. It wasn't something she had spent much time considering.

"I don't know. You and I believe in different things. I don't think there's anything wrong with that. We should be able to accept it. But I'm open to listening if you're open to talking about Steph. That might really help me."

Andrew paused. He seemed to be thinking.

"You say we believe in different things, but what do you believe in, Trish? You wear a cross around your neck. You keep it tucked inside your shirt, but every now and then it pops out. I've seen it."

And here we go. She steeled herself. *Be willing to give.*

"The cross was a gift. From my father."

"So your dad believed...what happened to you?"

"Not to me. To him. Dad was a police officer in New York. A homicide detective. He bought the cross and necklace for my birthday, but I was angry with him after he and Mom divorced. I refused the gift, so he wore it instead. He was wearing it the day he was killed in the line of duty."

Trish waited. She expected to hear an obligatory "I'm sorry to hear that" or some form of sympathy for the poor girl who'd lost her daddy.

Andrew sat silent.

"Anyway," Trish continued. "He spent his life solving crimes. Protecting others. Doing the right thing. He should have been the hero. He deserved that. Instead, he was murdered. Needlessly. Senselessly. And the world went on. For everybody but him." She levelled her gaze on Andrew. "How could a so-called God of love let something like that happen?"

Trish didn't wait for a response. The question was rhetorical. Andrew wouldn't have an answer for it because there was no answer.

"So I'm not big on church and Bible study and all that. I'm big on truth. I don't expect you to feel the same way, but I do want you to understand where I'm coming from. Truth is what I have. Not much in the way of family or friends, Steph was pretty much it, so I want to know the truth about her. I need to know. And you're my only hope on that front, Andrew."

When she finished, he nodded once.

"Fair enough. Thank you for being honest." He glanced at his watch again. "I have to go."

Shitty-shit-shit. Trish balled her fists under the table and squeezed until her fingernails left purple crescents in her palm. She had opened up. She had been honest. It hadn't worked. She should've stuck with trying to be clever and subtle.

Andrew stood and pushed his chair back.

"Hey, one thing," Trish ventured. "What I just told you...about my dad? Nobody else knows that. Even Steph didn't know."

Andrew paused in the midst of shouldering his backpack, then pulled the straps snug onto his shoulders.

"I won't tell anyone."

"I'd ask you to swear, but I know better."

This time, the slightest grin did crack.

He took two steps then stopped. "Listen, I appreciate you being honest. That probably wasn't easy for you. It's a good start. Maybe we can talk some more. Let me..."

He hesitated. What was going through his mind?

"Let me think about it. You think about what I said, too."

Trish unclenched her fists and pushed her own chair back, but she didn't get up. *Let him go. Let him think. It's a start.*

"I will. Thanks. I hope we can talk more. Maybe tomorrow?"

"Maybe. See you around."

He walked out of the annex. Trish took a deep breath. She had played her hand. Andrew was either going to think about it and perhaps help her, or he was going to go straight to Christian Berry and tell him everything. The question was whether Trish was going to have another visit from Slade soon, before reinforcements could arrive.

CHAPTER 19

IT WAS ERIC JOHNSON'S FIRST TIME in Texas, and his visit was not off to a promising start. He flashed his most charming smile at the woman on the other side of the airport rental car counter.

"It doesn't have to be full size. I'm fine with midsize. Anything you've got."

"I'm sorry, sir," the woman replied. Her hair had likely been pulled back at the start of her shift, but much of it had escaped containment and now framed her face with tangled strands. "We don't have any sedans available. This is your only option at the moment."

"I understand," Eric drew out the last syllable while he withdrew the leather bifold from his front pocket. He laid it on the counter to extract his driver's license and credit card. His NYPD badge showed prominently.

"You're a police officer?"

Eric upped the wattage on his smile. "I am. Detective. New York proud. Any chance a newly available sedan has popped up on your screen?"

"No sir," she said without looking at her computer. "It's a busy weekend. Sedans are gone."

Eric's smile dimmed.

"Any chance this is because I'm black?"

"Afraid not. We have zero sedans for all races, religions and sexual orientations."

"Yeah, I figured. Thought I'd ask." The last traces of smile vanished as Eric resigned himself to his fate. He had brushed fame a couple of years prior but had rejected it with a *'just-doing-my-job'* mentality. He now wondered whether he might be receiving his preferred vehicle if he had instead chosen to pursue the path of celebrated police hero.

Missed opportunities.

"I really am sorry," the woman said as she took his credit card and driver's license. "It's a home game for the Cowboys this weekend. Our cars vanish on Fridays before a home game. It'll be the same at all the rental counters."

"That's fine," he sighed. "As long as it gets me from here to there."

Eric gripped the steering wheel with both hands as two semi-trucks passed him on either side in unison. He leaned harder into the accelerator and the vehicle gradually increased its velocity but not enough to overtake the speeding eighteen-wheelers. The minivan was built for family comfort, not aggressive highway driving.

It had already been a long day since he had received the phone call that morning, and he still had a long drive ahead of him. Even though the minivan wouldn't have been his first choice in transportation—or his second choice or ninth—at least he was now on the road and not cooped up in an airline seat. He was not a frequent flier and not a fan of the experience in general, but there was no choice in the matter. Based on the way Trish had sounded on the phone and the details she had given him, he wanted to be on-site as soon as possible.

He had only seen Trish once since she had left for school the prior year. She had come home that summer and made sure to have lunch with him while she was in the city. The two of them weren't exactly close, but they shared a bond. She was George's daughter, and George had been more than a partner to Eric; he had been his mentor when Eric became the youngest member of the NYPD homicide department several years ago. George had also been his friend, and he owed a debt to his friend that he would never be able to repay. That extended to Trish. She was his family now.

And if some jock dickhead broke into her dorm room in the middle of the night and threatened her, well, Eric took that personally. He had thrown clothes and a toothbrush into a carry-on bag, headed to the airport and been lucky to catch a flight with only minutes to spare.

He wasn't certain what to think about the other things Trish told him. Before the phone call, he hadn't even known the girl with the knives at the Dallas Opera House had been Trish's roommate. Plus, the WiFi had been down on the plane so he wasn't able to do any research during the flight over. He was forced to read the airline magazine in the seat pocket—a special kind of torture—though he did discover a pair of noise-cancelling headphones he planned to order soon, and he learned that DFW Airport is larger than the entire island of Manhattan. No wonder he had lost his way twice while trying to reach the highway.

He did, however, have an opportunity while waiting in line at the car rental counter to watch the video of Trish confronting the preacher at the bonfire. That had proved entertaining. She had balls. He gave her that. The question now was just how deep of trouble those balls had gotten her into. He wouldn't know until he sat down with Trish and had a real conversation.

He nudged a bit more speed out of the minivan and continued south.

CHAPTER 20

JOHN SHIFTED HIS HIPS in an attempt to get more comfortable. The passenger side of the bench seat was, to be kind, rather well-worn, much like Cutter's pickup truck in general. On the driver's side, Cutter rested on a seat cover consisting of hundreds of wooden beads—each the size of a marble—that worked together to compose a type of upholstery chainmail. John's seat bore an ancient coffee stain, two strips of duct tape repairing old tears and a spring under the vinyl surface determined to poke John's ass with an intensity varying between annoyance and low-grade pain.

"It really would have been fine to take my car," John said. He had successfully maneuvered himself so the spring had settled into the center of his left buttock, still uncomfortable but preferable to the little bastard poking his tailbone. "It's new and...comfortable."

"I'm sure it is, but it lacks a couple of things," Cutter replied. He glanced at John as he spoke, but his eyes always returned quickly to the road. "There are a million of these trucks in Texas, from good ol' boys to lawn crews to grandpas. It's the most non-threatening, forgettable vehicle possible for the area. That works in our favor when doing surveillance."

"Fair enough," John said, uncertain if the tradeoff of riding the spring was worth it. "What else?"

"No rear window rack in your car. I prefer to keep my shotgun handy."

"God bless Texas."

"Damn right," Cutter said with a wink.

John pushed his hand into the brown paper sack that sat between them on the bench and extracted a teacake. He had eaten about a dozen since they'd hit the road.

"One more," he said as he took a bite.

"Sure," Cutter grinned.

"So what do you think we're walking into?" John asked, careful not to spray crumbs while he chewed even though they would have just blended into the dirt on the floorboard.

"Probably nothing, and that's something you need to prepare yourself for, John. I respect you enough to go along and play this out, but you have to understand we're most likely hunting snipe here."

"Huh?"

"A snipe hunt. A wild goose chase. A fool's errand. Call it whatever you want, I'm just saying the likelihood that the preacher in that video is Hiram Kane's son is about two degrees shy of slim. We need to be realistic about that fact going in."

John gazed out the window at a small herd of black and white cows huddled together under the shade of a large oak tree at the edge of a passing field.

"The odds are long, I'm aware of that, and I don't plan to spend my life tilting at windmills and scouring the internet for signs of the Kane family. But Cutter, when I saw those eyes, I felt it."

"I know you did. I'm not denying the power of a gut feeling and if anyone deserves to be given the benefit of the doubt on this, it's you." Cutter raised one eyebrow. "And your gut."

"Good one," John said, rolling his eyes. The stab wounds in his abdomen had healed well. He had more trouble from his ulcer than any lingering issues with the injuries from the desert. "But it's more than just a gut feeling. I've been thinking about this, and there's a degree of logic to what may be happening."

John shifted his attention from the fields on his right and focused on the horizon ahead.

"What can we glean from the experience with Marcus Kane in the desert?" John mused aloud. "We know the program served as a testing facility, a vehicle for Kane and his psychiatrist partner to experiment on unsuspecting participants. We know drugs were involved. The supplement beverage they forced us to drink every morning was chemically manipulating our behavior and making us susceptible to Kane's influence."

"Right," Cutter inserted. "And we know it was all part of a bigger plan orchestrated by Marcus's father, Hiram."

"So the question becomes 'what is the bigger plan,' correct?" John asked.

"Seems to be the important issue."

"Up until now, the authorities have focused on the chemical aspect. That supplement beverage had presumably been given to every participant in every iteration of the program. The desert compound was a proving ground for the formula. Developing it. Improving it until the drugs accomplished whatever the end goal might be. So we've been worried about how he might use it or distribute it among an unsuspecting population."

"Things you and I have discussed before," Cutter mentioned. "What does that have to do with your preacher buddy in the video?"

"What if we've been focused on the wrong thing? Or maybe focused on only half the picture?"

"What are you getting at?"

"A big part of the program in its later stages was something Kane called 'spiritual awakenings.' Every night, the participants would gather in the center of the compound to listen to him. It was deemed part of the therapy. There'd be a fire that we would all sit around and listen to his admonitions. The man was downright charismatic. There's a reason people were willing to follow him, do whatever he wanted."

"More cult than therapy program?" Cutter inquired.

"At the end, absolutely. Why do we overlook that aspect? What if the testing ground in New Mexico wasn't simply to experiment with the effectiveness of the drugs? What if it was also testing the effectiveness of the spiritual awakenings? How to best manipulate your followers."

"But with Marcus Kane dead, the cult leader is no longer there. Unless..."

"Exactly," John nodded. "Unless someone else is taking the mantle of cult leader. Someone else is delivering the spiritual awakenings. And who would be in a better position to do that than—"

"—than a preacher like the man in the video," Cutter finished.

They sat in silence for a full minute, Cutter digesting the line of thought as he drove.

"You may have something there, John. You just might have something."

"Maybe something but not enough," John replied. "We have the first act of a movie. It's possible we know the who, but that gets us no closer to the what or the why. Those are the bigger questions."

"What was his name again?" Cutter asked.

"Christian Berry."

"Feel like an alias to you?"

"Tailor-made." John smiled. Cutter was probing the same thought-lines that had popped into John's mind since first seeing the video.

"Guess you've become real familiar with that the past few years."

"Plenty familiar. And Christian Berry is a good one. The best aliases sit just outside of the common. Something unique enough to sound real, but common enough to be forgettable. Go with 'Smith' or 'Jones' or 'Miller' and you already sound suspicious."

"I agree. And this one is tailor-made because?"

"The profession. If you want to be a preacher, what better name than Christian? But it's common enough to not sound manufactured. The name matched with the profession exudes a feeling of manifest destiny that this man would become a preacher and adds an ethereal credibility to him without even knowing the person. And if you want to convey the sense of being harmless, you couldn't ask for a gentler name than Berry. In an age where Apple is a trusted brand, fruit-based aliases are winners. I was John Mellon for a few weeks last year."

Cutter snorted a short laugh as he changed lanes.

"Yep, you've gotten the hang of it."

"Good teacher," John said.

"So let's fast forward your movie to the end. What are they doing?"

"I don't know, but..." John's voice trailed off.

"What is it?" Cutter asked.

"Something he said," John spoke softly, his eyes surveying the horizon but not seeing anything outside his own mind.

"Who said?"

"Marcus Kane. Something he said when he was torturing me." John swallowed. He could feel the acid in his stomach building. Damn ulcer. "He said if you want to kill ten people, you make a compound in the desert, but if you want to kill *ten-thousand*, you need something more." John turned to face Cutter. "I'm worried Christian Berry is the something more."

Cutter must have felt the same chill as John. He turned the fan on the air conditioner down a notch and took his foot off the accelerator. As the truck slowed, a minivan passed on the left.

John pulled himself back into the moment. "Why are we taking this exit?"

"We're making a stop on the way. Someone we need to talk to. May prove worthwhile."

The truck hit a pothole on the exit ramp and the spring under John's seat poked him with vigor. He hoped the proposed stop was near.

CHAPTER 21

IT WAS THE MACHINE GUNS that made John nervous. He had no particular reason to be. Cutter had driven them to the military base, and he was the one talking to the corporal manning the booth to the side of the gate. But the two soldiers standing guard on either side of the entrance to Fort Braun—the two soldiers staring through the windshield at John and Cutter—were carrying M4 Carbines. The guns weren't pointed at them, and they weren't even being held in an aggressive manner, but they were at the ready. It was something John never encountered in his everyday life, and he found it disconcerting.

"No appointment, son," Cutter was informing the corporal. "This is a drop-in visit. Please inform Lieutenant General Butler that Cutter Valentine is calling. He'll either see us or he won't, but I 'spect he will."

The corporal was nonplussed and returned to the booth's interior to pick up a black phone and make a call. The sentries with the machine guns stood as they were. No conversation between them. Faces serious but not menacing. John remembered that there was a loaded shotgun in the rear window gun rack behind his head. The firearm was in full view of the soldiers, but Cutter didn't seem concerned.

John tore his gaze from the soldiers and looked around the base. When they pulled into the entry road, there was a tank on either side of the opening. They were dated and clearly out of service, but they were genuine army tanks. John had never seen one up close before. They were intimidating.

There was no equipment close to the main gate, but in the distance, he could see rows of Humvees, transports and a handful of more modern-looking tanks. Far to one side stood two helicopters. They looked big enough to transport troops but were single rotor helicopters, not the giant kind with two rotors on the top.

The corporal returned to Cutter's window with the good news that the commanding officer would see them. Cutter opened his door and stepped out of the truck, glancing over at John with a "you too" as he exited. John did likewise and stood a few feet from the pickup as the sentries moved to inspect.

"12-gauge in the rack. Handgun under the driver's seat," Cutter informed the men.

The guns were taken from the vehicle and stored in the booth, and a mirror on a pole was used for a quick examination of the truck's undercarriage. Cutter and John were then invited to return to their vehicle as another soldier pulled up in a Jeep that would escort them through the base to the building where they'd meet Lieutenant General Butler.

John sat at the same table as the two older gentlemen, but he listened far more than he spoke. Lieutenant General "Bobcat" Butler had greeted Cutter with a smile on his hawkish face. The two men were of a masculine generation that forewent hugs, but the handshake shared by the men was vigorous and even a casual observer could see it was heartfelt. When Bobcat shook John's hand upon introduction, it was a firm and authoritative double-pump.

The office in which they sat was nice but not ostentatious. When John had worked in corporate acquisitions, he would always visit a target's headquarters and viewing the office of the CEO was of particular interest for him. If the office was extravagant and appointed with fine furniture and expensive artwork, it served as a Bat-Signal to direct John toward what he would focus on during his due diligence and strategy planning. On the other hand, an office like General Butler's—which held dated furniture and family pictures instead of artwork—conveyed a different story. He may be the leader, but he's also a working man.

The fact that he had chosen for the conversation to take place at a small four-seat conference table in the corner of his office rather than sitting behind the desk with Cutter and John in the guest chairs also told John a story about the relationship between the two men.

As he learned through a couple of questions and inferring from the catch-up stories, Bobcat and Cutter had enlisted at the same time and served together. Following his four-year tour, Cutter left the military to enter the Texas Rangers. Bobcat stayed in the service as a career man and had met obvious success.

Beyond those initial questions, John had simply sat and listened, partly because he didn't want to intrude on the reunion but mainly because he knew Cutter had a reason for being here that John was completely in the dark about, and he wanted to observe Cutter's game plan.

"I swear," Cutter exclaimed through a grin, "Sergeant Swynn turned so red I thought he might have a stroke."

Bobcat guffawed a mighty laugh. "And that," he said glancing at John but levelling a finger at Cutter, "is why you can never trust this man when he tells you to take a bite of something."

John smiled. It had been an entertaining story. He suspected these two could spend the better part of an afternoon sharing them, but he was impatient to hear something that might be relevant to the mission at hand.

"So I know you well enough to know you didn't come out here just to relive the good times, Cutter. What can I do you for?"

John leaned forward. Progress. Bobcat was a doer and not just a talker.

"Well you've helped me out a number of times before, Bobcat." Cutter leaned back in his chair as he talked. "And you know I'm retired. This isn't official business."

"So noted," Bobcat replied. "What's the story?"

"Just wondering. When your boys are off duty, where do they usually go for fun?"

Bobcat furrowed his brow as he answered. "Mostly Abramsville. About twenty-five minutes south of here. College town so there's plenty of bars and dance halls and other activities that get my boys reprimanded from time to time."

"You spend much time there?"

"Not really. It's the closest town of size so Frannie and I will go in a couple times a month for shopping and dinner, that sort of thing." Bobcat stood, walked behind his desk and opened a drawer while he spoke.

"Okay," Cutter appeared thoughtful. "You hear about anything unusual happening down there lately? Any talk from your boys about the locals or anything?"

"How do you mean?" Bobcat extracted a pouch of chewing tobacco from the drawer and returned to his chair at the table.

"Nothing in particular. Just curious if there've been any incidents lately. Disturbances. Townsfolk acting strange or anything like that."

Bobcat furrowed his eyebrows again as he opened the pouch and procured a sizeable wad of dark brown strings. "Nothing springs to mind. TSC has got the big football game coming up next weekend so there'll be the usual craziness surrounding the bonfire and the game, but that's about it." He stuffed the wad of tobacco into his mouth. "Against regulations. Don't say anything."

"No scuttlebutt from the troops on anything unusual? Doesn't need to be anything big, maybe even something as small as people acting differently than they normally would."

"You're being awfully vague, Cutter." Bobcat leaned forward as he spoke. "I may need a little more information here." He picked up an empty Styrofoam coffee cup from the table and spit brown juice into it. He was an accomplished spitter. No trace to be found on his chin. "What have you got?"

Cutter sighed. "Nothing really. John and I are just going to spend a few days in Abramsville. Look around. I don't think there's anything there, but you usually have your ear to the ground, and you have a good antenna for when something is out of whack."

"Hold on there, amigo," Bobcat's eyes took on a serious glint. "You may say you're retired, but I didn't see a boat with fishing poles behind your truck. You're on the hunt. Is this something I need to be concerned about?"

"Couldn't say," Cutter replied. "I don't think so. We're just checking into things."

Bobcat leaned back in his chair and shifted his gaze from Cutter to John and back again. There was a minute of silence. John normally bore such silences well. His business success had been amplified by his ability to endure uncomfortable quiet periods. If the other guy spoke first, he often said something that ultimately gave John the upper hand. In this case, he was more concerned with a need to interrupt Bobcat's train of thought before the general inserted himself too far into the matter at hand.

"Sir?" John began. "I'm just curious. I thought this base was used for training troops for international conflict. Do you often find yourself looking into local trouble?"

Bobcat's gaze left Cutter and shifted to John. He gave a half-smile. "My duty is to protect this great nation from all threats, foreign *and* domestic. 9/11 may seem like a long time ago, but we're still feeling the effect. The state of Texas on a stand-alone basis represents the ninth largest GDP in the entire world. It's ripe for economic terrorism. Plus, there's damn near two-hundred colleges and universities in the state. A dozen of those hold sporting events—mostly football games—that attract upwards of fifty-thousand fans. That's not mentioning the professional teams. There are a lot of potential bad things that can happen, and our base gets the call if it does."

"I guess I hadn't thought about that sort of thing beyond local law enforcement."

"They're the most important part," Bobcat allowed. "But you may have noticed our two whirlybirds when you arrived. Those are Bell Venoms. Speed in excess of 166 knots. We can be in Abramsville in six minutes. Austin in forty. We're not the first line of defense," Bobcat spit into his cup again, "but we are the spear-tip of the offense."

"Speaking of your military-grade toys," Cutter interjected, "I'm guessing you have some mighty fine infrared tech. Scopes, goggles, that sort of thing."

The half-grin reappeared on Bobcat's face. "Nothing but the best."

Cutter nodded. "Any chance an old friend might borrow a few items for a week or two? If he promised to return it all in good shape?"

Bobcat shook his head, but the grin remained. "I knew you had something going on down there, you rascal." He spit. "I wish I could help you, Cutter, I really do, but we keep close tabs on equipment, particularly the high-tech stuff. Not the kind of thing I can look the other way on these days."

Cutter raised both palms. "Never hurts to ask."

Bobcat stroked his chin with one hand. "You're going hunting all right. I know you're not going to tell me anything, but if you get down there and find something I need to know about, you call me."

Cutter stood and John did likewise.

"I know the number by heart, amigo." He extended his hand. Bobcat stood and shook it, clapping his free hand onto Cutter's arm as he did so. Probably the closest thing to a hug either man could endure.

"You take care of yourself," Bobcat said, then looked at John. "And John, you watch yourself around this one."

John smiled and shook Bobcat's hand. "Yes, sir. It was a pleasure meeting you. Thank you for your time."

As they left the office, John didn't know whether Cutter would consider the meeting a success or failure, but he suspected the latter. Cutter's expression was inscrutable. For someone whose natural gift was an ability to read people well, John's inability to discern anything from the former Texas Ranger drove him crazy.

CHAPTER 22

AFTERNOON WAS TURNING TO EVENING. Hiram Kane opened a window of the dwelling he called home to allow the cool air to filter into the room. Roughly half the structure was a simple toolshed with the other half consisting of a modest studio space that served as sleeping quarters, living area and kitchen. There was a small bathroom attached. It was all he needed.

The toolshed portion of the structure was partly utilized for its intended purpose. Tools of various types and rust-levels adorned one wall above a sizeable worktable. The other half of the space was taken up by a large rack of weights, a sturdy workout bench and a duct-tape-wrapped hundred-pound heavy bag suspended by a large chain from an exposed ceiling rafter. What looked like a cheap wooden floor beneath the heavy bag masked the entrance to the underground tunnel that led to the church basement.

Hiram inhaled the crisp air and returned to the free-standing weight rack. The adjustable pins in the rack were set at a low height, the reinforced steel bar suspended at knee level. He slid another forty-five-pound plate on either side of the bar. There were now five plates per side.

He bent at the waist and gripped the bar, hands just outside his knees, one palm forward and the other with a reverse grip. He breathed deeply once followed by two shallow bursts of wind. He closed his eyes, lifted the weight from the rack and took two steps back.

His torso was tight. The trapezius muscles on either side of his neck were knotted sinew. He bent at the waist and lowered the bar until the plates almost touched the ground, then he straightened with a quiet grunt. He repeated the lift ten times, then, muscles shaking, took two steps forward and returned the bar onto the rack.

When he released the bar, his torso relaxed, and he felt the warmth spread through him. No lifting belt. No gloves. No chalk. Not bad for an old man. But no other old men had access to the secrets held by Hiram. Better living through chemistry.

Hiram smirked and returned to the window, looking across the yard at the back of the church. The deadlift set had been good. He was strong, far stronger than a man his age had any right to be, but he would increase the weight tomorrow. When things were headed in the right direction, you never stopped and admired your accomplishments. Complacency deserved a death sentence.

Things were going well, exactly as they should. All according to plan.

Light shone in the pastor's office and Hiram could see his son sitting at the computer. He should be readying himself for the night's spiritual awakening. The flock would be arriving in only a couple of hours. After they were settled into place and his son began the gathering, Hiram would return to the church to listen from the basement via closed circuit. At the appropriate time, he would fill the small plastic communion cups with that night's assigned batch of formula and leave it—along with the plates of tiny communion wafers—in the hallway outside the fellowship room.

As the sun set, the sky behind the church was colored an array of orange and pink. The church was perfect for Hiram's purposes. The town was perfect. The college was perfect. It was almost too much to ask for. Almost.

Before he exiled himself to life away from the prying eyes of law enforcement, Hiram had briefly worked at a rival university. Prior to his unfortunate notoriety, Hiram's credentials through MIT's chemical engineering program made him an easy hire at virtually any school he chose. The rival school had an excellent ancient history program and with it, access to certain scrolls which Hiram desired to study, but the truly fortuitous aspect of his time with the rival university was that it had led to his notice of Texas State College—the long-standing traditions of the school, the way the college was set up, the surrounding community of simple, unsuspecting folk; all of these attributes registered strongly on his strategic radar. Even then, he had an inkling that destiny would lead him here.

It was five years ago that the church had closed its doors, and the building was foreclosed upon. Hiram used his ample resources to purchase the property under the guise of a not-for-profit entity created for that sole purpose. He immediately paid an out-of-state contracting team to construct the tunnel between the church and the toolshed dwelling. He knew locals might scratch their heads at the dirt work being conducted at the church, but it would grass over, and people would simply forget about it over time as the church sat empty.

At the time Hiram purchased the property, Marcus was still alive, the program in New Mexico was still operating like clockwork, and Hiram and his youngest son were in southwest Texas where the man now known as Christian Berry went by the name Jonas Knight. The church they established in that town grew at an impressive rate. Jonas was, after all, an inspiring preacher, and the poor community who lived hand-to-mouth off the service-side tentacles of the oil industry was in need of hope.

What Marcus was doing in the desert with chemical and behavioral research on a targeted demographic basis, Jonas was doing on a softer but broader scale at the church. The formula advancements accomplished in New Mexico were incorporated at the church, with successes and failures researched and catalogued for future use. It was an ideal test run, a perfect dress rehearsal for the real thing.

Three years ago, when the testing had reached its conclusion, a terrible tragedy befell the little town when a previously undetected leak in the gas main under the church resulted in a massive explosion and fire during Sunday service. The explosion somehow jammed the doors of the main entrance, making escape from the fire and smoke an impossibility. Every parishioner died inside the church that fateful morning, an ironically hellish way for so many faithful to perish. The young preacher Jonas Knight was presumed dead along with his congregation. Remains were impossible to identify.

As dusk settled, it became easier to see into the pastor's office. Hiram watched as his son stood from the computer and began pacing back and forth, gesticulating with his hands and appearing to speak to himself. That was good. It meant he was rehearsing what he would say to the assembled group that evening. As usual, Jonas was on schedule.

Hiram returned to the weight rack and began removing the plates from either side. He needed to raise the pins, lift the bar and slide the bench underneath. Bench press was next.

CHAPTER 23

ERIC SIGNALED A LEFT TURN onto College Drive. It wasn't directly on his route to the motel, but he wanted to at least get a glimpse of the campus before dusk turned to dark. In two blocks, the hodge-podge of cheap restaurants, bookstores (which from the windows appeared to sell more t-shirts than textbooks) and pockets of old residential housing gave way to the main campus of Texas State College.

TSC's buildings were by no means ornate, but they were uniform in color and architectural style. At this hour, most classes would be finished for the day, but the sidewalks were still alive with students. Eric suspected the campus must be bustling during the daylight hours.

He rolled down the front windows of the minivan. The evening air was pleasant, and he wanted to hear the sounds of the college. He slowed as he reached a large field awash in light from portable floodlights. At least fifty students were hard at work lifting logs and bringing them to the center of the field where a growing wooden tower stood. The tower was bottom-heavy as the base layer was considerably wider than the recently begun second tier. The center pole was tall enough that Eric suspected another two tiers of logs would be added to the two already under construction.

Eric watched in fascination as young men wearing construction helmets deftly planted one end of a large log at the edge of the base level then worked as a team to push it to a fully vertical position against the other logs.

A horn blew and Eric realized he was holding up traffic. It had been a polite double-tap of a honk. He heard worse hourly in New York. He raised his hand in a *mea culpa* wave to the car behind him, returned to normal speed and corrected his course to reach the motel.

"Two queen rooms are available. What is the date of check-out?"

"Not sure yet," Eric said to the young man at the front desk. He looked like he was sixteen. "Let's just leave the booking open for now."

A look of consternation fell over the desk clerk's face. "Well, I can do that for now, but you'll have to check out by Friday next week. That's the night of the bonfire and the game is Saturday. Every hotel in town will be full those two nights. We usually book up months in advance."

"That's a full week," Eric smiled. "Maybe I can wrap up by then."

The young man ran Eric's credit card through the reader and then produced two paper envelopes with key cards inside each.

"We have a continental breakfast in the lobby every morning from six until ten," he said as he slid the room keys across the counter. "Thank you for staying at the Day Star Inn."

Eric took the keys and glanced at the room numbers. Both second floor. Since all the rooms in the motel opened up to the parking lot, the second floor was good. That meant no headlights blinding the windows at all hours.

He looked up as he took a step toward the door and saw her, auburn hair falling onto her shoulders in disarray and an embarrassed smile on her freckled face. Eric smiled in return and began walking her way. She covered the remaining distance in five quick steps and threw her arms around him, her face buried in his chest. Eric had seen this before.

He closed his arms around her and let her cry.

CHAPTER 24

CHRISTIAN BERRY HALF-SAT on the front of his desk, one foot on the floor with the other dangling in front of him. It was his relaxed pose. Intentional. He needed to radiate peace if there was any hope of calming Slade Stone.

Slade stood a few feet away, his hands on the back of a chair. Given his heated state, Berry knew the beast couldn't be persuaded to sit so he didn't bother asking. This was all part of dealing with lower life forms. They could be useful, but you had to handle them like children.

"Why else do you think she'd be talking to Andrew, huh?" Slade gripped the back of the chair hard enough that his fingertips were leaving indentions in the leather backing. "She's asking him questions. Trying to learn more about you. About us."

"That's possible, Slade. It's possible." Berry used a soothing voice. "But what if she is? What are you concerned will happen?"

"What if she finds out? What if she tries to stop the Reckoning?"

Berry smiled, lifted a glass from his desk and sipped ice water from it. "How could she possibly do that? And even if she's asking questions, who can tell her anything?"

"Andrew could. I don't trust him."

"I do," Berry replied. "He's one of us. And remember, not everyone has the same knowledge as you. You are my most trusted ally, Slade. My lieutenant. My swift right hand of justice. I have entrusted you with secrets far beyond the others."

Slade's grip on the chair loosened. His fingers darkened from white to pink as blood began to flow back into them. His internal rage was matched only by his ego, and Berry had meticulously cultivated that ego to be reliant on praise from him. He measured out such praise in calculated doses.

"I chose you for a reason, not only your physical strength but for your dedication to the cause. Your commitment. You are deserving of great rewards, but you must trust me if you are to receive those rewards."

Slade lowered his head. "Of course I trust you. I want to protect you."

"I know you do. And you will have plenty to accomplish in a very short time. Blood must be spilled to make us clean, to make us worthy. That will fall upon you as well as me. It will be no easy task, but it is not yet upon us. Sometimes the harder task is patience."

"Why not do away with her?"

"Because that's not yet necessary. The girl can do us no real harm. If things change, you will be my sword. For now, you must be my rock."

Slade huffed a sigh through clenched jaws, released the chair and straightened to his full height. His shoulders were back, his neck muscles flared. Not standing at military attention but certainly indicating a sense of readiness. If he had the appearance of a cobra rising from a wicker basket, then Berry was the peaceful snake charmer playing his pungi.

"As you wish," Slade intoned in a low voice.

"Excellent," Berry said as he stood from the desk and clapped a hand on Slade's meaty shoulder. "Come. The time draws near for our brothers and sisters to arrive. Let's make ready."

CHAPTER 25

"**I** HAVEN'T HAD ANYTHING since breakfast. I'm starving," Eric said.

"Well you come to the right place, hon," the waitress informed him. She was middle aged, chewed her gum with a vengeance, and smiled without ceasing.

"Great, what do you recommend?"

"We got good burgers and Freddy makes a mean turkey club, but breakfast-for-dinner is always popular around here, too."

"I see," Eric said as he skimmed the enormous plastic menu. It conveniently offered pictures of each meal alongside its description and price. "Sorry, my first time at Waffle House."

"Take your time, hon," she instructed between gum smacks.

"I'll go with the club sandwich. And fries, please." Trish chimed in from her seat opposite Eric in the booth.

"And I'll take the All Star," Eric decided. "Scrambled. Bacon. And that comes with a waffle, right?"

"You bet it does, sugar."

Eric and Trish handed their menus to the outstretched hand of the server, and she disappeared behind the counter which separated the open kitchen from the greater restaurant. If you sat at a barstool at that counter, you could watch your food being prepared by the skinny man in a stained t-shirt wielding a stainless-steel spatula whose name was apparently Freddy.

When Eric awoke that morning, he never would have expected that he'd be eating dinner in a Waffle House in Texas, but the restaurant sat in the lot adjacent to the motel, and Eric had been anxious to have a real conversation with Trish. Plus, he wanted to eat while they spoke. He truly was starving.

He wasn't prepared for the unexpected turn the conversation took.

CHAPTER 26

TRISH PUSHED A FRY INTO HER MOUTH and chewed the salty goodness. It was the first meal she'd had all day. Adrenaline—or perhaps lingering fear—had staved off the urge until now, but following her somewhat humiliating crying jag in Eric's arms in the lobby of the Day Star Inn, the knots in her stomach loosened and were replaced with ravenous hunger.

For the first time since waking to find Slade on her bed, Trish felt safe. Amazing what having a cop sitting across the table could do for your sense of security. And Eric hadn't blinked at her little breakdown in the motel lobby. She had been embarrassed, but it didn't seem to faze him. He had understood.

He was less understanding after the first few minutes of their conversation in the booth of the Waffle House.

"What do you mean you don't want me to confront him? That's the first thing I'm going to do!" Eric snapped before lowering his voice. "This Slade guy committed a crime, Trish. It may not have reached physical assault, but it was still unlawful entry at the very least. If you don't want to press charges, that's fine, but he can't believe he has free rein to do something like that without consequences. It might give him the idea he can take it further. We can't let that happen. This aggression will not stand."

Eric sat back in the booth and folded a piece of bacon into his mouth. "I know you think he's strong and tough, and I'm sure he is, but he's still just a kid. I guarantee I've seen tougher. I can handle him."

Trish smiled at him. *Men.* Eric was one of the smartest people she knew. She remembered her dad remarking on his intelligence several times when they were first paired as partners, before he and her mom had divorced. '*Intelligence and instinct can make up for a lot of shortcomings in this line of work,*' he had said. That was back when Trish was still speaking to him. She hadn't known what was to come.

But smart or not, Eric was acting like a typical male at the moment. Protective but overreactive. She wondered if he would be so quick to obstinacy if he was sitting across from a young man rather than a young woman.

"I appreciate the sentiment, Eric, but consider the bigger picture. The whole thing sparked because of what happened at the bonfire."

"I saw the video. Quite a show you put on."

"Not my finest moment. I'll admit that." She had a fry clasped between finger and thumb but put it back on the plate rather than in her mouth. "But I was there for a reason. Something happened with Stephanie to make her do what she did. I don't know what it was, but something pushed her into it. She was my friend, Eric. She wasn't crazy."

He didn't argue. She was worried he would play the pragmatic detective and say that Steph's actions offered more than reasonable evidence for premeditation and homicidal intent. But he stayed silent and listened.

"After I confronted Berry, Slade showed up in my room. He threatened me. Told me to drop it. Why would he say to drop it unless there was something there to drop?"

"I understand what you're saying, but Slade—"

"I don't care about Slade," she countered. "He's scary. I'll have nightmares for the rest of my life, but how could I live that life without finding out what happened to Stephanie? To at least *try* to figure it out. She was my friend, Eric. That means something to me. I know it does to you, too."

Eric was using his fork and knife to cut into his waffle. It was golden and round. Melted butter and maple syrup filled the tiny square pockets of the grid pattern. He finished sawing and set the knife next to the plate.

"And you're worried that if I confront Slade, he'll tell the preacher. And you think the preacher—or the church or whatever—is somehow responsible for what your roommate did. And you want to maintain a clandestine approach to an investigation." He speared a section of waffle with his fork and stuffed it into his mouth, speaking around the wad of syrupy dough. "Sound about right?"

What do you know? He didn't immediately argue the point. Perhaps intelligence and instinct *can* override male stubbornness.

"Yep. That's about right."

"If I'm investigating this preacher, I can't be with you all the time. Not allowing me to remove Slade from the equation puts your safety at risk. You understand that, right?"

"I'm willing to take that risk."

Eric appeared to be thinking while he chewed. "You do have balls. I'll give you that."

"Pretty sure I don't."

"Your dad would be proud."

"That his daughter has balls?" Trish asked.

"You know what I mean."

"What about you?" She bit into a long fry.

"Um, I'm proud of you, too."

"No," she smiled and pointed the other half of the fry at him. "I mean what about *you*? I appreciate you being here. I'm grateful beyond words." She paused as she swallowed the fry as well as the emotion that threatened to bubble up again. "But I'm sure you can't just take off from work at a moment's notice and be gone for days. I mean, is this okay?"

Eric dabbed syrup from his chin with his napkin. "Yeah, well, here's the thing. I got promoted last year. It was nice of them, but my new job isn't exactly thrilling. I seem to spend all my time doing paperwork and helping other cops do their jobs. I haven't solved a case in months." He sighed. "I told my captain I had a family emergency." He shrugged his shoulders. "Worst thing they can do is fire me."

"Whoa. I don't want to be responsible for that," Trish said.

"No big deal. I have options."

Trish shook her head as she lifted her sandwich from the plate with both hands. "Okay then. What now?"

"Now?" Eric seemed to think about it before speaking. "We start with the basics. Where you should always start. We'll pop by your dorm tonight to get whatever you need, and then come back to the hotel so you can get some rest. Tomorrow morning, we kick it. Seven o'clock."

Trish took a bite of her sandwich. Her hunger was subsiding and being replaced with a tiredness both deep and profound. She hadn't slept in a long time. She was grateful Eric had gotten her a room at the motel. She wasn't sure she could ever sleep in her dorm room again.

She swallowed the bite and stifled a yawn. "Can we make it eight?"

"Yes, we can," he smiled. "Basic training starts then. Be ready."

CHAPTER 27

"ABOVE ALL, MY BROTHERS AND SISTERS, know this," Christian Berry intoned the words with solemnity, "I remain in constant prayer for enlightenment. My eyes have been opened in ways not seen since the prophets. There is truth beyond human knowledge. Truth beyond what is found in the book."

He dropped his voice to convey the sense of a secret, but he made certain each of the forty-four seated in the circle of chairs could hear every word. "A reckoning." Dramatic pause. "Perhaps you've heard the word whispered, but you don't know what it means. You will learn in the coming days. I will free your minds. For you must be free—and you must have faith—at the time of the Reckoning."

Berry stood from his chair and walked to the center of the circle. It was awkward since he would have to slowly spin while speaking to reach meaningful eye contact with each of them, but this was the big finish. Communion had already been taken. Time to wrap it up after planting the seed of the Reckoning. It was the first time he'd used the word to this group outside of a very select few. It was a significant milestone. One that would be built upon tomorrow.

"The Reckoning is coming. And soon. I don't yet know the day, but I can feel it in my soul. I have been gifted this knowledge. You must stay by my side, attentive, faithful in every breath. I will guide you. Protect you."

His gaze reached Andrew, his intentional stopping point when he began the rotation.

"Your loyalty is the only thing that will save you. And you will be rewarded for that loyalty a multitude over."

In days past, any church meeting would be closed with a prayer. Berry had been phasing out that aspect for the forty-four the past several weeks. For the final meetings, there would be no prayer at all. He would tell them about his own prayer activities—implying that he'd handle the praying for the entire group—but he wanted to be certain their focus rested solely on him at all times going forward, not some invisible entity.

"Return home. Handle your worldly obligations as necessary but return here tomorrow night at the same time. More will be revealed."

The forty-four stood almost as one and headed toward the exit.

"Andrew," Berry took two steps toward him, "may I have a word with you?"

From the corner of his eye, Berry saw Slade smile.

Berry sat in the guest chair rather than behind his desk. Andrew occupied the other guest chair. Berry wanted this to be an intimate conversation, to make Andrew feel safe. And open. Little more than a decade separated them in age, but in Berry's judgment, the difference in intellectual maturity could only be measured in eons.

The windows in the office revealed only darkness outside. Little could be seen in the blackness of the night beyond a streetlamp. By contrast, the overhead fluorescent lights of the office cast a stark whiteness upon their conversation. He wondered if Slade was somewhere in the darkness, spying on the conversation from afar, struggling to read lips. Berry didn't care.

"I owe you an apology, Andrew," he said. "It's been two days since Stephanie died. I've prayed mightily about the situation, I've consoled our congregation, but I haven't sat down one-on-one with you. That was remiss of me, and I am sorry."

"That's okay," Andrew replied. He wasn't making eye contact, but Berry suspected it was from youthful awkwardness rather than anything more. "You have more important things at the moment. What you said tonight. The Reckoning—"

"—Is the most important thing imaginable, but that doesn't diminish *your* importance. You matter to me. Didn't I just promise to care for you?" Berry waited for a brief nod from Andrew. Perfect. "You were close with Stephanie, correct?"

Berry knew everything about Andrew's relationship with Stephanie. She had told him every intimate detail while being considerably more intimate with him in ways the boy in the chair across from him had probably never dared whisper. But Andrew didn't know that Berry knew, so the dance must be danced.

"She was my girlfriend," Andrew said. "We'd been dating a long time."

"I'm so sorry," Berry offered with empathy. "It's hard to lose someone you love. Particularly under these circumstances."

Andrew nodded but didn't display any noticeable emotional response. No anger. No tears. Exactly as it should be. He was too far into the final phases of the formula to exhibit such weakness.

"Would you like to talk about how you're feeling?" Berry asked.

"What's there to talk about?" Andrew questioned in return. Excellent. "Steph is dead. She did it to herself. It was her choice. And when she chose to end her life, that meant ending our relationship as well. Questioning the situation won't change it."

"No, it won't." Berry agreed.

"All I can do is keep my focus." Andrew established eye contact with Berry. "It's like you said earlier. These are end times. I'm not going to be distracted from my true meaning."

"You have more meaning than you know, brother." Berry leaned forward and clasped his slender fingers around Andrew's knee. There was a small hole in the denim. Berry didn't know if that was the style or if the young man was just ill-kempt. "Maintain that strength. I may have special need of you in the coming days."

"I will. Thank you."

They said their goodbyes, Berry escorted him from the church and locked the door behind them. Everything was as it should be, but it never hurts to reassess.

And perhaps to reassess again.

CHAPTER 28

JOHN CRADLED THE CELL PHONE between his ear and the pillow. It was an older model flip-phone. It lacked many of the conveniences of today's far smarter devices, but it also lacked any software that maintained an active microphone on the unit. If your phone responds when you say "hey, Siri," or "hey, Alexa," then that means it's listening all the time. John didn't trust anything that eavesdropped on his every conversation, and he didn't think that was an unreasonable position.

Outdated phone or not, the voice on the other end had been exactly what he needed to hear. They had only been talking a few minutes, but it soothed him like a two-hour massage.

"I think he's cautiously skeptical," he said in answer to his wife's last question, "but he is taking it seriously. That's all I asked. We'll start looking into things tomorrow. I'm not sure exactly what that means, but I'll let Cutter take the lead."

Laughter on the other end at John's generosity to the Ranger. John missed that laugh already. Another question, more poignant.

"I don't know," he responded. "One thing at a time. If it turns out to be him—or them—then we'll think of something."

A quiet request.

"I promise. Besides, I'm always careful. You know that. And we'll keep our distance. They'll never even know we're here. Cutter knows what he's doing."

He grabbed the bottle of antacid from the end table and shook two tablets into his mouth without raising his head from the pillow.

"The ulcer is fine," he lied as he crunched the tablets. "I barely notice it." He shifted his hand to hold the phone to his ear as he raised up on one arm. "You need your sleep. I suspect DJ will be up bright and early."

A clear sigh and another entreaty.

"I told you, I promise. This is a *good* thing that's happening, Sarah. If this is really it, then it's a once-in-a-lifetime opportunity."

A mumbled response.

"Didn't catch all that but I'm assuming you said 'I love you' and 'go get 'em, tiger' or something to that effect."

Softer laughter. A softer moment.

"I love you, too. Kiss DJ for me. Sweet dreams."

John flipped the phone shut with a satisfying clack (an underrated perk of the old flip phone). The bedside lamp illuminated the hotel room. It was nothing fancy. He had learned there was no such thing as a fancy hotel in Abramsville. But it was clean and had the flag of a reputable brand. He and Cutter both had rooms on the fourth floor—the highest at the hotel—and he suspected the Ranger was already sawing logs. It had been a long day.

John had put both rooms on a credit card under a previously unused alias. It was completely clean and untraceable to his existing name, the one attached to the house in which his wife and daughter slept. Cutter didn't say a word about the card but agreed it was smarter to use John's alias than Cutter's name.

John needed sleep as well. Tomorrow would be a big day. He turned off the lamp and stared at the ceiling, knowing sleep would elude him for quite some time. Still, he gave it his best effort and closed his eyes. He wondered if the nightmare would visit him. Vernon's death on the sundial. And when he looked into the eyes with fire dancing in them, would they belong to Marcus Kane or would they be the eyes of Christian Berry?

CHAPTER 29

BY THE TIME EIGHT O'CLOCK ROLLED AROUND on Saturday morning, Eric had been up for more than two hours and had already bypassed the motel's continental breakfast in favor of another "All Star" at the Waffle House next door. He had literally dreamed about that damned waffle.

Now he was back in his room, sitting in the plastic chair on rollers that accompanied the small desk with a Formica laminate top. Trish sat on the bed across from him. She looked rested and much better overall than the prior day. That was good. She bounced back strong.

"First things first," he said. "Before we talk investigation, before we start looking into what happened with your roommate, I need to be sure you know how to take of yourself."

"I can take care of myself."

"Really? If Slade was sitting here instead of me, and he lunged for you, what would you do?"

"I'd...think of something."

"But you wouldn't. Situations like that don't allow for thought, only reaction," Eric explained. "Slade comes at you and what's your first instinct?"

"Shit," Trish stammered. She appeared to be searching for what Eric would deem a correct answer. "Something to do with his groin?"

"Your first instinct should be to do whatever it takes to get the hell away from him. I don't want you fighting people, Trish. I want you safe. Get away."

"Okay. That's a better plan," she admitted.

Eric stood and Trish did the same. "Before you left for school your freshman year, we spent an afternoon together. Do you remember that? Your dad wouldn't have trusted college guys any more than I do. We went over the four rules."

Trish wrinkled her nose at him, freckles bunched together. "Yeah, so I appreciated that gesture, but I kind of felt like it was overkill at the time." She paused. "I don't remember any of the rules."

Eric sighed. "Rule One: Be a weasel."

"Ooohhhh...I *do* remember that rule."

"What is it?"

"Get out of the situation any way you can. Lie, cheat, steal. Just get out of it."

"Exactly. This is your chance to escape violence before it starts. Find a way to defuse the situation however possible. Talk your way out of it. Look around for help. Cause a scene. Draw attention to yourself. Whatever it takes. If there is a way to remove yourself from a violent situation, use it."

"Be a weasel," Trish repeated. "Got it."

"Rule Two: Find your exit. If you can't weasel your way out of the situation, determine whether or not you can run. If it's a choice between fight or flight, I want you to fly like an eagle. Fighting is your last resort."

"And if it comes down to that?"

"Then you still find your exit to take from the fight. Figure out the best way to reach that exit *before* you engage. You won't be able to think about it once the action starts. If you have to fight, you only need to be good enough to buy yourself a couple of seconds, because that will give you the time you need to make that predetermined exit, to find the shortest path to help. Got it?"

"Yes, Obi Wan."

Eric's breath caught in his throat. Only for a moment. How many times had he called his former partner 'Obi Wan' while George imparted his older and wiser wisdom?

"You okay?" Trish asked.

"Yeah," Eric said as he cleared his throat. "So you've tried to weasel and failed. You've now determined your exit; you just have to buy yourself time to make it." He cleared his throat a second time. Back on track. "Rule Three: Weaponize. Look around you. Take an assessment. Is there anything you can reach that would work as a weapon? Qualifications are something you can reach quickly and use quickly. I don't want you grabbing something heavy and swinging it. Takes too much time and your attacker will get inside your personal zone before you can use it effectively. Look for something light and sharp. Think 'stab,' not 'swing.' A knife. A ballpoint-pen. Scissors. A screwdriver. Is there anything easily in reach?"

Trish looked around. "There's a pen on the desk."

"Great," he said. "Think you could reach past me, grab it and then stab me with it?"

"Probably not."

"Then that's not your weapon. Look, the reality is if that you don't have the weapon already on you, there's a good chance you're not going to have an option for one. That's okay. I just want you to keep it in mind. A sharp stick is better than nothing."

"Noted," she smiled.

He returned the smile. "So now you know you have to fight. No other choice. You either have a weapon or you don't, either way, Rule Four: ETG."

"ETG?"

"Eyes," he pointed to his eyes as he spoke, then lowered his hands with each level, "then throat, then groin. Those are your three attack points."

"I aim for all three?"

"No, you pick whichever one looks most likely to succeed."

"You know," she said, "a better acronym for Rule Four would be G-E-T. Groin-eyes-throat. Spells 'get.' Easier to remember. You're welcome."

"Clever but the wrong order of importance. I know kicking a guy in the gonads seems like the end-all, and if you do it well, it *can* be really effective, but the nuts are also the easiest thing to miss. If you don't connect perfectly, you're just pissing the guy off and losing your two seconds to escape."

"Oh."

"So it's eyes first. They're the prime weak spot. E-T-G. Roger?"

"Roger," she sighed.

"All right. We're going to go over a couple of moves." Eric stood one foot in front of the other. His ready stance. "The first is if the guy is in front of you, and he's reaching out to grab you."

"Are you going to teach me to Judo flip you? There's not much room in here."

"No, there's not, but a confrontation might take place in a confined space like this. Better to learn here and fight in the open than to be accustomed to fighting in the open and getting cramped when the time comes."

"Makes sense," she said.

"Okay," Eric admitted. "Truth be told, I had planned to do this on that little lawn outside, but it occurred to me over breakfast that a black man even fake-attacking a white girl might not be looked upon with tolerance around here. I don't want to get shot before we can explain the situation."

Trish hiccupped an unexpected laugh. "Good point. It's not that bad around here, but good point."

Eric raised his hands as if he were going to grab her. "All right then, get ready."

CHAPTER 30

CUTTER HUNKERED DOWN to take a better look at the merchandise under the glass counter in the back of the giant sporting goods store. Along the wall behind the counter was a long row of rifles and shotguns. For most of the counter, handguns of various brands and sizes occupied the tiered shelves under the glass top, but the section in which Cutter and John were stationed was labeled 'Optics.' The store boasted an impressive selection of binoculars and scopes—even an array of infrared beyond what Cutter had hoped—but the price tags displayed made him shake his head. Things were durned expensive these days.

"What do we need?" John asked. He was kneeling next to him, eyeing the same product but without the knowledge to make an informed decision.

No salesclerk had walked in their direction yet, so Cutter spoke freely.

"Surveillance gear. We need eyes from a distance."

"Like a big telephoto lens?"

"Only if you're planning to take pictures. I'm not worried about recording the preacher's actions. This isn't some official operation where we need to document evidence. I just want to get a good look at what he's up to."

"So some binoculars for daytime plus night vision gear for after dark?" John inquired.

"Yep, but I'd also like a spotting scope. More challenging to use but a significant upgrade in magnification versus binoculars. Can mean the difference of a few blocks in a stakeout. That's significant."

The clerk at the far end of the counter finished helping a customer and took notice of them. He began walking their way.

"Being retired makes this complicated," Cutter spoke in low tones. "The Rangers had good equipment for this sort of thing, but I couldn't ask for a loan without raising eyebrows. I had hoped Bobcat could spot us some gear but that didn't pan out." He glanced again at the selection behind the glass. "Stuff is pricey."

The clerk covered the final steps to join Cutter and John from across the counter. Cutter straightened. He had bent over for less than a minute, and his lower back was already tight. It wasn't only being retired that made things complicated. Being old didn't help either.

"Can I assist you gentlemen?" the clerk asked with a smile. He wore a brown vest over his gray polo shirt. The vest was emblazoned with the name 'Dave' in red stitching.

Cutter started to answer, but John spoke first.

"Yes, please. We'd like to see a spotting scope. Top of the line. Same for a set of binoculars. We'll need two pair of those actually."

"Certainly, sir," Dave said as he selected a small key attached to a ring hanging from his belt. He unlocked the sliding partition behind the counter. The key zipped back on its retractable cord, returning to the unit on the belt.

Dave removed a sizeable spotting scope from the lower level of the counter. It was olive green and larger than a loaf of bread. Cutter looked at the displayed price. The scope was six-thousand dollars.

"This is the best we have," the clerk said as he removed the lens cap and handed the scope to John. "What's the intended use? You may not need this much magnification."

"Birds," John replied. "Little ones." He handed the scope to Cutter without testing it for himself.

Cutter leaned against the counter to steady himself—the single lens and high magnification of the scope made it difficult to hold steady if it wasn't affixed to a tripod—and aimed the scope down the long aisles of merchandise toward the front of the store more than two football fields away. A man was checking out at the register. Cutter could see he was buying a box of Top-Flite golf balls and a bag of wooden tees. Cutter could also read the hour and minute on the man's watch. It was a Timex.

"Yeah," Cutter said as he placed the scope on the glass countertop. "You could spot some tiny birds with this."

"We'll take it," John informed the clerk. "Tell us about your infrared."

Dave seemed pleased to have the discussion.

They crossed the parking lot to Cutter's truck, each man carrying bags weighted with expensive equipment. Between the surveillance gear and some other accessories—including John buying himself a ballcap and sunglasses—the final tab exceeded twenty-thousand dollars. The infrared tech was particularly expensive. John didn't blink.

Cutter noticed that John paid with a different credit card than the one he had used at the hotel. It was a corporate card with a business name Cutter didn't recognize, and John signed the name of an alias Cutter hadn't yet seen. He was full of surprises these days. There were no problems at checkout—John's mysterious company was apparently good for the money—and they were now equipped with gear worth far more than the pickup truck in which it would all be carried.

Cutter opened the driver door and climbed behind the steering wheel. He watched as John opened the passenger door, placed the shopping bags in the floorboard and fished his other unusual purchase out of the largest one. He placed the foam rubber stadium seat cushion—to be used for sporting events and the like—onto the passenger seat then clambered on top of it.

"Better," he sighed. "What's next on the list? Listening gear? Parabolic microphone?"

Cutter chuckled. "You'd make a fine spy, John, but no. You can't get the grade of parabolic microphone we'd need on the retail market. I could put together a homemade one that would surprise you with its effectiveness, but you still have to be closer to use it than we'd like."

"Surely you can buy that stuff somewhere. We just bought night vision goggles."

"That's because hunters swing a big pocketbook, and they're catered to accordingly. But hunters want to *see* their targeted buck. They aren't interested in listening to what the furry feller has to say." Cutter started the truck and put it in gear. "Besides, the use of parabolic mics skates well into the gray area of wiretapping laws. That's why you can't buy a decent one in Walmart or this here store, even if you just want to hear what the coach of the opposing team is telling his players."

"Fair enough," John acquiesced. "No mics. So what do we do now? Get into Berry's house? The church?"

"Your mind is on the right track, but you're getting ahead of yourself," Cutter replied. "First, we watch. We monitor. We observe patterns. The worst thing that can happen is for us to break into the man's house and be discovered. If he's innocent, we'd get charged with B-and-E or trespassing. But if he is who you think he is, the outcome could be far worse."

Cutter pulled out of the parking lot and entered traffic.

"I know patience isn't always your strong suit, John, but get ready to work on it. Better safe than sorry. It's going to be a long, dull few days of sitting in this truck, eating corn chips and pissing in bottles before we do anything like what you've got in mind."

John grimaced. "Glad I bought the cushion."

CHAPTER 31

HIRAM KANE OPENED THE DOOR from the tunnel and stepped into the lab in the basement below the church. The overhead fluorescents glowed as well as the track lighting above the lab table. The room was considerably brighter than the mostly earthen tunnel, and it took Hiram's eyes a moment to adjust.

Jonas Kane—for he was only Christian Berry to the outside world—stood in front of the table. He had an eyedropper filled with purple liquid between his fingers, and he was administering careful drops into a glass beaker. He paused to swirl the beaker's contents and glanced toward the tunnel door.

"Hello, Father," he said before turning his attention back to the swirling chemical solution.

Hiram observed him.

"Tonight's batch of formula?" he asked.

"Tomorrow's," Jonas replied.

"I thought it was already stabilized. Was there a problem?"

"No problem," his son said as he dispensed a single additional drop then set the eyedropper on the table. "Just a minor tweak. I don't want to take any chances."

"A tweak can create a chance," Hiram informed him. "Don't overthink and don't fiddle with the formula any more than necessary. We've run our tests. We know what we have."

Hiram wasn't actually worried about whatever minor adjustment Jonas was making. When it came to the chemical compounds in the formula, Jonas knew them as well as he did. Perhaps better. Still, he felt the young needed a measure of guidance on sheer principle.

Jonas walked to the glass-front refrigerator along the wall, opened the door and placed the beaker on a shelf alongside half-a-dozen similar containers of identically colored liquid. He turned and held up his palms.

"Finished," he said. "No more fiddling."

"Good." Hiram closed the door to the tunnel. Unlike the trapdoor in the toolshed, this one was left unhidden. There was no need. The entrance to the basement itself from the interior of the church was well concealed. "Leave me be. It's time."

Jonas turned and walked up the stairs leading to the ground floor of the church without a word. That was good. Jonas was so different than his older brothers—not just in appearance but in demeanor and personality—that Hiram often found him to be a conundrum, difficult to read. Perhaps he was too much like his father. But he followed direction, not always without questioning, but ultimately following. That was very good. Jonas would play a critical role going forward. His brothers were dead. Jonas was Hiram's sole heir now.

Hiram turned from the lab table and faced the opposite wall. It held only a door and a full-length mirror, with an ancient, ornate table resting between them. The basement consisted of two rooms—the lab in which he now stood and the vault. The sanctum.

The door to the sanctum was reinforced steel and could be opened only by Hiram. A digital keypad requiring a nine-digit code and a scan of his left thumbprint assured him of that unique privilege.

He stood before the mirror and removed his shirt, dropping it to the floor at his feet. He inhaled deeply and pushed his shoulders back. The width of the mirror was insufficient to reflect his entire body. That was fine. It adequately displayed his massive barrel-chested torso.

He gazed down upon the ornate table. It was more than five hundred years old. Reclaimed from a Catholic church in Spain. It was assumed to have been used during the Inquisition. Hiram surveyed the surgical tools lined neatly on the black velvet pad. He selected a number eight scalpel handle affixed with a number twenty-two blade. The blade's gauge and shape were designed for incisions through thick skin.

Hiram returned his focus to the mirror. His chest and stomach were almost entirely hairless, adorned instead with scars beyond counting. Each precisely three inches long. Perfectly horizontal. They were stacked one upon another in two vertical rows separated by his navel at the bottom and his sternum at the top. The twin stacks of scars began at his waist and ended at his collarbones, each scar a pink worm rising from pale skin.

He held the scalpel in his right hand while the fingertips of his left traced the ladder of tightly packed scar tissue. He closed his eyes. His body was a symphony of braille conveying a story of both horror and glory. His fingers stopped midway up his left pectoral muscle. He opened his eyes and peered closely in the mirror. He pushed his index and middle fingers against two adjacent scars and separated them. A tiny line of untouched white skin showed between them.

He lifted the scalpel and steadied the blade between his fingers.

The ritual demanded blood. Every time.

He pressed on the blade, and it sank into the skin. Dark crimson welled up on either side. With a steady hand, he drew the blade from his shoulder toward his sternum, trailing blood in its wake. He stopped when the blade's tip fell perfectly in line with the edge of the other scars and withdrew the scalpel, placing it back on the table to the side of the velvet pad.

He felt nothing. Pain was for lesser men. He flexed his pectoral muscles, corded sinew beneath ravaged skin. More blood welled from the open incision and trickled down the ladder of scars in uneven rivulets. Kane nodded at the man in the mirror.

He entered the code on the keypad, scanned his thumb and heard the electromechanical lock disengage. He opened the door to the sanctum and stepped into the dark interior. There was much to be done.

CHAPTER 32

TRISH GESTURED TO THE OLD BELL that sat in the middle of the quad as she walked alongside Eric.

"And that's the Victory Bell. Almost two hundred years old. It gets rung after a football game," she paused, "well, if we win. I've only heard it a few times since I've been here. It's become controversial this year. Someone researched its history and found out it was once used on a plantation to call the slaves or something like that. Students are either enraged that TSC would be so unfeeling to continue using the bell when it's a hurtful symbol of oppression, or they're enraged that people are trying to drag down a great tradition of today because of something that happened two centuries ago."

"Yeah?" Eric grinned. "What are your feelings on the matter?"

Trish shrugged. "It's a bell. I don't have any feelings about it one way or the other."

"What's that over there?" Eric asked, pointing at a building.

"Bailey Hall," she answered. "Men's dorm. Oldest one on campus. No air conditioning. You'd think that would mean no one would want to live there, but it's cheap housing and there are quite a few upperclassmen in it."

Trish pushed her hands into her pockets as she walked. It was another nice day. The sun was shining. The breeze was cool but not cold. And she was giving her very first campus tour. No one else she knew had ever visited her here—probably because she'd never invited anyone—and she was surprised at how many facts she had retained about the college. Eric just soaked it in. The tour had been his request.

Said he wanted to get a feel for the campus, for the places Stephanie went, the things she saw and did.

It was an eye-opening experience for Trish. She had always considered herself intuitive. She was called to journalism for a number of reasons, but part of her felt it was simple destiny. She knew she would be good at it. She was smart. She knew the questions to ask. What to look for. She felt like a natural investigator of the human condition. Spending time with an actual homicide investigator was sobering. Eric asked a lot of basic questions about the campus—the sort of things a prospective student might ask—but then he would slip in questions about Stephanie that made Trish stop and think. He was exploring paths she hadn't considered.

She knew she shouldn't feel bad. Eric was a professional. He did this for a living. He had training—a lot of it provided by Trish's own father—but she felt humbled regardless.

Trish shrugged toward the large oak tree where she had first encountered Andrew following Steph's death. "That's where Steph and Andrew used to hang out and study together."

"Tell me more about Andrew. How long had they been dating?"

"About nine months. They were really in love." She shook her head. "I mean, I guess. I thought they were in love. Steph did, too, for a while at least, but now, I just don't know."

"How has he been holding up?"

They paused under the shade of the tree. "It's weird. I thought he would be really upset. Traumatized. Like me. But his attitude has been so strange. It's like he's just dusting off his hands and saying '*que sera, sera*' about the whole thing."

"Hmm," Eric muttered.

"What?"

"Any suspicion on your part?"

"Suspicion like...Andrew may have influenced her to do it?" Trish asked. "No. He may be putting on an emotionless religious robot act, but I don't think he had anything to do with it."

"Fair enough," he said. "Listen to your gut. It's won't always be right, but it usually will be."

They started walking again, heading toward the football stadium. It was far and away the largest structure on campus.

"Listen," Eric began, "speaking of your gut, I know it's telling you that the preacher or his church had something to do with what happened to Stephanie—and I'm not saying you're wrong—but we do need to consider all avenues. Focusing on a single suspect without proof is a good way to miss something else important or, worse, convict the innocent."

"I don't think Berry is innocent."

"Yeah, you may have mentioned that, but humor me. Did Stephanie have any other significant influences in her life besides the church group? Did she belong to any clubs? A sorority? Intramural sports? Anything like that?"

Trish tried to consider possibilities along those lines. Nothing leapt to mind, but based on what Eric had just said, she did want to be fair. At last, she shook her head.

"No. Stephanie was pretty much just focused on being a student. She told me that she had been poor growing up. Her dad's company had done better lately, but she remembered how stressed her parents had always been about money. That can affect a kid, you know?"

"Been there," Eric nodded.

"Anyway, she wanted to be a doctor. She figured that was a sure path to financial security, so she'd never have to worry about money. And she thought her parents would be proud."

Trish's voice trailed off. It still seemed unreal that her friend was gone. Forevermore a past tense in any conversation.

Eric allowed the silence to extend before he spoke again. "So she was a good student, any influences in that area?"

Trish sniffed as a mental light bulb brightened.

"Yes! Well, maybe," she said. "Professor Garber. He teaches chemistry and courses like that. He was her favorite professor last year. She was having trouble in freshmen chem, and he helped her out. Took extra time to make sure she understood the concepts. She really appreciated that. She signed up for another class with him this semester."

"Okay," Eric encouraged. "Do you think he would be someone she might have confided in?"

"I don't know. I mean, I don't think of a professor as someone you really *confide* in, you know?"

"Think we should talk to him anyway?"

Trish wondered if this was a test. Part of detective training.

"Yes, we should talk to him. Couldn't hurt. I'll find out when he has office hours."

"Good. Now can you think of anyone else who should be on our talk-to list? Any other professors? Students? Friends?"

Trish furrowed her brow and thought about it, but no one came to mind. They were almost to the stadium. They wouldn't be able to go inside. The gates stayed locked outside of game day.

"Can't think of anybody," she said.

"I know your chief suspect is Berry, but what if we expand that net? You keep mentioning that Steph was part of a church group.

Group usually means more than two. Any friends in the church group who might be a connection outside of Andrew?"

Trish considered the question. They reached the iron fence around the stadium and stopped. She gripped the bars and stared through them at the mass of gray concrete and steel support beams. You couldn't actually see the football field itself unless you were inside the stadium.

"No."

Eric sighed. "That's a short list. No other emotionless robots at the church?"

A hiccup in Trish's mind. A flash of something. She tried to chase it. Felt she was losing it. She closed her eyes and stopped chasing. Tried to think of nothing. Eric was silent. Maybe he knew what she was doing. She dared not ask for fear the thing would be lost forever.

The breeze lifted her hair. A swarm of grackles filling the branches of a nearby tree chattered with the sound of a warehouse full of machinery badly in need of lubrication.

The thought crystallized. She was disappointed in the revelation. It wasn't big. Just weird. A mental rabbit chase for nothing.

She opened her eyes.

"Find what you were looking for?" Eric asked. Turned out he did understand.

"Yeah, but it was nothing. Just something you said. About the emotionless robots."

"You said it first. What was it?"

"It was when you asked about friends and the church *group*," she turned away from the stadium and leaned back against the painted iron bars of the fence. "Groups like that tend to be close, right?"

"Often, yeah," Eric agreed.

"It's just weird. The other night at the memorial service around the bonfire, you know, when I did the thing," Trish rolled her eyes.

"I recall the thing."

"Everything that happened that night may not be one-hundred-percent crystal clear in my memory," she admitted, "but I do remember something vividly. I didn't think about it at the time, but now, looking back, it just seems weird."

Eric raised his eyebrows in an expectant expression.

"They were all there for Stephanie, right? This special service to remember her. Preacher and all. And the weird thing," Trish paused again to consider it further before continuing, "there were no tears. Andrew told me earlier that day that he hadn't cried for Steph. That night, at the bonfire, *no one* was crying. All these young adults who are filled to the brim with hormones—half the girls on this campus weep when the humidity gives them a bad hair day—but not a single person was crying at a memorial service for a deceased friend, one of their own, not to mention any of the other victims."

Trish chewed on her lip. Just a mental rabbit chase, but something about it stuck with her.

CHAPTER 33

A S THE SMALL GROUP OF STUDENTS FILED OUT THE DOOR of the Physical Sciences building, Christian Berry held the door and clapped the last young man on the back while offering an encouraging word. He then stepped inside and closed the door behind him, giving it a final hard tug to ensure it was locked.

The Physical Sciences building—like most of the classroom buildings on campus—stayed locked on the weekends. Faculty had keys, naturally, along with maintenance staff and a few individuals with special dispensation. Berry was one of a handful of non-employees who enjoyed such privilege.

His counseling group met on most Saturdays in addition to the weekly early-morning donut session on Wednesdays. Since the group was categorized under mental health rather than any religious association, few people asked questions. Berry wasn't the only pastor who pulled double duty to also provide group counseling, and he often wondered how the others managed to voluntarily listen to the mewling of the undergraduate brats on a regular basis. The so-called "problems" of the students would be laughable if not so annoyingly predictable. They were stressed. College was hard, especially those darn science courses. Their high schools hadn't adequately prepared them for the rigors. Their professors were unfair. They expected too much. Blah-blah-blah.

But running the counseling group was a necessary—if tedious—component of the greater plan. Success required sacrifice. To lead this group, Berry had sacrificed three hours per week and the loss of countless valuable brain cells surely killed off as a consequence of absorbing the inane prattle.

This too shall pass. And soon.

Berry's footsteps echoed on the concrete floor as he progressed down the empty hallway to the elevator bank. The basement of the church was functional, but the below-ground level of TSC's Physical Sciences building held one of the best public university labs in the state. It was more than adequate for what was required by the plan, and leading the counseling group meant he had been provided his own key which in turn granted reasonable no-questions-asked access to the building during times which the facilities were generally unused.

In the grand scheme of things, it was worth the sacrifice.

TSC didn't utilize video surveillance in any of the campus buildings, but Berry paused to look up and down the hall, just to ensure there were no human eyes present. When he reached the elevator bank, he spun a tight circle, a dance move to music that only he could hear. At the end of his rotation, he punched the "down" button with one long finger.

As the elevator doors opened, Berry burst into song for an audience of none, belting out that—much like one of our nation's founding fathers—he was not going to throw away his shot. His own father would approve of neither the song nor the momentary lapse in caution, but Berry was not concerned. He excelled at keeping secrets.

He entered the elevator, touched the button labelled "B" and smiled as the doors closed. Time was growing short, and there was much to be done.

CHAPTER 34

CUTTER VALENTINE CLOSED ONE EYE and used the other to peer through the viewfinder of the spotting scope. Nothing had changed. The driveway to the small house behind the church was empty. No vehicle. Christian Berry still wasn't home.

Cutter leaned back into the driver's seat of the pickup. The spotting scope rested on a tripod which he and John had modified to fit the interior of the truck. It sat between them and was camouflaged with an old sweatshirt plus a few air fresheners hanging low from the rearview mirror. The dashboard held various fast food and convenience store trash as well. The pickup looked unkempt, exactly like a thousand other trucks.

The windows were down. A cool breeze filtered through the truck bringing the sounds of a fall Saturday along with it. The skittering chatter of grackles. The occasional engine noise of a vehicle passing their curbside parking spot five blocks from the pastor's house. And the thrumming of John's fingertips on the armrest of the passenger door.

"It's only been an hour, John. Remember what I said about patience. Surveillance is boring as hell. Drop your mind into low gear, or this will drive you crazy."

John flashed a half-second fake grin then tilted his ballcap back on his head so he could glance into the spotting scope himself. A moment later, he straightened and slumped against the passenger door.

"Sorry," he said. "Too much on my mind. I'm just anxious for some results."

Cutter nodded. He knew John well enough to know the man would be jittery as a long-tailed cat in a room full of rocking chairs until they could clearly ascertain whether or not Christian Berry was, in fact, the son of Hiram Kane, but Cutter was experienced enough to realize accomplishing that would be no easy feat. There wasn't going to be any billboard advertising the truth. This was going to take time.

"So is there anything else we can be doing?" John asked.

"Nope. Not today," Cutter responded. "On Monday, we'll start doing some background work. Learn a little more about our new friend Mr. Berry."

"Why Monday?"

"Because the people I need to talk to don't work on weekends. These are government employees, mind you, so Monday it is."

John sighed. "You could put me on a computer somewhere. We could get moving now."

"Afraid not," Cutter replied with a single shake of his head. "A man like Kane doesn't stay hidden for so long without some impressive fencing constructed around him. Part of that might be connections he has in the system, part of it might be just lying very low, but as sophisticated and smart as we believe him to be, I suspect he also has tripwires when it comes to internet searches."

"But we found his address on the internet."

"Right," Cutter agreed, "but not through a direct search. We used the tax appraisal district site to check out the church real estate and accompanying property of like ownership. Never entered the name 'Christian Berry' once."

"So what kind of background check happens on Monday?"

"The other stuff that's virtually impossible to detect. IRS, social security administration, birth records...all done directly through department mainline computers. Normal course of business stuff. Shouldn't trigger any alarms. That's why we'll be accomplishing this by using nice little old ladies who work there and not through your laptop at the hotel."

John nodded and looked out the window.

"Good points, one and all. I'll try to be more patient," John offered. "Just curious, you didn't mention anything about a criminal records check. Is that on the list?"

"Absolutely not," Cutter chuckled. "That's the one thing that—even if it's done directly through a department computer—I can guarantee Kane would have tripwires all over the place. We'd be firing a flare into a night sky letting him know someone was checking him out."

"Guess we'll pass on that one then," John said as he leaned toward the viewfinder of the scope again.

Cutter smiled and closed his eyes for a short nap.

CHAPTER 35

ERIC JOHNSON NOTICED TRISH making her way across the room toward him. Good timing. He was wrapping up his phone conversation.

"That's perfect," he said. "Just give me a call when you get the results. I owe you one."

He touched the red button on the screen and slid the cell phone into his front pocket just as Trish returned to the table with a tray of food. She had offered to buy dinner, and TSC's student union had a food court with a variety of options.

"Who was that?" she asked as she sat and moved the paper boat filled with tacos from the plastic tray to the center of the table.

"Buddy of mine in homicide,' Eric responded, selecting a taco and dolloping a generous helping of salsa into its interior. "He's going to run a criminal records search and general background check on Berry. We should get the results back tomorrow or Monday."

He watched as Trish crunched into her own taco. They had spent much of the day walking around the campus. He was famished, and it looked like she was as well.

The day had been productive. He felt a closer connection to student life on the college campus and what surrounded Stephanie before her death. He had been impressed with Trish. She never tired or grew bored with his questions. She had a tenacity that reminded him of his former partner, along with a number of other personality traits that Trish shared with her father which she probably didn't even realize.

"Hey, can I borrow your phone?" She asked between bites. "I want to look up office hours for Professor Garber."

Eric fished the phone back out of his pocket and passed it across the table. They had stopped by Walmart earlier that day and purchased a temporary phone for her. She called it a 'burner' and he laughed because that's exactly what it was, useless for anything but phone calls and simple texting. Great for doing drug deals. Not so much for investigative research. But the important thing was that she had a device to call for help if needed. Internet connectivity was much lower on the list in terms of importance.

"I realize you've only missed a couple of days," he said, "but you will need to start going to class again at some point. Education, good grades, all that—still important."

"Yeah, I know," she mumbled as she navigated the screen on the phone. "Just not yet."

Eric finished his first taco and reached for another.

"What's next?" she asked.

"Well, tomorrow morning, I'm putting on my nice shirt and attending church."

She raised her eyebrows while she navigated the screen on Eric's phone. "Belly of the beast? Is that wise?"

"Pretty sure I can handle it. Great opportunity for me to observe this guy without him knowing it. You showed me the church earlier. Looks big enough that I can blend in with the congregation. And to answer what you're about to ask, no, you may not come with me. You're too visible at this point. I'll be flying under the radar."

"Can I ask you a different question then?" Trish smirked as she changed the subject. Her eyes were still on the phone. "Just wondering, where do you hide your gun? We've been together all day, and I haven't noticed it."

She raised her gaze from the screen to him. Attention to detail. Eric was again impressed.

"You didn't notice it because I'm not carrying," he admitted. "I caught a flight quickly yesterday. No time to check in luggage. Carry-on only."

"But you're a cop—they wouldn't let you bring your gun on board?"

Eric shook his head. "Once upon a time, but not today. Law enforcement can get special permission to bring aboard, but that requires lots of paperwork in advance of the flight. No time yesterday so I'm left with only my wits and charming smile to defend us."

Trish stopped chewing her taco. An anxious expression crossed her face before she caught herself and made it disappear, but Eric noticed. She felt less safe.

He leaned forward and spoke softly. "Trish, I know you're worried, but listen, this isn't war. We're dealing with lots of maybes here. The preacher may be a bad guy. Slade is obviously a bad guy. But I can deal with either of them. And if we turn up any dirt, any evidence at all of criminal behavior, we're going to the authorities. I won't need a gun for any of that. Okay?"

She resumed chewing her taco, swallowed and offered a self-conscious smile. "Yeah, of course. I was just being dumb. That's all."

"There's nothing to worry about," Eric assured her. "It's all under control. It may not feel like it, but we're in the driver's seat right now. They don't even know we're investigating them."

CHAPTER 36

HIRAM KANE GRUNTED AN ACKNOWLEDGEMENT and hung up the phone. The call had been short, a simple notification that a criminal records check had been initiated on Christian Berry of Abramsville, Texas. Kane wasn't concerned about the outcome of such a report—the Berry persona was clean—but the fact that someone out there had actually initiated a check on his son was of great interest.

He leaned over the table and retrieved a container of honing oil from the shelf along the wall of the toolshed. The tin container was smaller than the palm of his meaty hand. He uncapped the spigot and placed three drops onto the sharpening stone. He selected the first of the daggers ordered neatly on the large square of old cloth on the worktable and held it to the lamp. The blade was ancient but not rusted or in ill-repair. This knife had been well cared for over the centuries just as the other four daggers on the table had been.

He used the flat portion of the tip of the blade to massage the oil into the stone in a slow swirling pattern as his thoughts consumed him. The background check on his son had been initiated out of New York. There was no name available—his resources were not perfect—but it had originated from the Homicide Department of the NYPD.

Kane altered his grip on the dagger's handle and lowered the blade's edge against the glistening stone. He drew the blade along the coarse gray rectangle at a precise angle from heel to tip, feeling the light abrasion travel from his fingers into his wrist, then repeated the motion.

Why now? Who from New York would be looking into Christian Berry? Had Jonas been recognized through that accursed video from the bonfire site? His son had been careless about the possible reaction of that Mexican whore's roommate. Jonas should have known better. He should have been prepared.

Still, Hiram hadn't expected the final stage to be without challenges. This was no more than a warning to avoid complacency. He glanced behind him and assured the blinds were drawn over the toolshed's only window. He himself had grown lax, allowing the window to remain open during the daylight hours. Walking in the open air between the church and home. No more. Windows would remain closed. Going forward, he would only utilize the tunnel between the toolshed dwelling and the church basement. He would be on guard and would instruct Jonas to be likewise.

Whoever had initiated the background check on Jonas had already made one mistake. They would make another. And Hiram would identify and deal with them before any possible interference in the grand plan.

He glanced at the clock on the wall, caked in years of dust but still functional. The spiritual awakening would be starting soon. Afterwards, he would tell Jonas of the research initiated on his alias.

Hiram rotated the dagger and began sharpening the other side of the double-edged blade. Long, slow strokes. It must be honed to perfection. Each of the daggers held a special purpose for the Reckoning. In only a few short days, each would taste blood.

CHAPTER 37

"**D**EATH IS COMING!" Despite the wireless microphone affixed to the lapel of his shirt, Christian Berry was shouting. "The question is—will *you* be prepared?" He emphasized the last word with enough force that spittle flew from his mouth.

The front-row members of the congregation didn't flinch. They were, after all, part of the forty-four. Though more than three hundred people had packed into the church's sanctuary, the front rows of the center section of pews were populated almost wholly by the forty-four. They had arrived early.

The sermon Berry was delivering was not for his chosen few, however. He had written it to be absorbed by the mainstream attendees, those whose devotion was focused—perhaps if only on Sundays—to things above and not solely on the preacher who stood before them. His messages to the forty-four were more carefully crafted and delivered with greater force at the nightly spiritual awakenings. His efforts this Sunday morning represented one more case of keeping up appearances while such appearances remained necessary. But he had also crafted this particular message with purpose and in such a way that his most devoted sect would be enthralled and filled with expectancy for what was to come next.

Berry softened his voice to repeat the question. "Are you prepared?"

He glanced down at the open book on the lectern. The words were already committed to memory, but he felt it added emphasis when the sheep saw him read directly from the book.

"When the Lamb opened the fourth seal, I heard the voice say, 'Come!' I looked, and there before me was a pale horse! Its rider was named Death, and Hades was following close behind him."

He paused for dramatic emphasis and raised his eyes to the congregation, slowly scanning them so each felt they had received eye contact. It was a basic technique used by speakers to keep an audience's attention fixed on his words, but Berry's piercing eyes made it particularly effective. As he trailed his eyes from one end of the sanctuary to the other, something registered.

He returned his gaze to the book.

"And they were given power over a fourth of the earth to kill by sword, famine and plague, and by the wild beasts of the earth."

What was it? What had he seen?

He raised his eyes to the congregation again and transitioned into his closing remarks. No one knows when the end will arrive, but it will be fierce. Blah-blah. Have faith in something greater than yourself. Yada-yada.

His delivery remained polished, but his mind was elsewhere. Was he distracted from the news delivered by his father the previous night—that a background check had been initiated on his Christian Berry identity? He was not accustomed to losing focus while performing, and it did not sit well with him.

As he called the congregation to repentance and salvation, he continued to survey them with his eyes. He inhaled and straightened his posture.

"Every head shall bow, and every eye shall close," he directed as he raised both hands to deliver the closing prayer. The heads of his forty-four immediately dropped as did the remainder of the congregation. It felt good to be obeyed, even if the sheep were easy to command.

"Oh, Lord," he began before his breath caught in his throat. One head unbowed. One set of eyes on him. A black man three rows from the back, sitting on an aisle. For a moment, surprise choked Berry. The feeling passed. He resumed his prayer. Polished. No one would know the difference. He raised his gaze above the congregation toward the ceiling. His performance was impeccable.

But he had seen him. His remarkable memory wasn't just useful for sermons. He never forgot a face. The face of the man in the back of the church was that of a policeman. The homicide detective responsible for the capture of his middle brother. The infamy of Silas Kane's killing spree and the sensationalism of his death had generated plenty of news. Berry had seen the detective's photo on countless occasions. And now he was here. In the church. *His* church.

"Amen," Berry intoned, and the congregation followed suit.

He stepped away from the lectern as music filled the sanctuary. He would not be shaking hands with departing guests today. He had to speak with his father. The answer to last night's mystery had been gifted to them on a silver platter.

CHAPTER 38

JOHN MICHAELS WATCHED as the front door of the church opened and parishioners began filing out. Cutter had moved the truck much closer to the building during the service. They now sat in the parking lot of a public middle school situated across the street from the church. The school had multiple other vehicles from spillover of the church parking lot (Christian Berry was apparently a big draw).

Their nearer proximity to the church was necessary as Cutter wanted them to be able to observe without using binoculars or the spotting scope. Just as the large number of people and vehicles would make it more conspicuous to use the optics—too many eyes who might notice unusual behavior like that—the mass of people also made the truck and its occupants less noticeable to the casual observer...such as a pastor whom they would prefer not know he was being monitored.

John reached down and retrieved the plastic jar of antacids from the floorboard. He opened the lid and shook two pastel-colored discs into his open palm. He popped them into his mouth and crunched loudly.

"Ulcer?" Cutter asked.

"I'll live," John replied. He hated talking about himself—and old habits made him particularly reluctant to impart any details that could convey personal weakness—but after two days of sharing the pickup's bench seat with Cutter and nothing to do but watch and talk, the former Texas Ranger now knew almost everything about John's life.

Almost.

"Drink plenty of water," Cutter offered.

"Thank you for the advice, but the more I drink, the more I seem to urinate. And that's not exactly high on my list of fun activities here in the cab of your truck."

Cutter smiled and returned his gaze to the church. "You get used to it."

"Looking forward to that," John mumbled as he swallowed the chalky remains of the tablets and observed the procession of people filing from the church. They looked like...regular people. He wasn't certain exactly what he had expected to see, or what notions Cutter might have, but there seemed nothing particularly noteworthy about the exodus. The congregation seemed to skew toward the younger generation—not an abundance of little old ladies—but that would seem normal for a church located only a few blocks from a college. There were a decent number of families, a few with young children, and even a handful of gray-headed attendees to balance out the student-aged population.

What John did not see was the man he most wanted to observe. Pastor Christian Berry was not in sight.

John would have loved to have attended the service, to watch Berry from a seat among the congregation, to listen to him speak, to hear his voice and see his eyes and resolve whether or not what he felt in his gut was true. But that wasn't practical. John hadn't even suggested the idea to Cutter.

Following the desert nightmare with Marcus Kane, John was quite certain that Hiram Kane or his youngest son would recognize him or Cutter on sight. Any observing they would do must be from a distance. And that's what they had done since yesterday when Berry finally showed up at his home.

So far, Cutter had been right. This was boring as hell. John craved movement. *Progress.* His former life as a corporate raider had required a degree of patience when orchestrating a hostile takeover of an acquisition target, but even in the mind-numbing diligence and contractual documentation phases, he was always moving forward, building momentum. Surveillance felt like treading water in hopes that the shark swimming in the murk below you chose to pop its head above the surface for a selfie rather than taking off your leg.

"We're not going to know anything until we can search his house," John spoke while watching the activity. "Any proof that he's not who he pretends to be won't be on display for the public. We need to be inside, to see what no one else gets to see."

"And I told you we're not even tiptoeing outside the law—you may recall that trespassing is illegal—until we've logged patterns and know when it would be safest to do that kind of extralegal research." He paused. "Probable cause would be nice, too."

"You're the boss," John said as he watched twin preschool girls run in circles on the church's front lawn while their mother spoke to her friends. In the observation thus far, Berry had given them nothing that could be construed as probable cause. He had barely left the house except to walk across the grass to his church.

John had promised Sarah that he would take his cues from Cutter. That he would be conservative and safe. He wondered how long he could go without breaking that promise.

CHAPTER 39

HIRAM KANE ADJUSTED THE VOLUME CONTROL on the speaker as he listened to the spiritual awakening taking place above him. Jonas had a habit of undulating how loudly he spoke to force his audience into active listening mode. He used this tactic to great effect during the spiritual awakenings. It worked well, but Hiram found it annoying to be forced to compensate by using the volume control.

Sunday was slipping into Monday, but the late hour was undetectable under the constant fluorescent lights of the church basement. Though his son was impressive as always in his delivery, Hiram's thoughts strayed.

The detective was here. Not in the church, not at this moment, but Eric Johnson was in Abramsville. He had attended the service that morning. He had watched Jonas—as the preacher Christian Berry—deliver a sermon. The detective had initiated a criminal search on Berry and had come all the way to Texas to observe him in person. Remarkable.

Hiram's gaze was fixed on the vault. The ancient texts lay behind the great steel door. The time was growing so near. Hiram had suspected that the closer he drew to the Reckoning; extraordinary things would begin to occur. The detective's presence here was no coincidence but was it an obstacle or a gift?

The temptation was almost overwhelming for Hiram to find him and dispose of him in an exquisitely painful manner. The detective's culpability in the death of his second son could not be overlooked.

When Silas had been killed, Hiram had been furious. It had removed his only insurance. If anything had happened to Jonas after that, all would have been lost.

But Jonas was fine. Beyond fine, he had proven himself to be more than Hiram had dared hope. Like a precision scalpel in the hands of a skilled surgeon, Jonas was Hiram's most valuable instrument. Hiram had no need of direct contact with the rabble of humanity. The forty-four acolytes above followed Jonas, and Jonas followed him.

Even now, the sound of his son's voice commanding the attention of all those surrounding him assured Hiram that everything would fall into place. Destiny would dictate it to be so. The detective had become an unexpected part of that destiny. It would be up to Hiram to determine what role—and what end—Eric Johnson would meet. It was only a small part of a greater reality.

CHAPTER 40

ERIC CROSSED HIS ARMS against the cool morning breeze. He should have worn a jacket, but he knew it would warm up later. He leaned back against the front of the minivan and lifted one heel onto the fender. The extensive mileage from trekking around the campus on Saturday had resulted in some serious aches on Sunday. His leg had recovered almost fully from the damage done by Silas Kane two years before, but Eric still paid the price if he overused it. The leg was better today, but he intended to be cautious.

He had parked in the student lot near the Physical Sciences building so Trish could meet with her roommate's professor. He had office hours on Monday and Wednesday mornings. Her parting advice to Eric had been clear: "Stay with the vehicle so you can talk yourself out of a ticket when the campus parking squad comes around." He glanced around the lot. Seemed safe thus far.

He returned his attention to the scene in front of him. The bonfire construction was at full tilt with students moving around the massive field next to the Physical Sciences building like ants obsessed with matchsticks. The logs were being stacked upright, bound together and reinforced with more wiring. The tiers were growing around the center pole. It was impressive.

The students involved all wore hardhats and leather gloves. Logs were trimmed and cut to size as necessary. The young men responsible for this duty all utilized axes. Chainsaws would have been much faster and more practical, but the axes were apparently part of the tradition.

Eric wondered if he would recognize any of the faces of those working on the bonfire—there had been a decent number of college kids at the church service he had attended the prior morning—but he didn't see anyone that looked familiar.

Attending the service had proven worthwhile. He had been able to watch Christian Berry up close. From that observation, he walked away with two things. First, Berry was a charismatic preacher who did absolutely nothing in the service that would spark suspicion of any unsavory leanings. Second, Eric determined that he did not care for Berry one bit. There was just something about the guy. Perhaps it was instinct. After all, Eric did have strong instincts once upon a time when he worked the street, before he had been moved into his current paper-pushing management role.

Whatever the vibe was, the preacher left a bad taste in Eric's mouth, and he didn't like it.

His cell phone vibrated along his leg. Eric pulled it out long enough to glance at the screen then returned it to his pocket. Speaking of his paper-pushing management role, that was his Captain's second attempt to reach him that morning. Eric didn't feel like engaging in that conversation yet. Another voicemail would be fine.

His thoughts returned to the church service. Another thing he didn't like was what he saw out of Slade Stone. Trish had given him a description, and Eric had found plenty of pictures of him as well. Slade had been a ferocious athlete so there was no shortage of online presence.

Based on what Trish had told him, Eric assumed he would see Slade at the church service. He was not disappointed, and upon seeing him, he could readily understand Trish's fear. Slade was a beast. An ugly beast. He sat on the front row accompanied by four fellow jock-looking monsters. The five of them overloaded an entire pew that probably could have seated ten normal humans.

Thinking about what Slade had done—and what he had threatened to do—to Trish that night in her dorm room made his blood boil. The fact that Berry apparently kept close company with this thug further cemented Eric's dislike of the preacher. There was something wrong there. Was that something also responsible for the suicide of Trish's roommate? Eric didn't know. Worse, he truly had no idea of how they would be able to learn the truth. But you had to start somewhere. Observing the preacher in action yesterday had been a start. Trish meeting with the professor was another step.

He glanced from the bonfire field to the Physical Sciences building and wondered how that step was progressing.

CHAPTER 41

THE OFFICE DOOR WAS OPEN, but Trish remained in the hallway and gently rapped her knuckles on the doorframe twice.

"Professor Garber?"

The middle-aged man seated at the cluttered desk pulled his attention from the computer screen to look toward the door. His shirt was wrinkled, and his hair looked like he had slept on it badly overnight then hadn't bothered to look in a mirror before leaving the house.

"Doctor," he said.

"I'm sorry?"

"It's *Doctor* Garber. I have a PhD." He pointed to a framed diploma on the wall.

Trish opened her mouth then closed it again. She remained in the doorway.

"I'm sorry," the man said as he stood, the paunch of his belly hung over the first inch of the knit fabric belt of his khakis. He had missed a beltloop. "That sounded so condescending and rather haughty, didn't it?"

"Um," Trish stammered.

"It did. My fault. I'm sorry. Rough day thus far." Garber walked from behind the desk and bent to remove a stack of notebooks from a plastic chair in front of it. "Please, come in. How may I help you?"

He dropped the notebooks on the floor along the wall and gestured toward the now empty seat.

Trish entered the small office and sat. The room smelled of dry erase markers. "I'm sorry, Dr. Garber. I didn't mean to disturb you. I thought these were your office hours."

He returned behind the desk and plopped into the chair. "These are my office hours, but I didn't expect anyone. I've taught here for years, and bonfire week is usually quiet for me. Students rarely seem focused on their studies during this time." He cocked his head. "Speaking of...are you one of my students? Forgive me, but you don't look familiar."

"Oh, I'm not. My name is Trish O'Brien. I go to school here, but I'm a journalism major."

"Fair enough, Trish O'Brien, journalism major, what brings you to my humble office?"

"I was hoping we could talk about one of your students. Stephanie Espinosa."

Dr. Garber nodded slowly. "I see. Are you doing a story on the tragedy? School paper, perhaps?"

"Oh no!" Trish responded, a little too emphatically. She chastised herself. *Keep it cool.* "No story. It's just that Stephanie is my—" She stopped herself. "Stephanie *was* my roommate."

"I'm sorry for your loss." His eyes looked past Trish as he spoke. "I knew Stephanie. I still can't believe what happened. What she did." His voice trailed off. "So unlike her."

"Yes. Exactly." Trish leaned forward. "And I want to know why. I know she respected you. She told me how much you helped her in the past. I was hoping maybe you could offer some insight."

Dr. Garber leaned back in his chair and ran his hands through his thinning hair, leaving it more disheveled than before.

"I'm afraid I must disappoint you, Miss O'Brien. I have no idea why someone—anyone—would do something so terrible. The knives. The people." He trailed off again before returning his gaze to Trish. "I spent quite a bit of time with Stephanie, but it was always academic. She was bright but was having a difficult time. I've seen it a thousand times. It's usually not the material that's the challenge. It's the adjustment to college life. Large classes. Higher expectations. I wanted to help her through that, and she did very well. Passed with flying colors."

Trish smiled. "I remember. She was more excited about her Chem grade than any other class that semester. We celebrated. She was also appreciative of you."

Dr. Garber sniffed. "I'm glad to hear that. I wish things had been different for her. Whatever demons she had, she kept them hidden quite well. But then, I wasn't looking for them either. Perhaps I should have been."

Trish leaned forward. "None of us were looking." She paused. "Did she ever talk to you about the church group she was part of?"

Garber's eyebrows lifted. "No. Not something we ever discussed. Why do you ask?"

"Are you certain?" Trish pressed. "She was part of a church group with a bunch of other students. Her boyfriend, Andrew Kraft, was also part of it. Led by Christian Berry."

Garber smirked. "I know Berry. I also know Andrew. He's one of my students. Smart young man. I hope he's doing okay given the circumstances."

"He's working through it," she offered. "Why did you make that face when I mentioned Berry?"

"Oh, it's nothing. He leads a gathering of some sort on Wednesday mornings in this building. Supposed to be non-religious, but I'm ninety-percent certain he worms it in anyway."

"That bothers you?"

"I'm a man of science. I believe our job as educators is to fill the minds of young people with facts, not myth. This is a state-funded college, and there should be a separation between church and state. I don't believe Berry adheres to that policy."

"Have you seen any students affected by Berry in a negative way? Did Stephanie ever give any indication of that?"

"Such an interesting question." His eyes crinkled at the corners with the remark. "Anything along the lines of insidious religious teaching is a negative in my eyes, but no, I didn't see any specific issues from Stephanie related to that nor from any other students."

"Oh," Trish hoped the disappointment didn't register in her voice. She was supposed to be keeping it cool.

"For what it's worth," Garber offered, "I've met Christian Berry several times. I'm not a fan."

"Really?"

"Really. But be aware that he does have his fans. Ardent ones. Some of them here in the chemistry department. Not all my colleagues share my worldview. There's a reason Berry is allowed to have his group meetings in this building, even though I personally believe those should take place in a more neutral location rather than an institute of learning."

Trish nodded. Her disappointment was still palpable. She hadn't entered the office with any specific outcome in mind, but there were so few avenues to pursue in trying to find answers, in trying to solve the mystery surrounding her friend's death. While the professor seemed willing to help, whatever hope she held that he would be a possible solution to the mystery had faded to nothing in only a few short minutes of conversation.

"Thank you for your time, Dr. Garber." She rose and extended her hand. "I really appreciate it."

He stood and shook the offered hand. "I sense that I have, indeed, disappointed you, Miss O'Brien. I'm sorry. I wish I could give you some sort of insight into what happened with Stephanie. The whole situation is tragic. For all those affected." He released her hand. "And it's not my place to say, but don't set your hopes too highly on resolving the reason behind this tragedy. As much as I wish answers always came clearly— as we like them to do in the scientific world—my experience is that matters involving the behavior of human beings are often impossible to understand. Don't drive yourself crazy trying to do so. Grieve for your friend, then move on. It's the only thing any of us can do."

Trish nodded and thanked the professor again before walking out the door. As she proceeded down the hallway toward the elevators, she wondered if he might be right.

CHAPTER 42

"**I**'M GLAD WE HAD THIS CONVERSATION. I hope you feel the same." Christian Berry put his arm around Andrew's shoulders as he escorted him from the office to the front door of the church. "Though I do apologize for the late hour."

"That's okay," Andrew replied as he walked alongside the pastor toward the exit. "I'm not tired."

Berry held open the door as Andrew proceeded through. "Rest anyway. Tomorrow will be a big day. Great events are upon the horizon."

Andrew nodded and ambled down the sidewalk. Berry watched as the young man receded into the darkness. It had been an engaging evening thus far, and his one-on-one with Andrew was not the end of it. The spiritual awakening that night had been frenzied. This was the gathering in which Berry redirected the mindset of the forty-four, fully altering their trajectory from following an unseen God to devoting themselves wholly to the shepherd standing before them.

Berry had considered this to be the most dangerous time. The act itself wasn't unprecedented. This was a basic page from the handbook of any run-of-the-mill cult leader. The difference was that those cult leaders generally had the advantage of isolating their sheep from other influences. Plus, they didn't have the same unforgiving timetable to which Berry was subject.

On the other hand, those generic cult leaders didn't have the meticulous planning skills of Berry and Hiram Kane. Didn't have the background. Or the formula. Or the benefit of what was kept behind the vault in the church basement.

They also didn't have the same aspirations. No one ever had.

Based on the reactions from the forty-four during the awakening, the waters had been navigated to success. The seeds planted by Berry over the weeks, the subtle alterations in their worship the past several days, the focus of a communion that no longer emphasized the historic underlying meaning of the sacraments, all of these elements combined to ensure a smooth and calculated transition for his flock in the direction he wished them to go. And there was more to come.

Berry glanced at his watch. His follow-up meeting with Andrew had taken longer than planned, but it had been important. His next meeting would be important as well. It was a big night.

He stopped by his office to retrieve a folder from his desk then returned to the fellowship room where the spiritual awakenings took place. The chairs were still arranged in a large circle. Five of them were occupied. Slade and his four friends.

The Elite Guard.

Though Berry had selected these individuals—had researched and profiled and engineered events to lead them into his flock for this eventual purpose—he had not branded the group with that particular moniker. When he and Slade had first brought these four additional individuals together in Berry's office and described their role as a special task force that would be devoted to undertaking necessary action for Berry—and to do so with a no-questions-asked utter faithfulness—one of them had asked, "like an Elite Guard?" The name stuck. Berry didn't care. They could call themselves the Ferocious Five or the Freaks from Fremont, as long as they did what he asked of them.

He walked into the circle, selected a chair and moved it in front of the row of hulking young men. Among them were three football players (including Slade), a power lifter and a track and field athlete that specialized in shot put and discus. Berry reversed the chair so he could straddle it, his thin frame leaning forward over the backrest.

He scanned their faces. None appeared annoyed or anxious about the amount of time they had had to remain in the room while Berry attended to other matters.

"You have been patient. Thank you for waiting," Berry offered.

Smiles from the group at the compliment, like dogs receiving praise from their master. Good.

"No problem. We're here to serve," Slade responded. "Right?"

Grunts of agreement from his cohorts. A self-assured smile lit Slade's face. He was no longer permitted to lead TSC's defense onto the gladiatorial gridiron of the football field, but Berry had given him a role of leadership here, and Berry could tell the monster reveled in it. Also good.

"Excellent," Berry nodded. "Because I have need of you. I have told you of this group's importance in the Reckoning. You will be integral, and I will provide you details as they are made clear to me through prayer and meditation." Berry paused and spoke in a low voice. "But there is something you don't yet know."

The beasts leaned forward. Faces expectant.

"There will be forces at work to prevent us from succeeding, to prevent the righteousness of the Reckoning to occur. We must be on guard."

Berry saw a flash of anger cross Slade's face. Berry knew it was rage at any who would dare be at odds with this mission. That fury would be easily directed, but the trick to the matter would be reining it to a controllable level. Berry didn't need loose cannons. He needed sniper rifles. Powerful but accurate.

"Tomorrow, you will truly become an elite guard unit. You will begin watching me from afar. *Keep your distance.*"

"Like I did with that girl, Trish."

"Yes, Slade. Like that. You proved quite valuable on that front."

Another satisfied smile from Slade. Good dog.

"You will be on alert to anyone who may, in turn, be following me. I suspect someone else may be watching. A man with ill intentions toward our cause. Your role is to spot that man."

Eyebrows raised. Berry opened the folder and distributed the contents among his five soldiers. Photos of Eric Johnson culled from the internet. From the time the detective had helped kill Berry's middle brother.

"Now allow me to explain who this man is, and what you will do when you find him."

CHAPTER 43

JOHN MICHAELS SAID GOODNIGHT to his wife and hung up the phone. It had been the best of calls and the worst of calls. Hearing Sarah's voice, knowing she and DJ were still safe, granted him a sense of peace otherwise unattainable while he stalked the man calling himself Christian Berry. He didn't realize how much he needed that peace, that balm, until Sarah's voice was in his ear.

What she had to say was less soothing.

She was trying to be understanding—John knew that without being told though she mentioned it anyway—but how long did he plan to continue this campaign? He had left their home four days ago. Had he or Cutter discovered *anything* in that time supporting the notion that the preacher was actually Jonas Kane?

It probably didn't help that John had called so late. The glowing red numbers on the digital clock by his bed in the hotel room had long since passed midnight. He was wide awake—and would be for a while yet—but Sarah had been sleeping. Their daughter was too young to politely adjust her sleep schedule according to the slumber needs of her parents. DJ would be up early. John was keeping Sarah up late.

Calling while DJ was asleep also meant that John didn't get to talk to her. He missed her voice. The most precious two syllables in the world were "Dad-dee" when spoken in all her toddler adorableness. But he didn't like calling during the daylight hours. He was with Cutter then. And while he respected the older man—and even considered him a friend—John valued privacy when speaking to his own family.

The phone conversation hadn't been especially long. John had little to report, still nothing to support his position beyond what he felt in his gut. Sarah didn't ask him to stop. She didn't tell him to come home. No ultimatums. But she was a smart woman, and her inquiries regarding whether Cutter felt this was a worthwhile endeavor were clearly a proxy for her own sentiment.

He knew this was hard on Sarah, too. They had endured much in the four years since New Mexico, but they had always done it together. That partnership and the ability to share the burden—the work and the worry amid the constant undercurrent of fear—is what had allowed them to weather the ongoing storm. John had never been away this long during that time, particularly since DJ had arrived. Four days may not seem like much, but to a toddler, it could be an eternity. Sarah told him DJ was feeling his absence.

Four days also felt longer given the lack of any definitive end in sight. The endeavor in Abramsville was open-ended with only John's instinct holding him here. That left Sarah at home, bearing the emotional weight on her own.

There were two options. Possibility Number One: Christian Berry was *not* the son of Hiram Kane. That would mean this venture was not only a waste of time, but that John had left Sarah and DJ exposed in their home since the "real" Kane family would still be out there somewhere. Sarah knew how to use the security equipment, and she was well-versed in escape routes and contingency plans, but that did little to comfort John when he couldn't be with her. On the other hand, Possibility Number Two was that Berry was, indeed, Jonas Kane. That meant John was smack in the middle of enemy territory, at constant risk of being identified, putting himself in danger and—much worse—possibly endangering Sarah and DJ if he were eventually discovered.

He sighed and reclined on the bed. He knew he needed sleep. Cutter was taking the first half of the overnight watch, but John would be on duty soon enough. The two had decided to monitor Berry jointly during the day when he was most likely to be active, but to take turns observing during the night.

John hated being in the hotel room. Nothing would be revealed here. He was supposed to rest, an impossibility under the circumstances. He wanted proof. He wanted to know Berry's true identity. Once that was proven, action could be taken. Only then could John hope to rest. When he knew his family would be safe.

There was something else beyond the evident. Something more than what he was seeing. Whatever Hiram Kane and his son were doing in Abramsville, it wasn't resting. They were up to something. John knew it. But how could he uncover the truth?

John took a deep breath, pushed the back of his head into the pillow and laid his forearm over his eyes. Sleep would mean dreams. Bad ones. His thoughts turned to his daughter. What would he be willing to do to ensure DJ never had to endure nightmares like this?

CHAPTER 44

T RISH SCANNED THE LOUNGE of the student union again. He
still wasn't here. That was bad. What was worse was the news Eric
seemed to be preparing to deliver.

"What are you saying, Eric?"

Eric sighed from his seat at the end of the sofa. "I had another less-
than-pleasant conversation with my captain this morning. He's not
pleased with my abrupt vacation plans."

Trish occupied the other end of the sofa. The chair next to her spot
remained empty. That meant he was either late, or he wasn't coming
at all.

"So what does that mean?"

"It means I'm in a tight spot. I came down here because you're
family to me, Trish. I would never let something happen to you. And I
respect your need to find answers in Stephanie's death. I want to help,
but we're hitting brick walls, and I may be running out of time."

Trish knew he was right. After an entire weekend walking around
the campus, talking about her roommate, probing her memory for any
possible connections Steph may have had who might possibly provide
insight into what happened, Trish had eked out a whopping five
possibilities that weren't named Christian Berry. She had met with four
of them yesterday, starting with Dr. Garber. All four of them had
combined to yield a total of zip. Nada. Nothing. And number five
hadn't shown up for the arranged meeting today.

"You can't leave," she said in a low voice. "I need you. I can't do
this without you."

"I'm not leaving yet. I want to solve this thing, too, but we have to face facts. We haven't found anything on Berry yet beyond the fact that neither of us like him. But his background check was choirboy clean. The guy has never even had a speeding ticket. And no one you talked to yesterday seemed to think the church was a problem."

"Just because that's what they think, it doesn't mean they're right!"

Eric nodded at her. He at least looked sympathetic. "I don't disagree. And I'm not saying Berry isn't slimy. And there is no denying his Slade connection and what that asshole threatened you with. Those things are smoke. I want to see if there's a fire, but I can't spend weeks away from work trying to develop this and being your bodyguard."

Trish sank in her seat. "I don't need a bodyguard."

"Didn't say you did. That's my debt to your dad. I can't shake it. Protecting you comes with the territory whether you like it or not. And I won't leave unless I'm certain you're safe enough for me to do so."

"I don't need protection. I need to find out what happened to Steph."

"I get that. And if this was New York, and I could work on it a little every day, I would. But we're in Texas, and I have a real job with a real boss two-thousand miles away. I can't do both. And right now, I'm a cop out of his jurisdiction. That hinders me more than it helps."

"What...what if..." Trish stammered. She wanted to finish the sentence, but she didn't know how. What *could* she do? What would need to happen for Eric to stay and help her solve this thing?

"The answer to the question you can't quite form is *progress*," he said. "I want to be here. I really do. But we need to have a next step in place. Right now, we're at a standstill. There's not much else we can do on the whole Berry investigation. I'm sorry, Trish. We need something more."

Trish looked to the ceiling and blinked several times. She didn't want to cry, it's just that she was so damn *frustrated*. There had to be an answer. She would not give up. But...what? What could she do? What would give them the break they needed?

She blinked twice more, clearing away the threatening tears, and turned to Eric. He wasn't looking at her. She followed his eyes to see Andrew Kraft standing right in front of her.

"Sorry I'm late," he said and dropped into the empty chair next to her.

CHAPTER 45

HIRAM KANE INCHED HIS FRAME FORWARD, leaning closer to the computer monitor and the camera attached to it. He disliked being on video, and he had a severe distaste for conducting business via the internet—even with rigorous safety protocols in place—but it wasn't prudent for him to leave the underground lair with the blasted policeman poking around.

The High Council needed to meet. It was important for the other members to feel his presence, and it was important to Hiram that he look them in the eye in advance of the Reckoning. He would have preferred the meeting to be in person but would make do with what was available.

"Is everyone clear on exactly what is to occur this week and your personal responsibility?" he asked. The heads of four men nodded and murmured compliance, each in their own video square of the conference grid on Hiram's monitor.

"Excellent." Hiram again shifted his position in front of the camera as he spoke. He watched his own video square to ensure his adjustments accomplished his goal. He was trying to take up as much of the screen as possible. He didn't want anything visible in the background. Not the vault door. Not the mirror. Nothing. These men represented his innermost circle, his most trusted allies, but he had no intention of allowing them to see anything more than his face. He had no doubt as to the High Council's loyalty to the cause, but trust was a fool's crutch. He brooked no such weakness in himself.

"We will not meet again prior to the event," he reminded the council. More nodding of heads. There had been fewer questions during this meeting than Hiram had expected. With the Reckoning almost at hand, he had anticipated some level of nervousness among this group. Anxiety always led to questions. But they had impressed him by only making the most essential of inquiries, almost all related to practical specifics of their roles this week. That was a positive sign. Their faith was strong. He was about to test it.

"There is one more thing before we close," he said. "And this is directed at Barnes but all of you should be aware."

Leonard Barnes, the Abramsville Chief of Police, cocked his head in expectation.

"A man has arrived. An interloper. His name is Eric Johnson. About thirty. Black. He's a homicide detective for the NYPD." Hiram noticed Barnes cock his head the other direction. He had his attention. "If this man has the opportunity, he will interfere with our plans. We cannot allow that to happen."

"What do you propose?" Barnes asked.

"No action on your part. I will deal with this matter." He paused. "Discreetly. Now is not the time for rash behavior." Hiram thought he saw Barnes exhale at that. "But should anything occur, it will be your responsibility to obfuscate any procedural response."

"That could prove complicated."

"Beyond your capability?"

"Of course not."

"Then I'm not concerned. I won't be asking for miracles, only time. As you gentlemen know, the time draws near."

Barnes nodded assent.

Hiram shifted his gaze to the other three video squares. They were occupied by Henry Ralston, the owner of the largest construction company in the city, Victor McNabb, the CEO of a publicly traded tech corporation based out of Houston, and Lucas Blankshire, the head of TSC's Chemistry Department.

Hiram had contacts in various industries, academic institutions and federal agencies all over the country. Many of these connections were individuals of wealth and influence. Hiram's cause had never lacked for funding. Greed had a way of making men pliant, and Hiram had been gifted with an almost supernatural ability to identify and leverage that greed.

The four men who composed the High Council believed they had earned their places by virtue of their trusted service and value to the cause. They were partly right. Ultimately, they sat on the High Council because that was where Hiram needed them to be to satisfy his own plans.

"I will keep you individually apprised of any matters that require your involvement," he told them. "You will keep me updated as well."

He shifted his gaze from the screen to look directly into the camera. He wanted these men to feel his eyes.

"This meeting of the High Council has concluded. I will see you all at the appointed time. Be vigilant."

Hiram ended the virtual meeting with the click of his mouse. The grid of heads vanished from his screen. He leaned back, closed his eyes and pondered what was to come.

CHAPTER 46

A S TRISH WALKED ALONGSIDE ERIC, she couldn't help feeling uplifted at the morning's events. The sensation was accompanied by guilt. Stephanie was still dead—nothing could undo that tragedy—but perhaps a glimmer of hope now existed for uncovering the truth and enacting justice. It was hard to reconcile her excitement with her grief.

"This is something, right?" she asked. "Tell me this is something."

One side of Eric's mouth rose in a half-smile. "It *may* be something," he admitted. "It's certainly more than we had before, but let's not get ahead of ourselves."

"Sure." She stepped onto the grass to make room on the sidewalk for a small herd of students heading the other direction. They all wore t-shirts of red and gold with Texas State College or some variation of TSC splashed across them. She remembered the same thing happening last year. The week of the bonfire and the Woodson State University football game was accompanied by a tidal wave of school spirit with attire to match. There was red and gold everywhere.

"What do you think changed his mind?"

Eric's question caught Trish off guard. Per usual.

"What do you mean?"

"You told me that Andrew had been something less than cooperative thus far. Why do you think he changed his tune?"

Trish mentally replayed the meeting in the student union. Andrew hadn't exactly been the zenith of cooperation—he hadn't even wanted to talk very long since he kept complaining about a headache—but he had told them he'd thought about what Trish had said and that he'd be willing to talk to them about the church. He hadn't been too preachy during their time together, but Trish surmised that any willingness Andrew had to discuss Berry and the church would carry with it the price of Trish having to listen to a plea for her eternal soul. That was fine. If it meant making progress, it was a price she could endure.

"He had told me before that talking to me was the right thing to do, and that he'd think about helping me. I guess he thought about it and decided to take a chance on me." Trish spoke the words with minimal conviction. She was making assumptions. But at the end of the day, she didn't really care. She wasn't about to look the proverbial gift horse in the mouth.

"The conversation was pretty short," Eric commented. "Think he'll meet with us again when he's feeling better?"

"He said he would. I think he meant it."

Trish had watched Andrew throw back a double dose of Excedrin during their talk. She remembered he had complained about a headache once before, the day after Stephanie had died. Maybe it was the stress. Maybe his refusal to deal with Steph's death—to at least cry for his love forever lost—was wreaking havoc with his mind. That might help explain what had surprised Trish the most about the encounter—that Andrew seemed unfazed about Eric's involvement.

Trish and Eric had both planned for Eric to introduce himself as a family friend but then excuse himself. He knew that any connections from Steph's life would likely be far more comfortable talking to her roommate than to a homicide detective. He had no desire to leverage his law enforcement status by making it seem like there was an investigation. Eric had said that could end up either raising walls or creating trouble, and he had faith in Trish's ability to question these connections on her own. They had both assumed it would be the same with Andrew. But when Andrew had sat down and Eric offered to leave the conversation, Andrew invited him to stay. He seemed to not to care that Eric was even there.

That had been surprising.

Two female students cut between them on the sidewalk. They were laughing and moving quickly. Late for class but not appearing to care very much.

"Any sign of him?" she asked.

She watched as Eric scanned the area. She did the same. The Physical Sciences building was now in view.

"Nope. You?"

Trish shook her head. "Nothing. But I'm sure he would have driven so he'd be coming in from the parking lot." They veered onto a path in that direction.

Toward the end of the conversation in the student union, when Trish had asked what she hoped sounded like a nonthreatening question about Christian Berry, Andrew had responded by ticking off a list of the good things Berry did for the community. He included the student sessions Berry led at the Physical Sciences building on Wednesdays and Saturdays. Today was only Tuesday, but Andrew had mentioned that Berry had told him he was stopping by the building this morning and that he'd say "hi" if he saw him.

As soon as Andrew had ended the conversation and said goodbye, Trish and Eric had both started toward the Physical Sciences building. To what end, Trish had no idea, maybe because they had nowhere else to be and wanted to set eyes on Berry again, but the point was, they had been on the same page. And maybe that meant something. Maybe Eric was also sensing a possible break in the case—if that was the term a detective would use—by Andrew's willingness to help. Trish felt that had to be a good sign.

As they drew closer to the building, Trish scanned the area for the slender form of the preacher. Maybe things were finally moving in their favor for a change. It was about time.

That's when she saw the hulking form of Slade Stone step from behind a tree and begin walking straight toward them.

CHAPTER 47

CHRISTIAN BERRY GAZED OUT THE WINDOW at the scene unfolding next to the parking lot below. He was on the third floor of the Physical Sciences building in an empty office, and he had begun scanning the terrain outside as soon as he had received the text message from his Elite Guard. The location afforded him both privacy and a perfect view. He was glad he had thought to bring a pair of binoculars to watch the show. All was proceeding exactly as he had predicted.

He watched as Slade left his station under the tree and walked toward a black man and the girl he was with. The four other members of the Elite Guard were approaching the pair from behind, flanking them from two different directions.

Berry peered closer at the man, focusing the binoculars. It was definitely Eric Johnson. The upstart detective. He watched as the girl stopped in her tracks and put her hand on Johnson's arm. She had spotted Slade.

Berry lifted his free hand, placed his palm against the pane of glass and leaned forward until the binoculars touched the window. *The girl.* It was *her*. The one from the bonfire. Stephanie's roommate.

"What fresh hell is this?" Berry murmured.

Why was she with the detective? He searched his memory, what little he knew of her. Her name was Trish O'Brien. She was from New York. The detective was from New York. But so were millions of other people. What was the connection between these two?

He reached into his pocket for his phone, then took a calming breath and released it, leaving the device in his pocket. Greater forces were at work here. His father had mentioned his expectation for such things many times. Berry believed it to be true as well.

He returned his gaze to the activity below, anxious to see where fate would lead.

CHAPTER 48

CUTTER BACKED THE TRUCK into an open space in the service lot near the Physical Sciences building. They had followed Christian Berry from his home, watched him pull into the building's main parking lot then enter the building twenty minutes earlier. Cutter had driven a circuit twice before deciding the service lot was the best option to stake out the area. There were several maintenance vehicles there, and Cutter's truck blended well. Plus, the lot had a decent view of the entrance to the Physical Sciences building and its adjacent parking, not to mention the constant activity occurring in the big field next door where it looked like students were preparing for the world's biggest marshmallow roast.

He glanced to the passenger seat and noticed John scrawling notes on his yellow legal pad, documenting the time and location as they monitored Berry's behavior and tried to create an anticipated schedule from their observations.

"Any thoughts?" John asked as he clicked the pen closed. The legal pad remained on his lap.

"None," Cutter replied. "Not yet at least."

Cutter heard a low murmur from his companion that could have been a soft clearing of the throat or could have been a mumbled word. He didn't bother to ask for clarification. If John had something he wanted to say, Cutter knew he would say it clearly. And if he didn't, he wouldn't.

That was something Cutter had grown to appreciate about John. The man had his issues, of that there was no doubt, but he was unafraid of silence. The two of them had spent hours upon hours together in the cab of Cutter's pickup over the past few days and most of that time had been blissful quiet. John had felt no need to fill the air with small talk, and he hadn't expected to be entertained either. He was focused on the business at hand and doing it well, even if this particular type of business was dull as a bowling ball.

Cutter respected that. Over the years, he had spent too many stakeouts partnered with a variety of officers who couldn't keep their respective traps shut for more than five minutes. It was a social insecurity, a fear of silence, a need to fill the quiet with some sort of banter. Cutter had never felt it. He was glad John was of similar ilk.

In fact, John had maintained his quiet composure during Cutter's phone calls with Maggie, even when he was hearing one side of a conversation that clearly involved the other party asking pointed questions about John and the usefulness of the operation they were currently undertaking. That had to have been difficult, particularly since Cutter hadn't been able—or inclined—to mount a strong defense for the work they were doing. He wasn't going to puff up facts to assuage Maggie. They had been married too long for that. She deserved the unvarnished truth.

And for that matter, John needed to hear the truth as well.

Cutter was honest with himself. As boring as Level One surveillance was, he had engaged in this endeavor partly because retirement hadn't exactly been brimming with excitement either. He missed the thrill of the hunt, even when the hunt was just sitting and waiting. But that wasn't all. If it had been, he would have called this off by now.

In all the soft research Cutter had conducted through his various sources, Christian Berry had proved to be a spotless human being. A law-abiding, safe-driving, tax-paying citizen. A soul without blemish. And the physical observations they had conducted thus far hadn't pointed toward any alternative conclusions. In their days and nights of surveillance, he and John hadn't witnessed Berry do *anything* outside of what a normal college-town preacher would do.

But here Cutter sat. Despite all logic and evidence to the contrary. And despite a spouse who would much prefer to see him home rather than on a fool's errand. Cutter was here not just because it was a brief recapture of his former life. He was here because there was still a chance. And if all evidence pointed to a ninety-nine percent probability that Christian Berry was innocent as a dove, then that meant there was a one percent chance he was, indeed, Jonas Kane. Until that chance was zero, Cutter felt obligated to pursue it. Maggie would have to understand.

Beyond even that, wasn't there something more? Something that Cutter himself didn't even understand but had been niggling at the back of his mind for quite some time. Something about New Mexico and the way events had unfolded.

Cutter gazed out the windshield as the flow of students entering and leaving the Physical Sciences building tapered off. He checked his watch and figured class must have started. His thoughts returned to the Berry situation.

The challenge was in proving the matter either way. If Berry was just a guy and not an accessory to a madman's evil plans, how many days would they sacrifice in what would likely be a vain effort?

But how to resolve the issue? What would need to happen to give the operation a clear indicator one way or the other?

Cutter's train of thought was disrupted by a faint tickle at the back of his neck. A sense of something. What was he seeing? He picked up the small pair of binoculars—the lowest profile set from John's shopping spree at the sporting goods megastore—and raised them to his face. He only wanted a glance. There were hardly any people near the service lot, but no sense in a long gaze that might risk someone seeing him using the binoculars.

It didn't take long to zero in on what had made the hairs on his neck bristle. The young men he was watching stood out like buffalo in a cow herd. Two of them walking together. It was the recognition that did it.

"Look familiar to you?" Cutter passed the binoculars to John. "The big boys at your ten o'clock."

John sank back in his seat before raising the binoculars. For an amateur, he wasn't bad.

"We've seen them coming out of Berry's church," John said. "Sunday service and at every one of those weird late-night Bible studies Berry conducts."

"Affirmative," Cutter agreed. "And on my watch last night, those boys stayed at the church pretty durn late. Well after the rest of the crowd left."

But it wasn't just the recognition that had drawn Cutter's eye. He had seen other students around campus that he'd also marked as having attended the church—though none so visually arresting as the big boys here—it was something else. It was the way these guys were walking that had caught his attention.

"And two more," John said as he scanned the area with the binoculars.

Cutter tracked John's line of sight and sure enough, he was right. The additional two behemoths were approaching from a different direction but headed on a path that would intersect the first pair.

Cutter rubbed his chin with his thumb and forefinger as he surveyed the area between the Physical Sciences building and the main parking lot.

"Now this is interesting."

CHAPTER 49

IT TOOK ERIC ALL OF AN INSTANT to register why Trish had stopped on the sidewalk and grabbed his arm. Slade Stone was fifty yards away and impossible to miss. He was striding toward them with an unrushed pace. His hands were to his sides. They were empty, but he was clenching and unclenching his fingers as he walked.

He glanced toward Trish. "Look at me," he instructed. She did so, though it took obvious effort to avert her eyes from Slade's approach. "Good. It's going to be okay. Broad daylight. Public place. And I'm here with you."

Trish nodded. She was maintaining composure, but Eric could sense panic lurked not far below the surface. It kicked his protective instincts into overdrive and made him welcome the confrontation. It should have taken place days ago. He had promised Trish that he would not instigate anything against Slade. He had concurred that the investigation of Christian Berry demanded a clandestine approach and confronting Slade might endanger their research, but now that Slade was coming to him, those obligations were moot.

Of course, it would have been nice if he could flash his badge without further risking their investigation, but that was off the table. As Slade grew larger with each approaching step, Eric mused it would also have been nice to be carrying a gun. Damn airline regulations. *Thanks a lot, Bin Laden.* Still, the likelihood this would turn into a physical altercation was slim. Unless the beast approaching them was completely off his bean.

"It's going to be okay," Eric said in a low voice. He scanned the area to assess the number of bystanders. *Shit.* He didn't see any students nearby, but he did take quick note of four more gigantors approaching from behind in two pairs. Two of them wore tank tops despite the cool weather. They were walking with purpose, and they weren't headed for class. The situation had suddenly and aggressively changed for the worse.

Slade and the quadruplets from hell were still out of earshot, but not by much.

Eric put both hands on Trish's shoulders and turned her to face him completely.

"Remember the four rules of a confrontation?" he asked.

She looked down for a moment and blinked several times before responding. "Yeah, um, be a weasel, plan your exit, find a weapon and, um," she stammered, "eyes...eyes-throat-groin!"

"Not bad," Eric grinned. "Not bad." She had remembered, even in the heat of the moment. "Right now, I want you to focus on rule number two."

He saw her eyes grow wide as she noticed the contingent approaching from the rear. There was a healthy fear in those eyes, but she wouldn't have the experience to appreciate the full scope of their new predicament. What was happening here was coordinated. There would be no weaseling, but perhaps there was an alternative.

"What about you?" she asked.

"I may have to break all the rules," he muttered. "And if I signal, you run. Got it?"

She looked conflicted but nodded.

Eric scanned the area again. They could make a break for it right now. Could run through the parking lot toward the bonfire field. There were plenty of people there. They could yell and draw attention. There were options. But he wasn't going to do any of those things, not yet, and Trish would take her cues from him.

After all, Eric was still an officer of the law, even if he couldn't reveal that fact unless there was no other choice. Moreover, he maintained a confident hope this wouldn't devolve into a skirmish. Slade and his cronies might be physical monsters, but that didn't change the fact they were barely into their adult years. Eric believed this crew was about to put up a show of intimidation that he didn't believe they'd back up with action. Not in broad daylight. He could still take charge of the situation. At least he hoped that was the case.

He turned to face Slade. He saw Trish swallow and face the same way, turning her back on the incoming threat from behind.

As Slade grew near, Eric could see that his black eyes—set too far apart on his face—were trained on him. Made sense. Eric was the unknown and would be perceived as more of a threat to deal with by Slade and his crew. When he was only a few yards away, those reptilian eyes looked toward Trish, and Eric could have sworn he saw a double take of surprise on Slade's face.

"Well hi there, Trish," Slade spoke in an oily sing-song voice. "What an interesting development."

Eric furrowed his eyebrows. He heard heavy footsteps behind him and risked a half-glance over his shoulder. He saw the four steroid rhinos come to a halt a few paces away.

Whatever happened next, he and Trish were surrounded.

CHAPTER 50

TRISH CRINGED when Slade said her name. She hated the sound of it coming from his mouth. She hated the way his lips curled into a sneer as he spoke it. She hated the way he extended the last two letters an extra beat, so it sounded like he was demanding silence. Most of all, she hated the feeling of utter terror that was rising from her stomach into her throat.

She knew Eric was capable, and she had remembered her father saying his young partner was a fighter, but these were five huge guys. Athletes. Scary ones. Maybe unstable. In the case of Slade, definitely unstable. And if the other four were anything like him, it might not matter that they were on campus in the middle of the day. If they decided to hurt Eric, to hurt her, then even thirty seconds of violence could result in massive injuries. Or worse.

"Is your name Slade?" Eric sounded confident. He was trying to gain the upper hand.

Trish assessed the situation. Eric had told her to be ready to run. That would mean leaving him to face the onslaught alone. She had dragged him into this. Her fault. She wasn't about to abandon him.

Four rules of a confrontation. The first step was weaseling your way out. Eric was clearly going to take point on talking their way out of the situation. Next step was planning an exit, but she was determined not to leave him. No matter the consequences. So...weaponize. She glanced around. They were standing in the middle of a lawn next to the parking lot. Nothing within reach. Nothing on her, unless she wanted to wield the gold cross from the chain around her neck, a strategic move if these guys were vampires, but that appeared unlikely since they were standing in sunlight.

"Yeah, I'm Slade," the beefy human cobra replied. "And you're..."

"Inconvenienced," Eric inserted.

Trish groaned inside. Bravado was awesome in the movies, but this was real life. Escalating the situation seemed like a bad idea.

"I understand you've been going places to which you haven't been invited," Eric said.

He seemed calm. Confident. Trish wondered if it was an act. It had to be, but it was a good one.

"That makes two of us," Slade replied. "Or did *she* invite you?" His broad nose wrinkled as he cast a short glance at Trish before returning his attention to Eric. "What are you doing at TSC?"

"Not your concern. Yet." Eric took a step toward Slade and lowered his voice. "But if you come within a hundred yards of this young woman again, it will become your grave concern."

Slade's lips curled into a grin that turned Trish's stomach.

"Whoa, did you guys hear that?" Slade addressed the monsters standing behind Trish and Eric. "I believe that was a threat."

"Sounded like a threat to me." The words were spoken by the dark-haired guy standing behind Trish and to her right. His shoulder muscles were accentuated by the tank top he wore. The words 'Property of TSC Football' were imprinted in red on the gray fabric. "Downright unfriendly, I'd say." He spit on the grass. Trish was grateful the glob of saliva hadn't been directed at her.

"Yep, unfriendly," Slade echoed. "You show up here. Unfriendly. Making threats. Here in my house."

Eric looked around as if reassessing his geography. "Not your house. And not a threat. A warning. With potential consequences. Back off." Eric glanced over either shoulder before returning his eyes to Slade. "You and your chorus girls."

Trish's stomach clenched. She was afraid she'd feel arms encircle her from behind at any moment. That Slade and his friends would attack. And she couldn't figure out why Eric seemed to be provoking them. Unless he believed there was no way to talk their way out of this, and this was a different strategy.

"Chorus girls. You're funny." Slade smiled as he spoke, but no humor extended to his black eyes. "Or stupid." Slade tilted his head back and inhaled deeply through his flat nose, nostrils flaring, like he was tasting the air for scent. "I think stupid. There's a lot of that going around these days."

In that moment, Trish noticed two things. Slade's shoulders pushed back, his massive chest puffing out as he did so, and Eric shifted his feet apart and bent his knees. The point of no return was upon them.

No-no-no. This is not going to happen.

"I have an idea," Trish blurted out. The words were louder than she planned. And fast. But Slade's attention shifted to her. He didn't attack. But she didn't know what to say next.

"Um, why don't..." Her thoughts raced. "Why don't we just come to an understanding? Maybe we can all go get a drink together. Or something."

Trish kept her eyes on Slade—she wouldn't have diverted her attention from him any more than she would have looked away from a coiled rattlesnake in her path—but her peripheral vision did catch Eric's face scrunching into a puzzled expression.

Slade laughed. A terrible, guttural sound. She couldn't tell if the laugh was genuine or contrived.

"What do you know, guys?" he asked. "Trish wants to be friendly. Get drinks. Sounds to me like her friend here isn't cutting it. She needs the five of us." His eyes swept from her feet to her face in a quick glance, and he nodded. "We can be friends, red." She felt like she needed a shower. "But not until later."

Eric sidestepped, positioning himself closer to Trish. She appreciated the effort but knew it was in vain. There were five of them. Something was about to happen. Something bad.

"Don't mind us, folks." The voice—deep and clear and spoken with a Southern drawl—took her by surprise. "We're just passing through."

Trish looked in the direction of the sound and saw two men walking toward them from farther up the lawn. Neither of them students. The first looked to be about forty and had brown hair. He wore khakis and a blue polo shirt. Maybe a professor? The other man was considerably older. His face was shaded by a cowboy hat, but his thick gray mustache stood out. He was wearing jeans and a denim jacket faded by years of use. He resumed speaking as the two men continued walking their way.

"You know, come to think of it," the cowboy said. "Maybe y'all could help us. We're trying to find the football field. Wanted to get tickets for the big game."

Trish glanced behind her. The quadruplets shifted their eyes from the cowboy and back to Slade. Looking to him for guidance. When she turned to Slade, she saw rage boiling. His upper lip twitched.

She could have kissed the old cowboy.

"You're going the wrong way," Slade said. He pointed past the two incoming strangers. "The football field is that direction."

The men didn't change course. The cowboy glanced to his companion.

"Don't that beat all?" he asked. "You were right. I coulda swore it was this way."

The cowboy's friend nodded and produced a half-hearted smile, but his eyes never left the party they were joining. "As long as we're here," he said to the older man, "I bet these guys can tell us the best place to sit at the game." He looked at Slade. "What do you think? Is the upper deck better? Can you see more from up there?"

As the two men reached the larger group, Trish saw Slade's hands spasming as his fingers clenched and unclenched into fists. She glanced at Eric. His eyes remained on Slade.

"It doesn't matter where you sit," Slade growled. "You'll see fine. Now I told you the field is that way." He pointed with emphasis. "Head on out."

Trish saw the cowboy's friend tense. She noticed he was sweating. The cowboy, on the other hand, didn't seem to pick up on the threatening tone. "Well now, it's our first time here. I'd sure appreciate some friendly advice."

"My advice is to leave now," Slade snarled.

The cowboy shook his head. "Now son, I asked for *friendly* advice. Perhaps the young lady here would be willing to chat with us."

Trish expected to see Eric smile or relax a little given their unexpected rescue, but he remained in the same ready position, eyes fixed on Slade. He clearly sensed the danger had not diminished.

"I'd be happy to visit with you," Trish almost shouted. "We both would." She patted Eric on the arm. He didn't move. The old cowboy smiled.

"I tried to be nice." Slade spoke through a clenched jaw. His face was red. Trish could see the muscles beneath his t-shirt grow taut. His arms trembled. Thick veins were visible under the skin of his forearms and another emerged on his forehead.

Oh shit. He's about to hulk out.

Slade turned his eyes to the cowboy. "I tried to be friendly, old man. Now I'll be real. Get the fuck out of here."

Trish felt herself shaking. This wasn't supposed to happen. The situation was supposed to defuse. She saw Eric grow tense, ready to spring at Slade.

The cowboy chuckled. "Now before you go and do anything you'll regret, I need to ask you boys a question." Despite the smile under the gray mustache, the man's eyes were serious. Trish saw they were a sort of steel gray. "Any of you fellas have weapons on you? Guns? Knives? Anything like that?"

"Ha!" The harsh laugh burst from Slade. Trish heard the quadruplets chortling with derision behind her. "We don't need weapons for this, boomer."

"You might think that, son," the cowboy said in a low voice. His right hand pulled back the open denim jacket, revealing a pair of handcuffs secured on his belt immediately behind a large revolver holstered high on his hip. He tucked the jacket behind the butt of the gun. "But I'm afraid it's going to put you at a powerful disadvantage."

Slade's eyes grew wide. Not with fear. Rage. The blue vein on his forehead pulsed with blood. Trish glanced at the quadruplets. She would have expected at least one of them to see reason and back away. They hadn't moved. And each wore an expression of fury, not fear.

"Your move, son," the cowboy said. "Best to walk away."

"I see," Slade muttered. "I see everything. You're interlopers, too. Infidels. Heretics. All of you."

Trish gripped Eric's arm. Slade wasn't going to walk away. None of them were. People were about to die.

"Whoa! Hey now!" A new voice. Female but deep and strong.

Trish turned—as did all the faces of the group—toward the parking lot as a woman in a khaki campus police uniform sidestepped between two parked cars and proceeded toward them. She was huge, not *My-600-lb-Life* fat, but she well exceeded the status of husky. She had a robust frame that would have bordered on masculine had she not also possessed massive breasts that swayed with each clunky step she took in their direction.

"What's going on here?" she asked as she grew closer.

Trish looked at Slade. His expression had shifted from rage to uncertainty. The quadruplets were exchanging glances with each other and then back to their leader. The dynamics of the situation had changed further.

"These young fellas were just leaving," the cowboy informed the officer when she was a few yards away.

Slade didn't make a move to leave. His brow knit and his eyes vibrated left to right. Trish could tell he was debating options.

"Sir, is that a firearm?" the policewoman directed the question to the cowboy as she arrived at the group. She was breathing hard. A nametag above the badge affixed to her shirt read 'Nixon'. Both badge and nametag tilted upward on the slope of her ample chest.

"It is, ma'am," the cowboy replied. "I'm licensed."

"I'm sure you are, but there are no firearms permitted on campus." She spoke in bursts as she caught her breath. "Texas State College regulation."

"Well then, I apologize," he drawled. "Am I in much trouble?" He gave a wink to accompany his contrite expression.

Officer Nixon was no longer looking at the cowboy. She had turned her attention to the hulking young men on the perimeter of the group. Trish wondered if the woman sensed the tension of the situation, wondered if she recognized the powder keg she'd just entered and how perilously close the flame hovered. Nixon's right wrist stayed in contact with the side of her own holstered gun. On the opposite side of her belt, a large contraption hung along her sizeable hip. It was used for checking license plates and printing tickets. She was a parking cop.

"Let me ask again," she now directed the question at Slade. "What's going on here?"

Trish held her breath. No one spoke for what was probably five seconds but felt like an hour until Slade's gruff voice broke the silence.

"Nothing's going on," he said. "We were just leaving."

Without waiting for a response from the officer, Slade jerked his head to the side, signaling his pack to follow, then turned and walked toward the Physical Sciences building. His friends trailed after him.

Trish let out a slow breath. She hadn't realized how tightly every muscle in her body had been wound until she felt them loosen. She wanted to sit down right on the grass but, with effort, remained standing. For the first time, she saw Eric alter his stance, the action reminding her of a gunslinger whose opponent had just changed his mind and walked away.

"Thank you for stopping by, Officer," Eric said. "And nice instincts. I'm blue myself." He extended his hand to the woman. "Eric Johnson, NYPD."

She shook his hand while keeping her eyes on the departing group of athletes until they entered the building. "Norah Nixon. You're welcome." She turned toward the cowboy. "I don't know what this was all about, but I'm not gonna cite you for the firearm. Just keep it off campus, understand?"

The cowboy smiled, his mustache lifting. "Yes, ma'am. I'll do that."

Officer Nixon nodded as her eyes returned to the door of the Physical Sciences building. She backed up four steps before spinning with the grace of a barge in choppy water and returned toward the parking lot. "You folks have a nice day," she said over her shoulder.

Trish laughed to herself. *Have a nice day. Oh yeah.*

Eric extended his hand to the cowboy. "And thank *you*."

"You're welcome," the older man replied as he shook Eric's hand. "Name's Earl Valentine. Call me Cutter."

Trish thought she saw something pass across Eric's face. Something about the name.

"Pleased to meet you," he responded. "This is Trish O'Brien." Trish smiled at the cowboy as he tipped his hat to her. *Cutter Valentine.* She liked the name.

The cowboy's companion spoke. "Eric. Trish." He nodded at them both. "It might be a good idea if we had a conversation about what just happened."

CHAPTER 51

THE OUTDOOR DINING AREA behind The Lone Star Pit consisted of a diverse array of picnic tables, lawn furniture and colorful sun umbrellas splayed out over a huge yard which was more dirt and crushed granite than grass. Trees and bushes lined the perimeter to shield the dining area from neighboring businesses and lend the dining area a country sensibility. A horseshoe pit and two sets of cornhole boards were being ignored by the lunch crowd who chose to instead focus on consuming the barbecue served on butcher paper resting atop individual plastic trays. John expected the outdoor games were probably more used in the evenings when the bar portion of the restaurant likely did more business.

He and Cutter had agreed to meet Eric and Trish here following the confrontation on campus. John hated to leave Christian Berry unmonitored for any length of time but having a conversation with these two seemed a worthwhile exchange, especially after more complete introductions had been made.

While still standing in a small circle next to the parking lot of the Physical Sciences building, it came out that Cutter and Eric had met in the past. While hunting for Hiram Kane and his remaining offspring, Cutter found himself in New York where middle son Silas Kane was suspected of lurking. While doing research with NYPD's homicide division, Cutter had reviewed a small number of open case files with Eric. As it transpired, Eric would later have a hand in capturing Silas and then, following the madman's escape from custody, earn a starring role in the sensationalistic drama that ended with the death of Hiram Kane's second son.

Following the revelations of that conversation, very little had been said since they left the campus. They had later met in the parking lot of the restaurant—with Eric and Trish stepping out of a minivan—then proceeded inside, ordered their food and absconded to the back corner of the outdoor space, away from the other diners. It had seemed an unspoken agreement among the four of them that nothing further would be discussed until they were huddled in an environment where the real conversation could take place.

They now sat in pastel colored plastic chairs around a metal table whose sky-blue paint was losing its battle to conceal the underlying rust. Occasional drifts of smoke from the two gigantic cast iron barbecue pits on the side of the building wafted through the yard, giving the air a taste of roasted meat. With the other diners out of earshot, the awaited conversation was primed to take place.

John watched as Eric drained the top half of a frosted pint of beer. It looked so inviting that John's throat ached, but that was a callback to his old life. He instead took a long swallow of unsweet iced tea. He was already about to risk aggravating his ulcer with a half-pound of brisket and pinto beans, no sense in doubling-down with a Budweiser.

"Thirsty?" The young redhead, Trish, directed the question toward her friend with a laugh. She had a nice laugh. Genuine.

Eric set his glass on the table and a movie-star smile of perfect teeth bloomed on his face. "Trying to offset the gallon of adrenaline still pumping through my system. Might be hard to sit still for much of a conversation otherwise."

Something about the statement set John at ease. Perhaps it was the honesty. If nothing else, John was comforted to hear Eric had been anxious about the earlier situation as well. When they left the truck at the time, Cutter had told John there was about to be trouble. From the moment the two had walked across the grass toward the five behemoths surrounding Trish and Eric, John's nerves had been taut. He was sweating bullets in anticipation of what was about to happen. Cutter, meanwhile, seemed to display the same level of anxiety he might have had dealing with middle school bullies on a playground. And Eric hadn't seemed phased by the encounter at the time either. It was a relief to hear that despite appearances, even an NYPD detective had felt the tension of the situation.

"Glad I'm not the only one to have found the encounter a bit unnerving," John admitted.

"That's one word for it," Eric agreed. "Before you guys arrived like the Seventh Cavalry, things were going to get ugly. The demeanor of

Slade and his boys—the look in their eyes—I've seen it before, a bad combination of drugs and hostile intentions. I don't know whether that crew was using—they seemed fully coherent—but they had their minds set on something, and it wasn't conversation. We had hit a point where anything else I said was going to take us over the edge."

"You said the leader's name is Slade," Cutter interjected. "Big ol' galoot. You know him?"

"I do," Trish answered. "There's a lot of backstory to unpack though."

John saw the girl glance at Eric. A question in her eyes. He returned an expression that obviously translated to some form of '*up to you.*' She gave a brief nod and began speaking.

"The story actually begins with my roommate," she commenced.

As Trish's tale unfolded, puzzle pieces began to align in John's mind.

CHAPTER 52

ERIC JOHNSON EXITED The Lone Star Pit's restroom—its walls had been lined with framed artistic renditions of old-time cowboys gathered around campfires and driving cattle—then navigated his way through the dark wood interior of the restaurant and out the back door. The outdoor dining area was almost empty, but the clock would soon strike five and Eric assumed the place would begin to fill with an after-work crowd at that point. The four of them had been talking for several hours now. Despite that stretch of time, no servers or other restaurant employees had questioned the length of their stay. There was something to be said for southern hospitality.

He shaded his eyes with his hand against the late afternoon sunlight as he made his way through the empty picnic tables to return to their personal corner of the lawn. John Michaels was pacing next to the table again. Cutter and Trish moved their heads in unison with John's back-and-forth, as if they were watching a slow-motion one-man ping pong match.

For Eric, the afternoon had proved an interesting gradation, beginning as informative before escalating to intriguing and finally arriving at un-fucking-believable. Trish got the ball rolling with a recounting of Stephanie's death, the confrontation at the bonfire (it turned out both John and Cutter had seen the video footage, which seemed to embarrass Trish more than a little), the late-night visit from Slade (which drew some righteous anger from both Cutter and John that Eric appreciated), and her growing suspicion of Christian Berry. Trish wove the facts into a compelling tale, and Eric wondered more

than once if her ambitions in journalism would someday morph into a
career as a novelist.

The deeper Trish's story grew—particularly as it concerned their
investigation into Christian Berry—the more engaged Cutter and John
became. John would ask penetrating questions while cutting his eyes
at his cowboy companion, sharing some sort of unspoken urgency.

Prompted by some leading questions from John and Cutter, the
story expanded from the present mystery over the death of Stephanie
to an unexpected tangent of Eric's past investigation of Silas Kane,
including the tragic loss Trish had suffered in the death of her father at
the hands of the killer. John and Cutter knew most of the story—as did
much of America since the lurid saga had been the subject of multiple
media reports in the aftermath—but there were certain questions
posed by John that were never highlighted by the reporters. He wanted
to know of any connections to Hiram Kane though Eric had been
unable to provide any insight on that topic.

At that point, Eric had known little about John (certainly not his
real name) beyond the fact that he was partnering with Cutter on
whatever had brought the former Texas Ranger to Abramsville. Given
Cutter's past work on the Hiram Kane investigation, Eric assumed
John must be some sort of specialist related to that line of research. As
the conversation progressed, he learned just how true that was.

During the initial phase of the discussion, John seemed guarded
and reluctant to overshare. He asked plenty of questions, but inquiries
directed his way were deflected with a subtleness that impressed Eric.
Following the full recounting from Trish and Eric on their current
efforts in Abramsville, however, whatever barrier existed within John
seemed to fall away.

"What do you think?" John had asked Cutter.

"This is your show, amigo," the cowboy had replied. "But
something tells me this is a connection we'd be foolish not to invest in."

With that, John informed the table in a low voice that all cards
would be laid on the table. And lay those cards he did. It turned out
John was, in fact, John Michaels, *that guy* from the New Mexico
horror show orchestrated by Marcus Kane. That revelation brought an
array of questions from both Eric and Trish, whose developing
journalistic curiosity shone.

Eric knew the basics. The story of the years-long mass murder
experiment in the desert of New Mexico had been even more
sensational than his own tale in New York, and with good reason from
a media perspective, the body count in the desert had exceeded a
hundred during the length of Kane's program. What most impressed
Eric was how much had been successfully kept out of the public's

knowledge. Shielding John and his wife—the couple whose efforts had ultimately destroyed the program—from the media was one thing (witness protection can work wonders on that front), but the extent of the program itself and the manner in which Marcus Kane had been experimenting on the unknowing participants was beyond belief. Eric had known Marcus was the bad guy—and the involvement of Hiram Kane as the controlling mastermind had been a detail revealed to the public since it would also be spotlighted to law enforcement agencies—but hearing a firsthand account from John Michaels of what happened in the isolated desert compound, the psychological and emotional manipulation intensified by chemical influence, proved as gripping as any Hollywood thriller.

John emphasized the chemical aspect of the program. He described the green supplement beverage the program participants were encouraged (effectively forced) to drink each morning. He spoke of the behavioral changes in his fellow participants over the course of the program. The numbed emotional state with a gradual deadening of any sense of right and wrong. He detailed the remarkable events that led to his discovery of the formula, his mental battle against the effects and his attempt at a hostile takeover of the program in order to save his fellow participants.

When John recounted his conversation with Marcus Kane in which the killer described the desert program as merely laying groundwork for something much greater, goosebumps rose on Eric's skin despite the warmth of the afternoon.

And yet, during this riveting tale of terrible manipulation and murder, Eric sensed that the construction of the story was a work of manipulation itself. Not that Eric felt John was being dishonest—to the contrary, every word he spoke bore marks of raw truth—but it felt like John was building a case, that the events in the desert were calculated foreshadowing for a different tale.

When John's survival story was complete, and Trish asked the natural question of "so why are you here now," Eric's instincts proved accurate, but he could never have guessed the outlandish connection John was about to make between his suspicions and the investigation underway by Eric and Trish. By that point, they had long since finished lunch and were simply nursing drinks that a helpful server continued to refill every twenty minutes. Eric had been on his third beer but had been alternating with water. He wanted calm nerves but a sharp mind. Trish had been playing with her hair while enrapt with John's story. She had twisted several long strands in her fingers and had a segment of the auburn entanglement in her mouth—like a tango dancer clamping a rose between her teeth—when John revealed his hypothesis that Christian Berry was none other than Jonas Kane, the youngest son of the madman Hiram Kane.

Trish's mouth had dropped open, the twisted rope of hair falling forgotten from her fingers and coming to rest on her collarbone. Eric sat speechless himself. When Trish reached across the table, helped herself to Eric's glass of beer and knocked back several swallows, he made no attempt to stop her.

It was at this point that John had first stood and begun pacing. He would be in and out of his chair throughout the next chapter of conversation. Eric understood. He liked to move when deep in thought as well. John explained his reasoning in making the connection. Eric noted that John minimized his visceral reaction to the resemblance in the eyes of Christian Berry to those of Marcus Kane and instead emphasized the logic that someone planning to emotionally manipulate followers—as Marcus had done with his spiritual awakenings at the desert compound—would be well served to take on the role of a preacher or spiritual guide. Jonas Kane, as Pastor Christian Berry, could utilize his pulpit in quite the effective manner toward those ends. Moreover, the death of Stephanie and her actions—a previously healthy, normal girl as described by Trish who not only chose to end her life but to do so in a manner that inflicted bloody violence on innocents—portrayed hallmarks of numbed morals and outside manipulation.

Eric followed the logic but maintained a detective's skepticism. John was smart, that much was obvious, but he had still once been the victim of a dreadful crime. Victims suffered scars, whether in the form of post-traumatic stress disorder or forever wondering if another bad guy was lurking around the street corner or hiding in their closet at night.

John's personal vulnerability to those things would have been amplified when he walked out of the desert with his life but also with the certain knowledge that another bad guy *was* out there. It was the most natural thing in the world for him to see monsters in the shadows. In that respect, Eric could see where John's intelligence could be his undoing. He had a masterful ability to draw connections and manipulate facts to justify his conclusions, but that didn't make him right. The possibility that Christian Berry was actually Jonas Kane was beyond one-in-a-million.

But then there was Cutter Valentine.

Cutter was no victim. He was an old school lawman with a pedigree that could not be denied. Eric respected him. The very fact that the former Texas Ranger sat at the table gave credibility to John's theories. But still...

Eric reached the table from his post-restroom voyage and lowered himself onto the plastic lawn chair that had been his home all afternoon. He wondered if the plastic had begun to mold to the form of his ass cheeks. John was musing about whether Hiram Kane might be guiding actions from afar, as he had the program in New Mexico, or whether he might be closer at hand. His and Cutter's observations had not yet included any possible sightings of someone who could be the Kane patriarch. John dropped into his own chair without reaching any verbal conclusions. Then, Cutter Valentine read Eric's mind.

"Now we've been sitting for quite a spell," the old cowboy began, "and this has been some fine pickin'-and-grinnin' but let me make this clear, there is no hard evidence whatsoever at this point to prove that Christian Berry is Jonas Kane. If your radar is warning you that this all sounds like conjecture, that's because it is."

"Not the kind of thing a District Attorney would pursue," Eric offered.

"On the nose," Cutter replied. "Here's the thing. I'm no D.A. Hell, I'm not even a Ranger anymore. I'm just an old dog these days, but let me tell you something about old dogs, sometimes they have the most trustworthy noses because they've smelled it all before. It's hard to fool 'em." He leaned forward in his chair. "Right here, right now, I smell smoke and it ain't just coming from that barbecue pit. With what John and I have observed thus far—which doesn't point to any evidence— and with what you've told us this afternoon—which also doesn't offer any proof on its own—I'll be durned if the smoke doesn't smell even stronger. Now maybe there's a fire and maybe not, but I couldn't live with myself if I didn't find out one way or the other."

Eric smiled. Cutter had just described an almost mirror portrayal of what Trish had been eaten alive with in terms of getting to the bottom of Stephanie's death.

"The challenge," John said, "and I'll admit this is a real problem, is the near impossibility of proving it one way or the other. If a man isn't who he says, but he lives his life in perfect synchronicity of the identity he's undertaken, how do you prove his identity one way or the other?"

"What you're telling me is that Christian Berry is the damn Schrödinger's Cat of undercover bad guys," Eric mused. "Maybe he is or maybe he isn't, but until we open the box and see for ourselves, it's impossible to know."

Trish furrowed her brow at the reference, but John smiled and nodded.

"Look," Eric continued, "I'll agree that something smells funny here. Stephanie's death was tragic, and it sounds uncharacteristic of the girl Trish knew. Slade's threats against Trish were serious. The relationship of him and his gang to Christian Berry casts shade on the pastor. And this morning's confrontation with Satan's defensive line was unsettling."

"You're about to say 'but' aren't you?" John asked.

"*But...*" Eric put emphasis on the word. He respected Cutter Valentine, and he empathized with John Michaels, but someone needed to take control of the situation with a harsh dose of reality, even if it meant Eric had to pour a bucket of ice water over the festivities. "But what you're talking about is absurd. You need to recognize that. There is no evidence here. You're picking and choosing facts to support the narrative you want to believe, and you're asking us to buy into it."

He took a breath and held up a hand to preempt a rebuttal.

"I get it, John," Eric addressed him. "You live in fear of reprisal. You're worried about your family and because of that, you've created a solution. That's who you are, right? You're a problem solver. You're a man who gets things done."

John said nothing. He sat unmoving in his faded pink lawn chair, his face betraying no emotion.

"I can't imagine what it's like to live with something like that," Eric continued, "so it's perfectly understandable for you to want to do something. To fix it. If you find Hiram and Jonas Kane and remove them from the picture, your family is safe. Your life goes back to normal. I get it. I'd want that, too. It's an alluring solution. I'd give anything for that solution if I were you, so don't you think it's possible that you've manufactured a situation that allows for this possibility?" He paused. He didn't want to injure the man, just wanted him to face reality. "Look, Don Quixote was an honorable man with the best intentions, but that didn't make the giants he battled real. Don't you think it's possible that you're tilting at windmills here? How does that help your family?"

John remained silent. Eric had no idea if he was clicking through possible counterarguments or if he was genuinely reflecting on the truth of what had just been laid in front of him. Eric suspected the former, but Cutter spoke before John could respond.

"I don't disagree with you," Cutter said. "But let me ask you this— why are you here? Why come all the way from New York City to this little burg in Texas?"

"Simple." Eric looked at Trish as he answered. "I'm here because she asked me to come. I'm here to make sure that whatever is going on, she's safe."

"No," Trish interjected. "You're not. We covered this. You're here so we can solve what happened to Stephanie."

"And I do want to bring resolution for you on that," Eric sighed. "I believe that Slade is a bad guy, and I believe that Christian Berry may be more slimy than righteous, but we still have to be realistic about what we're doing. There is zero evidence against Berry, and if we push things too hard, there's a good chance he files harassment charges." He turned his attention to Cutter and John. "Now it's one thing if it's just Trish and me gently poking around, but if we're shown to be in league with you two, actively taking part in whatever the hell you're proposing, then that becomes serious. I'm already on shaky ground with my captain. I could lose my job if this thing escalates."

"Then lose your damn job!" John spat.

Eric's mouth fell open in surprise.

"Don't you see?" John continued. "*This is our chance.* Just because the facts aren't in view yet doesn't mean they aren't there. You can't see the moon right now, but there's all sorts of evidence that it exists. The tide still rises and falls. What you're seeing happen here is the tide of Kane. We have to stop it before it becomes a tidal wave."

John paused for a breath, and Eric noticed his face had tinged red. Was it from the sun or was this just a man unaccustomed to losing his own cool? Eric heard a quiet sniffle. He glanced at Trish and saw tears brimming in her eyes.

"And yes," John resumed, oblivious to Trish's emotional reaction, "stopping Kane protects my family. That means everything to me. My family is worth more than your job. I need your help here. We need Trish's connections on this campus. We could use your detective skills. If you lose your job, I'll make it up to you. Whatever your compensation, I'll double it. Triple it." Eric saw Cutter turn his head and raise an eyebrow at that remark. "But we need you in order to get this job done, before it's too late."

Eric spoke in a low voice, as if he were calming an uneasy stallion. He hoped the tone would resonate with Trish as well. "I appreciate the thought, John. It's not the money. I have a friend who sits among the Olympic Pantheon of wealth, and he's already offered to stake a business venture if I ever want to go out on my own. But I'm a cop. That means something to me—at least it used to."

John settled back into his chair. Was he sulking?

"It's not that I don't want to help," Eric said. "It's just that I need to be a realist. The facts don't support the risk of what you're proposing."

"If you don't mind my asking," Cutter interjected, "what do the facts support?"

"That Christian Berry may be, at worst, a minor league cult master. That his influence had such a negative effect on a young woman that she killed herself. That he may still exert an influence over a group of students including Slade and his cronies. But there is nothing, *nothing* that points toward a grand scale continuation of Kane's masterplan that started in the desert compound in New Mexico."

"You're wrong, Eric."

The words came from Trish. He looked at her and saw a hesitant smile on her tear-streaked face.

"And I can prove it."

CHAPTER 53

TRISH SNIFFED AND WIPED HER EYES with the backs of her hands. She hadn't wanted to cry, hadn't even realized she was doing it until the confrontation between Eric and John had escalated. But now, she was so very glad the tears had come.

"What do you mean you can prove it?" Eric asked. Skepticism exuded from his knit brow, his narrowed eyes, his pursed lips. Trish didn't care.

"I mean I can prove it," she repeated. "Evidence. Enough to substantiate what John and Cutter are saying, and beyond that, a way to definitively prove that Berry is drugging his followers."

John's expression had shifted from exasperation to anticipation. Cutter tilted his cowboy hat further back on his head as a half-smile lifted one corner of his mustache.

"This sounds right interesting, young lady," he drawled. "Do tell."

Trish smiled at him. She loved the old cowboy's deep voice. It was calming. And Cutter wouldn't know it, but she needed to be calmed against the conflicting emotions boiling in her mind. She was equal parts excited at the possibility of solving the mystery of Stephanie's terrible death, grief-stricken that her friend had died as a pawn in such a dreadful scheme, enraged at Christian Berry for the horrible plans he was enacting, and exhilarated at the possibility of being part of the team that would end those plans and save lives in the process. It was a maelstrom of feelings she could barely contain, but therein lay the answer.

"Don't you see?" she began. "It's everything John has pieced together but more. He already found the answer, he just didn't know there was actual evidence to back it up."

"Catch me up, Trish," Eric encouraged. "What am I missing?"

He wasn't dismissing her out of hand. That was good. He needed to listen to this.

"The question isn't whether Berry is an asshole—we know he is—but it's whether there is proof that links what was happening in New Mexico with what's going on right here at TSC today. And there is!" She took a deep breath. "It goes back to two things John told us about regarding his time in the desert. First, the deadened emotions, the lack of feeling or caring about anything one way or the other. Think about the people most likely to be infected with whatever Berry is doing to them. It would have to be his closest followers, right? The group that meets on their own outside the regular church services. All that extracurricular stuff. Stephanie was one of those. Andrew, too."

"Okay," Eric said. "What about them?"

"Remember me telling you about that night at the bonfire? Something that didn't strike me as strange until much later, when we were talking in front of the football stadium?"

Eric glanced away as he considered the question before answering. "You said that no one at Stephanie's memorial service was crying," he intoned. "No tears."

"Exactly! It's like all these people care enough to show up for a memorial, but no one cares enough to actually cry over their church sister who's dead or any of the victims from that night. Even Andrew had told me earlier that day that *he* hadn't cried for Steph either. She was his *girlfriend*! There should have been some kind of emotional reaction, right?"

"That sounds familiar," John said. His eyes had taken on a far-off look.

"But there's more," Trish continued, talking to John, words flying fast. "You told us about that girl at the compound—Denise—and how she told you how she started feeling wrong and having headaches and you thought it was probably a bad reaction to the drugs Marcus Kane was giving you guys but none of you knew he was giving you drugs at that point." The sentence trailed off as she ran out of breath, but John nodded.

"Yes, that was right before Kane killed her." He spoke with a bitterness that was palpable.

"Well, Andrew has been complaining of a headache for days now." She looked at Eric. "That can't be a coincidence."

"I'll be damned," Eric murmured. "That might be a coincidence, but we're getting into a whole new realm of coincidences coinciding. I didn't see it."

"Me either," Trish smiled. "Right up until I started crying a minute ago, and everything...just clicked."

"All right then," Cutter spoke. "We're halfway there. I think you've just drawn a line connecting enough dots to sway even our understandably skeptical detective, but this type of evidence is still what we call circumstantial. You said something about being able to *prove* Berry is drugging his followers."

"Oh...yeah." Trish winced at the thought. "We can. I know it. But this is where it gets really complicated."

CHAPTER 54

"**T**HIS HAPPENED HOURS AGO, in broad daylight."

Christian Berry nodded even though his father hadn't formed the words as a question. He had known his father would be upset—Hiram Kane didn't like events veering so far away from planned outcomes—but Berry hadn't made it to the best part yet.

"Why am I only hearing about this now?"

Berry had foreseen this inquiry as well. They were standing in an antechamber that connected the church's fellowship hall with the main sanctuary. Its only furniture was an antique pew resting against a wood-paneled wall. The translucent glass of the small window opposite the bench was a cool blue from the soft evening light outside. Twilight was upon them.

"I've spent the afternoon in research," Berry said. "We needed to know the connection."

Hiram grunted, but Berry knew his father couldn't disagree.

"And what did you find?"

"The persistent girl who's proving to be more than an annoyance— her name is Patricia O'Brien. She and the detective know each other."

"How?"

"She's the daughter of Eric Johnson's former partner in homicide. *Former* because he's now dead. Care to guess who killed him?"

Hiram gave him a look of apathy and paired it with a low grumble of irritation. His father never did like guessing games.

"My dear brother Silas."

That raised an eyebrow on the old man.

"Interesting," Hiram said. "And now fate has brought them both to me. And at such a pivotal time." He trailed off, lost in thought.

Berry stayed silent. He wanted to savor this moment longer, but alas, he still had preparations to make for the evening's spiritual awakening. It was time.

"That's not all," he said. Hiram returned his gaze and again lifted one eyebrow. "The two men that interrupted the confrontation this morning. You would remember them."

Hiram's other eyebrow rose in anticipation.

"One of them was an older gentleman. A former Texas Ranger by the name of Valentine."

Berry watched Hiram's eyes light up. He knew that would get his father's attention, and it was just the appetizer.

"Valentine is here? With Johnson?"

"Indeed," Berry said. "But that's not all." He breathed in the electricity of the moment. His father's expression turned sharp. It was perfect. "The other man was John Michaels."

Berry had never seen his father's breath taken away before, had never seen him at a loss for words, but he observed that very reaction at this moment. Hiram put his hand on the back of the pew to steady himself.

"Extraordinary," he whispered. "I never would have dreamed."

Berry smiled. It was a good day. Though unexpected, these events would serve the cause in a grand way. The Reckoning awaited.

A ghost of a smile appeared on Hiram's lips. Berry knew his father must be thinking the same thing, though certainly for different reasons.

"I must meditate on these developments," Hiram said. "Go about your preparations."

Hiram dropped his hand behind the pew and triggered the release switch. The wood panel on the wall swung open, revealing the hidden staircase that led to the basement. He stepped inside and pushed the panel back as he descended the steps.

Berry turned on his heel and proceeded to his office at the back of the church. He strode with purpose, excitement still prickling his nerves. Much was to be done.

Neither man noticed that the secret door failed to close all the way. The wood panel hung ajar. Only a few inches. Just enough.

CHAPTER 55

TRISH PAUSED INSIDE THE ENTRYWAY of Wright or Wrong so the door guy could stamp the back of her hand. She was under 21 so she got the red stamp. If you could produce a valid driver's license proving you were of legal age, you were entitled to the black stamp. That meant you could buy alcohol at the bar.

It was a time-honored tradition at TSC for underage students to come up with new and inventive ways to best this scheme of discrimination. Trish and Steph had experienced success last year by painting a clear adhesive on the backs of their hands then peeling the adhesive off immediately upon entry once out of sight of the crack security personnel holding down the folding chairs by the door. Of course, removing the red stamp was only half the battle. In order to achieve true victory, one needed a partner of legal age who would "share" her black stamp by pressing the back of her own hand—with a still wet stamp—against the now clean back of the underage hand. Accomplishing this usually involved the legal age partner surreptitiously licking the back of her own hand just prior to receiving the stamp, keeping it moist long enough to make it inside and conduct the transfer.

It was a complicated dance that produced mixed results but provided plenty of excitement in itself. She and Steph had had some good times.

Trish looked at the red stamp on her hand. She had made no effort to circumvent the rules. She had no interest in alcohol tonight. No interest in fun, possibly ever again.

She was here because it was Tuesday night, and that was another tradition. The owner of Wright or Wrong was a TSC alumnus who had once made a string of successful appearances on the game show *Jeopardy*. He parlayed his winnings into the risky bet of opening a bar and grill near campus. That bet had succeeded, and the establishment had weaved itself into the broad tapestry of TSC traditions.

On Tuesdays, Wright or Wrong offered half price beer and one-dollar grilled cheese sandwiches. Many a poor college student, whether they had plans to drink or not, came to the Wright or Wrong every Tuesday for the cheap meal. It didn't hurt that the grilled cheese sandwiches were cheesy-crispy-melty happiness served on a flimsy paper plate. But that wasn't for tonight. Trish wasn't hungry.

She scanned the interior. It was even more packed than usual. Chalk it up to Bonfire week and the excitement of Saturday's game against the Bulldogs. Pregame parties started days in advance if the game was important enough. Students were packed into the tables and crowded around the bar, placing their orders. Trish had taken a chance in coming here and knew it would probably yield nothing, but she had to try. Everyone was counting on her.

She spotted him.

Andrew was sitting by himself at the high-top counter that ran the length of the back wall. People were all around him—either standing or sitting on barstools—but no one was particularly close to him. He was eating a grilled cheese, sipping a Coke through a straw and staring at the blank wall two feet in front of him.

The first gamble of the night had paid off. Trish knew Andrew and Stephanie used to come here every Tuesday night. The promise of affordable cheese and bread seemed to maintain its allure to Andrew even after Steph's death. Or maybe he was on drug-induced autopilot and was going through the motions of the life he once knew.

Trish hesitated before walking his direction. Sitting at the table earlier that afternoon with Eric, John and Cutter, she had been excited about the prospect of the whole situation. Justice for Stephanie. Bringing down Christian Berry and his pet cobra Slade. Perhaps even writing her first serious journalism piece—the inside story of the Kane saga. She had no doubt there would be widespread interest. She would be pursued by major news organizations.

The afternoon seemed an eternity ago. Reality had set in on her later, when Eric had a heart-to-heart with her in the minivan. He had wanted to make certain she understood the risks involved if what Cutter and John had theorized was true. He had spoken to her like she was an adult—rational and capable of making her own decisions—but she also knew he would prefer she walk away from the whole thing.

She wasn't going to walk away, but the gravity of the situation was growing by the minute now that she was standing in Wright or Wrong. This was *her* plan. This is what she had proposed to the group. They had agreed it was a good idea. Cutter had been impressed. That had made her happy.

But everything was so different now. Before today's revelations, there had been a sense of danger. The memory of Slade pinning her to her bed had stayed with her every minute since it had occurred. But there had also been so much *unknown*. Until now. Slade was scary. Berry was slimy. That was bad enough, but now, if John and Cutter were right, the people involved were straight-up killers. Hiram Kane (and his last son? Could it really be true that Christian Berry was Jonas Kane?) was prepared to murder thousands, and that presumably meant anyone who stood in his way as well, a category that now included Trish.

She felt short of breath. She looked around to see if anyone was watching her. It was the usual crowd. People drinking and eating and laughing and playing dominos. A country song filled the background, but the music wasn't blaring. The smells of beer and fried food and sawdust and janitorial disinfectant combined to form a distinct yet not unpleasant aroma. No one seemed to be paying any attention to her as she stood frozen, wondering if she was about to hyperventilate.

She looked toward the front window. There was a table there. With one side pushed against the window, the table was a three-seater. That was where she and Stephanie usually sat last year when they would come here, feeling strong and independent and free the way only college freshmen can. There were three guys sitting at that table now, wearing red TSC t-shirts and blue jeans. Stephanie would never sit there again.

Trish took a deep breath and steadied herself. Andrew continued to stare at the wall while chewing his sandwich. He was the key.

This was it. Trish pushed her shoulders back and marched toward him.

CHAPTER 56

ERIC STRUMMED HIS FINGERS on the steering wheel as he gazed out the windshield of the minivan. He had moved parking spots twice since arriving in the lot, each time trading up for a better view of the front door. The vehicle's engine was off, as were the interior lights. The windows were down so he could enjoy the evening breeze and hear the sounds wafting from Wright or Wrong.

He glanced at his watch. He had promised Trish an uninterrupted hour. That had been forty-five minutes ago. She hadn't come out so that meant she had found Andrew Kraft, or that she had been accosted and escorted out the back door where Eric wouldn't have seen. The latter was unlikely. Even after this morning's encounter with Slade and his crew, Eric felt confident Trish would be safe in a crowded establishment like this. But that didn't make the clock tick any faster.

Fifteen more minutes. He strummed his fingers in escalated rhythm, debating what he would do when he went inside. He would locate her from a distance but hang back. Give her more time if she needed it. She had proven her instincts to be trustworthy. But he would still monitor. Just to be safe.

The plan was unnecessary. The door of Wright or Wrong opened and out stepped Trish O'Brien. She paused to look around the parking lot, staying in the light of the entryway. Good instincts. Eric started the engine and the headlights blazed twin beams of light in front of the minivan. Trish spotted him and opened the passenger door a moment later. She was breathing quickly, like she'd just run a race.

"How did it go?" he asked.

"Good," she smiled. "I think it went well."

Eric put the minivan into gear and navigated out of the parking lot.

"Talk to me," he said as he turned onto the street. "What was the conversation like? What did you learn?"

"Conversation was weird. He talked to me—and that was good because I wasn't certain he'd talk at all—but it was...clunky. Like he kept having to think about what he was saying." She looked out the window at the passing lights. "I don't know if he's tired or emotionally drained or if he was just debating how much to tell me, but we got where we needed to go."

"And where was that?"

"I think I know how Berry is drugging his followers."

Eric glanced away from the road long enough to assess his passenger's nervous grin.

"Don't keep me in suspense."

"It's crazy, Eric. This afternoon, when we got deep into conversation about the 'what ifs' around the whole Christian-Berry-is-Jonas-Kane possibility, John started ticking off the scenarios of how Berry could be using his preacher role. He had this whole outline. And I think he was right."

"We were there for hours. John talked about a lot of stuff in his scenarios. What was he right about?"

"He said that the drugs were only half the equation. That based on Marcus Kane's spiritual awakenings in New Mexico, Jonas would likely be doing something similar here, and that the closer the Kanes were to their end goal, the more frequent the awakenings would probably be."

Trish's voice stuttered. Eric realized she was shivering. Her teeth were even chattering. He rolled up the windows and turned on the heater. It wasn't that chilly in the minivan. Her reaction wasn't to the temperature, it was the magnitude of what she was saying.

"Go on," he encouraged.

"Andrew said that the special group at church he's part of is meeting every night now. They gather at the church to meet with Berry. And they take communion every time."

"Communion," Eric whispered.

"Yeah, John nailed it. He said that might be the case. That guy..."

"He's had some time to think about it," Eric mentioned. "And your conversation with Andrew has confirmed it. Now for the next step."

"Well," Trish began, "I may have already taken it."

"What?" Eric's tone was sharper than he planned.

"When I was talking to Andrew, he may have been reticent, but he was also being *open*. I hadn't expected that, but it felt right so I took a chance."

Eric gripped the steering wheel but said nothing.

"I asked him a favor," Trish said.

His hands tightened on the wheel until his knuckles were white. "What favor?"

"To bring me a sample of the communion wine."

"You did what?" He was dumbfounded at the risk she had taken. "What reason did you give him?"

"I didn't do anything stupid, Eric." He could tell she had been ready for an argument. "I didn't advertise anything. I didn't tell him about John or Cutter. And I sure didn't tell him what we suspect of Berry. I don't think his brain could handle that right now."

Eric took a deep breath. The temperature in the minivan was climbing. The heater worked too well. But Trish wasn't shivering any longer. That was a plus.

"You may not believe it, but I was smooth," she said. "I don't think Andrew would be part of something evil. Not knowingly."

"No one is accusing Berry's followers of taking part in this knowingly," Eric paused. "Well, not all of them."

"Right. And I just think that maybe Andrew could do more for us than we planned. Maybe he just needs guidance."

Eric sighed. This was dangerous. If even a hint of what they suspected made it back to Berry, the whole thing could blow up on them.

"And what did he say when you asked that particular favor?"

Trish stared straight ahead, chewing on her bottom lip. "He said he'd think about it and let me know."

Eric clenched his jaw and drove.

CHAPTER 57

HIRAM KANE BREATHED IN RHYTHM, in through his nose, out through his mouth. The air in the sanctum within the basement vault smelled of sandalwood and rare herbs. The aroma filled his nasal passages and cleared his mind. His knees were on a foam pad, flat and stiff and covered in faded crimson fabric.

He was leaned back on his haunches with most of his weight resting on his heels. Any other man of his age and substantial weight would not be able to remain in such a position for more than a few moments before his joints and muscles would cry out for relief. Kane was no ordinary man. He could maintain such repose for hours upon end. Mind over matter.

His hands were outstretched, resting on the book upon the stone table. The ancient texts.

His mind was quiet. He listened not to the silence within the soundproofed vault. His ears were tuned inward, to the message from the texts.

He had not planned to enter the vault today, but the events of which Jonas had informed him made a visit to the sanctum necessary.

John Michaels. Here. Hiram would not have thought it possible.

He had spent hours in the sanctum since first hearing the news, not even interrupting his meditation to listen to that night's spiritual awakening through the audio system outside the vault door. He trusted Jonas to deliver the message as planned.

Somewhere in the back of Hiram's mind, his mental clock retained a dull awareness of time in the outside world. He knew the awakening had long since completed. His son was probably settling into bed, seeking the rest he would need for tomorrow's work. For Hiram, rest would not come without enlightenment. He would not allow it.

Hiram's vague sense of the world outside his mind made him aware of moisture in his lap. In his haste to enter the vault, he may have allowed the scalpel to penetrate his abdomen too deeply. Blood had continued to seep from the perfect horizontal line cut into the skin to the left of his navel. It wasn't substantial blood loss. Not enough to make him lightheaded. An inconvenience of wet trouser fabric. Then again, in his haste, he hadn't conducted any of his other typical rituals in advance of entering the vault. He hadn't voided his bladder. Perhaps he had micturated while in deep concentration, his mind focused on more important matters. It had happened before. Inconsequential in the grand scheme.

What mattered was the book. It was all that had mattered since he first found it forty years ago. He had been in his twenties then. Lost. Frustrated. Hungry. Angry. But he couldn't put his finger on the underlying reason for any of those things. He simply knew the world was wrong.

Hiram had studied chemical engineering at MIT. It fit his skillset and intellect but did little to satisfy his curiosity. His mind needed to expand beyond the mere physical sciences. He coupled his engineering courses with studies in ancient history. He remained unsatiated. His subsequent graduate degree in philosophy from Berkley provided him insight to the great thinkers of civilization and left him disgusted with how wrong these supposedly insightful men were throughout history. Pontification and meaningless suppositions on the nature of self and the universe. Futile exercises in academic masturbation. Hiram knew there was more.

He filled his time. He took a job with an oil company. Unfulfilling but well paying. He took a wife. Moira. More fulfilling but incapable of ever understanding. They had a son. Marcus. An obligation.

Then came Syria. His employer had been engaged in a new drill site in an arid wilderness, but one of the workers had encountered unusual artifacts in a cave adjacent to where the preferred drilling would be conducted. Hiram was tasked with studying the contents of the cave and determining whether the company would be obligated to inform the local government—something which would delay or even halt drill plans—or whether the historical significance could be deemed inconsequential and drilling could begin with no report to any regulatory agencies.

Hiram knew what his answer would be even before he bade Moira goodbye and stepped on the plane. It would be the answer that allowed his employer to continue conducting the business that paid him handsomely. Hiram was apathetic to anything else.

When he arrived at the site, he followed his own protocol of entering the cave alone. He found the artifacts where the worker had said they'd be. A collection of dusty, mostly broken urns. Two were intact. Hiram kneeled to inspect them with his flashlight. Then he stood and kicked one with his heavy boot. It exploded. Remnants of the shattered vessel bounced against the cave wall.

That was when Hiram felt it. It wasn't some archaeological sixth sense that led him to inspect the wall and discover the optical illusion of what appeared to be an uneven sheet of stone that in fact, if examined from the proper angle up close, proved to be an entrance to a dark tangential tunnel within the cave. It was no sixth sense. It was a *beckoning*. Hiram felt it calling to him.

He entered.

He had walked for a long time through the winding blackness when his flashlight finally shone into the small chamber at the end of the tunnel. The air was stale. Dry. He licked his lips and knew his saliva was the first moisture the chamber had encountered in centuries.

There were stone pillars blending with the wall, impossible to discern if manmade or a natural phenomena. And there was a shelf of stone. Upon the shelf, a dusty relic. There was no physical activity occurring within the chamber beyond Hiram's breathing. All was perfectly still. And yet, even from across the room, the thing on the shelf felt alive. He could sense a gravitational pull emanating from it.

When he approached the shelf, he expected the thing to glow, for illumination beyond the shaft of his battery-powered light to fill the room. Nothing of the sort occurred. He reached the shelf in still darkness, with only the circle of his flashlight beam revealing the book.

For that's what the thing on the shelf was. A book. Old and powerful.

It was impossible for Hiram to know the age of the texts, but he could sense they were ancient. Old enough that he was surprised it was in book form. Something told him the pages predated the codex. Predated scrolls. Yet here they were. Ancient, yellowed pages stacked one upon another, bound in a covering of some sort. He spread his fingers apart and held his open palm above the book. His hand did not shake. Despite the palpable sense of power emanating from the thing, he was not afraid of the relic.

He did not fear power. He craved it.

He lowered his hand onto the book. He had expected it to feel brittle. Fragile. Had even wondered if it might disintegrate upon contact. To the contrary, the book was soft. Supple. Warm. The sensation in Hiram's fingertips was not unlike touching human skin, reminiscent of his wife's belly when she had been great with child. Hiram would place his hand on her rounded stomach and feel a hand or foot pressing against the other side. That had been Marcus. As his hand rested on the book, for just a moment Hiram could have sworn he felt something similar press against his palm, pushing outward from the soft cover.

He did not withdraw his hand. It was only his imagination. Nothing more.

He opened the book. The symbols within were unreadable by his untrained eyes. But he would learn. He knew in that moment that he would learn all that the texts could tell him.

That encounter redirected Hiram's life. It gave lucidity to the underpinnings of his vague frustration with the world. Focused his hunger.

He left the oil industry. It no longer served his purpose. He instead returned to the world of academia. As a student, he had viewed the university landscape as self-serving and vacuous, an endless disappointment. As a professor, he found those same qualities created a pliable structure with which he could pursue his new quest. The book spoke to him. Not in words but in purpose. Hiram studied ancient language and the occult. He transferred from one university to the next, selecting each institution based on what it offered that would meet the next stage of his endeavor. His future employers were eager to have him join their staff. His background was impressive. His presence was powerful. To each opportunity, Moira followed. They had another son. Silas. A nuisance.

At long last, Hiram encountered an evolutionary advancement in his quest by way of a university in England. A partner. A man named Jonas Warleggan. An expert in ancient symbology and writing. An explorer. A seeker of truth. Hiram sketched the first few pages of the book's texts—the mysterious symbols that he had yet to prove capable of deciphering—and shared these duplicates with Jonas as a challenge. The man tackled the contest with relish. It took him months. He determined the characters on the page predated Sumerian Cuneiform in origin. But eventually, Warleggan cracked the translation.

Hiram wondered if the texts had spoken to Warleggan in the way they spoke to him. Could even a handwritten facsimile of the symbols carry the same power as the book itself?

Hiram pored over the logic and reasoning of the translation with Warleggan. His partner was patient. He explained every detail. He even produced a handbook to serve as a key for additional translation. Jonas was enthralled with the symbols. The information he had already gleaned from the duplicate pages had captivated him. The secrets held by the texts. If what he had translated was true, no one had ever seen anything like it before.

Hiram had killed Jonas Warleggan later that night with a neurotoxin slipped into his tumbler of whiskey. Though he had considered such a thing at various times in his past and had often been tempted, it was the first time Hiram had ever taken a human life. It had not proven a significant moral hurdle.

As the man lay dying on the floor, Hiram dropped to one knee, placed his meaty hand on his shoulder and praised him for his impressive work. Hiram offered Warleggan his utmost gratitude and swore that his collaborator would never be forgotten, even going so far as to vow to name any future offspring after his partner.

With renewed vigor, Hiram took a hiatus from his university pursuits and went into hibernation, intent on nothing but the full translation of the texts. He rarely took meals and slept even less, but he completed his task. The blinding knowledge was his and his alone.

His time in solitude with the relic changed him. The book spoke to him more clearly than ever. Where before, he could glean purpose and a general sense of direction, now he could receive clear detail on execution. He could align his aims with the potent knowledge contained within the book's pages. It was like carrying an unloaded assault rifle for years, sensing its latent power, and then being given the ammunition to fire. He had only to choose his targets.

Within the deciphered content of the texts, Hiram discovered combinations of herbs and natural elements that extended life, heightened mental awareness and expanded strength. Many of these concoctions proved challenging since the ancient identity of certain plants did not translate to the modern world. When faced with such difficulties, Hiram turned to his own expertise in chemistry to manufacture the combinations he believed would result in the desired outcome. These determinations always came about as a result of extended periods of meditation and communion with the ancient texts. He knew they would guide him to a successful outcome.

Hiram was already a brilliant man—though he knew the jealous society at large would cast him to the other side of the tenuous divide between genius and madness—but the knowledge contained within the book elevated him to a new stratum of intellect. He not only possessed an expanded understanding of the physical world around him, but the reality of the unseen was his to behold. Spiritual powers. Demons. The forces that truly dictated the fates of humankind.

With guidance from the book, he was now able to subject his will on lesser men in a manner far beyond his rational persuasive abilities and natural physical intimidation, the smallest taste of power previously reserved for the gods. He could sense the desires of a corrupt humanity and harness their selfish longing for his own purposes.

He would need all these gifts for his final objective, the greatest secret within the ancient book.

The Reckoning.

At last, his true purpose in life. The reason he was put on this earth, this twirling blue ball afflicted with the pestilence of idiocy and the sin of inanity. But to accomplish this goal, much would have to be sacrificed. Hiram did not care. In the end, those sacrifices paled to the reward.

He returned to work in academia. It again served his purpose. The seed of a plan had been planted in his mind, but it would take years to realize. And much work.

Through university systems, he would have access to advanced laboratory equipment. He would be able to order specialized chemicals in specific quantities without raising suspicion. He would scout locations. He would expand his network in a manner that would prove necessary.

Moira became pregnant again. Two brats at home had not been enough of an imposition on his life. She chose to add another. And yet, there was unseen purpose in everything. He had come to understand that. The book had led him to this conclusion.

He did not share any of this with his wife. Moira was a fine spouse, but she could never understand. She was jealous of Hiram's endeavors. Resentful of his hours spent with the book rather than his family. She wanted him to dedicate a greater allocation of time to his sons. That wish would be granted.

Moira died in childbirth. Hiram had no hand in her passing. He wasn't even in the room. It was their new child who had done that, their third and final son.

Or perhaps it had been the book, jealous in its own way.

Hiram named the boy Jonas and took him home, leaving his dead wife and his last frayed tie to humanity at the hospital.

From that point forward, Hiram acquiesced to his wife's final wish. He spent more time with his three sons. They were his legacy after all. He raised them. He removed them from public school and taught them himself. In stages, he introduced them to his plans. He opened their eyes to the truth.

When he began sowing destruction—in doses both small and large—they revered him the way other children might admire their own father if he hit a homerun in the company softball league. Hiram's homeruns involved bombs delivered courtesy of the postal service, some early experimentation with airborne viruses released in hospitals, and exacting harsh retribution on a federal agent who uncovered Hiram's role in those crimes. At that point, it was time to disappear. He did so and took his boys with him. There was no whining, no demands for a "normal" life. They understood. They had seen the truth. Lived it.

Over the years, Hiram showed them many things but never the book. His sons had known of the book's existence, knew their father possessed it, but Hiram had kept it hidden. Even though they would perhaps mean well, sometimes the young had to be protected from themselves.

Now, all that was left of that legacy was Jonas. His nearest intellectual equal. The boy who entered this world by taking another life. The son who was the key to Hiram's ultimate objective. The Reckoning could only be achieved through four acts. The first had already been accomplished. The remainder would not be possible for Hiram without Jonas—the last of his bloodline. His youngest was yet unaware of the sacrifice required, and Hiram intended him to remain in the dark on that matter.

They were nearing the time. And now, he pondered the appearance not only of the detective from New York and the Texas Ranger—soldiers who had worked against Hiram's machinations—but also of John Michaels. Hiram had no particular ill will toward the soldiers. He planned to see them suffer and die, but they were merely doing their jobs. John Michaels on the other hand...

In all the time Hiram had worked toward his goals with the aid of the ancient texts, things had seemed to work in his favor. Dominos aligned and fell as he saw fit. His careful planning and meticulous execution had assured him of success.

And then came that corporate bastard John Michaels and his wife, walking into Hiram's desert testing program, and doing so at the invitation of Marcus no less. That had been hubris on the part of his oldest son. Marcus should have known better. And yet, he had done it. All without Hiram's knowledge. And the program had paid the price. It was the first time Hiram had felt as if an outside force equal to the strength of the book's power had worked against him.

It was infuriating. He had raged at the injustice and vowed to revisit suffering upon the head of John Michaels a hundred times over. But he would bide his time. The Reckoning took priority, and once it was complete, retribution on John Michaels would be child's play.

The thought had occupied the back of his mind ever since New Mexico and the death of his oldest son. It had been difficult to reconcile the fact that Marcus would not be the chosen one.

But all things happen for a reason. Secret reasons that work toward the greater end, even when you may not understand them at the time.

Now here Hiram was. The Reckoning upon him. The pieces in place. Everything ready. And John Michaels steps onto the scene.

Everything happens for a reason. Sometimes the best things for the best reasons.

Hiram Kane was being given a gift. Somehow, unseen elements had placed John Michaels here. He would be present at the Reckoning. And once complete, once Hiram had ascended, once the power was his, he would sacrifice John Michaels in a glorious display of gratitude to the dark forces that had granted him his fiercest desire.

Hiram opened his eyes. The candles on either side of the stone table had burned to their bases. The sanctum was growing dark. It mattered not. The length of time it had taken him to reach this conclusion was of no consequence. Enlightenment had been attained.

He stood, stretched his legs and back, and opened the vault door. A sensor triggered the overhead lights in the basement lab. The effect was blinding. Hiram sealed and locked the vault, opened the door to the tunnel leading to his toolshed dwelling and pressed the button to turn off the bright lights.

The time had come for him to rest. He would disinfect the cut on his abdomen. Rid himself of the damp trousers. And sleep. Peacefully.

John Michaels would be dead soon.

CHAPTER 58

JOHN STARED INTO THE NIGHT from behind the wheel of Cutter's pickup. From his vantage point, he could see Christian Berry's house and the church. Both were dark. Same for the middle school across the street. Same for all the houses lining the neighborhood avenue.

The spiritual awakening—for that's what John had grown to believe those evening meetings were even though it hadn't been confirmed—had ended two hours earlier. He had watched the group file out of the building. He counted forty-four. They all looked to be students. Among them were the beefy thugs whose intimidation of Eric and Trish that morning had led to the unfurling of such an interesting afternoon. A few minutes after the group left, the lights had turned off at the church, and Berry had locked the church door then walked across the lawn to his home. The lights were extinguished in his house less than thirty minutes later.

The day had been taxing, but John wasn't weary. He was invigorated. And terrified. The addition of Eric and Trish to the equation offered both positive and negative impacts. Adding a seasoned detective who, strangely enough, had past experience with the Kane family was a plus. Having an insider at the college campus was another unexpected gift, though John worried that Trish's judgment may be compromised by the emotional ties she had with the girl who killed herself. That concern also encapsulated the negatives of the situation. This operation was too important to screw up. The life of his family depended on it. Wild cards diminished the chances of success. John trusted Cutter to make smart calls on something of this nature, and John trusted himself to do the same. That trust did not extend to Eric and Trish.

Experienced cop or not, Eric had admitted to running a criminal record check on Christian Berry. That would have alerted Berry and likely his father, wherever Hiram Kane might be (John divided his thoughts on this matter toward first worrying that Hiram would leap from the bushes with a machete at any moment and then worrying that he was isolated in a hut in Angola or an igloo in the Arctic Circle and would be impossible to ever catch).

Regardless, their operation had been exposed. Berry knew someone was investigating him and probably watching him. Based on the confrontation that morning, Berry knew Eric and Trish were the culprits and ordered his hit squad to deal with them. That would have been bad, but his and Cutter's intervention made it so much worse. Now they were exposed as well.

John suspected Berry had likely been watching the encounter from afar. He would have recognized Cutter—who had a rather distinctive look—and would most likely have identified John as well. He doubted his role in New Mexico had escaped notice of the Kane family. Now they knew he was here.

That changed everything. Berry now knew he was being watched, *and* he knew who was watching him. The heat was on. The question was whether John and Cutter and their new allies could prove Berry's identity before the water around them boiled, before Berry fled, before he implemented whatever terrible plan was underway, before he had them arrested for harassment or perhaps before he just outright had them all killed.

But for now, there was nothing John could do but watch. He, Cutter and Eric had agreed to alternate shifts on surveillance duty. John had learned his lessons in rural camouflage well. The truck was parked a good distance from Berry's house. The next morning was apparently trash day for the neighborhood. Garbage cans lined the curb. John had selected his spot on the street so that anyone looking this direction from Berry's house or the church would have a difficult time spotting the truck given the layout of the trash receptacles, but it left a perfect view for John. He alternated between watching the house with his bare eye and intermittently using either the spotting scope or the night vision gear. He saw nothing. All was quiet.

John sighed. The waiting game was the least fun game of all time. He wanted action. Resolution. He wanted proof positive that Christian Berry was Jonas Kane. He wanted him behind bars. Or dead. That desire extended to Hiram Kane. But, as usual, Cutter had expressed caution. From a legal standpoint, until the evidence could move from circumstantial to irrefutable, they couldn't risk anything further, even with the additional insight provided by Trish and Eric earlier that day.

John thumped his fist against the steering wheel. Not hard. It was a contained frustration. He wanted to walk around. He wanted his ulcer to stop hurting. Above all, he wanted to see his daughter. It had been days but felt like an eternity. He pictured DJ in his mind as best he could. Had she grown? A lot could happen in a limited time with that girl. He had no actual pictures of her. None of Sarah either. That was on purpose. If something happened to him, he couldn't risk their pictures being found on him. Couldn't open the door even a crack for Kane to pursue them.

Something pulled John from his thoughts. A light in the church. He snatched the spotting scope from the seat next to him and held it to one eye. *There.* A small window on the side of the church. Translucent glass. Probably a frosted pane. The light was dim. Barely there, but unmistakable, and it hadn't been there before. He was certain of it. Every window in the church had been dark since Berry had left. And Berry had not returned to the church. He was positive of that as well.

The dull light extinguished. The frosted window was dark once more.

John looked through the spotting scope and examined every window. No more light. No movement from the darkness within. What had it been?

He lowered the scope and rested it on his lap. It was probably nothing. Maybe a mouse scampered across the floor and triggered a motion sensor on an interior light. But John hadn't seen any similar activity in the prior nights. Was it a one-time appearance for the mouse? Or was it something else entirely?

John watched the church. He watched Berry's house. And he considered the possibilities.

CHAPTER 59

THE MAN KNOWN AS CHRISTIAN BERRY walked from the parking lot to the door of the Physical Sciences building. The sun had just peeked above the horizon. He cradled four stacked boxes of donuts in one lanky arm and dug his keys out of his pocket with his other hand. He unlocked the door and pulled the handle, using his free hand and one foot to open the door wide enough for passage. The donuts began to slide. He clamped them against his body but only succeeded in stabilizing the bottom three. The top box slid, teetered and fell to the tiled floor of the lobby.

Berry didn't yell. He didn't curse.

He wanted to stomp on the box. Squish the sweetened dough inside the cardboard into mush then kick the box across the lobby. But that's not what a self-controlled pastor would do. Even though there was no one around, one never knew. Appearances must be maintained. For now.

He set the other three boxes of donuts on the floor and retrieved their fallen comrade. The dropped box hadn't come open. The donuts may be misshapen, but they would be edible. And if Berry had learned anything from the nigh-intolerable experience of leading the breakfast group for students, it was that young men of college age had impressionable minds, stupid opinions and bottomless stomachs.

Berry restacked the boxes, lifted them from the floor, then proceeded to the lecture hall where the usual meeting would take place. He would lay out the donuts on a table beside the door. He would listen to the meaningless problems of vapid youth. And he would smile, for this was the last such meeting he would have to endure.

But before the donuts were put on display, he would first attend to his real business of the morning. He set the donuts down inside the lecture hall and made his way to the elevator.

It was a good day.

CHAPTER 60

ERIC JOHNSON LOOKED to his right and left. Thankfully, it appeared that his outburst of laughter hadn't drawn any undue attention. He couldn't help it. Watching Berry fumble the donuts like a butterfingered halfback—his scarecrow arms flailing to catch the box—had been so unexpected and so freaking hilarious, the guffaws burst from Eric's mouth before he realized it was happening. Not exactly covert-mission behavior, but no harm, no foul.

Eric had stationed himself next to a small shed at the corner of the bonfire field, and he was leaned against one side of it now. The position gave him a reasonable view of the Physical Sciences building—a great place to watch donut slapstick—while being inconspicuous. There was a surprising amount of activity at the bonfire site for this early in the morning, but Eric was quickly appreciating the amount of work that went into the massive structure. Students in hardhats bustled around the wedding cake tiers of upright logs. The stack had grown more than three stories high, almost as tall as the four-story Physical Sciences building which stood adjacent to the field.

On the side of the building that faced the Bonfire, a stage was under construction that would be worthy of a rock concert. The base platform appeared to be complete while several rows of galvanized steel lattice trusses lined the grass in front of the stage. They were the type of beams that would lock together to form towers on either side of the stage. He suspected they would support a truss for spotlights if the stage did end up taking on a rock concert feel.

Eric continued to watch the entry to the building. There was no sign of Berry, but he wanted to give it a couple of minutes just to be safe.

"Excuse me."

The voice came from behind Eric, startling him.

"Sorry," the young man said. He was wearing a hardhat and a long-sleeve TSC t-shirt that was torn in several places, presumably his bonfire work shirt. His face had surrendered to the struggle against acne, but he had a friendly smile. Nothing threatening there. "I just needed to get in the shed." He pointed to the door that Eric was leaning against.

"My fault," Eric said as he returned a smile. He raised his palms and stepped away from the door. "Didn't meant to get in the way."

"No problem at all," the enterprising youth replied. He opened the door and stepped inside.

Through the opening, Eric could see row upon row of sharpened axes hung along the wall. The young man snatched one and stepped outside.

"Had to grab one of these," he said with a smile and walked away, headed toward a line of logs lying on the ground. Two of his fellow students were already there, using axes of their own to chop errant branches away from the logs, leaving them clean and ready to be added to the stack. A commercial grade crane rested on its twin treads nearby, a yellow-painted tank ready to be called to duty. Eric realized the crane was necessary to lift the logs to the upper tiers of the stack. This was a big-time operation for a bunch of kids.

His eyes returned to the Physical Sciences building. Still no sign of Berry.

Eric glanced at his watch. Berry's student counseling session would start in a few minutes. That should occupy him for at least an hour. Unless he cut it short. The window was now.

He fished his phone from his pocket and thumbed the text message to John and Cutter.

Greenlight.

CHAPTER 61

CUTTER INSERTED THE STEEL ROD of the snap gun into the deadbolt and pulled the trigger. The pop of the rod signaled the driver pins had been forced from the lock cylinder. With the quick application of a tension wrench, the bolt slid aside. The front door to Christian Berry's home was open.

Cutter pocketed the instruments and turned to John. He had been standing behind Cutter, clipboard in hand, pretending to write something while looking as if he was there for some legitimate purpose and effectively blocking the view from the sidewalk of what Cutter was doing. Fortunately, there was no one visible on the sidewalk or anywhere along the street.

"We're in," Cutter said. "Remember what I said. I lead. First walk through, every room, I go first. I'm not expecting any booby traps or fortifications, but we play it safe. You keep your head down, your cap low and your sunglasses on. This is officially criminal activity. If he has cameras in there, you want to make it as hard as possible for anyone watching to identify you."

"Got it," John replied. He glanced up toward the ceiling of the porch and above the doorframe, inspecting for cameras.

"Yep, right there, you just ignored what I told you."

John chuckled and lowered his chin. "Oops."

They had already inspected the exterior for cameras and found none. Cutter felt that translated to a pretty solid bet that there would be no interior cameras either. If Christian Berry was Jonas Kane, he would take great pains to play the part. The humble home of a preacher in a modest neighborhood would not have a camera system. Still, Cutter felt it best to play it safe.

"After the initial walkthrough, you're on your own. We have to split up to maximize coverage. You have an eye for detail. That's good. Before you touch anything, study it. When you're done, everything needs to be back exactly as you found it. Files in the same order. Books opened to the original page. The feet of chairs in the same place on the floor. Tiny clown figurines facing the right direction."

"Tiny clown figurines?"

"No telling what sort of sick stuff this guy has in his house," Cutter winked. "One more thing, you have a sense of people, John. That's good. When we get in there, don't try to be methodical. That's what we'd do if we had time, but we don't, so use your instinct. Look around. Get a feel for this guy. You have a knack for that. Then start looking in the places you think most likely."

"I'll do my best," John nodded. "Let's go."

Cutter pressed his hand against the door. His breath caught in his throat. For just a moment, he flashed back to that day in the rat-infested warehouse in Fort Worth. The place to which he had tracked the murderous cult leader known as The Baptist. When he and his partner had broken down the door to find the madman, surrounded by the bloody remains of his dead followers. The children.

Christian Berry's front door had no resemblance to the worn wooden door in the dusty hallway of that warehouse. There was no reason at all for Cutter to associate the two, but it came screaming into his mind, nevertheless. At the forefront of his memory was the girl. The one he had saved. The only one. But he hadn't really been able to save her. Only physically. And only temporarily. In the end, The Baptist's hold on her had proven unbreakable even after his death. She was beyond saving.

"You okay?" John asked.

Cutter shook his head. "Fine," he grimaced and pushed open the door.

He stepped inside and scanned the room. No alarms sounded. No security panel by the door. No visible cameras. Cutter glanced at his watch then beckoned John.

"Come on," he said. "Let's get to work."

CHAPTER 62

"SO, UM, HOW'S IT GOING?"

Perhaps a dumb question but Trish didn't know how else to start the conversation.

"Fine," Andrew replied from his seat across from her. They occupied a table in the food court at the student union. At this hour of the morning, it was not crowded. Most students forewent any type of breakfast beyond a latte.

"Okay. Good," Trish said.

"Here." Andrew opened his backpack and retrieved a plastic water bottle. The label read Dasani but there was no water within it. Instead, a half-inch of purple liquid rested at the bottom. Andrew handed her the container.

"Is this..." Trish hesitated as she held the bottle in front of her eyes and swirled the liquid.

"Yes, it is," Andrew sighed. "I snuck it out last night, and now you have it." He looked around the room. "I don't know why I did it. This isn't even wine, Trish. It's grape juice. The same thing we use for communion every time. What are you looking for?"

Last night, at Wright or Wrong, Andrew hadn't asked many questions, something for which Trish was grateful. The discussion of Trish's motivation for the strange request was brief. She assumed he would ask more today, but overall, she was thrilled that he had procured the sample at all. And at least she'd now had more time to develop a rational explanation in the event of further questioning.

"Like I said yesterday, the more I thought about it, the more I decided that what happened with Steph may have been triggered by physical symptoms. Maybe it wasn't Christian Berry at all, but maybe it was something in her system. Maybe an allergic reaction."

Andrew stared at her with glassy eyes, but she noticed his forehead furrow. He must be listening. Trish pressed on, speaking fast.

"So I got to thinking that I was around her all of last year and never saw anything out of sorts, but maybe she was ingesting something different this year. Her diet hadn't seemed to change so the more I thought about it, the communion stuff seemed like it might be the answer. That would mean it wasn't Pastor Berry's fault—I'm sure he wouldn't do anything to hurt her on purpose—but we still need to know so maybe it doesn't happen to anyone else. Right?"

She ran out of breath on the last word. Her story had plot holes large enough to drive a truck through, but it was the best she had.

"Yeah, I guess," he said. "Oh, this too then." He returned his hand to the interior of the backpack and brought out a clear plastic baggie with a miniature white cracker of some kind. It was broken, leaving tiny crumbs in the bag with it.

"Communion wafer," Andrew said as he passed it to Trish. "If you're doing this, you better check both. Whatever it takes to get you to see the church differently. We're here to help people, not hurt them."

Trish pushed the baggie with the wafer into her pocket. "Thank you, Andrew."

"So what now?" he asked.

"I'm going to have it analyzed."

"Where?"

"Well, I'm not sure yet, but I know someone who'll help."

"Right," Andrew said. He squeezed his eyes shut and pinched the top of his nose between his thumb and forefinger. After a few seconds, his eyes opened again. They were bloodshot but more focused than before. "I'll go with you."

Trish was taken aback. "That's not necessary."

"Let me help," he said. "I want to prove to you that the church is innocent."

Trish considered the proposition. Eric was watching Berry. Cutter and John were searching Berry's house. She was on her own, and it was a long trek across campus. She had promised to stick to crowded areas and walk with other people. Andrew would qualify as other people. Besides, she wanted to trust him.

What does your gut say?

Trish knew she was asking herself the question, but it was her father's voice in her mind. She touched the front of her shirt between her breasts and felt the outline of the gold cross beneath the fabric.

"Okay," she told Andrew. "Let's go."

CHAPTER 63

A COOL BREEZE SWEPT OVER CHRISTIAN BERRY as he stepped from the Physical Sciences building and into the fresh air of the morning. As he emerged from the shadow of the building, the sunlight warmed him, and the fall air transitioned from brisk to refreshing.

He strode toward the parking lot with a light step. The last donut session was blissfully behind him. Another necessary drudgery checked off to never again blight his time.

He pushed his hands in the pockets of his jacket as he neared the parking lot. His fingers encircled the glass tubes in either pocket. The larger 50 milliliter tube in his right pocket had a screw top. He rubbed his thumb along the grooves. No moisture around it. Just doublechecking. The contents would not be dangerous if spilled in his pocket, but that was no reason to allow for any waste. Because what it could do in the proper circumstances...

The smaller 25 milliliter tube in his left pocket had a rubber stopper. His left thumb circled the seam where the rubber met the glass tube. Also good.

One tube for the cause and one for his own secret purpose.

He whistled an upbeat tune. It was a fine day indeed.

CHAPTER 64

J OHN'S PHONE VIBRATED in his pocket. He extracted it and read the text message from Eric.

On the move. Clear out.

"Dammit!" he hissed between clenched teeth.

John was standing in Berry's closet. He put the lid back on the shoebox he had been inspecting—one of several that maddeningly contained only shoes—and returned the box to its place on the shelf. He looked around the closet, taking a visual inventory. Everything was exactly as it had been when he walked in. He had discovered nothing of significance. Shoes. Clothes. Belts. A few sundries that could have been found in any closet in America. He had felt along the walls for possible hidden cubby holes. He had slid his hands along the baseboard where the carpet met the wall for potential loose spots that would indicate a hiding place under the floor. Nothing.

Cutter appeared in the doorway of the closet.

"Time to go," he said.

John clenched his fists in frustration. Between the two of them, they had checked the drawers of the small desk in Berry's bedroom, searched the undersides of tables, examined the contents of kitchen drawers and cabinets, explored the freezer, looked under the bed and even checked inside the toilet tank. These efforts had yielded a big bag of nothing.

"Yeah, I know, I just—," John started.

"You just want to look around more," Cutter interjected. "One more place. One more possibility. I know what you want, but that's not how we do this. We don't take chances at this point."

John blew out a sigh of frustration, but he knew Cutter was right. Emotion clouds judgment. They couldn't afford to be clouded.

He looked around the closet once more, making certain the clothing was hung in the proper places on the metal bar (he had pushed them all to first one side of the bar and then the other during his search). The hangers were spaced out as he had found them.

"Okay, let's go," he agreed and followed Cutter out.

The house search was a bust, but John decided to consider it a temporary setback. A disappointment. Nothing more.

The game wasn't over yet. It had just begun.

CHAPTER 65

"I SUPPOSE I SHOULD HAVE EXPECTED that the only visit I would receive during my final office hours of bonfire week would be from a student who isn't enrolled in any of my classes. What brings you back to my office, Trish O'Brien, journalism student?"

Trish smiled at Dr. Garber. He was showing his school spirit by wearing a red pullover polo shirt with "TSC" stitched in gold letters above the left breast pocket. The twin caps of a blue pen and a red pen peeked over the top of the pocket. The moderate paunch of his stomach stretched the fabric at the base of the shirt. His thinning hair was again disheveled. Trish wondered if his hair was ever combed or if it just lived in a constant state of disarray.

"I'm sorry to intrude again," she said as she walked into the office. Andrew followed behind her. Trish was grateful to be inside the room. She had been worried ever since arriving that she might cross paths with Christian Berry, that he would have decided to stay at the Physical Sciences building after his student session and in the world's worst stroke of bad luck, she would run smack into him. She had kept her eyes peeled ever since arriving at the building but thankfully never saw him.

"No intrusion," Dr. Garber replied. "And Mr. Kraft, it's nice to see you outside the classroom as well."

"Thank you, sir," Andrew said. "Same to you," he added as he took a seat in one of the plastic chairs in front of Dr. Garber's desk. Trish did the same with the other chair.

"Now, you were saying?"

"Well," Trish began, "I know this is unusual, but I hoped to ask a favor. You seemed willing to help when you and I talked earlier this week, and I don't know where else to go."

Garber's eyes widened with interest. "Go on," he encouraged.

Trish extracted from her jacket pocket the plastic water bottle containing the small amount of purple liquid and the clear plastic baggie with the communion wafer. She set them both on the desk. Garber put on a pair of reading glasses and regarded the items with a dull stare.

"We discussed earlier my concern over Steph's actions. How unlike her those actions were."

"Yes?"

"These are samples of the communion wine and wafer used by Christian Berry for his church group. I was hoping to have them analyzed."

Garber's eyebrows raised as he looked from Trish to the items on his desk. He lifted the bottle and swirled the contents, viewing the purple liquid against the fluorescent light in the ceiling.

"Analyzed? What do you suspect? Poison?"

Trish heard a low grunt from Andrew, but he said nothing.

"No, not at all!" she tried to emphasize for her companion's benefit. "I'm just curious if perhaps there was something in these—maybe a food additive or something—that might have triggered a reaction in Stephanie. Nothing bad toward the church."

Garber's eyes lowered from the bottle to Trish.

Andrew wasn't looking at her. She took the opportunity to jerk her head and cut her eyes toward Andrew then back to Garber, speaking with no words and praying the simple motion would convey her request of *please-don't-tell-Andrew-but-yes-we're-investigating-Christian-Berry-and-you-don't-like-Berry-either-so-please-do-me-this-favor-without-asking-for-further-detail.*

For an instant, Trish thought she saw the corners of Garber's mouth rise in a grin but then his face returned to normal.

"I understand," he said.

He couldn't understand. The reasoning behind her request was ludicrous. Which meant he really did understand. Victory.

"I don't have the equipment here for a full analysis, but I'm sending some other samples to Bhucharoen Labs in Austin today—they're a private facility partner to TSC—and I'd be happy to include this. I have a friend there. He'll get results back to us as soon as possible."

Trish lit up inside. "That would be great! Thank you so much, Professor...I mean, *Doctor* Garber."

Garber rolled his eyes as he smiled. "Least I can do." He stood up, which cued Trish and Andrew to do the same. "I'll keep you posted on what I hear."

"The sooner, the better," Andrew said. "Thank you, Dr. Garber."

"Yes, thanks again," Trish added as they walked out the office door.

When they reached the elevator bank, Andrew pushed the button and stared straight ahead as he spoke.

"Grape juice and a cracker, Trish. You'll see."

CHAPTER 66

HIRAM KANE HELD THE LARGE SQUARE of plexiglass in front of him. It was four feet long by four feet wide. More than adequate to cover the top of the thirty-five-gallon galvanized metal tub on the concrete floor of the lab in the church basement. Technically, it was three metal tubs stacked within one another to offer a triple-wall of protection. The plexiglass was two inches thick, which should also be sufficient for their purposes.

A hole had been drilled through the sidewalls of the tubs with a black rubber hose threaded through, supplying gas to the Bunsen burner at the center of the tub. The collar on the burner's tube had been opened more than halfway, allowing oxygen to mix with the gas stream in a stoichiometric amount that yielded a nice blue flame. It wasn't the maximum heat for the burner, but it was the right amount.

Jonas had just unscrewed the top from a 50-milliliter test tube and poured a portion of its contents into a glass petri dish. He raised his eyes to his father. Hiram hefted the plexiglass and nodded.

Jonas lowered the petri dish onto the top of a metal tripod within the tub so that the dish rested immediately above the Bunsen burner's flame. He extracted his hand, and Hiram lowered the plexiglass onto the tub, completely covering the opening.

The plexiglass began to fog, partially obscuring the reaction taking place within the container. Hiram held his breath. Seconds ticked away.

And then it happened.

It was beautiful.

Hiram looked at his son. The mask of stoic indifference usually worn by Jonas had fallen away, in its place was an expression somewhere between excitement and giddiness. The exuberance of youth.

He smiled in return.

CHAPTER 67

CUTTER RELEASED HIS THUMB from the spigot, and the water ceased flowing into the small plastic cup in his other hand. He eyed with suspicion the slices of cucumber floating amongst the ice cubes inside the glass beverage dispenser. He liked his water to taste like water, not vegetables, but at least it was cold. As he crossed the foyer to rejoin John and Trish in the small alcove away from the main part of the hotel lobby, he overheard an exchange at the front desk, a muted argument between the desk clerk and a gentleman checking into the hotel. He wanted to stay through the weekend, but the clerk was informing him of the requirement to check out on Friday morning. The hotel was completely booked for Friday's bonfire and Saturday's big game.

The hotel was not extravagant, but it was clean and nicer than most hotels in which Cutter had stayed. He made his way through the mostly empty lounge area—there was only one guest sitting at a table, pounding on a laptop keyboard and wearing a pair of headphones that looked to Cutter large enough to fit an entire stereo inside—until he reached the sitting area where John and Trish were talking. It was a discreet place. The lounge filled only in the mornings when the hotel offered its guests a complimentary self-serve breakfast, and in the evenings when people would use the lobby as a meeting place before embarking on their night's adventure. The rest of the day, it made a fine place to relax and converse in a space where no one else would be paying attention to their conversation.

Cutter placed the cup of water on an end table and lowered himself into the cushioned chair opposite John. Trish sat on the small sofa between them. John was speaking but not in an animated fashion. He had been seething when they had had to leave Berry's residence with nothing to show for their search but had since calmed. He had returned to planning and analysis mode.

"Ultimately, that's the key," John said to Trish.

"What's the key?" Cutter asked.

"Goals," John explained. "If we can figure out what the Kane family is up to—if we could find their target—then we could align our investigation in that respect." He paused. "Still, I'd like to get a look inside the church."

"You know the agreement, amigo," Cutter said. "We wait for the results on the communion wine that Trish procured." He turned to Trish for an aside. "Nice work on that again, young lady."

He smiled and was gratified to see her smile in return. He didn't spend enough time with young people. There was something about being in their presence that invigorated you and pushed aside—even if temporarily—the cynicism of age. He returned his attention to John.

"If that juice shows any kind of chemical abnormalities, we will search the church that very night. Until then," he held up one finger, "a single count of B-and-E and trespassing is all we're risking."

"So what do you guys think?" Trish interjected. "I mean, what are they up to? How do we focus the investigation?"

"You know, it's funny," John said, "the more I've thought about it, I realize that I've been getting in my own way on this. Trying to determine the reasons behind Hiram Kane and his sons doing whatever it is they've been doing. Trying to get inside their demented heads. Looking for motive. Now I think that was a mistake. We need to step back. Kiss."

"Huh?" Trish asked.

"It's the KISS Principle. K-I-S-S," John spelled. "Stands for 'Keep It Simple, Stupid.' Things work best when they're kept straightforward. Avoid unnecessary complexity. That's what we should be doing here."

"Keep talking," Cutter said. Sometimes it was best to get out of the way and let John wander a bit.

"There's plenty of things we don't know about the Kane family—as we've discussed, most of what we don't know relates to *why* and *how*—but we do know *what*. They want to kill people. Thousands. They're here in Abramsville. Kane's son is a preacher. These are things we know."

"He could be planning to kill his followers," Trish offered.

"He may well be," Cutter said, "but the church is too small to meet the thousands requirement."

"Which is why we need to start thinking of his followers as a means to an end," John commented. "I think Kane-Berry plans to use them to execute his plan."

Cutter narrowed his eyes. "Rein back, John. We've only counted forty-some-odd followers at those late-night church meetings. Even if we believe he could induce them to do it—through drugs or charisma—I don't think they'd be capable of killing thousands. Not without training. And weaponry. These aren't Bobcat's soldiers we're talking about."

"What's a bobcat soldier?" Trish asked.

Cutter smiled. "Bobcat is a friend. He's the general in charge of Fort Braun up the road a piece."

"Oh," she replied. "So for what purpose *could* Berry be using his followers? Could it be a pyramid scheme? Like he gets each follower to recruit two more followers and build an army?"

"I don't think so," John said as he shook his head. "I don't think Berry would allow any layers between himself and his minions. He wouldn't want to rely on middle management."

"Figure he requires more direct control?" Cutter mused.

"That would be part of it, but there's also ego. One thing I learned in the desert was that Marcus Kane was prone to arrogance. You could smell it on him. I'd be willing to bet that's an inherited trait shared by his bothers. Berry wouldn't want any distance between himself and his followers. He'd insist on the thrill of direct command."

Cutter sipped water from the plastic cup. It was cold enough to bite into his jaw. He glanced out the window at the parking lot as he pondered the matter of the followers. The gentleman who'd been having the argument with the desk clerk walked past, heading toward his vehicle, suitcase still in hand. He was apparently going to try his luck at another establishment.

And there it was. Staring them straight in the face the whole time. Cutter's blood ran cold. If it was true, they were almost out of time.

"Trish," he turned his head toward the girl, "do you go to the TSC football games?"

"Sure," she hesitated. Her eyes widened. He must not be hiding his anxiety very well. "Pretty much everybody goes to them."

"The people who work the football games—concession stands, ticket sales, gates, custodial—are they students or adults?"

Her brow knit as she considered the question. "A lot of them are students. Probably at least half the people working at the game."

"Son of a bitch," John whispered.

"Yep," Cutter nodded. It never took long for John to process information.

"The football game," Trish said in a low tone. Turned out she was quick on her mental feet as well.

Cutter leaned forward as he directed a question at his companions. "What are the odds these followers who attend Berry's late-night meetings and find themselves open to his suggestions also happen to be work various jobs at the football stadium?"

"I keep hearing about this weekend's game," John said. "Biggest of the year?"

"Yeah," Trish nodded, "like, forty or fifty thousand people. You don't think—"

"I do," John interrupted. "This is the target." He sat back in his chair. "Today is Wednesday. That's not much time."

"Let's take it one step at a time," Cutter emphasized. "We're still waiting on the lab results on the communion wine. That hasn't changed. It's still possible we're working ourselves up for nothing." He paused. "But I do think it's worthwhile to hash this out and start some groundwork. It already feels like we've been caught on our heels with this."

"Do you think he's going to plant a bomb?" Trish asked quietly.

"That's one possibility," Cutter said. Part of him hated to discuss the macabre scenarios in front of Trish, but young or not, she was an adult and part of the team. "An explosive device could kill a lot of people, but the stadium is an open venue. An explosion causes the most damage when it's in an enclosed area. It focuses the blast wave, and that's what does the most damage beyond the actual point of explosion. If a bomb goes off in a stadium, the blast wave would disburse into the open air and cause less harm."

"Same problem with a gas attack, I assume," John mentioned.

Cutter nodded. "I'd think so. Release a nerve gas in the stadium, and you'd kill plenty of people, but a gust of wind would impact your radius. You'd end up with more victims, but the toxicity would diminish."

"Other options?" John asked.

"There is straight-up poison," Cutter offered. "Put something deadly in the water supply or the beer or the soft drinks."

"But once people start keeling over in the stands," John countered, "it wouldn't take long for someone to figure it out and shut off the beer taps. Unless it was some sort of slow acting poison with a generous lag before people felt the effect."

"By then, they might be home," Trish said. "Does that fit the ego profile? Seems like he would want something with more of a bang." She stopped herself. "So to speak."

"Back to the explosives," John said. "What if he were to blow up the supports in the stadium, cause a major collapse with people filling the stands?"

"Complicated," Cutter replied. "But they are smart. And if they were to have access well in advance of the game—and if security turned a blind eye—that would be possible. But that would be quite an undertaking."

"Ego and ambition," John said. "The Kane family isn't short on either."

Cutter returned his gaze to the parking lot. Only a few cars decorated the lot at this time of day. But there would be many more starting on Friday. And on Saturday, the drivers of those cars would be enjoying a football game with no idea of the possibly fatal consequences.

"We should be cautious," he said. "But we need to start taking steps."

"I'll see if I can reach Dr. Garber and ask him to hurry with the analysis," Trish offered.

"Good idea," Cutter said. "We'll keep watching Berry, but in the meantime, maybe there's some extracurricular investigating we should undertake."

CHAPTER 68

TRISH STUDIED THE GENERIC TIMEPIECE ticking away on the wall as the woman at the front of the classroom droned on. Only a few more minutes until four o'clock. The professor should be wrapping up, but she continued to belabor some point about ethics in relation to social media. Trish had stopped listening halfway through the lecture.

It was Trish's first day in class since Stephanie's death. She didn't want to be here. It felt wrong. She felt as if she should be *doing* something. Not just sitting in a plastic chair surrounded by a handful of other students who also seemed to be paying the minimal required amount of attention to the professor. It was the day before Bonfire. The class normally had fifty students. Today, a total of seven students inhabited the chairs with armrest desktops. Many professors didn't even hold classes the Thursday or Friday of bonfire week. This class was the exception. Joy.

Trish wondered if Eric had insisted she return to class because, as he said, there would be life after this investigation and she needed to protect her grades, or if he had decided she would be safer attending class than helping in the investigation. She didn't *feel* safer. Even sticking with crowds when she walked around campus, Slade and his crew were still out there. She wouldn't feel safe until all of this was done...whatever *this* was.

She still had a difficult time processing current events. Was she truly in the middle of a life and death crisis, and not just her own life but the lives of thousands of potential victims at stake? Was Christian Berry really Jonas Kane? Was there an additional mysterious psychopath by the name of Hiram Kane lurking in the shadows? It strained her imagination, but it also felt true.

What would her father say about her involvement in this?

Would he want her to stay far away from the danger, or would he be ashamed that she was sitting in a classroom when she could be out there doing something?

She felt obligated to listen to Eric. He and Cutter were exploring the football stadium today. Checking security. Keeping watch. John was monitoring Berry. At least she knew what was happening, but she fumed at not being included in the actual action. She wasn't a child. Not helpless.

She had embarked on this investigation for a reason. Stephanie had been *her* friend. Not Eric's friend or John's or Cutter's. Trish loved Steph, and she was dead. And whether his name was Christian Berry or Jonas Kane, Trish felt certain that the scarecrow preacher had a hand in Steph's death. She wasn't going to sit on the sidelines.

Her phone vibrated on the small desktop in front of her. A couple of her classmates glanced her direction at the noise—anything to distract from the ethics lecture—but the professor continued to hammer whatever point she was making in the world's blandest monotone.

Trish looked at the screen. She missed her old phone, but at least the burner phone was functional. It was a message from Dr. Garber.

Meet in my office at 5pm.

CHAPTER 69

THE ELEVATOR DOORS OPENED, and Trish stepped out. Andrew was at her side. They proceeded down the hall to Dr. Garber's office without a word.

Butterflies fluttered in her stomach. She hadn't let Eric know she was coming here, much less informed him that she invited Andrew to join her. She didn't know why, and she didn't want to turn her introspection flashlight on too brightly. She knew she wouldn't like what it illuminated. If only dimly, she suspected that she wanted to learn the results of the analysis on the communion wine and have that information to herself, if only for a little while. She wanted to feel like she was doing something. No, not just doing but *in charge* of something important.

As for Andrew's presence, she credited her gut. She believed in him. He had come through for her by delivering the wine and wafer samples. If he was mixed up in something bad—knowingly or most likely not—she needed to help him find his way out. That was what Steph would have wanted. The key to that was to have him present when Dr. Garber delivered the results from the lab. Andrew respected Dr. Garber. If he heard it from his voice of authority—that Christian Berry was including something suspicious in the communion wine that he was drinking—then his eyes would be opened. He could be saved from whatever bad thing Berry was attempting.

They reached the open door of Dr. Garber's office. Trish looked inside and found him standing at a whiteboard, jotting notes in blue dry erase marker. The red polo with gold TSC stitching had been replaced with a yellow polo with red stitching of TSC above the breast pocket. His school spirit was all apparently purchased from the same sales rack.

"Ah," he said as he noticed their heads poking in his door, "Trish O'Brien, journalism major. And Mr. Kraft. I'm glad you came as well. This topic seems to be of keen interest to you both."

"Thank you, sir," Andrew said. He plopped into his usual seat without a look in Trish's direction. Trish remained standing.

"Does this mean you have the results back from the lab?" she asked.

"It does," he replied. He placed the cap on his blue marker, put on his reading glasses and turned his attention to his desk. "I printed it off for you..." He shuffled through a mountain of papers stacked at various points on his desk. "Somewhere."

At last, his search yielded results. He snatched the page off a stack.

"Ah-ha!" he exclaimed, then cleared his throat and began to list components. "Water. Glucose. Fructose. Malic acid. Tartaric acid. Citric acid. Ascorbic Acid."

"That's a lot of acid," Trish said.

Dr. Garber lowered the paper to his desk and peered at Trish over the top of his reading glasses. He turned his gaze to Andrew then back to her.

"It is a lot of acid," he said, "but grapes are highly acidic. Just a shade less than lemons and limes." He sighed. "Allow me to summarize the findings in this report rather than go over every trace chemical."

"Yes?" Trish asked.

"The chemical compound in what you provided me adds up to be...grape juice. Probably Welch's but we can't be certain. There is nothing in the sample outside the normal parameters for what you would purchase at the grocery store."

"But...I don't understand," Trish sputtered.

Andrew remained impassive.

"I'm afraid there's very little to explain, Trish," Dr. Garber said. "You brought me grape juice and a wafer."

"And did it—" Trish began.

Dr. Garber held up a hand. "The wafer ingredients were comprised of what you'd expect to find in bread, unleavened so no yeast." His shoulders lifted in a *what-are-you-gonna-do* shrug. "It was even gluten free."

"You called us to your office to tell us that?" Trish asked. She was in a state of disbelief. There had to be something more.

Dr. Garber looked at her in surprise. "This seemed to be a matter of great importance to you. I thought it was best to deliver the news in person."

"Thank you for that, Dr. Garber," Andrew stated. "This has been very helpful whether she's admitting it or not."

"No," Trish said. She was at a loss for words. "It's not, I mean, it's just...is there anything else? Are the tests conclusive? Is there something else we should be analyzing?"

"I'm sorry, Trish," Dr. Garber said. "This is conclusive. The equipment doesn't lie."

Trish's mind raced. If the wine and wafer were clean, what did that mean?

Andrew stood. "Thank you again for your time, Dr. Garber. We won't trouble you anymore." He touched Trish on her arm as he stepped past her and walked out of the office.

"Um, yeah, thank you," she said to Dr. Garber as she turned to go.

"I'm not certain exactly what you were looking for," he told her, "but I'm sorry to disappoint you yet again. I wish there was something I could do to help."

"That's okay," she said over her shoulder as she walked out the door. "It's fine."

Andrew was ten steps in front of her, heading for the elevator where he would undoubtedly deliver an '*I told you so*' along with a request for an apology and maybe even a guilt-heavy invitation for her to join a Bible study.

This had not gone according to plan. And what was she going to tell Eric? And Cutter and John? She had been the lynchpin. She was supposed to deliver the evidence needed. Instead, she had failed.

She was going to get together with the group soon. She had to think about how she was going to deliver the news. And what that news would mean for all of them.

CHAPTER 70

THE MAN KNOWN AS CHRISTIAN BERRY knelt on the wooden decking. Despite the hard floor, his bony knees pained him not. The temperature outside was pleasant, a brisk fall evening, but it had been a sunny day. The attic had absorbed the heat from the sun throughout the day and retained it well into evening. Even close to sunset, the space above Berry's modest home was a slow roasting oven. He didn't care. He could stay for hours.

The attic had no windows but the exhaust vents in the roof allowed a remnant of evening light into the space. The only other illumination came from the two candles which burned in front of him. The air smelled of old insulation mixed with the aroma of sandalwood and rare herbs.

Perspiration coated his bare upper torso. It dripped from his forehead onto the unfinished plywood upon which he knelt. A puddle had formed between his knees. He raised his chin toward the ceiling, the back of his hair touched the base of his neck. Drops of sweat fell from it and ran in rivulets down his spine, tracing the bony contours of each vertebrae pushing against his pale skin. His ribs were prominent and slickened with the perspiration seeping from his armpits.

This was his sanctuary. Private. Here, he was neither Christian Berry nor Jonas Kane. Here, he had no name. His physical weakness mattered not. In this space, he was not the runt of the Kane litter. Flesh and bone mattered little in contrast to the powers of the mind and the spirit. There were forces far greater than those of muscle and sinew.

In this place of meditation, his mind was free. No longer slave to linear thought, his psyche processed multiple threads with both speed and clarity.

He planned the night's upcoming spiritual awakening. It would be the last to take place within the church. He would reinforce his message to his followers, prime them for what was to come and inform them of the new meeting place for the next night. They were ready. Of that he was certain. The forty-four would fulfill their part in the Reckoning in disciplined fashion.

Physical pain intruded upon his mental plane. He opened his eyes and glanced at his abdomen and the railroad track of scars upon it. Row upon tightly packed row of scar tissue laddered from his navel to his collarbones. Sweat had mingled with the blood from tonight's incision, entering the cut. The salt from the perspiration burned where it met the exposed subcutaneous tissue.

No danger there. It was safe to ignore it.

He closed his eyes and returned to a state of transcendence. It was a quick journey. His mental faculties had long trained for such rapid ascent.

The pain was forgotten. The latest cut was another necessary step on the road to destiny. A minor one. There were major steps as well. Requirements to achieve the Reckoning. Stephanie had been the first. Her act had been an epic achievement to signal the beginning.

It had been the scars that had first sparked the conversation. At that point, she had already advanced far down the course he had meticulously laid out. She had needed some encouragement—even beyond the steady progression of chemical assistance—and he had found it necessary to selectively exploit the most prominent of the litany of emotional vulnerabilities she had revealed in their time together, but she had taken the bait each time, and with each step down the path he had laid toward her spiritual enlightenment, she became easier to manipulate.

The fragile psyche of a teenage girl—her fears and misgivings and frailties—was a beautiful phenomenon. If only everything in his journey to the Reckoning had been so simple.

By the time he had allowed her to see him without a shirt, she already belonged to him. He viewed her not so much as a pet, but as a working animal with a specific purpose. A German shepherd trained to sniff and detect explosives could be excellent at his job but would have no understanding of *why* such a job was necessary. The why was not required of him. But it was still possible to care for such an animal, and Berry did care for Stephanie in a fashion. She had proven quite adept at pleasing him. She was a pleaser by nature. And though the things he had her do served a purpose—each action a barrier for her to break that she would not have thought herself capable of doing prior to giving herself to her mentor and lover and guide—that did not mean Berry couldn't enjoy the steps of her descent. All work and no play makes Jack a dull boy.

The intimate conversations, the baring of her soul to him, the sexual taboos (the breaking of which she found exhilarating as her commitment to pleasing him deepened), all of the small steps down the path had been but groundwork. It was the sight of his scars that had widened her eyes and elevated her conversion into the final phase. She had given of herself every step of the way, had opened herself to him like a flower both physically and spiritually, but this would be the turning point. The opportunity for him to reveal something about himself to her. A secret with which she could be entrusted. And he did trust her exactly as a man would utterly trust his faithful dog. As they lay in bed together, his torso bared for the first time, she traced her fingertips over the scars that covered his chest. Her finger trailing the ridges of lined scar tissue down his abdomen. Her eyes wide with wonder.

It was then that he first uttered the word 'Reckoning' to her and informed her that the spiritual world was so much greater than anything she had known, that their studies together thus far had been but the merest taste of the fruit of enlightenment, that his was a journey that exceeded the simplistic walk of the common man, and that it was her destiny to join him on that journey and achieve a spiritual reward heretofore unimaginable. She was special. Remarkable. *Chosen.*

She bought it. Hook, line and sinker. She kept his secrets, and she did almost exactly what she was supposed to. Her little flourish with the knives was beyond the call of duty. That had infuriated his father. It was outside the necessary actions to achieve that part of the plan. *The self-sacrifice of an acolyte was a simple thing*, he had said. Hiram viewed Stephanie's media-grabbing measures as a risk to the plan. Jonas viewed Stephanie's overkill with a mixture of amusement and appreciation. Beyond killing herself—which is really all she had been trained to do—she went above and beyond and proved not only the effectiveness of the formula but the power of his own influence.

She had been the first.

The last was near at hand.

With that thought, he opened his eyes and held up his hands. He licked each palm then lowered them onto the burning candles, extinguishing the flames in pinpoints of exquisite pain. Darkness fell over the table between the candles. Upon the table were the sheets of yellowed notebook paper upon which he had copied the ancient texts so long ago. His greatest secret. The cover binding the book was not pretty. It was unprofessional, but that was understandable. After all, he had barely been a teenager when he made it. Finally, a use for the skin he had tanned years earlier, the hide he had found in the woods near a railroad track one day when he had been following his older brothers. It wasn't easy tracking Marcus and Silas. They were bigger and faster, but Jonas was quieter. And determined. That had been an exceptional day in the woods. He didn't know what had led to his brothers killing the man—particularly in such a gruesome fashion—but it had happened, and after they had left, Jonas had an opportunity to perform research on a real cadaver. And he had taken home a trophy.

Destiny works in mysterious ways. The smallest events proved to be crucial junctures in the unfolding of an epic journey. The runt of the litter scavenges from the rest of the pack, and in the end, emerges as the strongest of them all. The power gifted by the texts—identifying the base desires of lesser men, manipulating them, controlling them—was not solely possessed by his father. The charisma of the preacher Christian Berry was remarkable indeed. More power awaited at the Reckoning. Far more.

Jonas Kane rested in the dark for another moment. He needed to go downstairs and shower, prepare himself for the spiritual awakening. But he didn't want to give up this time quite yet.

He savored the smell of the smoke from the smoldering candle wicks.

Let the world burn.

CHAPTER 71

ERIC PUT HIS HAND on Trish's shoulder and squeezed gently. She had just apologized for probably the fourth or fifth time. There were no tears in her eyes, but he could read a sense of desperation on her face.

"It's not your fault," he emphasized. Again. "It was a lab report. You had nothing to do with it. You're delivering news. That's all."

"I know," she said. "But still, I just thought..."

"We all did, kiddo," Cutter interjected. His deep drawl would sooth her. Eric knew Trish had developed a quick fondness to Cutter. That probably made the situation worse. Did she think she was disappointing the former Ranger with the lab results? Eric could see that possibility. He and Cutter had spent much of the day around the football stadium, checking access points, scrutinizing security and walking away without a sense of having accomplished much. Perhaps because there had been no danger to guard against in the first place. Perhaps because they were chasing ghosts.

"What if they falsified the report?" she asked. "The lab in Austin, I mean."

"That's a stretch, Trish. You're reaching," Eric said. "Why would the report be falsified?"

"I don't know," she responded. "We were so sure. Everything added up." She paused. "What if Berry stopped using the chemicals? He suspects we're onto him, right? Maybe he's being more careful."

Cutter smiled. "That could be possible, but not likely. If Christian Berry were Jonas Kane, then he'd be working toward a specific goal. I don't think he'd hit the pause button on our account. It really comes down to this, either the sample included some kind of brain-altering chemical compound and the lab couldn't spot it—or they falsified the results—or the sample *didn't* include any nefarious chemical compound and it was truly just grape juice. If we accept the *just-grape-juice* scenario—which we have to admit is most likely—then the conclusions we can draw are pretty narrow."

"Ultimately culminating into one difficult conclusion," Eric pointed out. "Even if none of us like it."

Trish sighed. "That Christian Berry isn't drugging his followers. He's not actually Jonas Kane."

"That's what the evidence would indicate," Eric assured her.

"Or lack of evidence, to be more exact," Cutter added.

"Occam's Razor," Eric mused. "When faced with multiple possible explanations, the simplest solution is probably the right one." A thought occurred to him. "John is watching Berry now. This is going to be hard on him."

Cutter nodded. "Yep."

"Wait," Trish said. "This still doesn't solve anything. This doesn't change what happened to Stephanie. Or Slade showing up in my room. Or him and his goon-squad threatening us." She slapped the back of her hand against Eric's chest on the last word. It wasn't a light smack. "What are we going to do now?"

"Well," Cutter began as he pushed his cowboy hat back on his head, "I'm going to call John. He needs to know what we know."

Eric didn't have any ready answers for Trish, but one thing he did know—he didn't envy Cutter Valentine that phone call.

CHAPTER 72

JOHN MICHAELS HAD BEEN LEANING far to his right, over the center console of the minivan, to keep his head low. He hadn't wanted the glow from his cell phone to be seen through the windshield. He was parked a good distance from Christian Berry's home—seeing any detail required the use of the spotting scope—but he hadn't wanted to take any chances.

Upon hearing Cutter deliver his news, John sat upright, his concern about being seen erased in the shock of what he'd just heard.

"It's a mistake," John muttered. "Or intentional." He paused while thoughts clicked into place leading to the obvious solution. "It was the kid. Trish's friend Andrew. He gave her a false sample."

Cutter tried to interrupt him, but John was on a roll.

"You've got to see it, Cutter. Too many pieces fit together," he declared. "I don't care what the lab results indicate. We know what we're dealing with here, and the stakes are too high."

Cutter said something else. He was using his calming voice. John wasn't listening. His mind was moving too fast to pay attention. He had been on watch most of the day. True to form, he hadn't seen Christian Berry do anything suspicious. No surprise there. The man put on a good front.

John was grateful to have the minivan. Eric had been gracious enough to loan it to him, and it had proved immensely more comfortable than Cutter's old pickup truck, but the comfy driver's seat did nothing to soften the blow from the phone call.

Cutter was telling him to come back to the hotel. They needed to regroup. Talk about things.

"No," John heard himself say. He was still processing. "I'm staying on watch. I need to think, and it's not like I'd sleep tonight anyway. I'll see you in the morning."

He ended the call without a goodbye.

CHAPTER 73

CUTTER SAT ON THE SIDE OF THE BED in his hotel room and sipped the bottle of beer. He wasn't a big drinker—and rarely felt the need to indulge so late at night—but it had been one hell of a day. The beer was cold. He had pulled it from the minibar in the compact refrigerator under the television. Had probably cost him five bucks, but he'd worry about that later. John's mystery corporation was picking up the tab anyway.

Following the day's events, the beer was soothing but only half as much the comfort he took from the voice on the other end of the phone.

"This is your time to say it, Darlin'," he said with a smile.

"Say what?" Maggie replied, but he could hear the smile in her voice, too.

"Go ahead, you don't need me to prompt you, and you've never needed permission."

"Now, Earl," she said, "you know I'm not the kind to say I told you so." She paused. "But I have to admit I'm glad. I've been worried."

"Nothing to worry about here," he reassured her. "Besides, you know what a cautious guy I am."

"You can't see me but just know I'm rolling my eyes. How did John take the news?"

Cutter humphed. "He's in denial, I'm afraid. He really believed this was it."

"Well, who can blame him? This was his chance to protect his family. I may have been upset with him, but I can understand the need to protect your loved ones."

Cutter smiled. Maggie could be a spitfire, but she could also empathize with the best of them. She was something special.

"He's still watching Berry right now," he said. "And that's fine. Can't hurt anything. The preacher may be some kind of creep, but if he's not Jonas Kane, I'm not too worried about John doing surveillance. I'll have a heart-to-heart with him tomorrow."

"How about the other two you told me about? The detective from New York and the girl...Trish you said her name was?"

"They're okay," he sighed. "Still some stuff in the air on their end. The girl has been through the wringer—some powerful bad events—and she doesn't deserve to have been pulled into whatever this is. She's innocent." He raised the bottle and swallowed a mouthful of cold beer. "But I think she'll be okay. She's strong as hell. More than she realizes. And I have faith in Eric. He'll watch out for her. I can tell."

"You're not getting yourself involved in their situation too, are you?"

Cutter laughed. "Nope. I promise."

"So you're coming home?"

"Soon," he said, "particularly since they're going to kick us out of the hotel tomorrow. I just need to wrap things up here."

He took another sip from the bottle and looked into the dark rectangle of the television. It wasn't on. The dark screen showed only a blurry image of an old man drinking a beer on a hotel bed.

"I can't blame, John," he said. "This may have turned out to be a wild goose chase, but danged if it hasn't smelled funny every step of the way."

"John will be fine," Maggie stated. "Sarah will talk some sense into him. I'm sure of it. He's a smart man. He'll figure out what's right soon enough."

It was an offhand remark, but something about it resonated with Cutter.

For any other faults he had, John *was* smart. That comment he made on the phone earlier—his immediate reaction to Cutter's news about the lab results on the communion wine—he had said Trish's friend had substituted the sample, gave them grape juice instead of the actual communion wine. John hadn't even spent time thinking about it. It just popped out.

Cutter told Maggie he loved her and said goodnight. He got undressed and slipped under the sheets of the fine and comfortable hotel bed. John's comment never left his mind.

What was it that Eric had called it? Occam's Razor. The simplest solution is probably the right one.

He closed his eyes and fell into a restless sleep.

CHAPTER 74

JOHN MICHAELS STOOD BENEATH A TREE across the street from the church. The exterior lights of the middle school behind him didn't reach quite this far. He was in shadow. For now.

He held the infrared goggles to his face and scanned the exterior of the building. He saw no activity. It was late. The night was still. The spiritual awakening had wrapped up hours ago. He had watched the brainwashed mass of students exit the building. They seemed more worked up than in prior nights, talking to each other with animated gestures as they walked out the door and to their cars or down the sidewalk back to campus. Christian Berry must have delivered a jolting oration to pump them up like that.

John's thoughts flitted to Marcus Kane's charismatic speeches at the desert compound. Jonas Kane certainly shared none of his big brother's physical traits, but perhaps they had that one thing in common.

He lowered the goggles and took a quick assessment. This was it. Once he crossed the street, there was no turning back. But this was his last chance. He knew Cutter was prepared to end the investigation. He had heard it in his voice. John wouldn't get any support from Eric either. Maybe Trish, but she was just a kid.

John had promised Cutter that he'd listen, that they'd do things Cutter's way. He was about to break that promise. John didn't like it, but his family's safety trumped his own probity. The preacher they had been investigating *was* Jonas Kane. John knew it. He didn't give a damn what the test results said about the communion wine. Christian

Berry was Jonas Kane. Period. John was just as certain that Hiram Kane was here. Somewhere. In shadows of his own.

The clock had ticked past midnight. That meant it was now Friday. If the Kane family was targeting Saturday's football game for the execution of their grand plan, then they had to be stopped now.

John had no internal pretense of being a hero. He was aware that thousands of lives were on the line, but the cold reality was that he only cared about the two that were currently asleep in an ugly house in a suburb of Tulsa. Despite his efforts at living in anonymity, John believed the only thing that had kept the Kanes from focusing their efforts on finding him and Sarah had been their more important grand plan. If they successfully completed that plan, there was no telling what would happen next, but it might involve finding John and Sarah. And DJ.

John couldn't let that happen. He had to stop them now, while he knew where they were and *who* they were. If they escaped into the wind, he might not see them again until he woke up one night to find his wife and daughter murdered.

If he had to stop this thing on his own, then that's exactly what he'd do.

He squatted and retrieved the large rock he had found while walking to the church from the minivan's parking spot three blocks over. He took a deep breath, stepped out of the shadows and crossed the pavement in plain view under the streetlights.

He strode up the walkway to the back door of the church. It was partially in shadow. He glanced around for a closer inspection. He hadn't seen any exterior cameras from across the street, and he found none now. The church was an older building and the rear door was as dated as the rest of the structure. The door had a paneled window in the top half and seemed to bear only a simple deadbolt lock. Old paint peeled around the edges of the door.

John tried the handle—just in case this was his lucky night—and though the handle turned, the deadbolt was engaged. So be it. He'd make his own luck.

He glanced over each shoulder. The street remained empty. He took off his jacket, placed the rock inside it to muffle the sound—he had seen that trick in a movie or on TV at some point—and punched the jacket-covered rock through the pane of glass in the window panel adjacent to the deadbolt.

It turned out the movies had lied. Breaking glass sounds like breaking glass regardless of whether you use a jacket to muffle the sound. Go figure.

John sprinted back across the street and stood behind the tree. He glanced at the luminous hands on his watch. Five minutes minimum. Ten if he could be patient.

He heard no alarm from within the building, but that didn't mean there was no security system. If a silent alarm had been tripped, someone would show up within a few minutes. Police. Or perhaps Jonas or Hiram Kane.

John knelt low, making himself as small as possible within the shadows, and he waited.

CHAPTER 75

THE HANDS OF JOHN'S WRISTWATCH stood out in relief when viewed through the night vision goggles. They told an ugly story. He had been in the church almost three hours, and it wasn't long until daylight would threaten to expose his exit. He had searched everything. Some rooms were easy. They held only chairs with no place to hide anything. He had spent much more time in the pastor's office, opening every drawer and cabinet. He had brought a red light mini-flashlight that he used for viewing papers, being ever conscious that the windows of the office faced the pastor's home. He hadn't bothered turning on the computer. The light from the monitor would be too risky, and he was certain it would be password protected anyway. He needed hard proof. Something he could walk away with, get in the minivan and drive the evidence to Cutter.

He had found nothing.

And it pissed him off.

He had searched every room in the church and eventually returned to the sanctuary. He walked down the aisle, passing row after row of pews.

Where are your secrets, Kane?

He climbed the steps onto the stage, stood behind the lectern and looked out over the nonexistent congregation. The air smelled of old wood. Total silence.

All alone.

As seen through John's goggles, the large room was coated in transitional shades of green. No heat signatures. No living thing was within it.

Not a creature was stirring, not even the tiny glow from the body heat of a church mouse, he thought.

His breath caught at the triggered memory.

John raced off the stage, holding the goggles to his face so his quick steps wouldn't jostle them off his head.

The light.

He had to find the window.

He exited a door to the left of the stage that would return him to the church's interior. He was only a few steps into the antechamber when he saw it. He removed the goggles and walked to the window, ran his fingertips lightly over the surface. Frosted glass. This was the window he saw while on watch the other night. The light came from here. A light that appeared when no one was in the church.

He returned the goggles to his eyes and began scanning the room. The light he saw wouldn't have come from the overhead fixture. That bulb would have been too bright. He looked toward the doors on either side of the hall. Could the light he witnessed have come from there?

No, he thought, *any light emanating from there would also have illuminated the exterior windows in those rooms. I would have seen it.*

So that meant the light had to have come from within the antechamber in which he now stood. But what was the source?

He dropped to his hands and knees and scanned the walls, peered underneath the antique-looking wooden pew that sat against the interior wall, searching for a malfunctioning nightlight of some kind. There was nothing.

He rose from his knees and sat on the pew, resting his forearms on his knees. He looked around the room again from his seated position. Nothing. Just the exterior wall with the frosted window in the middle of it.

He sighed and leaned back in frustration. The back of his head smacked into the wall behind him with a hollow thud. He pulled forward and reached a hand to the back of his head. It hadn't hurt that bad—grabbing his head was a reflex—but anytime you hit your head hard enough to make a sound, it was only natural to...

John stopped mid-thought.

He stood and faced the wall upon which he'd thumped his head. It was covered in wood paneling and comprised of several large, framed panels. He softly rapped his knuckles in the place his head had struck. He took one step to the right and knocked on the next panel. It was a completely different sound. A dull thunk. He stepped to the other side of the pew and knocked on the panel to the left. The same dull thunk. He returned to the original panel and knocked.

Hollow.

John's pulse sped. *The wall behind the pew was hollow.*

He bent his knees, gripped the side of the bench and moved it away from the wall. He ran his fingers along the edges of the framing, starting at the top and working his way down. Nothing on the right side. He did the same along the left side of the frame. A few inches from the bottom, his fingers encountered an extrusion in the wood. He pressed and heard a click.

The wood panel opened along the seam of the frame. Just a crack. John pushed with his fingertips and the secret door swung inward without a creak.

John pulled the pew back to its original position and stepped into the opening. He was standing in a small space. Through the goggles, he saw a green stairway descending into empty blackness.

Behold the gates of Hell, he thought.

Every instinct John possessed, every scary movie he'd ever watched, every shred of common sense told him to walk away from this darkness. To get help. To return later.

He hesitated. He thought of Sarah and DJ. Despite the stale air within the space, for just a moment, John could smell the baby shampoo scent of DJ's hair.

He closed the panel behind him and descended one step at a time.

CHAPTER 76

JOHN HAD HIT THE JACKPOT. The secrets of the Kane family laid bare. The evidence they needed filled the hidden basement beneath the church, and John saw it all in night vision shades of green.

Their basement seemed to serve as an operating hub. Part office and part laboratory. Though he didn't dare to turn on the computer—and again assumed it would be secured anyway—there were actual paper files stacked on one corner of the table that ran along the wall. John only scanned the folders using his red light mini-flashlight. He planned to take them with him. He could look more carefully later. Some of the files had names of people. John guessed they belonged to Christian Berry's followers, the latest unwitting participants in Hiram Kane's mysterious plans.

The lab bench had an array of beakers and test tubes on display. There was a stack of metal tubs on the floor covered with a thick panel of what looked like plexiglass. There was a large refrigerator on one wall. It was a commercial model with a glass front. Within, John could make out shelves full of chemicals, no doubt the latest and greatest iteration of the formula for which John himself had once been a test subject.

Everything was here. John cursed himself for not bringing a camera.

He was sweating despite the cool air within the room. The last time he'd been in a basement, he'd been hanging from a chain while Marcus Kane tortured him for information. There had been a large mirror in that room. John had seen the man hanging there and barely recognized himself. That had been the worst night of his life. By far.

There was a mirror in this basement as well. He had jumped a foot in the air when he first entered the basement and saw someone step toward him from across the room. His heart kept pounding even after he watched the man in the mirror jump in exactly the same frightened way. It should have been funny. John couldn't bring himself to laugh. Even on the inside.

He had since calmed a little, but his nerves were frayed. He stepped closer to the mirror and inspected the table next to it. There were medical instruments aligned on its surface. Scalpels. Goosebumps broke out on John's arms and neck, rising on his sweaty skin.

Still, it wasn't the table that he cared about. It was the door next to the table, the heavy steel door that would be right at home in a bank vault but seemed quite out of place in the basement beneath a small-town church. There was a security panel on the wall next to it.

John wanted to leave. He wanted to grab the files in his sweaty hands and race up the stairs and burst through the back door of the church and sprint to the minivan and drive like a bat out of hell.

What he wanted more was to know what was behind that door. What was so important that it had to be protected by security borrowed from Fort Knox?

He studied the security panel, its buttons pinpoints of white against a sea of dark green through his goggles. He touched his hand to the door. The steel was cool beneath his fingertips.

As John studied the surface, the greens of the door suddenly exploded into a blinding white intensity. Wincing, he squeezed his eyes shut and snatched the goggles from his face, dropping them on the floor. He pushed his palms against his eyes and risked cracking one eyelid open, struggling to adjust to the brightness.

It was the overhead light. Fluorescent and blinding.

Someone had turned on the light.

John dropped his hands from his eyes. The room was a brilliant blur, but he could make out an immense form striding toward him. It was Marcus Kane. Not dead. He was here.

"Hello, John," the deep voice rumbled.

Pain exploded in John's head, and the world went from unbearable brightness to a far worse black.

CHAPTER 77

HIRAM KANE STOOD AT THE EDGE of the roof of the Physical Sciences building and observed the activity unfolding below. Three of the four members of his High Council stood with him. On his left was Victor McNabb, the CEO of a major tech corporation based out of Houston. At his right hand was Leonard Barnes, Chief of Police for the city of Abramsville. Next to Barnes stood Lucas Blankshire, the head of TSC's Chemistry Department. It was Blankshire who had been key to all the arrangements involving the Physical Sciences building.

The council members leaned forward, elbows resting on the solid railing surrounding the roof's perimeter. The wall was a little lower than waist-height for those men. Hiram's taller stature meant the railing only reached to his mid-thigh. He didn't lean over it. He stood upright, shoulders back, and breathed the crisp morning air.

The vantage from the roof allowed a perfect view of the adjacent bonfire field. The stack had been completed at sunset the prior evening. Even Hiram was impressed with the accomplishment of what amounted to a bunch of kids. The architecture had been passed down, revised and perfected over the years. It stood three stories high, tier upon tier of upright logs packed—but not so tightly as to impede proper air circulation—around the high center pole.

The top five feet of that pole rose from the upmost layer of logs like the fuse of a bottom-heavy stick of dynamite. Hiram smiled at the thought.

He surveyed the action taking place around the bonfire stack. Immediately below his place on the roof, the stage had been completed for the night's festivities. The steel platform was large and dull gray. Two towers rose on either side of the stage with a steel truss suspended between them upon which various spotlights were secured. The towers were anchored via guy wires to the ground from the front and on either side of the stage with similar steel cables counter-anchored to the Physical Sciences building. Hiram glanced down at the heavy eyebolts jutting from the wall a few feet below him. The guy wires had been secured well. Solid engineering.

On the stage were five members of the TSC Pioneers marching band, all drummers pounding out an ever-changing rhythm to accompany the morning ceremony. Under ordinary circumstances, Hiram would have found their efforts at what they believed to be music somewhere between annoying and excruciating. But today was different—today was the day—and so the thumping beats emanating from below were exhilarating.

The ceremony itself engendered no formality. It was unofficial to say the least, a tradition in which the work crew whose sweat and labor had built the stack would gather to watch the hoisting of the doghouse.

The doghouse in question was dangling from the end of a steel cable retracting into the arm of the yellow industrial crane to the side of the bonfire. Piloting the crane was Henry Ralston, the owner of the largest construction company in the city, alumnus of TSC, former bonfire crew chief and final member of Hiram's High Council.

Ralston's company provided the equipment for the bonfire construction every year at no cost to the school but with a stipulation that Ralston himself had the honor of lifting the famed "Woodson State University Doghouse" into place on top of the bonfire. As the bonfire burned, the flames would rise and eventually incinerate the symbolic home of the WSU Bulldog, apparently casting the Texas State College Pioneers into the dubious role of arsonists specializing in canine dwellings, but that mattered little to Hiram. Let them have their ridiculous traditions. They proved of great use to him. After all, it was these traditions that had first sparked the ideas that built upon each other, evolved and culminated in Hiram's final plan to achieve the Reckoning.

Now that day was here. At long last. There would be no stopping it. The Reckoning was his destiny. Before he ever translated the ancient writings—when the contents of the book still appeared to him only as indecipherable symbols—he could feel the power within and know that his fate was tied within its knowledge.

What else but the forces of destiny could have ensured this day was reached in such a manner? How else to describe the remarkable accomplishment of each meticulous step of his complex plan? The right players in the right places doing the right things, and the unplanned gifts bestowed upon him by forces unknown. To wake up this morning, to begin this auspicious and glorious day to find John Michaels standing in the church basement, nothing less than a Christmas present from the gods, such rewards on this day of the Reckoning defied belief.

Incapacitating Michaels had been child's play. He was weak. The next challenge had been surveying the grounds, ensuring his comrades—the Texas Ranger, the NYPD detective or the pesky girl— were not with him. The church had been empty. And there was no sign of any of them in the surrounding area. Michaels had come alone. Arrogant little prick.

Transporting his unconscious body had also been simple. Stowing him away within the Physical Sciences building was an obvious choice. The building would be empty the day of bonfire. No classes. Professors enjoying the first day of an unofficial three-day weekend. Besides, John had been stashed in a place where it would be impossible for him to cause any trouble. He would have to wait his turn in the destiny fulfilment line. Hiram would come first. After the Reckoning was complete, John would learn what role he was born to play. Executing John Michaels would be Hiram's first act—an act which excited Hiram almost as much as the Reckoning itself.

The drumbeat escalated into a feverish rhythm as the oversized doghouse was lowered with precision onto the center pole. There was no wind this morning. Another gift. Nothing that hindered the exact placement of the wooden structure onto the pole.

From within the pilot's cab of the crane, Ralston triggered the switch to release the doghouse from the hoist and the steel cable swung free. The arm of the crane turned away, leaving the bonfire and its new top-piece unobstructed. The doghouse didn't shift an inch. Gravity and clever engineering ensured it would remain exactly in place until the bonfire flames rose to devour it that night.

From this place on the roof, Hiram would have a perfect view of the cleansing blaze.

CHAPTER 78

CUTTER VALENTINE TERMINATED THE CALL before the beep sounded. He had no desire to leave John another voicemail. He glanced to his hotel bed. His aged leather duffel bag sat on the disheveled covers. It was packed and zipped. On top was the white envelope that had been slid under his door while he slept. It contained the summary of charges for his stay at the hotel—the front desk's subtle reminder that checkout was today.

A similar envelope lay on the floor of John's room. Cutter knew this because he had seen it only a few minutes ago. Cutter had given John time. He knew the man was unhappy with the lab results of the communion wine so he had shrugged off the lack of response to his calls. Cutter had even wrangled a late checkout to allow John time to decompress. But when the lunch hour came and went with no response, Cutter had had enough.

He had let himself into John's room using an extra card key after his repeated knocking on the door had yielded no results. He had found John's bed neatly made. It had not been used. His clothes were still hanging in the closet. Toiletries on the bathroom counter. The room had been untouched since housekeeping had serviced it the prior day.

That meant John hadn't returned from his evening watch of Christian Berry. And he wasn't answering his phone now.

John wasn't off somewhere sulking. Something was wrong. Cutter could feel it. And he had wasted hours doing nothing.

He swore under his breath, pocketed the envelope, grabbed his duffel and walked out the door, heading for his truck. He would call Eric once he was on the road.

CHAPTER 79

IN HIS FORMER LIFE, John Michaels had not only been a successful corporate raider but also an accomplished alcoholic. It wasn't the first time he had woken up with a pounding headache and his arms wrapped around a toilet. John did find the current experience unique, however, in that his wrists were shackled with handcuffs at the base of the commode. That was new.

He looked around the room through one open eye. He figured keeping the other eye closed alleviated by fifty percent the amount of painful light boring into his brain. The bathroom was a shock of harsh whiteness. Stark white fluorescent light from above. White tile floor below. White porcelain commode. White porcelain sink. Institutional stainless-steel piping running to both. The door was closed. It was white, too. The room was a small lavatory. No bathtub or shower. No window either. He could be anywhere.

John tried to piece together all that had happened. The effort at thought pained him. He opened his other eye and his vision swam. The whites surrounding him congealed together in a blur. He was going to be sick.

He leaned over the commode—grateful there was no lid covering the seat—and retched into the bowl. Acidic bile splashed into the water and filled his sinuses. It wasn't the taste of alcohol puke. He hadn't been drunk.

He finished and slumped over, dropping his cheek to the cool surface of the seat, his face assuredly resting upon unseen remnants of dried ass-sweat from the toilet's last user. John couldn't find it in himself to care.

He wanted to unroll a few squares of toilet paper and blow the nastiness from his nose, but the handcuffs made it impossible. He couldn't reach that high. He wiped his nose on his shoulder, leaving a thin trail of mucus on his shirt, and lowered himself to the floor. At least his mouth hadn't been taped shut. He'd be dead right now, choked on his own vomit.

His stomach ached. No mystery there. He hadn't eaten in hours and his ulcer was crying out. He wondered if he still had a roll of antacids in his pocket but realized he wouldn't be able to reach them anyway.

He was a prisoner.

He searched his mind for his last prior moments of consciousness until they emerged through the haze. He had been exploring the church. The hidden staircase to hell. The basement. The lab. The steel door. The blinding light.

Marcus Kane.

John pushed himself into a sitting position. His head rebelled in dizzy protest against the movement. He braced himself against the toilet as a fresh surge of nausea threatened to overwhelm him. He looked to the ceiling and took long, slow breaths.

He had a concussion. All the symptoms.

And it hadn't been Marcus Kane in the basement. He was dead. John had been there. The massive figure that had pummeled him into unconsciousness had resembled Marcus, but it wasn't him. He was older. It had to have been Hiram Kane. Daddy of them all.

It marked the second time John had been knocked out by a giant Kane humanoid. Marcus had done almost the exact same thing to John in New Mexico. He wondered how many other people could say they were the recipient of generational concussions.

The wave of nausea passed without John throwing up again. A small victory.

His head was starting to clear. His thoughts were still foggy, but the jackhammer pounding his skull had muted into a dull throb. The harsh light no longer hurt his eyes. He inspected his surroundings more carefully. There was a mirror above the white pedestal sink. It was simple, not decorative. The lavatory felt commercial, not residential. It certainly didn't give the impression of something you'd find in an old church building. John wondered where he was being held. Perhaps a warehouse or an industrial plant or maybe an office building?

He noticed the surface of the walls was textured rather than flat. On closer inspection, he recognized the texture as foam eggshell panels secured throughout. They were white also. Even the back of the door was covered in it. It was a material used for soundproofing, for people who wanted all the noise created in the bathroom to remain within the bathroom, lest folks outside the door overhear the user taking a particularly noisy shit.

Shit, indeed, so much for crying out for help.

The thought of making any type of loud noise pained John's head anyway.

No idea where he was. No clue how to escape. Pounding headache. Aching body presumably from being manhandled from the basement to wherever he was now. A room that smelled like puke, and sore wrists from the handcuffs.

John took little comfort in knowing he had been right all along.

CHAPTER 80

ERIC JOHNSON KNEELED at the back door of the church, inspecting the concrete. It had been freshly swept, but he would have bet his life savings—if he had any—that there had been shards of broken glass there earlier in the day. The pane of glass in the paneled window nearest to the deadbolt had been replaced with a cut-to-fit piece of cardboard secured within the frame with duct tape.

What was that southern saying? If you can't fix it with duct tape, you're not using enough duct tape.

He stood and tried the door. Locked. No surprise there. He peered through one of the intact panels of glass, forehead leaned against it, cupped hands framing his eyes to block outside light and maximize what he could see inside. He didn't see much. Lights were off. No activity. The same thing he saw when he looked through several other windows of the building.

He wanted to kick the door down and charge into the church. John had been in there. Eric was certain of it. John had balked against the news that Christian Berry was not Jonas Kane, and he had taken it upon himself to do some breaking and entering to try to prove his own theory.

And something had happened to him. He hadn't been taken into custody by the police. A quick phone call had taken care of that notion. That meant something worse had happened to him.

Eric clenched his fists in impotent frustration. He had only known John a couple of days—didn't even really consider him a friend for that matter—but Eric did respect John and, most importantly, viewed him as part of his team. He felt the same about Cutter.

He looked across the lawn and saw Cutter walking toward him, cowboy boots tromping through the dry grass in the afternoon heat. He had been further inspecting Berry's house. Based on his expression, he hadn't found anything.

After Cutter picked up Eric and Trish at their hotel—with Trish getting the dubious honor of riding in the center of the pickup's not-luxurious bench seat—they had agreed to come straight to Berry's house to try to find John. They had driven the neighborhood in concentric circles to eventually find the minivan parked nearby, but no sign of John.

They had parked the truck, and Eric and Cutter had walked straight up Christian Berry's sidewalk and banged on the front door loud enough to make a dog bark across the street. Trish watched from the cab of Cutter's truck, her cell phone at the ready to call the police if something went askew, but the door went unanswered. No one had been home.

Cutter proceeded to inspect the perimeter of the house, looking through windows for any sign of John. Eric had done the same with the church.

The fresh replacement of the pane of glass in the church's back door told Eric all the story he needed about John's activities last night, but as he'd encountered again and again the past week, it gave no evidence. In order to justify kicking down a door with no warrant (which he wouldn't get two-thousand miles outside his own jurisdiction anyway), he needed hard evidence.

It was the Catch-22 of being a cop. He was paid to enforce the law, but in so doing, he was held to a stricter set of rules than normal citizens. In the movies, the hero cop could bend rules at will, and he was celebrated for it when he brought the bad guy to justice (as he always did). In real life, a cop who bent the rules found himself on the receiving end of a public outcry and often the loss of his own job.

His badge should be a shield, but it lately felt more like an anchor.

What was he supposed to do when lives were at stake?

And did he believe that was the case now? Just yesterday, Eric was convinced that the theory constructed by John and Cutter—that this slimy nobody preacher in a nothing college town was in reality the son of a notorious psychopath bent on some grand scheme of mass murder—was utter bullshit. But now his gut was screaming out that something was seriously wrong. And as a cop, he was rendered ineffectual in investigating and stopping it. It infuriated him.

He waved to Cutter, gesturing to join him on the stoop. Eric suspected that when he showed Cutter the replaced pane of glass, it might be Cutter's booted heel that kicked open the door. Would Eric be a willing accomplice? In a few moments, he would have to make that decision.

His mental sparring session ended when he heard Trish yelling. She was running toward them from the truck. Cutter stopped in his tracks, scanning the area, his right hand hovering at his side. Eric knew his revolver was holstered beneath his jacket there.

Eric took two steps toward Trish and checked the area himself. He didn't see any activity. He noticed Trish was holding her cell phone. A few more steps and she was within a more comfortable range. She was winded from the sprint but spoke clearly.

"Dr. Garber just called," she managed before sucking in a sharp breath. "He found something with the communion wine. Wants me to come to the lab at his office."

Eric looked at Cutter. The Ranger nodded at him with a grim expression.

They would be joining Trish at this meeting. Right now.

CHAPTER 81

CHRISTIAN BERRY STOPPED WALKING and turned to face the five hulking young men who had been following his footsteps. His Elite Guard halted when he turned. They had been hiking the perimeter of the bonfire field. He wanted his men to build a sense of anticipation and an appreciation for the enormity of what was upon them.

The bonfire field was moderately quiet. A few industrious workers were testing the sound system on the stage. Security personnel monitored the stack of logs, protecting it from anyone from the rival school who might try to set it ablaze early and ruin the fun of the TSC fans who would shortly gather on this patch of land to drink cheap beer and cheer for their team and then die in agony.

The first of the revelers should arrive within the hour. A crowd would grow thereafter. By the time dusk settled on the field, an estimated thirty-thousand people would be packed shoulder-to-shoulder, singing school fight songs and smelling like a sweaty brewery. There would be a large contingent of current students but an even greater number of alumni and fans and even people from the rival university who placed the value of a good party above the contrived animosity between the institutions. Families everywhere. But not children. At least, not many.

The bonfire wasn't exactly a kid-friendly event. That was why accommodations were made for the children every year to have an age-appropriate party of their own in the gymnasium of the local middle school. To keep the innocent lambs safe from the debauchery of adult fun.

Berry smiled.

Slade and the other four members of the Elite Guard looked to each other with hesitant grins as well. They didn't get the unspoken joke. They were just playing follow-the-leader. That was fine.

Their position on the outskirts of the field was remote enough that no one could hear them. It was why Berry had chosen this spot. He wanted them to feel the late afternoon sun and breathe the electricity in the air, for this time was special, it *was* electric, as if nature itself knew of the importance of this moment in history and amplified the current running through the lowest levels of the troposphere.

Berry told his Elite Guard to close their eyes. To visualize what was to come. They knew their roles in detail. Though none of them were in danger of being labeled as smart, they knew how to follow orders. Berry had laid out the playbook for the night in painstaking detail over the past few days. He would brook no mistakes. They understood, and he believed them to be ready.

He transitioned into a combination sermon and pep talk. These were athletes—something in their brains was wired to respond to a coach's pregame speech—so Berry would deliver exactly that. In only a few short hours, he would need their utmost performance.

By the time he was finished speaking, the five men could not stand still. They were bouncing on their toes, ready to take the field of battle. But it was not yet time. He needed them to contain the energy and unleash it when called upon.

He put his hand on Slade's shoulder and asked if he would give them some words. Slade's eyes widened with appreciation. It was an honor. He proceeded to babble something about a gridiron and warriors and gladiators and honor and some other nonsense. That was fine, too. The other four young men ate it up, and it intoxicated Slade with the high of leadership, and that was what Berry needed. The time was right for the last priming.

Content that they were in the proper frame of mind, Berry dismissed them all except Slade. He would see them again soon. Once the others were out of hearing range, he turned to Slade and spoke in a low voice.

"That was excellent, Slade," he said. "You are a born leader. *Exactly* what is needed for the cause."

Slade beamed. "Thank you. It's my honor."

"And your duty. We all have our duty in the cause, and tonight, yours will be the most important of all. I could trust it to no one else."

Slade nodded but was there any hesitation in his eyes? There could not be. Berry would not allow it, and that was why he intended to give the final push, a verbal steroid to the ego.

"It's time I told you, Slade," he intoned in a manner of conveying a most precious secret. "You truly are special. Have you ever wondered how it is that you've excelled in sports? How you've succeeded where others have failed? How you have crushed lesser men?"

Slade looked perplexed. "Hard work," he responded with hesitation. "Desire. Toughness."

Berry nodded. "Of course all of those play a part, but Slade, it goes beyond those things. You were gifted at birth by forces you cannot comprehend, provided all you would need to fulfill a destiny meant for you alone. You were born for what you will do tonight."

Slade's brow knit. Berry pushed harder. He needed to make certain this got through that thick skull.

"You know what is going to happen tonight. I don't want you to be afraid because, Slade, tonight you will be untouchable. Invulnerable." He paused. "Invincible."

Slade's eyes widened.

"Nothing can harm you. Not man nor beast nor fire. Tonight, you will be made into an unstoppable warrior. What will kill those around you will fall away from you as nothing." Berry put his hands to Slade's bowling ball shoulders and squeezed. "Do you understand what I'm saying? Tonight will not be the end. It will be the *beginning*. You are destined to rule with me at my right hand. Do you understand?"

An incredulous expression crossed Slade's face. Berry knew the young man had been willing to die for the cause, but many men were willing to die in theory only to shrink from their duties when it came time to actually meet that death. He could not afford for Slade to hesitate, to doubt, to wonder whether he should turn and run rather than face his responsibilities.

So Berry told him he'd be indestructible.

The corners of Slade's mouth rose in a knowing grin and he nodded to Berry. "I knew it. I think I've always known it. I will not fail you."

Berry nodded, squeezed the sinew of Slade's shoulders once more and released him to his fate. Slade walked away and Berry stood alone.

He gazed at the mammoth stack of logs, tiered like a wedding cake with a doghouse perched at the top. Slade had bought it. The brute honestly thought he had spiritually gifted superpowers. That was perfect.

Everything was falling into place. Exactly as it should.

CHAPTER 82

A SINGLE *DING* ECHOED through the vacant hallway of the Physical Sciences building as the elevator doors slid open. Trish had never seen a building on campus so empty. She suspected they were all like this at the moment. With Bonfire only a couple of hours away, there would be no classes, most students would be gearing up for the big party and most professors would either be doing the same or staying as far away from the drunken merriment on campus as possible.

The tomb-like silence of the building was a stark juxtaposition to the controlled chaos happening on the field just outside. People had already begun gathering in order to secure premium positions near the bonfire. Trish didn't envy them. She and Stephanie had attended the event last year—a freshman requirement if you wanted to truly experience TSC—and her two most vivid memories involved a too-young-to-legally-imbibe student in a t-shirt with Greek letters stumbling between them and upchucking in the dirt (some had gotten on both her and Steph's shoes, which was beyond disgusting but also a source of shared laughter for the rest of the year) and the unbearable heat emanating from the bonfire itself.

It had been a two-stage process. The bonfire itself was lit by the work crew chiefs who carried torches, marched the circumference, then threw them into the stack. Prior to the lighting ceremony, a team of firefighters from the Abramsville airport had soaked the stack with jet fuel to ensure certain ignition once torch flame touched log, and to guarantee a fast and even burn to minimize the risk of one side burning too quickly and the stack collapsing in an uneven heap. The first few moments after lighting, the flames of the bonfire were beautiful against the night sky. A minute later—once the tiered stacks of logs were really roaring—the crowds pushed back as one when the first intense heatwave washed over them.

That was Trish's memory. Scorching heat, even from a hundred yards away.

Trish stepped through the elevator doors and pushed the "B" button to proceed to the basement level lab as Dr. Garber had asked. She kept the doors open while Eric and Cutter filed in behind her with Andrew in between them.

They were late in arriving at the Physical Sciences building. It wasn't just the impossibility of finding a place to park—they had ended up parking in a lot two buildings down and walking the rest of the way—but finding Andrew and bringing him along had taken time. Still, Cutter had insisted. He hadn't elaborated beyond saying he felt Andrew should be with them to hear whatever Dr. Garber had to say, but Trish suspected he didn't trust Andrew and wanted him close at hand for whatever came next.

That was fine with Trish. In her heart, she still believed Andrew wouldn't do anything wrong on purpose. If he had, it was because he was under the influence of Christian Berry, so she felt it better that Andrew stay with them and keep far away from the scarecrow preacher.

As the doors slid shut and the elevator began its short descent to one floor below, she glanced at Andrew. He was staring straight ahead, his eyes betraying neither guilt nor innocence. When they had picked him up, he hadn't argued. He had, in fact, seemed interested in what Dr. Garber might have to tell them. Trish decided she still trusted him.

The elevator doors opened onto the basement level and a long hallway with working laboratory spaces on either side. The end of the hall held a different looking entryway bearing a stark yellow and black sign reading *Hazardous Materials Lab*.

Since he was familiar with the building from his own chem lab course requirements, Andrew led the way. Trish glanced into open doors as they walked. The lab spaces varied in size with some holding a dozen tables—each equipped with a sink and Bunsen burners and all the accompanying chemistry paraphernalia—while other labs were much smaller with only one or two worktables. One of these small labs bore the number designation Dr. Garber had given Trish. Still in front, Andrew was the first to walk through the door while Trish, Eric and Cutter filed in behind him. They found the professor standing at a raised table.

"Ah, welcome!" Dr. Garber greeted them.

Trish offered quick introductions of Eric and Cutter. Names only. No explanation for their presence. Hands were awkwardly shaken in greeting as the group crowded around the table which appeared to be designed for two people to perform experiments but not so much for five people to huddle around.

"Though you didn't elaborate," Dr. Garber offered a nervous smile as he addressed the two new faces, "something tells me you gentlemen may be looking into the affairs of one Christian Berry. Am I correct?"

"I wouldn't say you were wrong," Cutter drawled.

"I suspected as much." Dr. Garber looked at Trish. "You could have been honest with me, Miss O'Brien. And you, Mr. Kraft," he said as he nodded to Andrew.

Andrew raised his hands, palms up. "I have nothing to do with this. I just brought the sample to prove a point, and I thought the lab results accomplished that."

One corner of Dr. Garber's mouth rose in a half-smile. "That's what I thought, too," he said. And was that a glimmer in his eye? "But there was something about the whole thing which bothered me."

Dr. Garber directed his next comment to Trish. "I suspected there was more to the story than you shared. Let's just say there was an undercurrent of urgency that belied the reasoning you provided for the requested lab tests. Plus, knowing this had something to do with Berry..." He lifted his shoulders in a slight shrug and raised his eyebrows.

"I'm sorry I wasn't able to be more straightforward with you, Dr. Garber," Trish offered. She noticed Andrew looking at her with an expression of dulled betrayal. He didn't appear shocked. She wondered if his emotional state was beyond such feelings. Was he under a chemical influence after all?

"Think nothing of it," Dr. Garber said. "I surmised your situation was delicate but also of great importance, so I took it upon myself to explore the matter further. If you'll indulge me..."

Dr. Garber turned in the tight quarters and retrieved a beaker from a bench that ran along the wall. The glass container was the size of a small coffee pot and was filled to the halfway point with a dark purple solution. He placed it at the center of the table.

"Now, you'll recall the original sample size provided by Mr. Kraft was of a small amount," he said. "We forwarded that sample to the lab in Austin. However, with the detailed results from the chromatography, I was able to synthesize an identical compound in a larger volume."

"And this is that compound?" Eric asked.

"Indeed," Dr. Garber nodded. "Exactly the same in substance as what was provided by Mr. Kraft, but of a volume that I could siphon off necessary amounts for additional experimentation."

"Experimentation...not analysis?"

Trish glanced at Eric when he asked the question. How did he always pick up on the word clues? It was a talent she hoped to develop for herself.

"Exactly," Dr. Garber said with a smile as he pointed a finger at Eric. "You see, I knew that Trish's concern had to be less about the compound itself and more about how the communion wine may have interacted with Stephanie's constitution, and whether it could have resulted in a negative outcome." He paused to glance at Trish. "This much, you essentially told me though masked in what I presume to be a cover story."

Andrew again glanced toward Trish before returning his attention to Dr. Garber. He may be annoyed, but they were all enrapt now— Andrew, Cutter, Eric and her—wondering where this was headed.

"So the question was never really about the chemical composition of the communion wine," Dr. Garber explained. "The real question was how this compound would react once introduced to the human body."

"Wait," Andrew interrupted. "You said the analysis showed it was grape juice. Half the world drinks grape juice. There is no reaction."

"So it would seem, Mr. Kraft," the professor said as he pivoted back to the bench along the wall. He pulled a glass test tube from one end of a small wooden rack of such tubes, turned and held it up to the group gathered around the table. It was full of clear liquid and capped with a black rubber stopper.

"What's that?" Trish asked.

"This," Dr. Garber shook the tube as he spoke, the liquid splashing inside, "is a synthesized representation of the acid found within your stomach, Miss O'Brien." He shook his head. "Anyone's stomach really."

Andrew's eyebrows furrowed as he looked at the test tube. Eric and Cutter were also peering at it, eyeballs in tracking motion as Dr. Garber waved the tube while he spoke.

"Don't you see? We need to know how this supposed grape juice reacts once it encounters the stomach lining and how it might change when it's absorbed into the bloodstream. If it was really grape juice, no problem. But what if it was something more? Something that you wouldn't even notice when looking at the results of the analysis."

"I'm sorry, doc," Cutter's deep voice interrupted. "It's been many a year since I sat in a science class. You may need to spell this out for us slow folk."

"Actually, what I want is to show you. It will make so much more sense when I do."

Dr. Garber handed the test tube to Andrew.

"Mr. Kraft, if you'll do the honors."

Andrew looked at the test tube in his hand, shrugged and pulled the stopper.

"Wait," Dr. Garber said. "Let me give you some room." He edged his way around the group toward the door, allowing Trish, Eric, Cutter and Andrew to each have their own unobstructed side of the lab table. "I want you to be able to see this clearly. When Mr. Kraft pours in the solution, watch the reaction within the beaker very closely. You won't believe this. Go ahead, Mr. Kraft."

Trish leaned close to the beaker. Cutter and Eric did the same. Andrew held the uncapped test tube an inch over the top of the beaker and tilted it, pouring the clear liquid into the purple solution. He lay the tube on the table and leaned close to the beaker, scrutinizing the reaction occurring.

The purple liquid effervesced. Tiny bubbles growing larger. A film of smoky gas formed on the surface, a thin layer of undulating fog over a miniature purple sea. Fumes rose from the glass container. They weren't altogether visible. It reminded Trish of watching heat rising from sunbaked pavement on a blistering summer day. The fumes smelled sweet. Sickly sweet.

Trish heard the door close, glanced behind her and realized Dr. Garber had stepped out of the room. She put one hand on the table to steady herself. She was lightheaded. It was the smell.

Her other hand found the table, she meant to brace herself from the dizziness. Whatever was coming from the beaker, she was having a strange reaction to the scent. She started to say something to Eric. He appeared to be wobbling. But was it him or her?

Her knees went weak then buckled.

"I don't—" she began as she fell.

Black.

CHAPTER 83

HIRAM KANE STOOD at the window, hands clasped behind his massive back like a soldier at rest. He wasn't a soldier. Nor a general. Nor a king. But soon, he would be a god.

The mass of humanity on the bonfire field below was growing by the minute. Dusk was almost upon them. In less than an hour, the Master of Ceremonies would take the stage and begin the pre-bonfire ceremonies. Speeches would be given. Music would be played. Cheers would be led. And once the crowd of thousands was worked into an adequate froth of school spirit—and upon the arrival of the time loosely referred to as "dark-thirty"—the real event would begin. The lighting of the Bonfire. What the crowd will have been waiting for all evening. And what Hiram had waited for his entire life.

The Master of Ceremonies title was an honorary one and rotated on a yearly basis to the chairs of each department within the college. This allowed each of them an opportunity at the distinction of basking in the glow of the canned lights while bumbling through opening remarks with jokes found via a clumsy Google search. This year's honorary emcee was Lucas Blankshire, the head of TSC's chemistry department and coincidental member of Hiram's High Council.

Blankshire was somewhere down there now, schmoozing the various faculty and donors while waiting for his chance to take the stage. Hiram, meanwhile, stood in Blankshire's corner office on the fourth floor of the Physical Sciences building. The office was well-appointed with fine art and elegant furniture. A large teakwood desk was fronted by guest chairs covered in supple leather. A conference table constructed of African Blackwood was surrounded by six suede-upholstered chairs. A centerpiece of undefinable crystal captured the light in a prismatic glow. A rustic cabinet sat against the far wall. Behind its closed doors, Hiram knew Blankshire kept a full bar replete with custom glassware.

Blankshire prided himself on what he believed to be his sophisticated taste. Hiram wondered how much of the cost of the furnishings in the office had been assigned to the department budget and how much Blankshire had funded himself through his non-institutional sources of income (of which Hiram knew Blankshire had several).

Regardless, the vanity of the department head afforded Hiram two important things in use tonight. The first was a private bathroom. Windowless. Soundproof. It couldn't have been more perfect to meet an unexpected yet exquisite need—the ideal place to stash a troublesome pest. Hiram glanced to the bathroom's closed door. John Michaels was on the other side, chained to the toilet like an ill-behaved dog. Hiram smiled.

The second thing Blankshire's narcissism provided was perhaps less important but instead served a sentimental purpose. The office itself was nice. That appealed to Hiram. He wasn't an unfeeling monster. Just a man with a purpose. His thoughts went to his late wife. Moira would not approve of this evening, but perhaps she would appreciate his efforts at conducting this necessary business in a luxurious and comfortable place. Perhaps that would soften the impact.

The entrance to the office opened and a lanky frame attired in white dress shirt with black slacks stepped inside from the empty receptionist's space and closed the door behind him. Jonas Kane. Hiram's son would be Christian Berry no longer. The burden of that mask would at long last be lifted from him. Hiram himself would conduct the final spiritual awakening. The followers of Christian Berry were primed for instruction, and when Hiram gave direction in place of their former guide, they would listen and obey. To this, there was no doubt in Hiram's mind. Such was the power he held. Likewise, Berry's Elite Guard would follow Hiram's instruction. They had an important role in what was to occur on the roof later.

For Jonas, who had played such a pivotal part in all that had transpired to bring them to this glorious evening—for this young man who was at once nothing like his father and yet completely like him—his most critical role could not be accomplished as the fictional Christian Berry, but only as the true son of Hiram Kane.

Jonas was carrying a canvas bag which he placed on the conference table next to the unfolded leather knife roll. The ancient daggers rested upon the leather. The blade of each had been sharpened to a razor's edge. They did not gleam in the light. Their age had dulled any reflective capacity. The ancient metal instead seemed to absorb the light. These blades existed in a world of shadow. There were four daggers on the table. The fifth was wrapped in a separate cloth and rested in Hiram's jacket pocket. No need to display that one.

Jonas gazed at the daggers with an expression of appreciation. He glanced up to his father.

"May I?"

"Of course," Hiram responded.

Jonas lifted one of the knives by its hilt and held it up. He caressed the flat of the blade with the tip of one bony finger then returned it to the leather alongside its brothers.

"Did you bring the bottle?" Hiram asked.

Jonas smiled. "I've looked forward to this moment for years," he said as he reached within the canvas bag and produced a dark bottle. "I know it's been even longer for you."

Hiram crossed from the window to the table and took the bottle from his son.

"It has. Well done," he said as he examined the label. He had indeed waited a long time. He had purchased this bottle before Jonas was born especially for this day. Even then, he believed that the fulfillment of the promises within the ancient texts should be accompanied by ceremony. This particular bottle had remained with Hiram for decades, unopened, just for this purpose, for this occasion.

He cradled the bottle in one meaty hand and returned to the window, soaking in the anticipation of the moment. The Reckoning was here. There was nothing to stop him. Unseen forces of unspeakable darkness and might propelled him in his journey. His taste of power from the texts—the supernatural gift of persuasion used on those of his High Council and so many others—had aided his quest thus far. He would have more of that power. Michaels couldn't stop him. Nor the Texas Ranger, nor the police detective. Hiram's destiny was manifest. And since that calling required sacrifice, he would make it, even of his own flesh and blood.

He watched the people scurrying around the bonfire field. Hugging and laughing and yelling and toasting each other's idiocy. They would burn. All of them. Then he would ascend. The power would be his. Hell would follow.

Jonas sidled next to him. He, too, watched the mortals below.

"Is everything ready?" Hiram asked.

"All is prepared," Jonas replied, not taking his eyes from the bonfire field. "The Elite Guard and my followers believe this to be the end time. They know to expect the unexpected." He turned to face Hiram. "I will be on the roof, overseeing. You will command the sheep. I know it's important for the order to come from you, and it will be so. By the end of the night, the three rites of the Reckoning will be fulfilled. The power will be ours." He tilted his head to Hiram. "You shall lead, with me as your heir, your partner and right hand."

Hiram took in a great breath. *The three rites of the Reckoning.* Jonas was a good boy. He hadn't needed to know there were in fact four rites.

"You have made me proud," he said, knowing that he'd never before given such a compliment to Jonas during his lifetime. He wondered how his son would process it. "I'll pour."

Jonas turned his attention back to the window while Hiram walked to the bar cabinet. He set the bottle on the counter, opened the doors and removed two etched crystal tumblers from the shelf. He found a penknife and traced a slow circle through the wax at the top of the bottle, unsealing the cork. Hiram had never been an ambitious drinker, but he had learned a few lessons from the aristocratic oil executives for whom he had once worked. Unlike certain types of wine which continued to perfect with age even after bottling, whiskey aged only in a cask. Once the spirit was bottled, it ceased to improve in flavor profile.

That was true except for a very few varieties, one of which sat before Hiram now. This limited bottle of whiskey was infused with select drops of a rare Amontillado wine upon bottling. Over the years, a slow chemical reaction would take place within the bottle creating a wholly unique spirit, which is exactly what Hiram had always known this occasion would call for.

He gripped the top of the cork, the fat upper half sat above the rim of the bottle while the lower half sealed the neck, and gently worked it from the bottle. It came free with a subtle pop. The aroma of the whiskey filled his nostrils.

He glanced over his shoulder at Jonas. His son continued to observe the growing masses on the bonfire field. Hiram used one hand to pour the amber whiskey into the tumblers, filling each to the halfway point. His other hand reached into his pocket and extracted a small vial of fine gray powder. He set the bottle down, opened the vial and poured the powder into the glass on the left, then dipped his finger into it and swirled. The powder blended with the whiskey. There was no change in color. It was perfect. Hiram wiped his finger on his sleeve and pocketed the vial. He had kept his back to Jonas just in case, but when he turned, a glass in each hand, his son was still looking out the window.

He crossed the room and handed Jonas the left-hand glass. His son took the tumbler and raised it to his father.

"To a day of glory," Jonas said. "Well-earned and well-deserved glory."

Hiram raised his glass in response. He was glad of this ceremony. It was casual, even commonplace, to toast success, but it felt right.

"To glory for us both," he said, "and to my son, to whom I am grateful."

Hiram believed he saw color rise in the cheeks of his son. He had never seen Jonas blush before, perhaps had never given him occasion for that reaction. But now, at the end, he was glad to have done so. Jonas was a good boy. He had done all Hiram had ever asked of him. His loyalty was his hallmark, and like Isaac, who had allowed his father Abraham to bind him as a sacrifice to God, Jonas would fulfill his part in faith. Isaac's life had been spared. Alas, this could not be so for Jonas.

The two tumblers came together with a soft clink. Hiram brought his glass to his lips and drank of the whiskey. The taste filled his mouth and bit into his jaw. He watched as Jonas did the same. His son sipped at first, then swallowed the entire contents of the glass. Hiram finished his as well. The whiskey burned his throat and warmed his stomach. It was excellent.

"I meant what I said," he told Jonas. "I truly am proud of you."

"I know, Father," Jonas replied. "And I'm grateful for you to say so."

Hiram cocked his head. He had expected a faster reaction to the drug, but Jonas was still standing.

"Well, sometimes..." Hiram paused. He was slurring. His lips felt thick. Jonas was watching him with clear eyes.

"Perhaps you should sit down," Jonas offered. He stepped to the table, grabbed the back of one of the suede-upholstered chairs and rotated it so the seat faced his father.

Hiram grew unsteady on his feet. He staggered toward the chair and turned, sitting heavily onto its thick padding. He glanced at the tumbler in his hand. It dropped from his fingers onto the carpet. He no longer had the strength to hold it.

Jonas stood in front of him. His expression impassive. His eyes cold. What had he done?

"It's okay, Father," Jonas said. His voice was emotionless. "This is how it had to be."

CHAPTER 84

J ONAS KANE PLACED HIS HANDS on his knees and bent forward, studying his father's face. Hiram's jaw was slack. A thin rivulet of saliva trailed from his mouth down the side of his chin. The corners of his eyelids drooped, but the eyes themselves were clear. He was awake.

"You're wondering what happened," Jonas sighed. "You put the paralyzing agent into *my* glass so why am I standing while you're a vegetable?"

He straightened and placed his hands on his hips. "The answer, Father, is something you would appreciate. *Chemistry.*" He said the word with a flourish, but of course, no reaction from his seated audience. He smiled. "It represents, in fact, my highest achievement in the field. It was also my greatest gamble." He leaned close to his father and spoke with his voice lowered. "I spent years in psychological agony, wondering how you would do it, applying my mind to the deduction of the most likely scenario for how you would choose to end the life of your own son. And I must tell you, it is tremendously rewarding to have been right."

He began pacing as he spoke. "But how? But when? But why? But where? So many questions racing through your mind right now. Here, let me get that for you." Jonas removed a handkerchief from his trouser pocket and wiped drool from Hiram's chin. "All valid questions, and I have a few minutes, so I am more than happy to answer them."

He pulled a chair from the table, placed it in front of his father and sat so they were face-to-face.

"We'll start with the most important bit of information. *I know.* I have known all along. There are no secrets. You took great pains to secure away the ancient texts, your precious book. Ever since I was in middle school—which I suspect is when you translated the rites required for the Reckoning and realized what must occur—you secreted away your treasure. You told me of it, of course. You shared much of its knowledge, but you never let me see the book itself."

Jonas sighed. "You're wondering how I managed to circumvent your security. How I could have studied the book without your knowledge. You were so careful. Perhaps it will make you feel better— if you could feel anything at all in this moment—to tell you that I never even tried. I didn't have to. You see, there was a time when you weren't so careful. When I was but a boy, you kept the book in a metal strongbox in your closet. The key was under the lamp on your nightstand. I found it. Quite by accident at the time, or so I thought." His eyes remained on his father, though he now looked beyond him. "But the more I've pondered it, I do believe it called to me."

He shook his head, clearing his thoughts. "Anyway, I may have been young, but I knew the book was important." He paused. "No, that's not it. I knew the *writings* within the book were important. So I began to copy them. Every day, while you were working and Marcus and Silas were outside terrorizing the world beyond our home, I returned to the closet with my pen and paper. One symbol, one line, one page at a time, until I had copied the entirety of the writings, a precious book of my very own."

He leaned back in his chair. His father was still slumped in the chair across from him. Jonas had a few more minutes before he would need to take final action.

"The key—no pun intended—was in fact *the key*, the deciphering instrument. You didn't leave that locked up. I found it in your desk. Once I copied the key, I was able to begin translating the writings myself, a special hobby cultivated over the years of my youth. What wonders they hold!"

He smiled. "Of course, you know that. But, oh, the things I learned from the book. My secret companion. And the insight it's given me into *you* over these years. The things you would tell me, and the things you chose not to reveal. Let's call them lies of omission, shall we?"

Jonas rose from the chair and went to the window, with all the activity below.

"And the greatest lie of all is the Reckoning. That we would share in its power." He shook his head. "A soul must be prepared to ascend to power. You told me of some of the preparatory work required but not all. You prepared yourself in secret in the vault, assuming I would remain oblivious. Fortunately, I have made myself ready in all respects. I have undertaken the rituals of preparation, just as you have. Your deception could not forestall my destiny."

He turned from the window to look at Hiram. "And the lie within the lie. You shared with me the *three* rites required of the Reckoning. The self-sacrifice of an acolyte. The killing of trusted generals. The slaying of ten thousand innocents. But you never mentioned the *fourth* rite." He raised his eyebrows with the remark. "And with good reason, eh?"

Jonas walked to Hiram, placed his hands upon the arms of the chair and leaned close to his father's face. "The sacrifice of a son." He cocked his head. "I wonder if you had planned to use Marcus for that purpose. Or Silas? Or—even if my brothers had lived—was I always your chosen sacrificial lamb? Or perhaps you would have killed all three of us." He sighed. "I suppose it doesn't matter. All that matters is the truth within the ancient texts. And the truth encompasses the flexibility within the translation. The symbols refer to the relationship of the sacrifice, but it may be interpreted either direction." Jonas put his lips almost to Hiram's ear and whispered. "The father sacrifices his son. Or the son sacrifices his father."

He straightened and turned to the table. "The Reckoning was always to be mine, Father. Not yours. Every action that occurred, every step that has been taken, every aspect of your plan has favored me. Stephanie was not your acolyte. She was mine. The followers who will fulfill tonight's slaughter follow me. You have kept yourself a step above the entire time, believing in the transitive—that those who serve me must therefore also serve my master, but *I am my own master*. Your generals—your preening High Council—may believe themselves to be your friends, but all their actions in helping bring about the Reckoning will ultimately serve me. They will be sacrificed as mine."

Jonas glanced at his father. Perspiration covered the old man's forehead. His eyes no longer drooped. They were wider now. Rage burned within them. It was time.

"So we return to the magic of chemistry on this night. You needed to sacrifice me, but I didn't believe you would do so in a crude manner. You're a man who believes in ceremony."

Jonas opened the canvas bag on the table and felt inside until his fingers touched cold metal.

"I gambled that you would choose to incapacitate me with a paralytic agent, then bind me and end my life with whatever pomp and circumstance you deemed appropriate."

He withdrew his hand from the bag, the scalpel held in his long fingers. He removed the guard from the blade. It gleamed in the light. He saw Hiram's eyes fix upon it.

"I know you well enough to know your preferred methods. I extended my gamble to cover exactly which paralytic agent you would choose. I then—and this is what will really impress you—set about the process of developing a mirrored counteragent. It took years to perfect, but I effectively synthesized a clone of your agent, a bizarro formula, so to speak. This formula would mimic the effects of the agent in identical fashion, but if it came into contact with the original agent, the two chemicals would null one another, cancel each other out."

Jonas passed the scalpel from one hand to the other as he walked behind his father.

"I created this specimen in the labs here in the basement of this very facility. Two days ago, I took a test tube of the formula and used a heavy gauge hypodermic needle to pierce the cork of that bottle and inject the solution into the whiskey. I then even used a candle to melt and smooth the wax over the cork. Just to be thorough."

He held the scalpel in his right hand, ran his left hand through his father's short gray hair, then traced his fingers down the back of his head and onto his neck.

"As you can tell, the formula worked like a charm. I feel no ill-effects whatsoever."

Jonas placed the tip of the scalpel at the base of his father's neck, between two vertebrae. He noticed the muscles on either side tensing. Sinew responding to stress.

"And to think, if you hadn't chosen to poison me, we *both* would have drank the pure agent I had injected. Then we'd both be in trouble. But no, you did exactly what I expected. That's why I feel no remorse in doing the same."

Jonas stabbed the scalpel forward, pushing through skin, meeting resistance after the first inch before the blade plunged deep between the vertebrae, severing the spinal cord. Clear fluid welled along either side of the blade and ran down Hiram's spine. It tinged a slight pink color as trace amounts of blood began to commingle with it. The muscles on either side of Hiram's neck went slack.

Jonas sighed. It was done.

"There now, that wasn't so bad, was it?" he asked. "You probably didn't feel a thing."

He thumbed the release on the blade, leaving the sharp steel embedded in Hiram's spine, and set the handle of the scalpel onto the table.

"You remain in perfect health, except for your new lifestyle as a permanent quadriplegic. But worry not, you won't have to endure this ignominy for long."

He opened the bag again and removed a square padding of gauze and a roll of surgical tape. In moments, the wound was covered.

"I wish it didn't have to be this way, Father," he said. He again stood in front of the massive man slumped in the chair, once so intimidating, but no longer. "How does the line go from that movie—'there can be only one'?"

He reached down and felt in the pockets of Hiram's jacket, searching until he extracted the ancient dagger. He set it on the table alongside its four brethren, then returned his attention to the burning gaze of his helpless paterfamilias.

"I am the one, Father."

Jonas crossed the room and opened the door. Slade Stone stood on the other side along with the four other members of the Elite Guard. One of them had a tall dolly, the kind used for moving refrigerators or large items of furniture. A backboard was secured to it.

"Enter," Jonas said to the group, "and prepare my father for his destiny."

He leveled his eyes at Slade. "You come with me. And bring John Michaels."

CHAPTER 85

BEFORE TRISH OPENED HER EYES, her first conscious thought was that her nose itched. Not the outside but the inside, like she had inhaled a cloud of pepper, but rather than triggering a sneezing response, the spice had left an irritating itch within both nostrils. She wanted to rub her nose, squeeze the nostrils together, do anything she could to relieve the itch, but when she went to do so, her hand would not move.

She opened her eyes, a more difficult task than she expected. It was bright in the room. She was sitting on a tiled floor with her back propped against a wall. She turned her head, the room swam with the movement, causing her to close her eyes again before reopening them. Eric was seated next to her. He was looking at her.

Her nose still itched. She again made to scratch it, but still couldn't move her hands.

"Are you okay?"

Eric had asked the question.

She wasn't okay. Her nose itched.

She started to respond but found it challenging to form words. Her mouth felt like it was full of cotton balls. She moved her tongue around. It felt swollen. No cotton in there. Just dry, fuzzy mouth. Yuck.

"I'm fine," she managed to reply.

She glanced away from Eric to her other side. Andrew was sitting there. He had one eye open. The other looked like it couldn't quite get there. Cutter was sitting on the floor to the other side of Andrew. He wasn't wearing his cowboy hat. His gray hair had a soft matted ring where the hat would normally encircle it. Cutter's eyes were open. More than that, they were blazing with anger. Could gray eyes blaze?

She looked up to see what had irked him so. Dr. Garber stood a few feet in front of them. He was leaning against a stainless-steel lab table. His hair was more disheveled than usual, if that was possible. He was perspiring. His shirt was wet from it, the sweat beneath his armpits so heavy the stains met at Garber's chest, forming dark saddlebags of moisture on the shirt. He was breathing like he had been exerting himself.

He was also smiling.

Trish's head began to clear. As the mental fog lifted, her memory returned, bit by bit. With it, her mind began piecing together her current situation. The lab. The beaker on the table. Dr. Garber stepping out the door while she and her friends leaned close. The sweet fumes.

"What the hell?" she asked.

Dr. Garber crossed his arms and maintained the smile but said nothing.

"A double-cross," Cutter spat.

The gravity of the situation settled into Trish's sharpening mind. She looked down. One of her shoes had come off. One sleeve of her shirt was pushed up. Her gold cross rested on the outside of her shirt rather than being tucked underneath between her breasts.

She sat up straighter, attempting to extricate her hands from behind her back. They didn't budge. Her wrists were bound.

"Duct tape," Eric said.

"Huh?" It was Andrew. Both of his eyes were now open. Trish watched him attempt to tug his hands apart, but they remained securely behind his back as well.

"You'll have to forgive me," Dr. Garber said, breathing hard. He walked to a rack of open shelves that sported various glassware and lab equipment along with a stack of folded white towels. Garber plucked the top towel from the stack and mopped his sweaty forehead. "I haven't found it necessary to do that much physical labor since my youth. I'm just glad to have managed to get you all in here before the effect wore off."

"I don't understand," Trish said, shaking her head. It didn't make sense. Dr. Garber was supposed to be helping them.

"Allow me to sum up," Garber responded. "You, Trish O'Brien, journalism major, are a pest of the highest order, along with your friends. Pests should be caged. Or exterminated. That's not for me to decide, but I have a strong suspicion about which direction that will go."

"*You* dragged us in here?" Trish asked.

"Yes! It was exhausting," Garber sighed. "I didn't have a cage handy but the haz-mat lab—while perhaps not comfortable—will serve nicely to keep you out from underfoot. Extraordinary forces are at work this night."

Her missing shoe and tousled clothing made sense now. What didn't make sense was why this was occurring at all. And what was going to happen to them.

"The only extraordinary force you're going to feel tonight is my boot in your ass." There was a menace in Cutter's voice that Trish wouldn't have thought possible.

Garber turned his head to Cutter with a look that Trish suspected was meant to be intimidation, but when their eyes met, Garber took a step back. She saw him swallow hard before reaching to the table and picking up a large handgun. He pointed Cutter's own revolver at him.

"I don't think you're in a position to do that," Garber informed the former Ranger.

"Not yet," Cutter said. He popped his wrists apart and Trish heard a clink. The sound of handcuffs. Garber must have used Cutter's handcuffs to bind him but duct-taped the rest of them. Cutter's hands stayed behind his back, but even bound and sitting on the floor, he looked scary.

"I don't want to shoot you," Garber said. "But I will. I know how to use a gun perfectly well. I've had lessons."

"Why are you doing this?" The question came from Andrew. Trish could tell from the look in his eyes that he was still disoriented, but it wasn't just from the knockout gas. He was bewildered at what was happening. After all, hadn't Garber been a trusted authority figure to him as well as to Stephanie?

Garber shifted his gaze to Andrew though his eyes returned to Cutter with regularity. "I am doing this, Mr. Kraft, because I value alliances that provide dividends—immeasurable dividends. I think you'll find that betraying such alliances is never in your best interest."

"So Andrew *did* give you the real sample of Berry's communion wine," Eric interjected. "And you dumped it and sent a sample of grape juice to the lab." He paused. "Or you didn't send anything at all and just faked the whole report. Threw us off the scent completely."

"But why?" Trish asked. "You hate Christian Berry. Why would you help him?"

"Are you so naïve, Trish?" Garber rolled his eyes. "Appearances can be deceiving. You would have made a lousy journalist. The world won't miss you."

The words cut into Trish. It wasn't the insult. It was the dismissiveness of the statement. The finality. The world wouldn't miss her because she was going to die. Garber wasn't going to lose sleep over it. It wasn't a challenge to which she could rise up. She was helpless. So was Andrew. And Eric. Even Cutter. It wasn't a question of bravery. Garber had a gun. She and her friends could do nothing. Their lives were in his hands, and he had made clear what little value he placed on those lives.

They were going to die.

Would it be painful? Would they do anything to her or just shoot her? And her friends? Would she watch them die first or would they see her go? And what happened after that? Was there anything after the light left your eyes in this world? She had once believed so, but that was a long time ago.

The door opened behind Garber. He turned, gun at the ready, then lowered it as Christian Berry walked into the lab. Close at his heels, angling his shoulders to enter the door was Slade. Trish gasped as she saw Slade jerk his arm forward and yank into the room a stumbling John Michaels. His wrists were bound in handcuffs. One eye was darkly bloodshot, like he had taken a devastating blow to the head. He looked terrible.

Slade pushed John against the wall next to Cutter but left him standing, then stepped next to Berry and crossed his arms over his bulging chest. He surveyed the prisoners on the floor. Slade's eyes stopped on Trish, and his lips curled into a hideous reptilian grin.

Christian Berry clapped his hands together then held them clasped in front of him as he glanced about the room.

"I see the gang is all here," he said. "How very exciting..."

CHAPTER 86

JOHN MICHAELS SCANNED THE ROOM and assessed the situation. His head was pounding, his stomach burned from his ulcer, his body ached, but his mind was clear.

His assessment was clear, too.

They were fucked.

He had been dragged by the man-beast with the cobra-looking neck muscles from the restroom on the fourth floor. As he was pulled through what appeared to be a nice office, he saw the other four gigantors who had been accosting Trish and Eric on campus the other morning prior to his and Cutter's intervention. In hindsight, given the current situation and his expected fate, John mused that perhaps getting involved hadn't been the smartest move.

Trish had said the leader was named Slade. He hadn't been gentle in unshackling John's wrists from the toilet or in re-shackling them. He had passed the handcuff key to Jonas Kane—to Christian Berry, the scarecrow preacher—and had then yanked John up and out the restroom door.

The other four apes had been surrounding a barrel-chested older man seated in a chair. John saw knives laid out on the table next to him. No introductions took place, but John had a strong suspicion the helpless brute was Hiram Kane. The future did not appear bright for the old man.

John had been pulled by the wrists by Slade through the office, down a hallway, onto an elevator and then down another hallway on the basement level. Seeing the lab spaces lining either side, John knew he was in the Physical Sciences building.

He had tried to get Jonas to talk along the way, to learn something, but the only response he received was '*soon.*' Not helpful at all.

When they reached the end of the hall, Jonas Kane leading the way, they passed through the clean room for the hazardous materials lab. White haz-mat suits replete with plastic face masks and the whole nine yards lined one wall. There was a decontamination pod as well. Jonas Kane ignored these protocols and proceeded straight into the lab.

Now, John stood with his back to the wall. He saw Cutter on the floor, wrists behind him. Trish and Eric and a young man unfamiliar to John were bound the same way. They looked okay. No one appeared hurt.

Standing at the center of the room was some sweaty asshole with messy hair holding what John was ninety-nine percent certain was Cutter's gun. John couldn't recall having previously seen the guy with dark stains on his shirt under his armpits, but it was safe to say he wasn't siding with the good guys.

The fact that all of them had been gathered into a basement lab that was designed to be hosed down with bleach or whatever you use to make a hazardous materials work area sterile again was not lost on John. If a serial killer could dream up a perfect place to do his murdering then clean it up and get away with it scot-free, this was what he would describe.

Yep. Fucked. One and all.

When Jonas Kane began to speak, it did not make John feel better.

"I see the gang is all here. How very exciting."

"They await your judgment, Christian," said the perspiring guy with the revolver.

John mused that Pit Stains there must not be in the know about Christian Berry's true identity. He wondered if that could be used in some way. It wasn't much, but John had no other ammunition to speak of at this point.

"Judgment will wait," Jonas said in a soothing voice. "This is a time to be savored, my friend. But you've done very well in assembling our congregation here. It's as if every desire is granted to me with but a wish."

Pit Stains beamed. Asshole.

John looked down at Cutter. His hat was missing, but he didn't look too bad.

"Hey," John said. Clever as it was.

Cutter regarded him. "How you faring?"

"Same as always."

"That bad, huh?" Cutter grinned. "You look like it."

"I love reunions," Jonas interjected.

Was the faux preacher annoyed that he had lost the spotlight for a moment? John thought so.

"Let's all take a moment to appreciate this," he continued. "Think about the cosmic forces at work that somehow drew this group together for this momentous occasion."

"What occasion would that be?" Eric asked from his place on the floor.

"The Reckoning." Jonas smiled.

From the corner of his eye, John saw the young man on the floor between Cutter and Trish shudder. His jaw had dropped open at the remark. John wondered if this was the Andrew kid who Trish had talked about. The one John suspected had given them a false sample of the communion wine. If so, then based on the kid's current predicament, John must have been wrong about him.

"A reckoning of what?" Eric inquired.

"Not *a* reckoning," Jonas said dismissively. "*The* Reckoning. An ascension to otherworldly power never before achieved by mortal man."

"Oh...that," Eric muttered.

Eric might be flippant, but John felt an electricity in the air—what he used to experience in a board room when reaching the final stages of negotiation in a corporate takeover, when the cards were all laid on the table (often reluctantly by the other party) and John could at last see the final gameboard and what moves were required to dismantle the opposition and achieve victory. One critical card had just been laid by Jonas Kane, whether he realized it or not.

"That's what this has all been about?" John asked. "The experiments at the program in New Mexico—the chemical and psychological manipulation—followed by what you've been doing here, the nightly spiritual awakenings, the drugged communion wine. It all leads to this Reckoning?"

"Very good, John," Jonas said. He brought his hands together in three quiet claps. "You've been doing homework. You really are quite perceptive, aren't you?"

"Not really," John admitted. "What I know pales compared to what I *don't* know. What you're planning with your followers, why you've drugged them, how you achieve this Reckoning...I don't know anything."

Jonas smiled. "You want me to tell you, don't you? Reveal my plans?"

This was it. Had John read the card correctly?

"I'd be very interested," he answered.

Jonas glanced at his watch, then backed up to the stainless-steel lab table and hopped onto it, sitting with his feet swinging beneath his bony knees. He placed his hands on either side and leaned forward, looking like a casual tech guru conducting an informal meeting.

"Sure! I've got time," Jonas said.

John saw Pit Stains and Slade exchange a look. They obviously didn't expect this basement encounter to become a tête-à-tête between their leader and his prisoners.

It was no surprise to John. Some cards are easier to read than others. Jonas had an ego. He liked an audience. It was a family trait he shared with his big brother. In the end, Marcus Kane's ego had proved a fatal flaw. John didn't know how things would play out with Jonas, but he did know that incentivizing him to talk would buy two things: more time and more information. Both of those could prove helpful if he could just keep Jonas talking.

"Would you like to ask me questions or should I just start monologuing?" he asked from his perch on the table.

"Let's start at the very beginning," John offered.

"A very good place to start," Jonas sang the words with a grin. Whatever was happening tonight, it had put him in high spirits. Thankfully, he reverted to a normal speaking voice as he continued. "I'd be happy to share the story with you, John." He paused to acknowledge his seated audience as well. "With all of you. You've all played such significant roles in the events that have ultimately led us to this evening." He gave a perfunctory nod of appreciation to his captives.

"The Reckoning," he continued, "is the fulfillment of a lifelong ambition. Foretold in ancient times and realized today. It is attainment of true power. For me and those whose faith will be rewarded." He looked to Pit Stains and Slade. Both of whom produced smug smiles to accompany nods of appreciation. Perhaps they didn't mind the conversation as long as they received adequate accolades during its course.

"But to achieve the Reckoning requires immense planning. You have but one opportunity to prove yourself worthy. The dark gods are not generous by nature. Sacrifices must be made."

"Sacrifices like Stephanie?" The question came from Trish. Her voice broke on her friend's name.

Jonas nodded. "Yes. She was the first. Her selfless act fulfilled the first rite. You should be proud of her. She did all that was asked and more. A fine example."

Trish looked away. Tears in her eyes.

John saw Andrew shake his head twice in silence, a look of disbelief on his face, then lower his gaze to the floor between his outstretched legs.

"What next?" John asked.

"Three more rites. I won't bore you with trifling details, but they will involve the death of several pompous men gathered on the roof at this moment, plus the sacrifice of my own father." He paused. "And the killing of ten-thousand innocents. That's the big one."

"You're not doing it at the football game," Cutter spoke. "It's the bonfire. That's been your plan all along."

"On the nose." Jonas touched the tip of his nose with one long finger. "At the top of yonder bonfire sits a doghouse. Inside that doghouse is a vessel containing a chemical compound that would take your breath away. I mean, literally," Jonas smiled, "it will suck up all the oxygen when it ignites. Once the flames from the bonfire reach the containment unit and it heats to critical temp, the compound will detonate. The housing unit will rupture and release the combusting chemical in a glorious umbrella of death that will cover half the bonfire field. It will rain fire on every reveler in a five-hundred-yard radius."

"You're talking about napalm,' Cutter said.

"I'm talking about what napalm dreams it could be...if incendiary bombs could dream. This is a new creation developed specifically for this evening along with a perfectly controlled disbursement pattern that will maximize fatalities of those below while providing for a perfectly safe viewing environment for those watching from above. Thousands upon thousands, dead in a flash." He paused and looked toward Slade. "Only the truly special will survive."

Slade smiled. John wasn't sure if the beast was an idiot or just fatally gullible. He decided he didn't care either way.

"I've been to the Bonfire before," Trish said. So she was still with them. She hadn't checked out. She might be young, but perhaps she was stronger than John had given her credit for. "I don't think you're hitting the right target if you're looking for innocents."

"How astute," Jonas replied. "Rest assured, that has crossed my mind. Realize that we're looking primarily at quantity, but quality should certainly be a consideration as well. You see, plenty of those families attending the bonfire have been dropping off their children at the middle school just across the street from my church. It's such a lovely gesture provided by the community every year. They've been doing it for decades. Free babysitting for well over a hundred children, from toddlers to tweens. Volunteers arrange games and snacks and movies. The kids pack into the gymnasium like adorable little lambs filling an abattoir, awaiting their turn at slaughter."

"You sick fuck," Trish spat.

"Well, I won't be killing the little darlings myself." Jonas looked to John. "*That's* the destiny of my followers, John. They will march to that middle school and proceed to dismember every tiny body in the place. And I assure you, Trish," he turned his gaze back to her, "that action will amplify the overall quality of innocence within tonight's sacrifice."

"They won't do it," Trish said. "They won't kill those kids."

"Yes, they will," Andrew said. He spoke at first to the floor then raised his gaze to Jonas. "How could you do that?"

"Through years of hard work and perseverance," Jonas replied, then turned to John and winked.

John felt sick. He knew Andrew was right. The followers would do whatever Jonas said. He knew from experience what it felt like, to lose your emotional anchor, to forget any sense of right or wrong. If the drugs used in New Mexico had been further refined, made more potent, John had no doubt the followers would murder their own families with no compunction.

"What does all this get you?" John asked. He wanted to keep him talking, but he was driven by genuine curiosity as well. What drives the mind of a psychopath? "What happens at the Reckoning?"

"What does it get me?" Jonas repeated. "Why, everything, John. It gets me everything. The Reckoning is the opening of a gateway from which untold power is bestowed upon one worthy individual. My body will become a vessel that will overflow with the might of forces beyond the realm of our reality. I will hold sway over nations. The lives of lesser mortals will be mine to do with as I please." He raised a clenched fist. "I will be a god."

"And rule our mortal plane with a power heretofore unknown on this earth," John said.

"Yes!" Jonas cried in excitement.

"Or check yourself into a mental institution," John added. "You know, whichever seems most appropriate."

The muscles in Jonas's long neck tensed. Veins were visible under the skin. His face reddened. Rage filled his eyes. John didn't care. This was the opportunity.

"I thought you would understand," Jonas whispered through a clenched jaw. Was he disappointed? What did he expect from John?

"I understand," John said. "You're talking about killing thousands of innocent people so you can be granted some sort of supernatural ghost power. That's the type of crazy usually diagnosed as 'batshit'." He spoke fast. Before Jonas could cut him off. "And speaking of killing, you're being pretty cavalier about sacrificing your own father. You just kind of threw that into the conversation. If a man will murder his own father, it makes it hard to trust him. Who's he going to betray next? If I were you guys," he directed his statement toward Slade and Pit Stains, "I'd think carefully about whether *this* is the path you want to walk. It's not too late. You can stop this. Save thousands of lives. You'll be heroes."

Jonas hopped off the table. His face was full crimson now.

"That's a fine effort, John. Clever to the end."

John looked to Pit Stains and Slade. Blank expressions. Neither ventured to stop Jonas. They didn't look moved by John's petition at all.

"He's right, you know," Eric added. "You can't trust a madman. Be heroes instead."

"History is brimming with instances of science ridiculed as madness by those too ignorant to understand," said the guy with the gun. Turned out Pit Stains was eloquent. "I am faithful to those in whom I believe."

Shit.

John had played his hand and lost.

He watched as Jonas regained his composure. The strain was diminishing from his face. His color was transitioning from red to its previous pale white.

"Thank you, my friend," Jonas said to Pit Stains. "Please continue to hold them here until my return." He glanced at his watch before returning his attention to his captives. "I'm afraid our time together has come to an end. But while we're on the subject of faithfulness..."

Jonas turned to the table and picked up a Bowie knife.

"That's mine," Cutter said.

"I found it hidden in his boot," Pit Stains informed his boss with a smug pride.

Jonas ran his thumb along the edge of the silver blade.

"It's quite nice," he said to Cutter. "Very sharp."

Jonas stepped toward Andrew, placed one hand on top of his head, intertwined his long fingers into the kid's hair then clenched his hand into a fist. Andrew winced as Jonas yanked his head back toward the wall, exposing his neck. In one swift motion, Jonas placed the blade under Andrew's left ear and drew it across his throat from one side to the other.

"No!" The same word was shouted by all of John's fellow captives. Eric and Cutter each bucked on the floor but were helpless to make any real movement. Andrew was silent. Fear covered his face. He appeared to be holding his breath, perhaps hoping that what he feared had not just actually occurred.

John saw blood surface where the blade had just traveled. A thin line for a scant moment, then a torrent of crimson poured from his neck.

Andrew's lips moved, but no words, only a wet gurgle emerged. John thought the sound may have come from the young man's throat rather than his mouth.

Trish was crying, frozen in place. John suspected she was torn between getting away from the bloody mess versus moving closer to Andrew in some misguided thought of helping. There would be no helping him.

And there would be no more observation.

"Say goodbye to your friends, John," Jonas said. "You won't see them again." He dropped the knife onto the steel table with a clatter and strode from the lab.

Before John could say a word, Slade's meaty paws grabbed his shoulders and shoved him forward. John stumbled through the lab door and into the clean room. The sound of Trish's sobs faded behind him.

CHAPTER 87

*T*HIS CAN'T BE HAPPENING.

That one thought reverberated through Trish's mind in an endless loop. It overrode all others. Coherence was lost to her, replaced by denial and rising panic and darkness.

This can't be happening.

"Breathe."

She heard the word. From the darkness. It failed to process.

"Trish...breathe."

Breathe. *What?* She wasn't breathing. There was no air in her lungs. She snatched a short breath. Gulping a small mouthful of oxygen. Again. Short, quick breaths like a pregnant woman might use to circumvent the pain of childbirth.

Wait. Hyperventilation. She was hyperventilating.

She took back control of her mind from whatever had seized it and forced herself to draw a long slow inhalation. Her head began to clear. She repeated the action.

She opened her eyes. The darkness left her. She was looking at Eric. It had been his voice.

He was blurry.

Tears. She was crying. That's why Eric was blurry. Her face was wet. She could feel snot on her upper lip. She had lost her breath. That's what had happened.

She was in shock.

Andrew.

She started to turn her head, but Eric's voice made her pause.

"Keep looking at me, Trish. You're okay."

She kept her eyes on Eric. Clarity had returned. As Eric instructed, she didn't look at Andrew, but she knew he was to her left. And he was not okay. He was dead. Horribly, gruesomely, irretrievably dead.

Trish had not been there when her father died. He had been shot in the neck and bled out on a rooftop while pursuing Silas Kane. Eric had been with him. Trish knew he had blamed himself for his partner's death.

The boy next to Trish hadn't been shot. His throat had been slashed. And he never would have been here if it hadn't been for Trish. The blame now lay with her.

She kept her gaze locked on Eric's eyes. She saw fear, anger, desperation. She knew he was already feeling guilty over what was about to happen to her, to all of them, but it wasn't his fault. It was hers.

Her hands were bound behind her. She wiped her nose on her shoulder and sniffed. She nodded to Eric. Her heart was still pounding, but she was okay. More or less.

"Thanks," she said. "Sorry."

"Nothing to be sorry for."

Oh yeah. There was plenty to be sorry for. She had dragged Eric to Texas. She had put him in the middle of this. And hadn't it been fun? She loathed to admit it to herself, but despite her grief over Stephanie's death—what she now knew to be a sacrifice to a psychopath's delusions of grandeur—the selfish truth was that it had been exhilarating to work a real case. She had been a power-combo of Nancy Drew and Lois Lane and Veronica Mars. Together, she and Eric were going to get to the bottom of the mystery.

They had reached the bottom all right.

She had been scared in the days since first confronting Christian Berry, but the fear had been that of a child. She knew something bad could happen, but even after learning that Berry might actually be the far more dangerous Jonas Kane, she had no appreciation for the magnitude of the consequences. Like a soldier with the confidence of basic training who enters his first battle in excitement only to feel that confidence vanish the moment he's spattered with the remains of a blown-apart friend, the visceral reality of her situation overwhelmed her.

The metallic scent of blood filled the air. This time, she did turn her head and look. Blood was pooling around Andrew. It had soaked through his shirt and done the same to his pants. It spread onto the tile floor from there. The blood hadn't yet reached her. She scooted a few inches away. Andrew's eyes were open. He faced forward. He wasn't looking at her. He would never look at anything again.

Trish didn't want that for herself. Or Eric. Or Cutter. But she was helpless.

Dr. Garber stood beside the table—gun still in his hand—staring at them. His expression was that of a curious boy who has kicked an anthill to watch them scurry.

She turned to Eric.

"What now?" she whispered.

He was no longer looking at her. He was scanning the room.

"Good question," he muttered in response.

She looked at Cutter. His eyes were fixed on Garber.

"It's fascinating to watch, isn't it?" Garber asked.

Trish looked up. To whom had he addressed his question?

"Death, I mean," he continued without waiting for a response. "This is the first time I've actually seen someone die, seen the life depart from their eyes. Fascinating."

"Why are you doing this?" Trish asked. They were helpless, and if they just sat here, she had no doubt that Andrew's fate—or something worse—would befall them all when Berry returned from his Reckoning. Garber was the answer. If they could convince him to let them go.

"You already have those answers," he responded. "Power. Authority. For Christian and for his trusted partners. You see, in this world, power is the only thing that really matters. Not fame. Not wealth. Those are the trappings of fools. Power trumps all."

"But you told me in your office that you're a man of science," she said. "That you don't believe in the supernatural."

"Don't put words in my mouth. What I don't believe is a *religion* whose outdated teachings have served to only provoke mankind over the centuries into countless wars and suffering in the name of what is holy while the one in whose name this terror is conducted remains absent from the scene. How could a supposed god of love allow these things to happen? It's self-contradictory. Irrational."

Garber shrugged as if the very concept was so elementary, he shouldn't have to explain it.

"You know, Trish," he continued. "I thought I sensed in you a similar thirst for truth, an ability to rise above the ridiculous blind faith of the weak-minded." He pointed to the gold cross that now hung outside her shirt. "I see that was a misevaluation on my part. You're as weak as the masses. Rest assured that if your god exists, he has forgotten about you. Or perhaps he just ignores you."

Trish winced. It wasn't the derision in Garber's voice that stung her, but the fact that he had just outlined every tenet with which she had struggled since her father had died.

And that she believed Garber was right.

"So you dismiss one religion for being foolish," Eric interjected, "while buying into the madness that Christian Berry is selling? Can't you see he's crazy? How can you believe him?"

Garber chuckled. "There are none so blind as those who will not see. I choose to see."

"Fine, but even if Berry's not crazy," Eric countered, "even if this whole insane theory is true, do you really believe he plans to share any of that power? You're going to be left behind. Maybe even sacrificed like the others."

Garber sighed then pointed the gun at Eric. "I could shoot you now."

"No, you can't," Cutter growled. "Your boss wouldn't like that. And for all that talk of friendship and faith, something tells me he scares you. Maybe you need to think about why that is."

Anger flashed on Garber's face. "I'm done listening. How about I tape your mouths shut?"

Trish saw a grin curl on Cutter's lips. "Maybe you should."

Again, she saw Garber take a step back, perhaps reconsidering the wisdom of leaning in close enough to Cutter to put tape over the cowboy's mouth.

"Please," Trish said. No manipulation. No games. For whatever evil Garber may seem capable of, he was still human. He still had a heart. "Please. Don't let him kill us. Please let us go."

"Ugh!" Garber coughed out the sound of exasperation like he was choking on her heartfelt plea. "I've had enough."

He retreated several steps to the door, whether it was to get away from Trish's entreaties or just to put distance between himself and Cutter, Trish didn't know. The top half of the door was a pane of safety glass with wire mesh interwoven within. He stepped into the clean room.

"I'd rather not listen to any more mewling, but I'll be watching through the window. If you try anything, I *will* shoot you. Make no mistake on that account."

"Wait!" Trish yelled.

The door closed. Garber stood on the other side.

"Please!" she cried again.

He cupped one hand behind his ear, pantomiming his inability to hear while wearing a comical expression of bewilderment. His face shifted to a serious countenance, and he raised the pistol, tapping the barrel on the glass.

Tears threatened Trish again. Garber had been their last chance.

She looked down at the cold tile upon which she sat. The spreading pool of Andrew's blood crept closer to her.

There was no hope.

CHAPTER 88

THE MAN KNOWN AS CHRISTIAN BERRY stood at the front of the lecture hall before his flock. It was the same room he had used for the tedious Wednesday morning group counseling sessions for students. Those were in the rearview mirror. His audience tonight was far more important. And more engaged.

Fervent was the word.

And for good reason. From the moment he had burst into the room of his assembled forty-four (minus select members of his Elite Guard and the recently departed Andrew Kraft), Berry had launched into a blistering performance of charismatic motivation. His speech had been scripted well in advance—he had crafted this final spiritual awakening as the climax of all the groundwork instilled in his followers during the escalation period—but his delivery exceeded his own expectations.

The heightened passion of his presentation was not at first genuine. The performance was a necessary one to ensure his assembled army carried out their duties with a thirst for blood and spiritual reward, but Berry had not expected to be swept along himself.

It began as overcompensation. Yanking open the door to the lecture hall and shouting that the time of the Reckoning had come, that the end times were upon them, displayed a zeal that had been the opposite of what he felt when entering the room. In truth, an air of melancholy had overtaken him. It had been the scene in the basement. The success of incapacitating his father had been euphoric, as if every fiber of his consciousness was attuned to the flow of the universe, as if his plans dictated the course of fate and not the other way around. Everything clicked into place within his meticulous design.

What had he expected from the gathering in the basement?

He had taken the opportunity to assemble into one place the entirety of what his father would have described as enemies of the Reckoning, chief among them John Michaels.

But why had Jonas done so? He had not given it any thought. Such an assembly was never part of his grand scheme. It couldn't have been. The presence of each of these adversaries was perhaps a gift from the forces that awaited to bestow the power upon him, but the gift was unexpected. Not part of the minute-to-minute plan he had long ago laid out for this night. So why assemble them at all?

Was he perhaps looking for affirmation? Respect?

He had labored in secret for so long. The constant threat of discovery from his father made it impossible to confide in anyone. Even Garber—for whom he had concocted an elaborate plan of feigned mutual animosity between them so Garber's supervisor, the head of the chemistry department, would never suspect an alliance and alert Hiram Kane—was a confidante in science only. He was privy to nothing of the real Jonas Kane. He knew only Christian Berry. That had been enough. The charisma, intelligence and supernaturally-gifted persuasive abilities of Christian Berry had been more than adequate to secure Garber's loyalty (that and promises of reward following the Reckoning—empty promises to be certain).

Gathering his foes into the basement had been an exercise in ego. A human frailty. Something to which Jonas should not be victim.

He had wanted shock and awe. He had wanted to see their faces as he described the culmination of his grand plans and witness their horror at the truth of his pending rule. He had perhaps wanted to hear them beg for mercy.

Instead, John Michaels had called him crazy. There had been no devastating realization on their part of his triumph. No wails of horror. No concession of his superior intellect. No pleading for mercy.

Mental institution. That's what Michaels had recommended.

The whole thing had been so utterly...disappointing.

It was the first letdown Jonas had experienced on this glorious day. The first sense of misalignment with destiny. He was disappointed not just with the encounter in the basement but in himself. He should be above such things.

So he first entered the lecture hall in a blaze of artificial excitement to compensate for that feeling of disappointment, but as he stoked the righteous passion of his followers, he found himself swept into the moment.

Over the course of the spiritual awakenings, he had used each engagement as an opportunity to erect a new metaphorical domino in the minds of his forty-four. Just a simple tenet that, individually, was both logical and meaningful. It stood on its own. Tonight, Christian Berry tipped the first domino, thus toppling the next and the next. He guided his flock on a journey of righteousness to which the only conclusion would be to execute whatever plans he laid out—no matter how heinous such a thing might have seemed in a previous life—and join him in everlasting glory on this day of Reckoning.

As he spoke, Berry's disappointment morphed into anger, first at himself, for his folly of ego. Then came the realization that ego was not a weakness. It was his *right*. He was the chosen one. The infidels in the basement were in the wrong. They *should* have begged. It was *their* egos that had skewed what should have been a magnificent encounter. To point, it was *his* ego. John Michaels.

Berry preached with escalating intensity. His followers were frothing now. Many had already risen from their seats. Only a few more dominos to fall and the outcome would be unstoppable.

He glanced at the clock at the back of the lecture hall. Almost out of time. Lucas Blankshire, the head of TSC's chemistry department, would be giving his speech on the stage outside at this moment. With the bonfire crowd tuned to the spotlighted speakers on the stage, no one would pay attention to Berry's followers when they filed out of the building.

Berry would then head to the roof. He would address the High Council. Then the Elite Guard would join them with his father. And with John Michaels.

Let Michaels witness the Reckoning in person. Then he will meet his fate.

Time for the finishing domino in his sermon, a diamond in the rough for any of his followers who still harbored an attachment of this current day of triumph with their old associations of religion.

"As we read in First Samuel," Berry shouted, sweat dripping from his hair as he raised an open Bible, "the Lord Almighty said to punish the Amalekites for what they did to his people. Now go and smite Amalek, he said, and utterly destroy all that they have and spare them not. Slay both man and woman, infant and suckling, ox and sheep, camel and ass."

Berry dropped the Bible onto the floor. He wasn't reading from it anyway. The book had just been for effect. The passage chosen only because it mentioned killing kids. That the verses were delivered starkly out of context mattered not; it gave his message some nice oomph. He raised both hands, palms toward his flock, and shouted.

"Man and woman! Infant and suckling! Destroy them! Spare them not!"

He clenched his fists and brought his elbows to his sides, like he was performing a chin-up on an invisible bar.

"Evil is upon us, brothers and sisters! We will spare them not! On this day of Reckoning, all will be made right, for it is *righteousness* that drives us!"

Scattered shouts of affirmation from the sheep soldiers.

"The children are gathered in the gymnasium of the school. Infant and suckling." He lowered his voice. "You will spare them not. For this is a cleansing of fire and of blood."

He pointed to the door. "Outside this building are the tools of your mission. Axes honed to a lethal edge. Weapons of righteousness."

Slade stood next to the door. Berry would not have thought it possible, but his lieutenant appeared even more invigorated than before. Slade had been swept into Berry's performance as well.

"Follow Slade from this room. He will guide you to the shed and distribute among your ranks the weapons you require to administer this cleansing. He will then remain at the bonfire to fulfill his mission. As for you, brothers and sisters, you will then march—not run nor walk—you will *march* to the school. For you are an army of justice, and you will execute this mission and eradicate the plague of sin and join me in glory upon the Reckoning."

He lowered his head in a dramatic pause, then raised it once more to sweep his eyes over his flock.

"The time is upon us. Go!"

His followers sprung from their seats and rushed toward the door. Slade kicked it open and led them out. Berry remained at the front of the room, supervising their exit.

There was no worry of anyone stopping them. The axe shed was on the outskirts of the bonfire field. No one would pay them any mind. Jonas's father had earlier negated the possibility of police interference. The Abramsville Chief of Police—conveniently on the roof at this very moment as part of the High Council—had ensured the 911 operators on duty had been informed of one campus fraternity's ill-conceived plan for a practical joke of calling in a band of hooligans armed with axes. Any such calls were to be ignored by the department this evening.

And within this room, the dominos had all fallen as planned. There were no objections. No last-minute challenges of "but wait, they're children!" The drugs and his planning and his charismatic persuasion had carried the day.

He deserved an ego. He deserved the power. He deserved to be the chosen one.

And it would all be his on this very night.

And once the power was his, once he had *become*, the first thing he would do is deal with his adversaries. John Michaels first, followed by all the enemies in the basement. One by one.

And then their families.

CHAPTER 89

JOHN MICHAELS SAT in the suede-upholstered chair, his handcuffed wrists in his lap. He had been returned to the well-appointed office on the fourth floor where he had earlier enjoyed a full day of quality time chained to the toilet. The chair was an upgrade from the bathroom floor. At least he had that going for him.

And as bad as things were, all he had to do was look across the room at Hiram Kane to see how things could be worse. During the time John had been in the basement for Jonas Kane's summit of self-congratulation, the four gigantors had stood Hiram up and secured him to a backboard on a rolling dolly. Thick cargo straps encircled Hiram's broad chest and shoulders, his waist, his legs and his feet, holding him tight against the backboard. A smaller nylon strap crossed his forehead, keeping his head upright. A tightly rolled hand towel had been placed behind his neck, ensuring his head didn't loll and causing his chin to jut upward. The towel was white. Must have come from the all-white bathroom.

John didn't know if Hiram's current condition had rendered him physically unable to speak or if he simply chose to remain silent, but no words were uttered by him to either John or to the four apes who guarded them both. The steroid crew each held one of the antique-looking daggers John had seen displayed on the table earlier.

John was surprised by the swell of pity he felt for the old man. It was like watching an aged lion surrounded by jackals. The once-feared king of the jungle reduced to prey for lesser predators. And yet, this was the man who had orchestrated the hell in New Mexico. All the innocent people who died there. Friends. And family. And in the years since the desert horror, the specter of Hiram Kane had loomed as a shadow over John and Sarah's life, the boogeyman John feared may someday hide in his daughter's closet.

A bitter smile twisted John's mouth. He had come to Abramsville in the hope of finding Hiram Kane, clinging to a thread of belief that the scarecrow preacher in the news footage was Jonas Kane. John had seen an opportunity to end the fear, to protect his family, to make certain DJ didn't have to grow up worrying about someone discovering her true identity and killing her in an act of psychotic revenge against her parents. John had seen this as his one chance to stop Hiram Kane.

Well, here they were. Hiram Kane was stopped. He would never terrorize anyone again. John's wish was fulfilled. But be careful what you wish for because you just might end up sharing a nicely furnished holding pen awaiting your own impending doom along with the guy you wished dead.

John's mind raced. Before Jonas left to lead what he referred to as the 'final meeting,' he commanded the fearsome foursome that if John spoke, they were to cut out his tongue. This was said right in front of John, so it was clearly a warning. And not very subtle.

John had briefly debated trying to engage in conversation anyway, but when he saw the way the brute squad fingered their new dagger toys, he decided they might be not only willing but eager to execute the tongue extraction plan.

A swell of noise could be heard from the bonfire field. It was fully dark now. The crowd was roaring over what someone had just said into the microphone on the stage outside. All those people out there who wanted their football team to beat the other football team tomorrow. Yay.

Tomorrow, all John wanted was for his wife and daughter to be safe. He would be dead. So would Cutter. Between the concussion and the unattended ulcer, John already felt like hammered dogshit. The added guilt of having gotten Cutter involved made it worse. And the trifecta was the fact that by dragging Cutter into this, John had also managed to eliminate a dedicated protector for Sarah and DJ. They would be on their own now.

A pulsing beat of music could be felt in the office again. Songs had been interspersed between the speakers outside for the past several minutes. Go, fight, win. Rah-rah. Thousands of people listening to that music were going to die tonight. None of them were on John's mind. Sarah and DJ occupied the entirety of his thoughts.

What would he give to save them?

The door to the office opened and Jonas Kane, the madman of the hour himself, poked his head in to address the four beasts.

"Give me five minutes then bring my father and Michaels to the roof. The time has come."

And with that, the door closed, and he was gone.

Five minutes until John would join Jonas Kane on the roof.

He looked at Hiram Kane. Still no words, no movement whatsoever, but there was a rage in the older man's eyes that could boil the sea.

It was a bad night all around.

CHAPTER 90

JONAS KANE HAD LEFT THE BOWIE KNIFE on the table.
Cutter couldn't see the surface of the lab table from his seated position on the floor, but he had seen Kane drop it there after he'd murdered the kid. In cold blood. The act of a coward. Cutter had heard the knife clatter onto the stainless steel when Kane walked out. And Garber hadn't picked it up at any point after that. Cutter had been paying close attention.

Now Garber was outside the lab. He was still watching—Cutter could see him on the other side of the safety glass in the door—but he could no longer hear them. That was good.

Getting Garber out of the room had been key. Cutter hadn't really expected it would happen—leaving his prisoners wasn't exactly professional—but sometimes things just worked out. And it's not like Garber was a trained enforcer. He was a chemistry professor. An amateur who had made a mistake befitting his status as such. Still, kind of dumb for a smart guy.

Between that mistake and the knife, there was a glimmer of hope that wouldn't have been present otherwise, and if you're in a dark enough place, a glimmer could shine awful bright.

In the end, it came down to something Jonas Kane had said, something that brought home a concept that had been floating in Cutter's mind for quite some time, and not just recently, ever since returning from the desert of New Mexico. It had been running through his thoughts like a song you can't get out of your head.

He looked to his right. After Kane had used the knife—Cutter's own knife—to slit Andrew's throat, the poor kid had simply slumped back against the wall. His hands duct-taped behind his back; the young man hadn't even been able to clutch at his own wounded neck. Without even a nominal staunching of the flow, he had bled out quickly. Minimal struggle.

Cutter regretted his assumptions about Andrew. The kid was innocent. He had even tried to help. And he sure as hell didn't deserve to go out like that at the hands of a monster like Jonas Kane.

The pool of liquid crimson expanded around Andrew. Because he hadn't fallen over to the side, the blood spread uniformly. It hadn't yet reached Cutter but would in a minute. That was fine. He needed that minute. To talk to her.

"How you holding up, Trish?"

The girl looked at him with wet eyes. She was crying, but it wasn't the same as before. Cutter didn't blame her for the outburst when Andrew died. Screaming. Crying. Those were natural reactions. Human. No fault in that. She had since fought back the shock and regained control of her emotions. That was admirable. And tears were okay. Wet or not, what was important was that she was looking at him with *clear* eyes. If things played out the way he expected, he was going to need her. So was John.

"Not so great," she sniffed, "if we're being honest."

"Always the best policy," Cutter agreed. "You hang in there. How you doing, hot shot?"

Eric was seated on the other side of Trish. He leaned forward so Cutter could see him. He smiled and made brief eye contact before he returned to scanning the room.

"No progress to report down here," he said.

Cutter nodded. Eric knew what he was asking but that had been a vague response. A new thought occurred to Cutter. One that had obviously already crossed Eric's mind. The detective was sharp.

Cutter glanced to the door. Garber was watching them through the window but not with scrutiny. Was he feigning disinterest? Cutter wondered if the clean room had a sound system which allowed visitors to listen in to the activity of the lab. He didn't see any microphones but couldn't take any chances. Maybe the professor wasn't so dumb after all.

Eric had been right to speak in generalities. Just in case.

And he had said nothing good was happening down there. That was what Cutter anticipated. Duct tape was a bitch. Cutter never thought he'd be glad to be shackled by his own handcuffs, but duct tape would have put him in the same poor situation in which Eric found himself.

But he wasn't worried about Eric. He had training. And moxie. Cutter could tell. When the time came, Eric would do what had to be done. Cutter's focus for the moment was on Trish, and not just because he had taken a shine to the young lady, but because if what Cutter suspected was true, then her role in this would be bigger than his own.

And there was one other reason.

"Trish, I want you to listen to me," Cutter stated. "And this is important."

"I'm listening," she said. Her voice had a sense of resignation to it. Cutter didn't like the sound of it.

"The other day at that barbecue restaurant, when we all first got together and told our stories and realized our connection to the Kane family, do you remember that?"

"I do."

"I told you both about my part of the story in New Mexico, but I didn't tell you why I was out there in the first place. Truth is, I was running from something," he cleared his throat. Honesty may be the best policy but that didn't make it the easiest. "A ghost. I was running from a ghost."

"Are you serious?" Trish asked.

"Not a floating-through-walls and rattling-chains ghost. Call it a memory that haunted me. Of a girl." He coughed. Even now it was hard to talk about. "When I was still with the Rangers, my partner and I had tracked down a very bad guy, a cult leader. The bastard liked children. And not unlike Jonas Kane under his Christian Berry guise, this guy twisted the words of the Bible to his own warped ends. That boils my blood."

Cutter glanced at the floor on the last word. The crimson pool continued to creep toward him, but not there yet.

"By the time we found him, it was too late. Thirteen kids were dead. One lived. But only for a while. The damage that had been done...it went deeper than her flesh." Cutter's voice dropped to a hoarse whisper. "I got the bad guy, but I wasn't able to save her. Not in any way that mattered."

"I'm sorry, Cutter," Trish said.

"I remember reading about that case," Eric added. "That sucked."

"Yep," Cutter nodded. "It did. And I couldn't live with that outcome—couldn't live with myself—so I ran off to the desert of New Mexico, and you know the rest."

"Why, Cutter?" Trish asked. "Not about the desert. You said it was important for me to hear this. Why now? Why at all?"

"I'm telling you all this for a reason. Because it may have taken a lot of time to beat some sense into me, but I learned a lesson out of it. I spent my life in law enforcement, trying to stop the bad guys and protect the innocent. What I learned is that saving the masses may be important, but sometimes saving just one person can make all the difference."

"Are you about to tell us the parable of the lost sheep?" Eric asked.

Cutter leaned forward and saw Eric grinning.

"What? I went to Sunday school," Eric said before returning to a scan of the room.

Cutter assumed Eric was still looking for a way out. Something with which to cut the duct tape. He wasn't going to find it. The best answer was the knife on the table, but having your hands bound behind you ensured a slow and awkward process of rising to your feet. None of them could scramble up and reach the knife before Garber would open the door and unload Cutter's revolver on them.

Not yet.

"Good allegory," Cutter agreed. "The shepherd leaves his flock of ninety-nine to save the one lost sheep, and he does it because that one sheep matters."

"It only matters if the shepherd cares," Trish muttered.

And there it was. Cutter had suspected it.

"Now, Trish, you didn't believe that horse pucky Garber was shoveling, did you?"

"What do you mean?" she asked.

"That God has forgotten us."

"Kind of hard for me to believe otherwise at the moment," she looked at Andrew's bleeding body as she spoke. "Life is a game, full of one random cruelty after another."

"Maybe it is a game, but it's not a game of chance," Cutter responded. "'God doesn't play dice.' Einstein said that. Smart man." He paused. Another element to his long-running train of thought clicked into place. "Maybe more like chess."

He looked toward the door again. Garber was still standing on the other side of the glass. He was playing on his phone. Son of a bitch was bored. Good.

"I'm no philosopher—and certainly no chess master—but I've had some time lately for thinking. Turns out retirement is good for that. So is surveillance. I've been thinking an awful lot about our current situation. About good and evil. Truth be told, I don't know if Jonas Kane is crazy or not. If he is, our little group here is in trouble. But if he's not crazy, if what he was telling us is somehow real, then the whole world is in a heap of trouble."

"Mark me down for a crazy vote," Eric remarked.

"Probably so, but I do believe he's going to make good on murdering thousands at the bonfire tonight," Cutter said, "and killing all those kids."

"Yeah," Eric agreed.

"That qualifies as crazy," Trish offered.

"No question," Cutter concurred, "but one thing he said tonight *didn't* strike me as crazy. In fact, given everything happening, it fits right into what I've come to believe."

"What's that?" Trish asked.

"Something I've seen through a life in law enforcement. There are plenty of wrong-place-wrong-time stories where bad things happen. Funny thing is, there are also lots of stories where against all likelihood someone was in the right place at the right time and managed to prevent something bad from happening."

"Sounds like coincidence on both sides," Trish said. "The random game."

"Or two sides playing against one another," Eric mused almost to himself, "making moves and countermoves."

Cutter smiled. The detective had a talent for deduction.

"Now go back to that barbecue joint," Cutter continued, "and the stories we told each other about our pasts. Think about the extraordinary series of events that allowed John to escape the desert, that allowed us to stop Marcus Kane's program, that allowed Eric and your father—because Trish, your dad is a part of this just like you are— to track Silas Kane, to stop him. A few minutes ago, Jonas Kane stood right there and spoke of the cosmic forces that had to have been at work to draw this group of people together. I believe that's true but not in the way he thinks. Because however it happened, here we are—all of us—just in time for Jonas Kane's Reckoning."

"And we're supposed to be what," Trish interrupted, "chess pieces moved into place on an unseen board?"

She sounded angry. That could be worse. Angry was better than defeated. Anger could find its way to resolve, and that's what Cutter needed from her. Without resolve, without *belief*, they were never going to stop Jonas Kane.

"Not quite," he responded. "Chess pieces don't get to make a choice. We do. Part of that whole idea of free will the good Lord gave us. Some people choose to walk a dark path and others suffer as a result, but some believe in something better, and those people can make a powerful difference in this world."

"And you think that's us?" Trish asked. "We're instruments of God gathered here to stop Jonas Kane?"

Cutter glanced to the window. Garber was still only half-watching. Still bored. Cutter looked to the floor. The pool of blood had almost finished its creeping expansion. It was just about time.

"Yes ma'am, that's the thought that's been running through my head. That for whatever reason, we're here to be the force for good."

"I hate to tell you this," she sighed. "But if that's the case, I'm a pretty poor choice." Her voice broke on the last word. Fresh tears.

"I ain't exactly an ideal candidate either, but here we are," he replied. "And I'm no Bible scholar, but I can tell you the good book is chock-full of stories of broken, unfit, poor-choice people who God picked anyway."

The spreading blood reached Cutter. It touched his jeans where he sat on the floor. Whenever he'd cut his hands back home while working with barbed wire—or doing whatever other fool thing—he would wipe the blood onto his jeans. Maggie would scold him. Remind him how hard it was to get blood out in the wash.

Maggie would not approve of anything he was about to do.

"God would choose those people and all he asked was for them to have faith, and they could move mountains. What we have in front of us is a big mountain."

"Damn big," Eric chimed in. The comment made Trish laugh. That was good.

Hands secured behind his back, Cutter pushed his left thumb into his right palm and wrapped his fingers tightly around it. This was going to hurt like hell.

"So what you need, Trish, is to dig deep and see if you can find that faith."

He tightened his fist around the thumb and began to pull. Keeping a straight face wasn't easy, but he couldn't risk Garber seeing something he shouldn't.

"Easier said than done," she said.

As Cutter struggled in quiet millimeters, one more thing leapt into his mind, something he hadn't noticed about Trish until seeing her tonight, something minor, but for some reason in this moment, it seemed important.

"Nothing worth doing is easy," Cutter said with a stilted grunt. He changed his grip on his thumb. "So listen close. That cross around your neck. Don't pretend it's just a keepsake or a piece of jewelry. It can save your life. And much more."

Cutter gritted his teeth, clenched his fist and punched toward the floor. There was a loud pop as his thumb fractured and dislodged from the joint. He closed his lips against a reflexive groan of pain. He sounded like a startled horse.

He looked to the door. Garber remained as he was on the other side of the glass. He hadn't noticed. Neither had Trish. The girl was dealing with a lot at the moment. Maybe mentioning the cross had been too much, but it had felt important, and he wasn't going to question his instincts. Not now.

"Cutter, I—" she started then choked back a small sob. "I don't know if I *can* believe."

He lowered his broken left hand into the blood that was finally pooled behind him, using his right hand to scoop and smear it from wrist to knuckles as well as possible.

He leaned forward and saw Eric staring at him, eyes wide. He had heard the crack. Cutter nodded.

"I know it sounds like a lot, Trish," Cutter said as he rotated his left hand back and forth, lubing the skin under the handcuff with blood. He gripped the steel bracelet with his right hand and began working his left out of the shackle. He suppressed another groan of pain as the steel slipped over the vacated indentation of his thumb joint. The useless digit flopped against the bracelet as it passed.

Couldn't do that with duct tape.

"Cutter..." Eric began.

"Look at me, Trish," Cutter interrupted, cutting Eric off. The time had come, and this was too important. Trish leaned forward and made eye contact. Her eyes were wet with tears but clear. Girl had grit. Now she needed resolve. And faith. "It's not always easy to believe, but when the chips are down, it's all that matters."

Cutter braced himself. He was no longer a young man. Quick moves hadn't been in his repertoire for quite some time, but he was only going to get one shot at this. If he failed, it wasn't just over for him, but for Trish and Eric and thousands more.

He'd been talking the talk for Trish. Time to walk the walk.

"Trish, I believe in something far bigger than myself," he said. He glanced at Eric. The steely expression on his face told Cutter that he was ready. "And because I believe, I'm not afraid to do this."

Cutter looked to the door and grinned as he brought his blood-smeared hands in front of him, mangled thumb hanging from his left hand and handcuffs dangling from his right wrist.

Garber's eyes went wide on the other side of the window as Cutter scrambled to his feet in a race against time.

CHAPTER 91

SLADE STONE REGARDED THE AXE in his hand. It was light. Just like all the others. An occasion as momentous as this deserved to have real weapons. Something with weight. Like those medieval battle axes that had big, curved blades extending on either side from the top of the handle. Those always seemed like they had *heft*.

He passed the too-light axe to the guy standing at the door of the shed. Slade had forgotten his name. It wasn't worth remembering. The guy took the axe and looked at the blade with reverence. He had skinny arms. Probably couldn't lift one of those battle axes anyway.

The guy stepped away from the door and was replaced by another dude. This one also had small arms, but he looked meaner. At least that was something.

These axes would do the job. They were sharp. And probably worked best for the group that would be using them. Christian had said so, and he always knew the right thing.

Slade could hear the yells and shouts of the bonfire crowd through the shed's thin walls. The noise made him think of a football game, when you were on the field and the roar of the crowd washed over you as you collided with a player on the other team. If it was a good hit, the other guy wouldn't get up. Then maybe accidentally step on his fingers while you walked back to the huddle. Cleats were excellent for that, though the plastic spikes were blunt at the ends. Metal spikes would be better.

He passed another axe through the door. The noise was pumping him up. He was ready for some action. He wanted to be right in the middle of it, but this was his job for the moment. And it was important.

When Slade started passing out the axes, he treated the first few with reverence, like he was presiding over a formal ceremony. That got old after the first dozen. Now, he was just handing them out. Get this group moving. Get this show on the road.

Slade was above these soldiers in Christian's hierarchy. He knew that. Slade was a leader. These people were followers. That was why he had the more important responsibilities. This group would go slaughter kids. That would be easy. Kids couldn't fight back. And, at best, they'd each kill a handful.

Slade's place was here at the bonfire. This is where the real action would take place. Thousands would die. Tens of thousands. And when it happened, the Reckoning would take place. And Slade would be here for it. He was impervious. Christian had told him. He had always known this to be true, and he felt it more than ever tonight.

He reached one hand to his back pocket and felt the outline of his phone. He had to be prepared if Christian needed him. Be on alert.

He passed another axe out the door. Almost done here. Couldn't be that many more outstretched hands. And once this task was complete, he would leave the shed and move into the crowd.

When the fire came down, he wanted to feel the heat and see faces melting all around him. These people deserved to die. They weren't worthy.

CHAPTER 92

JONAS KANE ASCENDED THE FINAL STEPS and pushed the metal bar to open the door. As he stepped through the opening onto the roof of the Physical Sciences building, a cool breeze caressed his face. The night was welcoming him. The air carried an aroma that left a taste of kerosene in his mouth. The bonfire logs had been soaked in jet fuel, an indication the time was very near.

The door closed behind him with a clank and the heads of the four men standing at the edge of the roof turned in unison. On the end was Lucas Blankshire. His duties as guest emcee complete, he had made his way to the roof as planned. That meant Jonas's timing was perfect. Of course.

The members of the High Council each offered him a curt nod of acknowledgement before returning their attention to the festivities below. Jonas was not the man upon whom they awaited. He was not worthy of their attention.

How that would soon change.

Jonas crossed the few steps to the men. With their backs to him, he was able to inspect them unnoticed. Of chief concern was the chief himself—Leonard Barnes, Chief of the Abramsville Police Department. Jonas stepped close behind him and scrutinized his belt, his lower back and his ankles. No holstered gun on his hip. No telltale bulges under his clothing. He was unarmed.

Jonas knew Hiram had long ago established that Barnes was not to carry a weapon in his presence. It was nice to see the Chief continued to follow orders. *Thanks, Dad,* thought Jonas.

A similar inspection of the other members of the High Council revealed they were similarly unarmed. As expected. Jonas would have been quite surprised to find any of them bearing weapons of any kind, but it was always better to be safe than sorry.

Everyone was accounted for. The Chief, who had ensured the school massacre would be executed without interference until it was far too late. The wealthy tech company CEO, who had funded much of the work to date. The owner of the construction company, who so ably placed the doghouse atop the bonfire which would rain cleansing fire upon the thousands gathered. And the head of TSC's chemistry department, who had arranged facilities, ordered necessary base compounds and mixtures through academic channels so they would not arouse suspicion, and provided them this lovely view of the pending carnage.

They had given so much to the cause. Tonight, they would give the remainder.

Jonas stepped to the waist-high wall at the edge of the roof to observe the activity. The crowd of TSC supporters was in a fervor. They were facing the stage to engage in the last of the rallying cries. The rhythmic beat of the drum corps erupted to punctuate whatever was happening. The throng below yelled something in unison about beating the bulldogs. Jonas wrinkled his nose. Layered on top of the kerosene scent in the air, he was certain he could smell the alcohol and body odor of the mass of humanity crowding the bonfire field.

He checked his watch. Almost there.

"Gentlemen," he addressed the men in the line, "if you'll please step back. I have a few words in advance of the commencement. If you'll indulge me, I'm certain you'll find it quite interesting."

The four members of the High Council took a few steps away from the wall, and Jonas positioned himself between them and the action on the bonfire field. They were looking at him with a mixture of expectation and annoyance.

His lips curled into a grin of excitement and menace.

The Reckoning was upon him.

CHAPTER 93

ERIC HAD SUSPECTED Cutter was about to do something, but that anticipation did not prepare him for the sight of the former Texas Ranger revealing his newly freed, blood-smeared hands (complete with one dangling, dislocated thumb). The spectacle was horrific, but there was no time to gag or gawk. Cutter was on his feet.

Across the room, the door handle was turning.

And Garber had a gun.

Getting up with your hands duct-taped behind your back under any circumstances falls somewhere on the spectrum between awkward and difficult, but Eric was an athlete. Thought left him and instinct took over. He pushed the back of his head against the wall, using the muscles in his neck to gain quick momentum for his upper body to arc forward. He heard the whoosh of the door opening and felt the change in the room's air pressure.

He tucked one knee low and rolled forward, his shoulder crashing into the floor in front of him. He heard the echo of Cutter's boots on the tile floor as the cowboy rushed toward the lab table.

Eric pressed his cheek against the cold tile, using his head and neck for leverage as he drew his knees to his chest and got his toes beneath him.

Two seconds had ticked away since Cutter had made his move. An eternity.

Eric's knee found purchase beneath him, limited stability but enough support to straighten his back. The boom of the heavy caliber handgun filled the room, echoing off the bare walls and tile floor. It was deafening.

Eric's ears rang as he pressed his weight upward using his stable leg, bringing his other foot beneath him, a clumsy action but the only thing he could do. He felt a harsh twinge in his hamstring.

Damn.

Another shot boomed. Eric could hear nothing else. Was that a shout? His ears were ringing.

He lunged forward, hands still bound behind him, legs pumping to drive his forward momentum, an uncontrolled headlong charge toward the other side of the lab table.

Four seconds gone by. He was too slow.

Several short, unbalanced strides and he risked shifting his eyes from the floor toward where he was hurtling.

A quick glance. Cutter stood between the lab table and the door. Garber right in front of him. Almost chest-to-chest. Garber's gun was pointed into Cutter's midsection.

Eric planted his outside foot and launched himself, an awkward human missile targeted at the bad guy with the gun.

His shoulder collided with Garber's ribs. They both careened toward the wall as a third shot erupted from the revolver, the sound so loud Eric felt it reverberate past his eardrum and into his jawbone.

He crashed to the floor next to Garber and rolled to the side. He wouldn't be able to regain his feet before Garber could fire, but he could kick the bastard.

He drew back his foot, targeting Garber's gun-hand, but saw the revolver lying on the tile. Garber had dropped the gun. Both of his hands were at his neck, fingers touching the hilt of the Bowie knife, its blade buried deep in the center of Garber's throat. His eyes were wide in shock. Crimson streams spurted from either side of the blade and coated the professor's fingers. He held the blood-covered digits in front of his face with a look of disbelief. It was the last thing he'd ever see.

Garber slumped to the floor.

Eric turned to Cutter. Three shots fired. Did he—?

Cutter was leaning against the lab table. One hand on the tabletop, supporting him. One hip against the side of the table, his blood-soaked jeans leaving a smear of red on the stainless steel.

He nodded to Eric. It had been less than half a minute since the cowboy's eyes had blazed with gray fire when he revealed his incredible escape artistry. Now, those eyes were drained of flame. Cutter looked tired. He said something to Eric—his lips moved—but in the aftermath of the gunfire, Eric couldn't hear anything except the ringing in his ears.

Cutter pushed himself away from the lab table, taking a halting step toward Eric. That's when Eric noticed.

The ringing in his ears diminished by degrees. Eric could hear something besides the echoing ghost of gunfire. He could hear Trish. She was screaming. She had seen the whole thing.

Cutter covered the remaining distance to Eric and dropped to his knees on the tile. His left hand—the one with the mangled thumb—was pressed to his stomach. Fresh blood seeped through his fingers. On that same arm, there was a hole in the sleeve of his denim jacket. The faded blue was soaked crimson from his bicep to his forearm.

In the movies, the hero gets shot and the wound transitions to the importance of a mosquito bite within minutes, an inconvenience about which to offer quips and wisecracks. In real life, bullets tear muscle, shatter bone, rip arteries and fire a code-red response through every nerve and pain receptor in that region of the body. It cripples the gunshot victim with blinding pain. Shock or unconsciousness typically follow.

And yet, here knelt Cutter Valentine, wits still about him, leaning over the bleeding body of Dr. Garber. His lips moved again. Eric heard words, but the ringing distorted them. He'd need a few more seconds.

Cutter kept his damaged left hand pressed to his damaged midsection while his right grasped the handle of the Bowie knife and pulled it from Garber's throat.

Eric's ears were definitely improving. He heard a wet sucking sound as the blade slipped free.

Knife still in hand, Cutter held the blade upright and twirled it twice. No words necessary.

Eric rolled to his other side, turning his back to Cutter. He felt the duct tape give way. One clean motion. No sawing necessary. Cutter's knife was sharp.

Eric pulled his hands apart, the adhesive tugging at his skin, and scrambled to his feet. The remnants of the tape clung to one wrist. Eric ripped it free and threw it to the floor.

Cutter coughed and sat on the tile. Eric leaned over and put his hand on Cutter's shoulder, above the bloody wound on that arm. Cutter looked at him and smiled. Beneath his thick mustache, his teeth were red with blood.

That came from the inside, Eric thought. *He coughed that up.*

That was a bad sign. Very bad.

Cutter proffered the knife. Eric took it and raced across the room to Trish. Her eyes never left Cutter. Fresh tears streamed down her cheeks.

Eric pushed her shoulders away from the wall, leaned behind her and sliced through the duct tape, careful not to nick the skin inside her wrists. The last thing they needed was more blood.

Trish was on her feet and kneeling beside Cutter in a flash, duct tape trailing from one wrist.

"Cutter, why?" she cried.

Her words were clear, the ringing in Eric's ears now a fading backdrop.

Cutter's eyes no longer blazed, but there was still steel in those gray orbs.

"Because sometimes," he told her, "saving one is just as important as saving thousands."

Eric squatted in front of Cutter and assessed his condition. The bullet wound in his arm was bad. The one in his abdomen was far worse. Eric raised his head to look around the room for something with which to staunch the blood flow, but Cutter grabbed the front of Eric's shirt and with surprising strength jerked his attention back to him.

"No time for fooling around," he drawled. "Don't worry about me."

"But Cutter—" Eric started.

The cowboy coughed then turned his head and spat blood onto the floor.

He glanced to Trish. "Pardon me," he muttered. "Now listen up. The clock is ticking, and innocent lives are on the line."

Cutter's good hand reached into his pants pocket and extracted a set of keys. He held them out to Eric.

"You take my truck. Shotgun in the rack. Get to that school. Protect them kids."

Eric nodded. No argument. Cutter turned his head toward Trish.

"You know how to use a handgun?"

She nodded. "Dad taught me."

"Then you take my gun. Get up to the roof. Stop Kane. Save John."

Trish retrieved the revolver from the floor, then shook her head. "Cutter, I can't."

"Yes, you can, kiddo." He touched her cheek with his good hand. "You have to."

She closed her eyes and pressed her cheek into his palm.

Cutter smiled, terrible crimson between his teeth, then lowered his hand. He pawed at Garber's body and retrieved the dead man's cell phone.

"You two get out of here," he snarled. "Time's wasting."

"But you—" Trish started.

"Go!" He raised his voice then coughed at the effort. An awful wet sound.

Eric straightened and took Trish by the arm, pulling her to her feet.

"We have to get moving," he told her. He didn't want to leave Cutter, but he also knew the Ranger was right, and he wasn't going to let this sacrifice be in vain.

He pushed Trish toward the door. She glanced at Cutter, then turned and ran out of the lab, pistol in hand. Eric followed but stopped at the doorway and looked back. Cutter sat on the floor. Bad hand against his bleeding stomach. Good hand cradling the cell phone.

He should be wearing his hat, Eric thought. *He looks wrong without the cowboy hat.*

"Call an ambulance," he admonished.

Cutter nodded.

Eric sprinted through the clean room and into the hallway after Trish.

CHAPTER 94

THE STAIRWELL OF THE PHYSICAL SCIENCES BUILDING consisted of concrete and steel. It was cold. John Michaels reached the platform at the top, a small square of flat concrete, descending steps behind him, a door to the roof in front of him.

The four apes were also to his rear, almost to the top of the stairs. They each toted a corner of the dolly and backboard to which Hiram Kane was strapped. He was a big man, but the brutes who carried him were strong. They had navigated the stairs without issue.

For a moment, John pictured himself turning around and kicking at the two beasts in front. He had the high ground. He could probably strike one in the face, perhaps even make him fall. But what good would it do? Best case scenario would be the crew would drop the dolly. It would clatter on the stairs along with Hiram's limp body. Perhaps a couple of them would stumble. Maybe twist an ankle. But they wouldn't fall far. The stairs doubled back on themselves every twelve steps. Their fall would stop at the next platform below. Injury would be a maybe; pissing them off would be a certainty. And each of these guys carried a dagger tucked into the back of his waistband.

And where would John go? He couldn't get past them and race down the stairs. Heading the other direction and going through the door would just put him on the roof. Not much of an escape plan there.

"Move it," said one of the brutes in front (this one wearing a red TSC t-shirt with the sleeves cut off), "it's time."

His wrists still shackled in front of him by the handcuffs, John put both hands onto the metal bar affixed to the door. He pushed, and the door opened.

His ears were met with the sound of thousands of people screaming.

CHAPTER 95

THE WORLD WAS GROWING DARK for Cutter Valentine. He had arranged himself into a seated position against the wall. Next to him lay Garber's lifeless body, a growing pool of blood spreading around him. A match set to the crimson pool surrounding Andrew's body across the room. One deserved it, the other didn't, but both were dead just the same.

Death comes to us all, thought Cutter.

He raised the cell phone in front of his face. It was hard to focus on the screen. The edges of his vision were fading, like looking through a soft tunnel.

The screen was still live. It hadn't locked. Thank the good Lord for that.

Cutter used his thumb to access the keypad screen for dialing.

His arm ached, but his stomach burned. On the plus side, the burn had gone from a searing pain to a throbbing warmth that pulsated from his gut in tendrils through the rest of his body.

That was shock. That was why the pain had transformed into something more bearable.

Probably.

But his mind was clear. Enough to make a phone call at least.

A succession of violent coughs racked his body causing him to almost drop the phone. He held on. When the coughing fit had passed, the taste of salt and copper was stronger in Cutter's mouth. He turned his head and spit out a greater quantity of blood than he expected. It spattered on the tile next to him, deep crimson into which was mixed an ominous, blackish bile.

Eric had told him to call an ambulance. That would be a waste. They wouldn't reach him in time. Cutter knew he was fading, and there wouldn't be time for more than one phone call.

He needed to help Eric and Trish. Save the kids. Save the people at the bonfire. He couldn't call the police. Doing so should have been his first instinct, but it didn't feel right. The Kane family had proven themselves to have connections far and wide. What if they had gotten to the Abramsville police, too?

Only one phone call before the world would finish dimming around him.

He wanted to call Maggie. To hear her voice one last time. She'd call him an old fool. She'd cry. She'd tell him how much she loved him. He'd say the same to her. He would use these last few moments to tell her she was the best thing that could have ever happened to this old cowboy. And he'd tell her to say goodbye to their son for him. Robert would be fine. He was a grown man now. He'd tell her to let him know how proud he was of him.

That was what he wanted with every fiber of his dying being.

Cutter focused on the keypad. The tunnel was narrowing. More dark in his vision than light. Time was almost out. One phone call only.

He punched in a number that was not his wife's and hit the green button.

I'm sorry, Maggie.

CHAPTER 96

THE DECIBEL LEVEL OF THE SCREAMING was unreal. It felt to John as if he'd stepped from the stairwell onto the roof above a rock concert. He could hear drums pounding a beat, and the crowds below yelling and cheering. He could hear an amplified voice—someone speaking through a microphone—but couldn't understand what he was saying. Whatever it was, the crowd was eating it up. They were excited. They didn't know they were also doomed.

John saw the architect of that doom now. Jonas Kane was standing on the other side of four men who were facing Jonas with their backs to John, and in the midst of what had to be a virtuoso performance of crazy. His eyes were wild. The wind swept across the rooftop, blowing his hair dramatically around his gaunt face. He was speaking in a forceful tone about destiny and power.

Jonas's eyes flicked toward John. He had spotted him through the space between two of the men in his small audience. He took a deep breath.

"Gentlemen," Jonas began, "we have a special guest who'll be joining us for the Reckoning. This is John. Say 'hi' to the men, John."

The men turned toward John. He noticed their eyes stayed on him for only a moment before looking past him to the door of the stairwell. With the assistance of the brute squad, Hiram Kane was making his not-so-grand entrance.

"Come here, John," Jonas said as he beckoned him forward. "I saved you an excellent spot to witness the night's glorious events."

John walked past the four men—he could see they were all older, probably in their sixties, and appeared to be professionals—and stopped at the edge of the roof where Jonas indicated, a few feet to the side of where the lunatic was running this sideshow.

The attention of the of the older men remained fixed upon the sight of Hiram Kane, secured to a backboard and being wheeled across the roof on a dolly.

John looked the other way. The field below the roof of the Physical Sciences building was pulsing with activity. The area was lit by clusters of floodlights at each corner of the field, the kind you might find at a construction site or sporting event. They illuminated not only the tiered levels of a massive assembly of logs in the center of the field but also the thousands of people surrounding the soon-to-be-ignited bonfire. The throng of people was beyond counting, but John estimated there had to be at least twenty thousand down there. Maybe thirty.

There was a firetruck parked to one side between the Physical Sciences building and the bonfire. The bright yellow stood out amongst the sea of people. DJ's most recent obsession was firetrucks. Who said girls don't like trucks? She and John watched firetruck videos together. Some were set to music. Some were educational, and some were just fun. DJ loved them all. Thanks to those videos, John knew the neon yellow of this vehicle meant it was an airport fire truck. It would spray foam rather than water like a standard city fire truck. Based on the stark scent of kerosene in the air, its presence made sense.

He continued scanning the scene below and saw the doghouse perched at the top of the center-pole above the bonfire stack. That was it. The hidden instrument of destruction for all those gathered around it. Burned alive from a napalm-spewing imitation doghouse.

John stepped closer to the edge of the waist-high half-wall encircling the roof and peered over the side. There was a stage constructed below. It was huge, accommodating not just the person talking with the mic but also band members on risers. Except the drummers. They stood in front of the rest of the band. John supposed they needed their freedom, wouldn't want to cramp the beat.

An enormous lighting array rose from the front of the stage, a cross platform supported by two steel towers. John noticed guywires anchored to the side of the Physical Sciences building just below the roof that stretched to the lighting array, helping to secure it in place. It was quite a setup, though a different definition of the word than what was taking place on the roof right now. John suspected Hiram Kane and the men with the shocked expressions at his helpless appearance had all been set up. Royally.

Jonas was smiling. He clapped his hands together.

"Welcome, Father," he said. "Now the night of the Reckoning has truly begun."

CHAPTER 97

A S TRISH RACED DOWN THE HALLWAY of the basement in the Physical Sciences building, she was conscious of the weight of the revolver in her hand. The gun was heavy.

Cutter's gun.

Her mind swam with the events of the night. Andrew had been murdered. John taken away. And Cutter was dying. Perhaps already dead.

He had died to save her.

She would not cry. There would be no more tears. Not until this was over.

She reached the elevator bank and pushed the button.

"No! Use the stairs!" Eric yelled.

He sprinted past her to a door on the other side of the elevator bank. A red-lettered "EXIT" sign hung from the ceiling in front of it.

She rushed to join him, but he didn't open the door. When she reached his side, he stood where he was and looked at her.

"Can you do this?" he asked. No doubt about what he meant.

"I don't know," she replied.

"Garber fired three times back there." He held up three fingers to reinforce his point. "That leaves you with three more. Make them count."

She nodded.

He pulled the handle and yanked open the door. He stepped through first, looking above, making certain no one was in the stairwell, then pounded up the stairs, taking them two at a time. Trish followed, keeping the handgun in front of her, compensating for its considerable weight as she pumped her arms.

By the time they reached the ground floor landing, her thighs already burned. Eric hesitated at the exit door, the keys to Cutter's truck still in his hand, and turned to her. She knew he didn't want to leave. He was supposed to be her protector, and walking out that door meant abandoning her to almost certain death.

"Trish, I—" he stammered.

Before he could say another word, she threw her arms around him in a tight embrace. The pistol clunked against his back. It probably hurt, but he didn't even wince.

"Shut up," she whispered into his ear. "Do what Cutter said. Save the kids."

She let go and continued up the stairs.

"Make sure the safety is off!" he called from behind her.

She glanced at the handgun. The safety was off. It was a live firearm. Ready for action even if she wasn't. She heard the exit door slam below.

She was on her own now.

She took the steps in twos, and for the first time in her adult life, Trish prayed.

CHAPTER 98

THE EXPRESSIONS ON THE FACES of the High Council as Hiram Kane was wheeled across the roof were priceless. Jonas Kane had long anticipated this moment with a mixture of eagerness and anxiety. What would it be like when he finally revealed himself to his father's collaborators, when he fulfilled the rite by sacrificing his own begetter, when he turned the daggers of old on the Council itself, and when he attained the final steps to the Reckoning and his ascension to power?

He had known it would be many things, but what he had never imagined was how much *fun* he would have.

As his Elite Guard rolled his motionless father past the open mouths and shocked faces of the High Council, Jonas considered his exuberance. He glanced to John Michaels, standing at the edge of the roof, and decided that therein may lie the source of his glee.

Overtaking his father, usurping his position of power, sacrificing his generals, these were feats for which Jonas had always known he was destined. They were all in his plans from the beginning. But having John Michaels here had not been planned.

Earlier, Jonas had transitioned from melancholy to anger, with Michaels the root of both emotional states, but that had been looking at the wrong side of the coin. The ancient texts had provided him a pathway to enlightenment. Unseen forces had put Michaels here for a reason. A gift. An opportunity for ultimate victory. After all, Michaels had defeated Marcus Kane (whom Jonas had always known was the favorite son), and Michaels had remained a thorn since then, an itch that his father had longed to scratch, a death he desired but could not fulfill while his eyes were focused on the Reckoning. Tonight, Jonas would achieve all that his father could not. Hiram Kane would not be alive to see it, but that mattered not to Jonas. This was his victory and for his own enjoyment. No one else.

The Elite Guard halted the dolly a few feet from the edge of the roof—exactly where Jonas had instructed them earlier in the day—and turned the unit so Hiram was facing the High Council, his back to the bonfire field. Jonas stepped next to him. The lighting on the roof was adequate at best. He could see his father's face well, but it was alas too dark to look deep into his eyes and read whatever may be churning there.

"What is the meaning of this, Christian?" The question was blurted by one of the High Council members. Jonas thought it was Ralston, tough guy owner of the local construction company.

"You needn't call me Christian Berry any longer," he replied.

He reflected that none of the High Council knew his real name. Because they knew he was the son of Hiram Kane, they were aware the Berry pseudonym was just that, but had any of them ever asked his real name? Perhaps the runt of the litter did not merit the trouble.

Was he not even worthy of a name in their eyes?

"Names will matter not after the Reckoning," Jonas continued. Though the name did matter right now, to him, the men standing before him were not worth the effort of explanation.

His Elite Guard stepped away from Hiram and retreated, slipping behind the High Council—blocking the exit—while their attention was fixed to the massive man strapped to the backboard. Drool ran down Hiram's chin and onto his shirt.

"You each came here tonight to witness something extraordinary," Jonas intoned. "The Reckoning will bestow power beyond measure unto the chosen one. You anticipated that to be my father, Hiram Kane. In that assumption, you were mistaken."

Murmurings from the four council members. They were looking from Hiram to Jonas and then to each other. This was an event for which they had planned and awaited with greedy expectation. They had been asked to give their time, their authority and much of their fortunes to this cause, and they had been promised fulfilment of their greatest desires as reward. Power, wealth, fame, women, whatever they could dream.

The night was not going as they had planned.

Jonas reveled in it.

"Before our guests arrived," he resumed, "I was describing the painstaking tasks that had to be fulfilled to lead us to this day. I'm certain you were listening and not just awaiting my father, eh?" Jonas raised his eyebrows. More murmuring from the group but no direct reply. Perhaps they sensed the situation had grown dire. He saw the Chief of Police glance over his shoulder. The Chief would see four very large college athletes standing between him and the exit.

"There are but a few tasks remaining to bring about the Reckoning and earn its power," Jonas continued. "You know of the death that will come to those on the bonfire field below. This is the sacrifice of numbers. A rite that will be magnificent to behold from this vantage." He swept one arm toward the field and the eyes of the council followed his gesture. They still wanted to see this act of mass murder. Like most men who had climbed to positions of power in society, they shared the sin of avarice, but they wouldn't be here now if a certain bloodlust didn't also burn within them.

"But that is not the only rite of blood required by the Reckoning," Jonas stated. He withdrew the ceremonial dagger from where he had secured it beneath his belt at his lower back and raised it in front of him to eye level. The ancient blade absorbed the limited light into its darkened steel.

The sounds from the High Council escalated from murmurs to hesitant protests. They didn't know what was about to happen. Humans hate uncertainty.

"Don't worry," Jonas soothed. "This sacrifice stays in the family."

He stepped closer to his father, then paused and turned his head to John Michaels, just to be certain he was watching. He didn't want Michaels to miss this.

Another step to the Reckoning. *Not* the mental institution.

Michaels was watching. Satisfied, Jonas returned his gaze to Hiram.

"You have worked with diligence, Father," he said, "you were a fine example. You made me the man I am. Tonight, forces greater than you will fashion me into the man I am meant to be."

Jonas raised the knife and uttered a phrase in Latin. It was meaningless. The ancient texts required no such thing—they weren't even written in Latin—but it made for a nice effect.

Let the record show, he thought, *that Jonas Kane earns high marks for showmanship.*

"Goodbye, Father," he said as he placed the edge of the ancient blade against Hiram Kane's sinewy neck. Jonas pressed hard, feeling the dagger slice into his father's skin, reaching the jugular and carotid, then pulled the blade across his throat. He was grateful to have practiced on Andrew in the basement earlier. It removed some uncertainty and allowed Jonas to complete this action as an experienced professional.

The rest of Hiram Kane's body may have been paralyzed, but his heart was strong. When the dagger opened the arteries, blood pumped forth in a pulsing jet of crimson. The spray reached far enough to strike the members of the High Council. They stepped back, away from the arterial mist, and each bumped into a member of Jonas's Elite Guard.

When giving his instructions to his guards earlier, Jonas had described the plan as man-to-man coverage, a strategy he knew the brutes would both understand and appreciate.

He glanced back to John Michaels. It was too dark to see for certain if the look on his face was one of disgust or terror. Jonas hoped it was the latter.

He returned his attention to the High Council.

"Don't leave yet, gentlemen," he intoned, "you're going to find this next part very interesting."

CHAPTER 99

ERIC SHOULDERED OPEN THE DOORS of the Physical Sciences building and bolted across the lawn. The bonfire festivities were taking place at the field on the opposite side of the building. Though four stories of concrete and glass separated him from the action, the noise generated by the thousands of fans was still impressive.

He sprinted—the keys in his hand jingling as he pumped his arms—covering the distance to reach the parking lot that held Cutter's pickup. He was at once frustrated that they'd had to park so far from the Physical Sciences building yet grateful that he would be able to exit the lot without having to contend with the crowds that had amassed for the bonfire.

The campus was almost empty. Everyone was behind him at the festivities, cheering the home team in blissful ignorance of the incendiary device that would kill most of them once the flames of the bonfire triggered it.

Could Trish stop it? Did she have any chance at all? She was just a kid. It wasn't right to expect something like this of her. It wasn't fair. His thoughts went to his former partner. George O'Brien's blood ran through Trish's veins. That was something at least.

Dwelling on it wouldn't do him any good. Eric had a job to do, and fair or not, Trish had the same.

He reached the parking lot and sidestepped through parked cars until he reached the familiar sight of Cutter's pickup. Had Kane's followers armed themselves yet? Did they have weapons in hand?

Were they already marching toward the school? It was only a few blocks from campus. He didn't have long.

He opened the driver's door of the truck and slid behind the wheel onto the wood-beaded seat cover. He inserted the key into the ignition, and for a moment, he was certain the old vehicle wouldn't start.

He clenched his jaw and turned the key. The truck's engine roared to life.

CHAPTER 100

JOHN RETREATED A STEP toward the edge of the roof. He was in no danger from the spray of blood that had erupted from the opened neck of Hiram Kane—the dying patriarch was turned away from him—but the sheer horror of watching Jonas slit his own father's throat had triggered an instinctive recoil from John. He felt the solidness of the half-wall press into his hip. He could retreat no farther.

"As I was saying," Jonas addressed the men in front of him, "what we have referred to as the Reckoning is actually a series of such rites. A settlement of account so to speak. You see, power comes with a price."

John watched as the four older men glanced nervously at each other. They hadn't yet been assaulted, but each was guarded by one of the steroid rhinos. He could tell that whatever confidence with which they had entered the evening had vanished, replaced by apprehension for what was to come.

"The price of the power I seek shall be paid in predetermined installments," Jonas continued. "The first was the loss of a dear friend who sacrificed herself to this great cause."

John never knew Stephanie Espinosa, but he felt sick on her behalf.

"The next installment, difficult as it was for me, was the loss of my own father. You all witnessed this moment of noble sacrifice on his part."

John flexed his arms in an attempt to separate his wrists. The handcuffs didn't budge. He hadn't expected the links between the steel bracelets to snap—he was no superhero (not even a weightlifter)—but he had to try *something*.

He could turn and shout to those below, scream with all his might for them to not light the bonfire, but he knew it would be a wasted effort. His position on the roof was too high above the stage. On a quiet day, someone on the ground might be able to detect his shouting, but with the heightened decibel level this evening, there was no hope.

"Of course, you are all aware of the accounting to take place with the bonfire and the school. Ten-thousand innocents cleansed in fire and blood." Kane glanced past John toward the bonfire field, then raised one eyebrow as he returned his attention to his main audience. "I think we're going to exceed that tally nicely this evening. That moment is almost upon us."

John debated charging Kane. Tackling him. But what good would it do? The odds were too slim. Even if John could separate the dagger from Kane's grip, there was no way he'd be able to use it on him before Kane's beasts fell upon them both. And they all had daggers as well.

"But before that moment, in order to attain ascension, to be deserving of the final Reckoning, there is another sacrifice that must be made."

John had never felt so helpless. There was nothing he could do. Death would come to so many tonight, and what would happen after that? He knew his own demise was on the agenda. What would happen to Sarah and DJ? Would Jonas seek them out? Would he be able to find them? Had John put enough safeguards in place to protect them?

"You have each given so much to this cause," Jonas informed the men assembled before him. "You were trusted generals to my father...and to me, whether you were aware of that fact or not. And for that, I salute you."

He lifted the dagger, touched the tip of the blade to one eyebrow and swished it forward in an awkward salute. A picture of homicidal insanity thought John.

"But there is alas one more sacrifice to which you, the High Council, are called."

Thus cued, in a synchronous motion from behind the older men, the four apes each wrapped one of their muscled arms around the neck of his assigned man and raised their daggers in unison with the other hand.

The four victims struggled but none was a match for the bull-strength of their captors. Jonas shouted something in what John suspected was Latin.

At that moment, the door to the stairs clanged open.

Trish burst onto the roof, pistol in hand.

CHAPTER 101

TRISH THOUGHT SHE WAS PREPARED for anything. During her race up the stairs—an endurance trial that left her thighs burning and heart pounding—she had steeled herself for whatever she might find on the roof. After all, Christian Berry—no, the bastard's real name was Jonas Kane—had revealed his plans in bragging detail to them in the basement lab. Trish knew he planned to kill his father along with several other—how did he describe them—*pompous men*. She assumed he intended to kill John as well. And he planned to watch from the rooftop as thousands burned to death, bathed in chemical fire on the bonfire field.

She had no idea how she could stop Jonas Kane and save John. Her four-story climb had been a frantic rush with no attempt at advance planning. She knew the clock was ticking. And she had a gun. With that, she had burst onto the roof.

Standing in front of the door, Cutter's revolver pointed forward, the weight of the gun a challenge in itself, out of breath and struggling to make sense of the scene in front of her, Trish felt neither strong nor heroic. She felt foolish and overwhelmed.

It wasn't just Jonas Kane. There were one-two-three-four huge guys with daggers. She placed them as the same linebacker thugs who had accosted her and Eric the other day on the lawn beneath this very rooftop. Each of the monsters held a struggling older man. Those men were spattered with blood, and their necks were choked in the crooks between four sets of bulging biceps and veiny forearms. There was another man, huge, strapped upright to some kind of backboard, his barrel-chest and belly were soaked crimson from a pulsing neck wound. Trish didn't let her eyes settle on him. She had seen more than enough blood today to last a lifetime.

And there was John. Standing at the edge of the roof. Still alive.

She swung the pistol in a wide arc, not knowing what to do next.

"Stop!" she cried as she settled on pointing the weapon at Jonas Kane.

His lips curled into a smirk.

"No," he replied with a flat voice.

Kane turned to his army of giants.

"Do it," he commanded.

Trish watched in horror as the four brutes swung their daggers in individual arcs, plunging the blades into the abdomens of the older men they held captive. Choked screams reached her ears as she witnessed the daggers twist and saw, eviscerating the helpless victims.

"You were saying?" Jonas asked.

CHAPTER 102

THE CLOCK WAS TICKING.

Eric blew past a stop sign. He would have welcomed the sight of flashing red and blue lights, the sound of a siren. They could follow him straight to the school.

He was given no such gift.

There were plenty of police at the bonfire. Security was a given at an event like that. But he hadn't bothered to go out of his way and flag one down. It would have taken too long to explain, and he couldn't spare a single minute on bullshit. Lives would be lost.

And there had been no police on his route toward the school.

Never a cop around when you need one, he mused.

He took a chance and cut one street over. Sure enough, he saw them. A loose formation of college kids advancing in some sort of half-assed march.

There had to be at least forty of them. Shit, that was a lot.

And what were they all carrying?

He peered closer. Axes. They all had axes. Double-shit.

He was tempted to turn Cutter's truck around and careen straight into them. See how much they wanted to follow their leader's orders when lying broken and bleeding on the pavement.

He didn't do it. Partly because he was afraid the drugs and the motivation of Kane would be so great that the group would scrape themselves off the road and continue shambling toward the middle school like a pack of zombies, but also because—and he had to remind himself of this—this pack of animals wasn't necessarily evil. They were under a terrible influence.

He didn't want to kill any of them, but if it came to that or saving the lives of innocent children, he would do what he had to do. Until he was overwhelmed by the mass of them.

Eric floored the accelerator. The school was close. If he was lucky, he'd beat the zombie mob by two whole minutes.

CHAPTER 103

FOR A SPLIT SECOND, Trish felt her finger spasm against the trigger. She stopped herself before the hammer drew back on the revolver. It had been a reflex spurred by the shock of the moment.

The four older men collapsed to the surface of the rooftop. She refused to look at their bodies. She knew she would see *stuff* emerging from the gashes in their stomachs. It went beyond blood.

She focused instead on Jonas Kane, and she tried to keep the gun steady. Her hands were uncooperative. The barrel of the gun wavered despite her efforts, an erratic metronome of nerves and steel.

"Stay back!" she yelled.

The four brutes—the four *murderers*—turned to face her, but none of them made a move in her direction. Not yet.

"Trish, such a surprise," Kane said, hands in front, palms separating as if he was welcoming an unexpected guest into his home.

She saw John walk her direction, so she took several steps to meet him halfway, gun trained on Kane and his thugs, skirting a wide berth around them. John was still handcuffed, but she felt better standing next to him. At least she wasn't alone.

"You okay?" he asked.

She shook her head once—surprised at how hard the simple question hit her—but she kept her cool. No tears. Nor would there be. Not until this was over.

"Perhaps it's time we all talked." The words emanated from Jonas Kane, but the smooth tone in which they were delivered was pure Christian Berry.

John ignored him.

"Cutter?" he asked her.

Trish shook her head again. Only once. The lights on the roof were dim, but she could see John swallow hard.

She noticed movement and saw Kane take two steps. Just enough to shift his position so the sizeable corpse on the backboard affixed to the dolly stood between him and Trish's revolver.

"Perhaps there's been a misunderstanding," Jonas said from the other side of the obstacle.

His goon squad remained rooted in place, but she saw fists clenching and unclenching in anticipation, like a foursome of attack dogs anxious to strike at his command. A total of five bad guys standing only a few feet away, and she had three bullets.

But they couldn't know that.

"There's no misunderstanding," she replied, her voice sounding stronger than she felt. "You're going to call this whole thing off right now."

She glanced to John and saw utter despair etched on his face.

"That's the problem, Trish," he said. "He can't call it off."

CHAPTER 104

"JOHN IS RIGHT, TRISH."

Jonas Kane employed his smoothest, most calming tone. The appearance of the pain-in-the-ass ginger bitch had taken him by surprise. Everything to this point had transpired in perfect alignment with his meticulous plans. Granted, the presence of John Michaels had not been in his original plan, but he had come to appreciate this gift from unseen forces as a supplement and, as it turned out, necessary catalyst for his greater plans to succeed.

Trish O'Brien showing up on his rooftop and interrupting this glorious moment did *not* feel like a gift. The fact that she was brandishing a firearm cemented her non-gift status and further complicated the present scenario. How had this happened? How had that moron Garber possibly have let this occur?

It's so hard to find good help these days, he mused.

If nothing else, the evening had grown more exciting, though not in a way Kane would have preferred. He may have convinced certain of his followers that they were bulletproof, but he knew he was not. Not yet. He needed to buy time.

"There is no 'off' button on the incendiary device," he explained to the girl. The barrel of the pistol bobbed and weaved. Either the gun was heavy, or she was far more nervous than she presented. "There's nothing I can do at this point. I can't make a phone call or cut the red wire. The device atop the bonfire is self-contained."

"Then we have to stop them from lighting it," Trish said. The girl was speaking to Michaels, but at least Jonas knew she was listening to him.

Jonas saw Michaels nod, then step toward the edge of the roof. He was scanning the area. Jonas knew what he was doing. He was searching possibilities and making calculations. Figuring out how to solve the problem. That's what John Michaels did. But not this time.

The math on the roof was simple. Five versus two. The girl held a revolver that carried six bullets, but how many were in the gun now? Had shots been expelled in the basement during the great escape?

"There is no stopping the bonfire," Jonas intoned. "It's too late. Any moment those floodlights are going to shut off and cast the whole field into darkness. It's quite theatrical. The crew leaders are going to light their ceremonial torches, march them around the bonfire and throw them into the stack." He delivered a nothing-I-can-do shrug. "I'm sure you've seen how fast the bonfire roars to life. There is no stopping this. Tell me, did you shoot Dr. Garber? Did you leave him in the haz-mat lab?"

Jonas saw her take a breath before Michaels interrupted.

"Don't answer that," he said.

Blast him.

"Key," Michaels commanded, raising his wrists to show off his shiny handcuffs.

"I don't have it," Jonas responded.

"Your right front pocket," Michaels said. He turned to Trish. "If he lies again, go ahead and shoot him. We don't have time for this."

How I've come to hate this fucking man, Jonas thought as he dug the small key from his pocket. Handcuffed or free, it wouldn't change anything. He stepped to the side and tossed the key in the direction of Michaels before returning to his prior place, keeping the corpse of his father positioned as well as possible between him and Trish's gun.

The girl's eyes moved from Jonas to his Elite Guard and back to Michaels. In that moment, the path became clear. His target wasn't the one with the gun, it was the one to whom the gun looked for guidance.

It wasn't five versus two. It never was. It had always been destined to be one against one.

Jonas Kane versus John Michaels.

And to win, all Kane had to do was buy time. Minutes. If that. Then the Reckoning would be realized, and the power would be his. At that point, the battle would be over.

Michaels retrieved the key from where it had landed, then turned to Trish. "Okay, here's what—"

"You haven't thought this through, John," Kane interrupted. *Now bait the hook.* "As smart as you are, you've missed something important."

Kane saw Michaels turn his attention from Trish to him. He knew Michaels wouldn't be able to resist the hook.

"Think about the big picture," Kane implored. Over the years, the ancient texts had augmented his natural abilities—seeing inside lesser men, identifying their desires—and it had enhanced his ability to persuade others to do his will. John Michaels was *not* above him.

"You're a smart man. You've calculated the probability, haven't you?" Kane asked. "You know this is impossible to stop. You may find it horrifying, but those people down there *are* going to die. The Reckoning *will* occur. The scenario upon which you should focus is what happens afterward."

Michaels said nothing.

He knows I'm right, Kane thought. He continued before momentum could be interrupted.

"Those people will die, but that doesn't mean you have to. You or Trish," Kane offered. "You need to realize that I am not my father, nor am I my brothers. They were obsessed with death and vengeance over whatever problems they had with the world. *That's not me.* With the power granted unto me, I can make this world a better place."

The handcuffs dropped from John's wrists onto the surface of the roof. He glanced off the side of the building at the field below. Trish continued looking from Kane to the Elite Guard to John. The gun shook, but she kept it up.

Not enough. Go for the heart. What makes John tick?

"And if not for yourself, think about Sarah."

John's head snapped back. *That did it.* Kane had his undivided attention.

"The Reckoning will take place. The pertinent question is what I decide to do next. Will you choose to join me, to simply stand aside and let destiny unfold as it will regardless—such an easy path—and in doing so *guarantee* that I will honor the safety of not just you but your wife as well? Or will you attempt to stop unstoppable events, and in so doing, force my hand? For if you do this thing, I pledge that I will find Sarah, and the damage inflicted will be slow and unspeakable."

That felt right. A simple choice. But the expression on John's face was unreadable. Was he weighing his options? That was fine. Let him weigh them another minute. Maybe two. By then it would be too late.

Could there be more? Think. He loves his wife. Happily married—blah-blah-blah—in hiding for four years. Wait, given their ages, and that look in his eyes. Of course.

Kane realized he held the winning card, an unexpected ace. Destiny was, after all, inevitable.

CHAPTER 105

THE BACK OF THE PICKUP FISHTAILED as Eric turned into the parking lot of the middle school. Cutter's truck was not a high-performance vehicle, but Eric managed to avoid the cars scattered throughout the lot. Whether they were the vehicles of volunteers watching the kids inside or from parents who dropped their kids off and walked the few blocks to the bonfire field, Eric didn't know.

On the other side of the lot was a large grassy lawn bisected by a sidewalk which ran from the parking lot to the backdoor of the school's gymnasium, where the kids would be running around and playing games and wholly unaware of the mob of axe-wielding cultists prepared to murder them all.

A huge, windowless brick box taller than the rest of the school building, the gym was easy to identify. And since it was a school facility, it would have limited access points—can't provide too many options for escape to the little tikes during the school day. That worked in Eric's favor. He had three goals: shut off access from the outside, call for reinforcements and somehow hold off the zombie horde until help arrived.

The problem was in the math. Regardless of the drugs or the cult-leader influence, tonight those people were a mob. Forty fanatics with axes hellbent on killing children—that was a big number—and they weren't going to stop. Even if the police showed up, how many of Kane's followers would still get through? How many would have already made it into the gym? How many kids would be dead on this night?

One problem at a time.

Eric took his foot off the gas but didn't bother braking when he reached the end of the parking lot. Cutter's truck jolted when the front wheels hit the curb, a strong possibility of a broken axle, but that wasn't on Eric's list of concerns at the moment.

He drove up the sidewalk, the pickup's tires eating into the grass on either side, finally hitting the brakes when he was a few feet from the gymnasium door. He slowed then stopped when the rusted bumper kissed the doorframe. The front of the truck completely blocked that entry to the gym.

Eric put the transmission in Park, jammed on the emergency brake and turned off the ignition. Keys in hand, he stepped out of the truck, pulled back his arm and launched them onto the roof in an arcing throw. He heard the keys jangle as they landed out of sight.

He reached back into the cab of the pickup and grabbed the shotgun from the rack in the rear window. God bless Texas.

Eric raced around the perimeter of the building toward the school's front door. The horde would approach from the side where he had parked the truck. With the back door blocked, the mob would bypass that option. Eric planned to funnel them into an alternate entrance where he could fortify his position and hold them off.

He made it past the high brick wall that delineated the gym and saw a line of floor-to-ceiling windows with the front doors—also glass—situated in the middle. They were all single-pane windows—the kind that would shatter with one well-placed swing of an axe. Lights blazed inside. Eric could see an open area—possibly a cafeteria—to one side. The interior entry to the gym would be along that side. It was bordered by a front lobby area that sported a receptionist window to the administrative office. Eric saw lockers line a hallway that trailed from the other side of the front lobby.

As far as fortifiable positions go, it sucked. So much for Plan A.

At least he didn't see any kids inside. They must all be restricted to the gym. That was something. In fact, he saw only one person in the front lobby area. She was wearing a gray security uniform. And Eric recognized her. He had plenty of friends on the force who moonlighted as private security. Apparently Abramsville police were paid such that they had a similar need for supplemental income.

The woman was sitting on a stool, the mass of her hips spreading wide on either side of the cushion. She was reading a magazine.

When Eric flung open the front door and charged in with the shotgun, he was shocked at the speed with which she moved. In a flash, she was off the stool and two steps toward him, her hand went to her side, but there was no gun there. That didn't surprise Eric. Security companies were fifty-fifty on whether they allowed off-duty cops to wear their sidearms. This one didn't. Probably meant they paid less. This officer deserved her money. Going for the gun had been a reflex, but when she didn't find it, her hands immediately rose in front of her, fists at the ready.

Eric's mind raced. He was good with names.

"Officer Nixon," he called. He thought harder. "Norah!"

She cocked her head, fists still raised, beefy right arm cocked and ready for delivery—Eric imagined a punch from this woman could pack a wallop if delivered—but her face softened, and her jaw unclenched.

"I know you," she said. "The other day on campus. Cop from New York. You were staring down a bunch of unfriendly jock types. What's going on?" Fists still up, she nodded toward the shotgun in his hands. "No firearms in the school."

He sensed nothing malevolent from her, but he had to ask.

"Norah," he looked into her eyes, "are you a follower of Christian Berry?"

"Who?" she asked. She was breathing hard from the excitement. Her enormous breasts rose and fell with each breath. "Is that a social media thing? I don't go on them internets. Rots your brain."

"Good enough," Eric said. He had no choice at this point. "Look, there's no time to explain. What you need to know is that right now there is a mob of forty people with axes coming to kill the kids in that gymnasium." He levelled a finger toward the doors he assumed must lead to the gym.

Norah's fists lowered as her eyebrows rose. "Say what?"

The doomsday clock ticked in Eric's mind. He didn't have time for an explanation, but he needed her.

"It's a cult. We've been investigating them. Think of them as terrorists, I don't care, but they will be at this school any minute."

He held out the shotgun with both hands, an offering. She accepted it with a look of doubt, as if she couldn't decide whether this was some sort of ill-conceived prank.

"This is life and death," he growled. "Right here. Right now. Believe me."

She looked at the shotgun in her hands, then back at Eric. She was getting the picture. He drilled into her eyes with his hardest stare.

"I need your help," he spoke slowly, driving home every word. "They are coming to kill these kids."

She glanced from Eric across the open space to the side of the front lobby, to the doors of the gymnasium. Bubbling laughter and muffled shouts of glee drifted from the other side. The children were having the time of their precious lives. Something snapped in Norah. She got it.

She held the shotgun upright, the forestock gripped in one brawny hand.

"No sir! Ain't nobody touching them babies!" She pumped her arm in an authoritative up-and-down motion, chambering a shell into the barrel of the 12-gauge with a loud clack. "Not today!"

Eric exhaled in relief. He wasn't alone in this. That was something.

"I've got the back door blocked," he told her. "Call for backup. Get somebody out here."

He turned and opened the door.

"Wait!" she called. "What are you gonna do?"

"I'm going to hold them off and buy you some time," he said, hoping he sounded more confident than the statement merited. He stepped through the doors but spoke over his shoulder. "Lock these doors! Be ready for anything!"

She was already in motion when he turned and sprinted back along the side of the building. They were almost out of time.

CHAPTER 106

JOHN WAS ALMOST OUT OF TIME (they all were), yet here he was, expending precious moments deliberating the words of a madman. Doing so seemed madness in itself, but there was undeniable truth in what Jonas Kane said. The odds were steep against any attempt to stop the events unfolding at this very moment. The deck was stacked in Kane's favor.

If an outcome is inevitable, does a smart man fight it or accept it and make the best of the situation? Hadn't John spent his life playing the odds and allowing the cold indifference of logic to override sentiment and chart his path?

A pounding rhythm of drums erupted from the stage below. Bonfire edged closer, the moment of glory when the lights would shut off and the torches would be lit. The whole scene was madness, and the constant drumbeat was its score.

He glanced to Trish. She had guts, and John respected the hell out of her for charging onto the roof, but that didn't change the fact that the revolver shook in her hands. He knew Kane suspected the gun was low on bullets. Five bad guys. Two good guys. And four of those five bad guys could bull-rush a three-hundred-pound offensive tackle and come out on top. John didn't scrape two-hundred pounds, and Trish was far less than that. If just one of those beasts got to them, it would not end well.

And Cutter wasn't here to help. John's friend. Once a knight in cowboy armor for Sarah and DJ. But never again.

Damn it all.

If Kane made good on his promise to seek out Sarah when this was over, she would be on her own. John will have left her exposed.

"It's a difficult choice, John, I'm certain," Kane said. He kept his position on the other side of dear-old-dead-dad as he spoke. "And keep in mind, we're not just talking about your wife." He paused. "We're talking about your *family*."

Son of a bitch. How could he know? Did he know?

"Kids are wonderful, aren't they?" Kane continued. "A man would do anything to protect his children. If he had a choice between doing something stupid that would result in the painful, nightmarish death of his child, or doing something smart and ensuring their safety, well, that's not much of a choice is it?"

With every moment of deliberation, stopping the planned slaughter of thousands grew more improbable. It was almost impossible already. When John had looked off the roof, he had seen only one possibility, and it was a million-to-one shot, if that. Almost certain suicide to even make the attempt.

For Kane's alternative, all John had to do was nothing. He didn't trust that Kane would spare his life, but he did think there was a decent possibility he was telling the truth about whether or not he'd hunt John's family when this was over. And wasn't the slimmest possibility of their safety worth more than the guaranty of their deaths if John chose to fight?

Logic dictated a clear choice in the matter.

He looked to Trish. The wind on the rooftop swirled her auburn hair. To save his wife and child, all he had to do was stand here. He'd tell Trish to run. Kane and his thugs wouldn't chase her, not with the threat of the gun she brandished. Kane wouldn't care if she fled as long as the bonfire was lit and his insane plan moved forward. By taking the easy road, John could save her, too.

The pulsing beat of the drums ceased.

CHAPTER 107

WHAT IS HE DOING? Trish wondered.

She took her eyes off the fearsome foursome and their sociopathic leader long enough to glance at John. When she moved her head, the stupid wind whipped her hair so that it flew in her face. Her ponytail had long ago surrendered to the chaos of the night. Some of the offending strands blew into her mouth. She didn't realize her jaw had been hanging open. She tried to spit the hair out, not wanting to take either hand off the pistol to brush the strands away. The handgun grew heavier by the moment.

Why wasn't John doing anything? Was he actually listening to this psycho?

The expression on his face told her that, yes, he was listening.

He was wavering.

Shit-shit-shit-shit.

Trish didn't have a plan. Cutter had told her to save John. She had stormed the roof and done just that—more or less—but that couldn't be the end. All the people down there. They would die.

The drums went silent. So did the crowd.

For the first time, the roof was quiet.

In a flash, inspiration hit Trish. She could fire the gun in the air, while it was quiet, people would hear. There were police down there. Security guards. *Somebody.* Someone would come investigate.

But would they stop the bonfire? And firing the pistol meant she would have fewer bullets. And the thugs would attack.

Jonas Kane's voice filled the silence.

"This may be hard to believe, John," he said (Trish didn't know whether to be relieved or pissed that Kane seemed to be ignoring her completely even though she was the one with the gun), "but I really don't want to kill you. Keep in mind, you were a gift to me. The final days leading to the Reckoning were the most dangerous for me—when the likelihood that my father might uncover my plans was highest—but then *you* arrived. Manna from heaven in my time of need. My father's focus was disrupted. You were the perfect distraction."

Trish glanced from John to Kane and back again. Why was he listening to him?

"Truth be told," Kane confessed, "I owe you one. Maybe more than that. First you get rid of my brother Marcus, then you help me eliminate my father. You've done the world, and me, a great service on both counts. You deserve to be rewarded."

Trish could hear a single voice from the stage below. Someone speaking through the microphone. The crowd remained quiet, respectful. Vague memories of something similar came to mind from her bonfire experience the year prior. She thought maybe someone was saying a prayer. Dr. Garber would hate that, but then again, that asshole didn't have to worry about such things anymore. The thought empowered her.

"Enough bullshit," she declared. "You can't listen to this, John."

The lights were dim on the roof but bright enough for her to see Kane glower her direction. She was tempted to attempt a shot at the part of his face she could see, but she was afraid of missing and hitting the upright corpse of Kane's father instead. That would be a wasted bullet.

"You know what Cutter told me before he broke us out?" she asked John. She kept her eyes on Kane and his goons, but she suspected her mention of Cutter had regained John's attention. She could feel it. "He said we were here for a reason. That out of all the people in the world, *we're* the ones who've been entrusted to stop this."

She aimed the barrel of the handgun from Kane back to the brute squad. Had one of them just taken a step toward her?

"I don't know if Kane is crazy," she continued, "but if the Reckoning is real, then this isn't just about saving the people down there, and it's not about saving your family." Her fingers tightened around the grip of the pistol—her shoulders ached from its heft—but she would not lower it. "We're here to save the world, John. And you can't do that by striking a bargain with the devil."

"Spoken like a child," Kane countered. "Naïve and hopeful. She doesn't understand cold reality like you and me, John. Negotiations are part of business, and when it comes down to it, this world isn't worth saving anyway."

The lone voice on the microphone ceased speaking with what was perhaps an amen, and the silence was shattered by a roar from the crowd.

Trish took her eyes off Kane and his brutes to look at John. No more words. It was time for action.

His eyes met hers for a moment, then he turned, took two swift steps to the edge of the roof and vaulted over the side.

Stunned, Trish turned her attention to the four goons. They were already in motion.

And she was alone.

CHAPTER 108

ERIC ROUNDED THE CORNER of the gymnasium and raced toward the truck parked on the sidewalk, nose-against-door. He looked past the half-filled parking lot and scanned the street beyond.

That's where they'll come from.

The glow of the streetlights illuminated nothing but a quiet neighborhood street. He still had time but not much.

He reached the pickup, stopping at the rear. He grabbed the handle to release the tailgate, but it resisted. A second hand and two grunting tugs succeeded in dropping the tailgate to its lowered, flat position. Cutter's truck seemed to consist of equal parts rust and dirt. It was a working truck. Eric hoped that meant it would have something he could use.

He climbed into the truck bed and scanned its contents. There was a flat-blade shovel (too heavy), a hoe (too long but call it a 'maybe'), pruning shears (scary but impractical) and some sort of contraption with two long wooden handles attached to what looked like a metal duckbill. Eric assumed it must be used for digging holes for fence posts, but still, too awkward for what he needed.

He pushed aside the implements to see if there was anything underneath.

He saw the axe handle and smiled.

Fight fire with fire.

He pulled the hickory handle from beneath the other tools like Arthur freeing Excalibur from the fabled stone.

His smile dissipated with the realization that the axe handle lacked an axe head. He wasn't holding an axe. Just a length of wood that would make a much more effective weapon if only a freaking blade was attached to it any fashion.

"Could've used a little more help than this, Cutter," he muttered.

Then again, beggars can't be choosers. The wood was strong. The heft was solid. It would be agile. Good for fighting multiple opponents. Kind of like a baseball bat but with a better balance of weight distribution.

Good enough, Eric thought.

He straightened and walked to the tailgate. This would be it. He'd stay in the truck bed for now. A better vantage from which to monitor their approach. The mob would come from the tree-lined street. They'd then have to traverse the parking lot and cross the expanse of lawn after that. The lawn itself had no trees and was well lit. It was wide open. That would be the battleground, for a few minutes at least, until Eric was torn apart by axes and the zombie horde attacked the front entrance of the school.

At least Norah would be able to take some out with the shotgun. Perhaps even barricade herself in the gym and keep her babies safe for another minute or two. Maybe five.

Movement in the street. Eric gripped the hickory handle in both hands and watched as the formation of axe wielding believers marched into sight.

The zombie horde was here.

CHAPTER 109

EVENTS ON THE ROOFTOP spun out of control. The last thing Jonas Kane expected was to witness John Michaels jump off the roof. They were four floors up. It was suicide.

The action sparked further chaos. Kane's Elite Guard rushed Trish. Only he hadn't ordered it, and he was supposed to be in control. So the girl did exactly what you would expect someone who was holding a gun in that situation to do, she opened fire.

As the first shot reverberated over the rooftop, Kane ducked close against the shield provided by his dead father and the backboard upon which the corpse was secured. He peered around the side to watch as his men advanced upon her. No fear. Trish had missed.

A second shot resonated and the front soldier jerked like he'd been kicked in the chest. He dropped to the surface of the rooftop without a sound. The remaining three soldiers bellowed on his behalf, their angry chorus blending with the roar of the crowd below. Kane was grateful for the masking noise.

The third shot snapped a soldier's head back. Kane saw blood spurt from the back of the young man's skull as well as the front. He was dead before he fell.

Two soldiers down. Blast it.

Out of control.

His remaining two soldiers were almost upon her. Despite the crowd's cheering below, Kane's ears were attuned to the rooftop. He heard the distinct clack of a hammer striking a spent shell casing. And then another. The little bitch was out of bullets.

He stood and stepped away from his hiding place. He saw Trish—gun still gripped in both hands—retreat a step. His soldiers were only a few feet away, daggers raised.

"No!" Kane screamed at them. "I want her alive!"

The girl was not going to have the benefit of a quick death. Not after this.

Kane sprinted toward the half-wall surrounding the perimeter of the rooftop. Had John fallen to the stage? Why hadn't the crowd silenced? A man dropping to his death onto the stage would stop the bonfire festivities indefinitely.

Kane pulled his cell phone from his back pocket—the number already queued up as a failsafe precaution—and initiated the call.

From the corner of his eye, he saw his pair of remaining Elite Guard subdue the girl. Not gently. The gun was knocked from her hand by one while the other struck her across the face. He used an open palm. That was good, it wouldn't kill her, but based on her scream, you'd think it had come close.

He reached the edge of the rooftop and looked over the side. Three college kids were at the front of the stage. They would be the work crew chiefs. They held their unlit torches over their heads as the crowd screamed and cheered. In a moment, those torches would be lit, and the crew would walk from the stage down a cleared path through the crowd to light the bonfire.

Though not if John Michaels lay dead on the stage.

Kane scanned the area below. There was no dead body. The show was going on.

Kane shifted his eyes from the stage and spotted him. John Michaels was dangling by one arm from the steel cable securing the lighting array above the stage to the Physical Sciences building.

The son of a bitch was still alive.

CHAPTER 110

JOHN HAD TAKEN NOTE of the guy wires earlier but was forced to make a best guess on the location of the closest one when he vaulted over the side of the roof. That had been a dangerous gamble. As it turned out, the guy wire had been about a foot to the left of what he anticipated, an error that had saved his life.

His intent was to dive off the roof and grab the guy wire with both hands, then proceed hand over hand down the thick steel cable to the lighting array. That was the kind of thing you'd see in the movies. For John—who had not attempted a chin-up since his teenage years—expecting to support his body mass with only his fingers was a mistake, a fact he realized the instant he made contact with the cable. The closer position of the guy wire resulted in one hand grabbing the cable while John's other arm struck the steel line just beneath his armpit. He curled his arm, so the crook of his elbow caught the cable, securing it tightly between his forearm and bicep, an action that saved his life.

The pain was immediate and intense. John had no idea he was so *heavy*. His other hand slipped from the wire. He hung from one arm, dangling four stories above the steel platform. He heard a gunshot.

The arm cradling the cable felt like it was being torn in half, an excruciating burn in his elbow that flamed outward to his wrist and shoulder. In desperation, he managed to reach his other hand back to the cable. The original concept of hand-over-hand descension of the guy wire was a bust—he wasn't strong enough—but he hadn't fallen yet. It could be worse. He swung his body, kicking his feet forward and up, gaining momentum. Another gunshot.

On the third try, he hooked an ankle on the cable then followed suit with the other leg. With his body weight now supported by all four limbs, the position was painful but at least a fatal fall was no longer imminent. Another shot. He hoped Trish killed them all, but he knew better.

She was willing to die to save the world.

Cutter had already made that sacrifice.

As much as Jonas Kane talked a good game, his comment that the world wasn't worth saving ended the negotiations. John's little girl was going to grow up in this world—messed up as it was—and what kind of world would it be if her dad let thousands die because the math denied his ability to stop it?

He glanced down—*never look down*—and saw three guys at the front of the crowded stage. They were each waving something over their heads. John shifted his eyes to the rooftop.

Jonas Kane stood at the wall, cellphone to his ear.

John began inching himself down the slope of the cable in the manner of a cocaine-fueled sloth, away from the building and toward the lighting array.

CHAPTER 111

THE PHONE VIBRATED IN HIS HAND only once before Slade answered the call. He pressed the phone tight against one ear while holding his other hand to his free ear to staunch the swell of cheering around him.

"Yes?" Slade spoke with the sharpness of a military commander. He was prepared for anything.

The voice on the other end was Christian Berry's—as Slade knew it would be—and he sounded angry. Furious. Downright pissed.

"Code red!" that pissed off voice said. "Light the fucking thing!"

"Yessir!" he shouted. He shoved the phone in his pocket and charged forward, elbowing people out of his way.

It had come down to him. Slade had known it would. And he would not disappoint Christian.

CHAPTER 112

JOHN REACHED THE END of the guy wire and gratefully clutched a handhold on the tower. His palms were raw from the braided steel of the cable, and the cool smoothness of the tower's piping was a relief. Traversing the guy wire had taken just under a minute. If the wire hadn't had a downhill slope from the building to the tower, John wasn't certain he could have completed the journey at all, much less in such a short span of time.

He lowered his feet to the security of footholds on the tower. It was a galvanized steel construction consisting of three vertical pipes creating a rising triangle intersected on all three sides with stabilizers in a z-pattern. Those braces provided structural integrity to the tower sections but also served as a ladder for anyone needing to climb it. Feet in place, John embraced the tower, pressing his cheek to the cool metal.

He looked back along the guy wire. It was empty. He had feared one of Kane's goons would follow him onto the cable and wondered if doing so would snap the line from its anchor and kill them both. Perhaps the goons had feared the same thing.

He looked to the roof. Kane was standing there, leaning over the railing and shouting something at him. It was lost in the wind and the cacophony of noise erupting from the crowds below. John had thought it was noisy on the roof, but the decibel level as he hovered directly above the stage was deafening.

He began to descend the tower. There was no time for further discussion with Kane. Trish had saved him—possibly sacrificing herself in doing so—with only one goal, to stop the slaughter from taking place. To stop the Reckoning.

John believed the Reckoning to be a product of a delusional, psychotic mind, but he had no doubt the murder of thousands was quite real and almost upon them.

For that, he had a plan.

He couldn't just interrupt the bonfire ceremony. Even if he reached the stage and grabbed a microphone and shouted that there was a bomb—and doing so would almost certainly result in the authorities putting a stop to the lighting of the bonfire—that still wouldn't change the fact that there was a gigantic stack of logs in the middle of this field, and based on the smell in the air, those logs were soaked through with jet fuel, aching to transform from potential energy to kinetic in an eruption of flame.

All it would take was a single match.

Even if John stopped the official ceremony, Slade was still out there. John had noticed his absence from the rooftop, and he suspected that meant Kane had stationed him on the bonfire field, a failsafe to make certain the bonfire would light no matter what. It was a smart move. It was what John would have done.

But he had a plan. One shot to stop it.

He just had to reach the bonfire before Slade.

CHAPTER 113

ERIC STOOD ON THE TRUCK'S TAILGATE and watched as the horde of Kane's followers emerged under the streetlights on the other side of the parking lot. When he saw them marching earlier, they had been in a loose formation approximating a two-by-two pattern. They had since bunched together as they grew closer to the school, perhaps each anxious to make the first righteous kill of an innocent child in the name of their demented master.

They reached the parking lot as a dense mass, a pulsing cloud of maniacs, and began making their way through the intermittent vehicles.

Fuck me, Eric thought. *That is a lot of axes.*

He looked down at his own weapon. The bare wooden handle inspired little confidence.

He couldn't take them all down. He knew that. But he hoped to buy time. Maybe reinforcements would arrive soon. He hoped Norah had called for back-up. Or he hoped that perhaps Cutter had reached the police before he—Eric swallowed—before he wasn't able to anymore.

He gripped the axe handle tighter.

That was a shitload of hope *and* maybe.

In the meantime, he was the first line of defense for the kids on the other side of the wall behind him. The gravity of the situation loomed over his thoughts. His pulse raced.

Standing in the bed of the pickup, Eric had the high ground. That would be helpful in a fight, but it wouldn't do anything to stop the mob from splitting up and sending plenty of axes to the school's front door and that vast line of floor-to-ceiling windows waiting to be shattered and walked through.

He would have to take the fight to them. Make the wide-open grassy lawn the focal point of attack, and hope they devoted their attention to him first before moving on to their main objective.

The zombie horde was at the edge of the parking lot, about to step onto the grass, this was it. Eric took a deep breath.

"Stop right there!" he yelled deep from his diaphragm in his most authoritative police voice. He held up one hand like a cop directing traffic.

To his great shock, the mob stopped. He saw the group exchange glances amongst themselves. They had marched from the Physical Sciences building to the axe shed and to the school without a soul interrupting their progress. Perhaps it was just the novelty of it that had halted them, but Eric would take what he could get.

"All right, listen up, people," he bellowed. "You will cease and desist this activity at once, or you will all be placed under arrest."

That lasted about a second. The front row of the horde shrugged and moved forward.

"Wait!" he shouted. "There's one more thing."

Again, the horde paused. Eric used the axe handle to point toward them, like a baseball player calling his shot. His heart was pounding hard enough he could feel it in his extremities.

"If we're going to do this," he yelled, "we're going to do it right. Hollywood style." He waved the axe handle from left to right, taking in the whole group. "I want you all to form a single-file line and attack one at a time, just like the movies. Come on, people, let's go!"

Without hesitation, the zombie horde charged in a massive wave.

"Shit, it was worth a try," Eric muttered.

He jumped from the tailgate of the truck onto the sidewalk that bisected the wide grassy lawn and raised the hickory axe handle like a samurai sword.

This was it.

CHAPTER 114

T HE BRIGHT SPOTS WERE FADING from her vision, but Trish was still lightheaded. The linebacker on her left had hit her across her face. Hard. The goon's hand was so big, it not only struck her cheek but managed to clap across her ear as well. The effect had been disorienting and excruciating. She may have even blacked out for a moment.

When she regained her senses, her whole body hurt. Well, maybe not her entire body, but lots of it. Her head pounded from Thing One's handiwork, and her left forearm ached thanks to Thing Two. He had knocked the gun from her hands with a hard, downward chop. She didn't think her arm was broken, but it was possible. Her ribs throbbed from when they tackled her following the initial strike, and her right breast flared with pain.

Had one of them hit her in the boob? Monsters. It hurt like crazy.

She now had a goon on either side, each holding one of her arms. She couldn't move. Her knees were weak, but the apes kept her upright.

"Bring her!"

That was the voice of Jonas Kane, scarecrow of evil.

Her over-muscled captors dragged her to the side of the roof. Would she see John? Dead on the stage below? Why had he done it?

When she arrived at the half-wall, Jonas put his hand to her face, cupping her chin, his thumb pressed into one cheek while his bony fingertips dug into the other.

"Keep your eyes open," he hissed. His breath was hot. Flecks of spittle landed on her forehead. "I want you to see this. *Nothing* you did matters."

He released his grip, and she lowered her chin. Scanning the stage below. No dead body. No John. She could see three guys at the front of the stage. They huddled together, shoulder to shoulder, holding long sticks.

Not sticks. Her mind returned to last year, watching the event with Stephanie. *Torches.* The crew leaders were lighting the torches.

On cue, she saw flames erupt from the enlarged heads of each torch.

This was it. They were about to march from the stage to the bonfire stack.

Movement caught her eye. She traced its source and spotted him. John was alive, climbing down the tower that rose from one side of the stage to support the crossbeam lighting array. He was almost to the ground.

The three crew leaders on stage raised their blazing torches above their heads, and the lights extinguished not only on the stage but all the floodlights surrounding the bonfire field as well.

Darkness descended, pierced only by the three burning torches.

The Reckoning was almost here.

CHAPTER 115

"**I** SAID GET OUT OF THE WAY!" Slade roared into the blackness. The instant the lights went off, his journey had grown both more challenging and more thrilling. It was difficult to see now, though the moon and ambient lighting from the buildings and streetlights outside the bonfire field perimeter provided slight illumination. Making his way through the cheering sheep had become a more hands-on operation. Rather than wedging himself between the excited fans, he decided power was better than stealth. Besides, he wasn't made for stealth. Leave that to the pansies. He was built to dominate.

He lowered his shoulder and charged ahead. He knocked people to the side. Red plastic cups of beer were lost. People shouted in anger. One lady fell forward, in front of him, rather than to the side. Slade felt no pity when he stepped on her spine between her shoulder blades as he ran. She would die soon anyway. They all would.

The other benefit of the darkness was the focus it provided. In his back pocket, he carried a lighter and a road flare. Two reliable ways to create fire. Two possibilities for when he reached the bonfire stack. But in the darkness, a third possibility presented itself. One far more magnificent.

He saw the three torches bobbing down the stage, starting their journey toward the bonfire. Three sets of flames danced, penetrating the night with their importance. Those guys would be walking down a precleared path through the crowd to reach the stack. In that moment, Slade knew what he must do. The torch would be his. The world would witness him light the bonfire—Christian would see him from the roof—

and know that Slade Stone had delivered unto him this night of power and glory.

He altered his trajectory to intersect the path of the torches and claim what was rightfully his.

CHAPTER 116

JOHN TOUCHED FOOT TO THE METAL PLATFORM of the stage just as the young men with the torches disappeared into the crowd toward the stack. From his excellent view while he descended the tower, John had noticed there was a precleared path for the torchbearers. Given the mass of people packed into the area between the stage and the bonfire stack, such a path would make life much easier for John—particularly given the relative darkness once the lights shut off—but John was headed a different direction.

He bolted from the stage and into the crowd of people. Squeezing between bodies and edging around clumps of people, muttering "pardon me" and "excuse me" the first several times before abandoning all vestiges of politeness and charging forward. He was rude. He was a bully. But if they knew, he was certain these people would rather spill their beer and stay alive than have their skin melted off their bodies.

At least his targeted destination was closer than the bonfire stack. Slade was out there. Possibly to the bonfire already. It wouldn't surprise him if Kane had given the order to light the bonfire early. No sense standing on ceremony when you intended to murder the audience.

John's heart was pounding. He had no idea how exerting it would be to run an obstacle course where all the obstacles were living beings who indignantly shouted "hey" and "watch it" in your wake. Then again, he'd had a long day with no food or water combined with a concussion, toilet shackling, jumping from buildings and climbing down towers. It was no wonder he couldn't catch his breath. But he was almost there. The bright yellow was easy to spot even in the darkness.

When he reached the fire truck, he didn't stop to ask for permission. The firefighters would likely be in the cab anyway. Airport fire trucks allowed control of the spray turrets from within the truck cabin, thus keeping the firefighters away from the scorching heat of a chemical fire erupting from an airplane's fuel tank. John had learned a lot watching the firetruck videos with DJ.

He located the ladder at the rear of the truck and scrambled to the roof. Once he reached the top, he paused to assess the situation. The three bobbing torches were almost to the stack. From the higher vantage of the truck's roof, he could see everything illuminated by the torches, including the giant human breaking through the edge of the crowd like a cobra emerging from its den.

Slade.

John couldn't see the entire encounter—the crowd blocked the lower portion, so he was watching heads and shoulders—but Slade levelled some kind of vicious attack on the lead torchbearer. The cacophonous cheers of the crowded thousands were distorted with shouts of anger and shock from the throngs closest to the torch path, the ones who had seen Slade's attack.

The wave of sound blended with the pounding of John's heart. He could feel it as well as hear it.

He saw a single torch race toward the bonfire stack, leaving the other two torches stationary, still on the path. *Slade had a torch.* He was steps away from the stack.

John raced to the front of the truck, to the primary turret with the massive deck gun. He prayed it was rigged for optional manual control and not solely guided by the firefighters in the cabin, and that he could figure it out in time. How hard could it be?

He scanned the rig. There was a functional platform below the turret. That was a good indicator that it was designed for someone to stand there. Huge nozzle on the gun. Twin vertical handles on the back. Large gray lever between the handles. And what looked like a locking mechanism on the base of the deck gun.

A lot more damn complicated than he had hoped.

He glanced up toward the bonfire stack. The torch was there, held aloft by Slade. He was standing right next to the base tier of upright logs. The area around the stack was clear of people. Spectators were kept far from the structure, partly for security and partly for the searing heat that would radiate immediately upon lighting.

John looked higher. The doghouse sat atop the stack. Symbolic home of the WSU Bulldogs, and when heated to critical temp, implement of death for everyone on the ground. Including John.

Slade touched the torch to the tower of logs. The instant contact was made, flames leaped from the torch and spread over the first log, then the logs to either side and the ones next to those. In the span of five seconds the entire bottom tier of logs was ablaze.

The mass of thousands roared their approval.

John watched in horror. The swell of cheers from the crowd was supplemented by the thumping in his ears from his pounding heart. The feeling was palpable.

The Reckoning was here.

CHAPTER 117

THE INSTANT ERIC JUMPED from the tailgate to the sidewalk, he was struck by his response to the situation. He had always considered himself cool under pressure. Now, with the pressure exceeding anything he had ever before experienced, his heart was pounding so hard he could feel it. It reverberated through his body.

Whump-whump-whump.

He knew this was the end. No time for self-reflection. No luxury for thoughts of roads not taken or what could have been. He was here, and he would protect the innocent until he could swing his bare axe handle no more.

The zombie horde charged, emerging from the parking lot onto the expanse of grass like army ants swarming an unfortunate mammal.

Eric bent his knees, ready to charge in return. He would hit them at the center, axe handle thrashing. He let out a battle cry he barely heard; his heartbeat had grown so deafening.

Whump-whump-whump.

That wasn't his heartbeat.

Just as the thought registered, the expanse of lawn between the charging mob and himself erupted in a thunderous explosion of dirt and grass. The zombie horde shrank back toward the parking lot, away from the shower of dirt and the roar of machine gun fire. An impossibly bright circle of light enveloped the group as the *whump-whump-whump* intensified and the helicopter settled into a hovering pattern just above the field.

A voice boomed over a loudspeaker secured to the bottom of the copter, overcoming even the thunder of the rotating blades.

"This is Lieutenant General Bobcat Butler of the United States Army. Drop your weapons and lie down on the ground," the voice commanded. "Now."

Eric watched as forty axes fell to the grass or clattered to the parking lot pavement. The true believers were lowering themselves onto their hands and knees, ready to embrace the earth below them. As strong as Jonas Kane's hold on these people may have been, the visceral shock of the military chopper's devastating display of firepower had broken through it.

As the helicopter decreased altitude, a smaller spotlight encircled Eric. He dropped his axe handle and held one hand in front of his face, shielding his eyes from the blazing light. The pulse of the rotating blades pumped through him as the driving wind from the turbines made him bend his knees and hunch his shoulders to maintain his balance.

"Now that's what I call reinforcements," he said aloud to himself. The scene was too noisy anyway. No one else could hear him. Except maybe one. "Thank you, cowboy."

The chopper settled onto the grass next to the irregular line of chewed up dirt where the machine gun had performed its handiwork. Eric saw half a dozen armed soldiers deploy from the interior, M4 Carbines held at the ready, moving into cover formation around the prostrate zombie horde.

Eric raised both hands, palms up, as he approached the chopper. He needed to talk to the general right away. Afterwards, he'd give him a hug.

CHAPTER 118

FLAMES ENGULFED THE SECOND TIER of the bonfire stack. The base of the structure was already blazing. Fire crawled upward toward the third tier and the doghouse above. The crowds closest to the structure were awash in orange light.

Time was up.

Atop the firetruck, John felt around the locking mechanism of the turret's base. It was already pointed the general direction of the bonfire, but he'd need control. He couldn't spare a moment knocking on the window of the firetruck cab and explaining to the nice firefighters why they needed to douse the bonfire that twenty thousand people had come here to see. By the time he got five sentences into the tale, they'd all be dead.

He discovered what felt like a latch and tugged it. Once, twice, harder, and it gave, unsnapping from its home position. The nozzle of the deck gun swung to the right. It was free.

John straightened and looked toward the bonfire. Slade was still standing in front of it, a black silhouette against the yellow flames, oblivious to the heat, his arms raised in triumph.

He wanted to turn the other way, scan the roof line of the Physical Sciences building. He was certain he would see Jonas Kane, watching his planned slaughter from the safety of his own private viewing area, but would he see Trish? Was she still alive?

No time to look.

He stood at the rear of the deck gun, grabbed both handles and swiveled the long nozzle in the direction of the bonfire's base. Should he start low and work higher or start high and work lower? How do you douse a jet-fuel-enhanced bonfire three stories tall? The videos he watched with DJ never covered that.

First things first, how to turn this thing on?

The gray lever between the handles looked promising, but when John pulled on it, nothing happened. He tried again, harder. Nothing.

It wouldn't budge.

CHAPTER 119

THE BONFIRE WAS ABLAZE. Jonas Kane felt metaphorically ablaze himself. Sensations of excitement, relief, anticipation and sweet vengeance coursed through him.

As the flames grew, rising from the lowest tier of the structure, crawling their way upward, his sense of destiny overshadowed all else.

The Reckoning was at hand.

He pulled Trish tight against him, wrapping one long arm around her neck in a makeshift headlock while ensuring she could still see, for there was so much to see.

"Behold," he whispered, "for all your struggles, for all your sacrifices, destiny sides with me."

She no longer fought him. She, too, was enrapt to the scene playing out on the field below. Something about fire has always attracted the attention of man. What must it have been like for the Neanderthal who saw lighting strike a tree, to watch with awe and wonder as the mystery of the orange flame devoured it? Fascination with fire was primal. It was beautiful. And dangerous.

In moments, the heat would intensify and rise to the doghouse. The chemical agent would ignite and deploy from the housing unit. They would then witness the real show. The real fire.

All the rites will have been completed. For him. For the Reckoning.

"Away from me," he commanded his remaining two Elite Guards.

They stepped back with what looked like a sense of relief. They had no idea what was coming. They just knew it would be powerful. Giving their master space was a wise decision.

Keeping Trish close to him was a choice of his own which Kane relished. She had been an irritant for far too long, had come so near to disrupting his plans this very evening. He wanted her close at hand when he was bestowed his new power.

He had plans for the girl that would chill her despite the rain of fire that would wash over the field below at any moment.

CHAPTER 120

JOHN LOOKED UP from the nonresponsive controls of the firetruck's upper turret. The top tier of the bonfire was burning. Flames licked the base of the doghouse. He could feel the heat from the blaze on his face.

He studied the gray lever between the handles—the one that had refused to budge—then glanced at a small adjacent panel. There was a freaking key inserted into a slot. John grabbed the base of the key and turned it. It clicked at a quarter-turn, and a green light popped on. He tried the gray lever again, as it lifted, an unsteady drizzle of white foam seeped from the end of the nozzle.

John aimed the deck gun and lifted the handle the rest of the way. The stabilizers and solvents of the fire-retardant foam mixed with the water in the truck's interior tank, then blasted from the nozzle with the force of a battering ram.

He aimed high, targeting the top tier. The water-and-foam mixture hit the structure with enough power to dislodge the exterior grouping of stacked vertical logs.

The crowd around the bonfire went silent.

John lowered the trajectory of the deck gun, maintaining max pressure. Foam against jet fuel. Thousands of lives at stake.

A voice from below him.

"Hey! What are you doing up there?"

He could ignore that.

As the jet of foam lowered, John saw Slade drop his arms, torch still in hand, looking first up at the white foam cascading over the fire and then shifting his gaze to the firetruck and the man responsible.

John held the handles of the turret like he was aiming a gatling gun and aligned the nozzle's trajectory with the base tier of the bonfire.

The blast of foam and water struck Slade in the chest, lifting him off his feet and slamming him back into the blazing structure. The beast's body was lost in the chaos of foam, fire and collapsing logs. John felt no pity. Not this time.

He continued shooting the foaming agent on the bonfire. The flames grew lower, diminishing at first, then extinguishing altogether as the white film coated the structure and the fire could find no suitable source of fuel.

The doghouse remained at the top of the center-pole, inert, perched above the thousands it was meant to destroy.

CHAPTER 121

"**N**O! IT'S NOT POSSIBLE!"

Kane's mouth was so close against the side of Trish's face, his scream almost burst her eardrum. The long arm around her neck tightened its hold, surprising strength in the ropy sinew beneath the fabric of his shirt.

Trish clutched at his forearm. The bonfire was out. John had done it. They had done it together. But alone on the rooftop with Kane and his two remaining goons, Trish knew her situation was beyond dire.

"This was you!" Kane hissed. "You're going to pay for this, you fucking whore!"

He was choking her. To death.

Her mind clutched at what to do. How to escape. To survive.

Eric's lessons.

There was no talking her way out. No exit. No weapon. And eyes-throat-groin only worked if she could reach them, and Kane was directly behind her, out of reach.

She bent hard at the waist, trying to buck him, and succeeded in smacking her forehead on the rooftop's half-wall railing. Her head already hurt. Much, much worse now.

And Kane hadn't loosened his grip.

She jerked herself from side to side, shifting her body weight each direction. He rotated his long torso to match her movements and tightened his chokehold.

A glint caught her eye. The hard swaying had caused her necklace to swing back and forth. The gold cross had arced in front of her face and snared the light for a fraction of a second.

She was starting to black out. Her lungs burned from lack of oxygen. In the growing darkness, a thought of Cutter pushed its way to the front of her mind. What had he said to her in the basement, right before he ripped the handcuffs from his bloody hands?

"*That cross around your neck,*" came the old cowboy's drawl, clear as a bell in her mind, "*it can save your life. And much more.*"

She groped her hands in front of her, first fumbling then finding the necklace and sliding her hand to its end, where the chain passed through a small loop at the top of the cross. She grabbed the cross, pinching the top section tight between thumb and forefinger, the sides of the cross extending over those digits like the hilt of the world's smallest sword.

With her last remaining strength, she bent her knees, dropping her weight like a stone. Kane stooped forward to maintain his chokehold. Trish planted her feet and drove her body straight up with all the force she could muster.

Kane's grip loosened at the reverse of momentum. His head was level with hers. It was just enough.

She jammed her thumb over her opposite shoulder, aiming for Kane's eye. The thumb found its mark, with the protruding two inches of the gold cross preceding it. When the cross stabbed into the orb, she felt a pop and liquid inside burst forth, spurting onto the back of her hand as the eye deflated within the socket like an exploded water balloon.

Kane screamed in pain and released his grip. He pressed a palm to the vacant space where his eye used to be.

Trish released her grip on the slimed cross and gulped air, oxygen rushing into her lungs, clearing her head. She saw the two goons advancing, perhaps slow on the uptake in understanding what had just happened to their boss but moving now.

Kane's cry of pain morphed into one of rage, and he leaned into her. This time, she was ready, again bending her knees, ducking low, letting Kane's momentum carry him forward. Trish grabbed at his legs behind his bony knees, put her shoulder into his groin and heaved up and back with all her might. It was the only defense she could muster.

If Kane had had both hands in front of him, it never would have worked. He could have stopped it. But with one hand pressed to his eye socket, he wasn't in position to brace himself at the railing, so he flipped over the side, free hand reaching back toward the building for purchase, finding none.

And then he was gone.

She spun, not watching him fall, aware that two more threats to her life were advancing upon her, but the two goons had stopped, dumbfounded expressions on their faces.

Despite the hush of the assembled crowd given the dousing of the bonfire, Trish didn't hear Kane's body strike the stage below, but she did hear a lone scream ring out, followed by another. Those were the shrieks of people who'd just witnessed a body splatter on a steel platform.

The shouting snapped the goons from their shock. For a moment, Trish hoped they would come to their senses, like servant vampires transformed back to normal when Dracula is stabbed with a wooden stake and disintegrates to ash. That didn't happen. Based on the shift in facial expression, they appeared ready to respond to the death of Jonas Kane with their most accessible emotion—rage.

Trish took a step back but bumped into the half-wall railing. There was no escape. She balled her fists and held them in front of her.

The beasts charged.

She expected to get one good hit in. A solid punch. That didn't happen. Thing One went low, punching her in the stomach with a quicker strike than she could even hope to block, and Thing Two repeated the same downward chop that almost broke her arm when he had earlier knocked the gun from her hand. This time, Thing Two directed the chop at her neck.

It was good fortune that Thing One landed the gut-punch first. When his fist went into her stomach, she bent forward, causing Thing Two's chop to strike her in the middle of the back, knocking her flat to the surface of the roof, but not snapping her neck like the originally targeted blow surely intended.

She managed to extend her hands when she fell. The grit of the rooftop bit into her palms, a feeling with which she became even greater acquainted when her momentum carried her face into the roof thereafter. Bits of white gravel dug into her lips. She smelled tar and tasted blood.

Her side exploded in pain as an oversized foot kicked her ribcage. That was a dick move. Probably the same goon that had hit her in the boob.

She couldn't get her breath. She was lying on one arm. It was useless. She swiped her other arm out, flailing. She may have scratched a leg. That should do it.

She was going to die. They would most likely pick her up and dump over the side. She'd land next to Jonas Kane and die looking at his corpse.

Another kick to her side. She thought she felt a rib crack. The pain was so intense her vision went white. Or maybe it was a hallucination. Pre-death delirium. It was snowing. A blizzard.

The goons were gone. She lifted her head from the surface of the roof, one cheek embedded with white flecks of grit. The goons were ten feet away. In a snowbank. She could only see their shoes sticking out. And more snow was landing on them. It wasn't falling from the sky. It was blowing in from the side.

The snow was wet. And foamy. It smelled like cleaning solution—the cheap industrial stuff used by the custodial staff in her dorm. Stephanie used to tell Trish that she liked the smell.

Maybe she was right. It wasn't bad.

The snow foam stopped streaming in from the side of the roof and started blowing every which way. Trish shielded her eyes as the foam covered her shirt, soaked her hair and invaded her mouth.

And what was that noise? Her head was pounding. No, not her head, her ears. She looked up to the source. It took a moment for her foggy mind to process the cause of the wind blowing the foam everywhere, but that was a helicopter hovering over the building.

Weird, she thought.

CHAPTER 122

THOUGH THE BONFIRE FIELD remained in relative darkness, the lights beaming from the Bell Venom helicopter onto the rooftop were stark. The attention of everyone on the ground had shifted from the extinguished bonfire to the action above the Physical Sciences building.

John wondered how many of them had seen Jonas Kane plummet the four stories to his death. Almost all of them had seen John direct the firetruck's deck gun at the rooftop. In fact, the crowd in front of the stage had been soaked in the foam. Oops. It couldn't be helped.

John was shocked by the power of the turret, the force of pressure necessary to achieve the distance to the rooftop. If the truck had been parked on the other side of the bonfire stack rather than near the stage, the jetting foam would never have reached that distance. In fact, if it had been parked anywhere else, John wouldn't have made it to the vehicle in time. Everyone would be dead. But they weren't. They were just confused and some of them were shaking white foam off their clothing and out of their hair. Not the evening they had planned.

John watched as three lines dropped from the military chopper to the roof and the dark shape of a soldier slid down each one. John assumed the foam hadn't killed anyone up there, but even if the goon squad lived, the soldiers would ensure Trish's safety.

She was going to be okay.

"Sir, get off the vehicle now!"

People had been yelling at him ever since he soaked the bonfire—most vocally the firefighters who had scrambled from the cab—but this voice was much closer. He turned and saw a police officer standing a few feet away on the roof of the firetruck. The officer extended his left hand in front of him, like he was attempting to calm a dangerous animal. His weapon remained in its holster, but the fingers of his right hand were wrapped around it, prepared to draw the firearm if necessary.

John raised his hands, palms up.

"I surrender," he said.

Then he started laughing. The police officer looked at him with a mixture of confusion and suspicion. That made John laugh even harder.

He couldn't help it.

EPILOGUE

JOHN DROPPED HIS PLASTIC FORK amidst the scattered remnants of brisket and potato salad on the butcher paper. The outdoor dining area of The Lone Star Pit was mostly unfilled. It was late for lunch, but that had worked out, what they considered to be 'their table' in the back corner of the grassy yard had been open, and they were able to speak with some privacy.

Three of the four seats were occupied, yet their table still felt empty. The vacant fourth chair pained John, and he knew Trish and Eric felt the same. It colored their conversation. Grief of loss blended with relief that the ordeal had ended. Sadness offset by laughter. Life.

He looked across the table to see Eric spear a piece of sausage, then turkey, then brisket onto the same fork. He rolled the contents in a puddle of barbecue sauce on his tray, then pushed the fork into his mouth.

"You know," he said between chews, cheeks full of meat, "I am going to miss the food. Best thing about Texas."

"It grows on you," Trish said with a smile, the bruises on her face noticeable despite her attempt to conceal them with makeup. Her meal was already finished; the tray taken away by a friendly server.

They were at ease, and it made John feel better. He had hoped that the outcome of ending the nightmare of the Kane family would feel like basking in warm sunlight after surviving a horrific storm. Instead, he felt anxious. The lightning and thunder may have passed, but gray clouds loomed, refusing to budge. He knew it was because he hadn't yet fully emerged from his own storm.

The three of them had spent the past two days answering questions. The Abramsville police department. The FBI. Even a private visit for John with Lieutenant General Butler. Bobcat had wanted answers, and John told him everything. He owed him that much and far more.

It had been a grueling time, but the toughest aspects were not yet over. There was still the funeral. And what needed to happen before.

Beyond any of that, John knew he wouldn't feel better until he could be home again, until he could embrace Sarah and DJ. They had spoken several times on the phone, but it wasn't the same. He had wanted to keep them far away from the messy aftermath in Abramsville, but he longed to hold them close.

"I'd still like to know what was in that vault beneath the church," John muttered. "They wouldn't tell you anything?"

Eric sipped his Coke through a straw. "I think the Abramsville PD would have told me, but they never had a chance to look. The FBI swooped in hard. They handled searching the church and the other buildings. When I asked the special agent in charge about the contents of the vault, all he told me was that it was being overseen by top men."

"Who?" John emphasized.

"I asked that same question," Eric grinned. "The guy just repeated himself. Told me '*top men*' again like that answered anything." He shrugged. "Feds."

John sighed.

Eric looked at his watch. "I've gotta go soon."

"Us, too," John agreed. He had already thanked Eric a hundred times but did so again anyway. "Thank you."

"Hey, you bought lunch," Eric replied. "But speaking of that," he began, a pensive look on his face, "if you want to do something for me, you could clear up a little mystery that's been bugging me."

John raised his eyebrows. "Go on."

A half-grin from Eric. "It's nothing really. None of my business, but it's a loose thread in my brain, and I hate those threads. They stick in there like a song you can't get rid of."

John had no idea where this was going.

"You've been in witness protection a long time, since the thing in New Mexico. The other day you offered to hire me for triple my salary. It was in the heat of the moment, granted, but I think you were serious." He paused and leaned over the table toward John. "A man in WITSEC doesn't have access to funds like that. So...what's up?"

Now it made sense. Eric was asking the question that Cutter had chosen to ignore.

"Before I respond, I need to know who's asking," John said. "My friend or a detective with the NYPD?"

A broad smile spread on Eric's face, and John had to admit it was a damn charming one.

"Your friend who happens to know a lot about police-type stuff and wants to make certain you're not doing something inadvisable."

"Fair enough," John replied. It *was* fair. And he did trust Eric. The man had earned it. "Sarah and I left the witness protection program years ago—with Cutter's help—and we've been on our own since then. It's allowed me a little more freedom."

"Freedom to do what?"

"To make money. I needed it to protect my family and ensure we could stay off the grid. What do you know about the stock market?"

"I know my 401k sucks."

John laughed. "Here's the nutshell version that will answer your question. Lay people think the stock market is controlled by investor sentiment. People like the stock of a particular company, it goes up. People don't like a stock, it goes down. That's incorrect. The people in the stock market are insignificant. They don't carry enough weight. A million investors can decide to buy or sell a stock, who cares? Millions of kids play little league. None of them can hit a homerun off a curveball in Fenway. You want to find that, you look for the point-oh-one-percent who have made it to the big leagues."

"Not following," Eric interjected.

"*Volume* drives the market. Who controls the volume? Hedge funds and certain foreign governments through their nationalized banking reserves. I've ignored the foreign governments for now. Too complicated. But the hedge funds are much easier."

"Easier for what?"

"Hedge funds control trillions of dollars as a group, and the top handful of funds represent a big portion of that. Most of the buying and selling of those funds is dictated by complex formulas and algorithms, but it's the fund manager's responsibility to provide direction on the shape of those algorithms."

"This is the nutshell version?"

"Sorry." John caught himself and took a breath. "When it comes down to it, I employ a number of informers—not insiders, these are mostly private detectives—whose job is to monitor the life activities of the heads of select hedge funds. My informants don't know each other, and they don't even know why they do what they do. They're paid to regularly report their mundane information to various online personas that could never be identified as me. That data helps me profile the fund managers and divine an informed opinion on the position their funds might take in the market."

He paused before relaying the last part. Though John trusted Eric, openness didn't exactly come easy. But he was trying to grow.

"Of course, I can't act on this information in a meaningful way as an individual, even through the use of created aliases—the IRS does have their moments—so I employ a number of somewhat fictional offshore corporate entities to manage the transactions in volume."

Eric looked at him with a blank expression.

"And that's not legal," John finished.

Eric nodded slowly. "So what I just heard was: 'I pay people to spy on rich dudes, blah-blah-blah, I make a lot of money off it, blah-blah-blah, no one gets hurt.' Does that about sum it up?"

"In a nutshell," John said.

"Fine by me."

"Did I just create an ethical dilemma for you?"

"Not as long as you keep paying for lunch," Eric responded with that half-grin.

◇ ◇ ◇

The man in front of Eric walked ahead when the lady at the station waved to him. Eric gripped his bag while he waited his turn. Airport security lines were the best.

It would be good to return to New York, but something weighed on Eric's mind. A major life decision that he was making while waiting in a queue of stressed-out airline passengers.

The man at the station cleared protocol and moved on to the baggage x-ray machine. The female agent beckoned Eric. She was smiling. She had smiled for everyone in line. Must be exhausting. Eric smiled back at her while offering his plane ticket and open leather bifold with his driver's license.

The agent scanned his ticket and looked from Eric's ID to his face and back again. She rubbed a thumb against the badge opposite his license in the bifold, as if to test for authenticity.

"You're a police officer?"

"NYPD," Eric replied. "But I'm retiring."

"Wow. You're young. Wish I could do that."

"Another adventure awaits."

She handed him back the ticket and bifold.

"Good luck. Have a nice flight."

He thanked her and moved on to the next stage of security.

That was it then. He had said it out loud. He set his bag on the roller belt and pushed it along as he progressed through the line one shuffling step at a time.

The past few days had been eye-opening, and not just because he had almost died. He had spent his life believing his destiny was to be a cop, but now, he no longer felt that was the case. In all the insanity that had just gone down, his badge hadn't made a difference. If anything, it had been an impediment. His brain had made a difference. And his guts.

And a whole lotta luck. Can't discount that.

What could he do if he wasn't held back by the restraints of being a formal member of law enforcement? What could he accomplish on his own? How much good could be done? Especially if he was backed by the right resources?

He slid his bag into the x-ray tunnel and prepared to step through the machine that would assure the agents he was unarmed and worthy to board his flight.

He grinned. Just like that, waiting in security, he had made up his mind. He was going to do it. When he got back to New York, he was going to drive upstate to Armstrong Island and take his best friend up on his offer. He was going to start his own agency.

Of course, in addition to being ludicrous rich, Dr. Grant Armstrong was also smart. Too smart for his own good. He'd probably want to involve himself in whatever cases Eric took on.

Eric shook his head at the thought. What a nightmare that idea was. Terrifying and fun.

"Adventure awaits," he repeated to himself and stepped forward with a smile.

◇ ◇ ◇

Trish swallowed hard as John turned off the dirt road at the bright red mailbox. He eased the sedan down the long driveway. Their windows were down. She heard gravel crunch under the tires. Clusters of oak trees surrounded them. She saw cows in a field on the other side of a barbed wire fence. They'd seen lots of cows on the drive up.

"You're not going to come inside?" she asked.

John shook his head. "Not now. It's best if I don't, not unless she invites me."

"And you're not going to attend the funeral tomorrow either?"

"Nope," he stated. "Probably better that I'm not there. I'll pay my respects another way. For what it's worth, I'm not abandoning you. I've arranged a rental car to be waiting at that little hotel we passed on the way in. It's yours for however long you need it. You can take it back to Abramsville, return it there. As for me, I'll leave the hotel at first light tomorrow morning. I'm anxious to get home."

Trish nodded. She knew that was true. She could hear it in his voice. Home meant more than a house.

"John, look at me." He did. He was driving slow enough that it wasn't a risk. "You know it wasn't your fault, right?"

"I know, but in the end, that doesn't change anything for her, does it?"

Trish's eyes followed the tilt of his head and saw the house—Cutter's house—and a woman that must be his wife standing on the front porch.

His widow.

"I guess not," she said.

The car stopped a decent distance from the house.

"I'll wait here," he told her. "Take your time. All you need."

Trish drew a deep breath and opened the passenger door. She walked across the packed dirt interspersed with gravel patches as she made her way to the front porch. The woman wiped her hands on the apron she wore and came down the steps to meet her.

◇ ◇ ◇

Maggie Valentine stepped away from the porch, wiping vestiges of flour and dough from her fingers onto the apron. The girl approaching her wore a simple dress. Her hair fell on her shoulders and captured the late day sun, vibrant auburn against the dark green fabric.

This would be Trish O'Brien.

The screen door behind Maggie creaked open, and Walker bolted out. The dog covered the porch steps in a single bound and raced past both women, heading toward the vehicle parked in the driveway. Maggie watched as John opened the driver's door. He remained seated but turned so his legs hung out of the car. Walker wedged into the opening, put his front paws in John's lap and accepted some ear ruffling.

A faint smile brightened Maggie's lined face. It was the first time she'd seen much life out of Walker the past few days. The dog had known. He'd somehow sensed it.

Maggie had been angry with John—still was, truth be told—but that was just her taking the easy bypass route, so she didn't have to meet the grief head-on. Fact was, John had been right. That man down there had indeed been Jonas Kane. And if John hadn't gone to

Abramsville—and if her Earl hadn't gone with him—a great many people would have died.

And after it was over, John had been the one to make the call. He had told Maggie what happened. The next day, they had had another call, much longer, when her mind had calmed enough to crave further explanation. She had said some awful things to John in both those conversations, but he had held on. That act had been worth something. Yes, the man in that car scratching Walker's neck was worth something.

But sweet mercy, Earl Valentine had been worth so very much to her.

"You must be Maggie," the girl in front of her offered, tentative smile on her bruised face. Bless her heart, she was young and uncomfortable, but here she was anyway. That was worth something, too.

"And you must be Trish," she replied. "Earl told me about you. We spoke every day he was gone; you know. He said nice things about you."

A blush crept into Trish's cheeks, her freckled skin almost mirroring her hair.

Earl had indeed said nice things about Trish. He had been taken with her, and Maggie thought she knew why. Just like Walker had sensed his master's fate from two hundred miles away, maybe Earl had a premonition of what was to come. Somewhere deep down, maybe he had known. And he had gone anyway. To right a wrong.

He had devoted his life to trying to help others, and despite countless successes, he had spent the past few years haunted by the one he had lost, the girl he couldn't save. He had feigned healing after returning from New Mexico, but a wife knows. It had never left him.

Tears threatened Maggie's eyes. Earl would never have to worry about it again. He had found peace.

"I'm sorry," the girl said. "Are you okay?"

"It's just—" Maggie's voice broke. She swallowed and took a breath. She held out her hands, and the girl clasped them in her own. "You're the one. After all this time, he finally saved you."

The girl had been on the verge of crying herself. With Maggie's statement, tears spilled from Trish's eyes. "In every way possible," she choked out as a large tear rolled down her cheek and fell to her dress, turning the green fabric even darker where it landed, right next to a gold cross she wore on a chain. The cross caught the evening sun and sparkled. It was pretty. The girl was pretty.

Maggie was glad she was here.

"Well, that's quite enough blubbering from us," she stated. "There's work to be done. Lots of people will be coming after the service tomorrow. My son is here. He's been helping out in the kitchen, but Robert's as bad as his father, sampling more than baking." She raised an eyebrow at the girl. "Have you ever made teacakes?"

Trish wiped her eyes with the sleeve of her dress. "No, ma'am, but I'd love to learn."

"Then come on in," Maggie paused before adding, "they were Earl's favorite."

She watched as Trish glanced back over her shoulder, toward the car in the driveway.

"John can join us in a bit," Maggie assured her. "Let him visit with Walker for a spell. It'll do them both good."

The girl nodded. She walked past Maggie, climbed the steps of the porch and waited at the front door. Maggie squinted at the late day sun. It would only be bright for a few more minutes before it would redden and sink to the horizon. Then it would rise again tomorrow.

She climbed the steps and escorted Trish into the house.

◇ ◇ ◇

John switched on his turn signal and prepared to enter his neighborhood. There were no other vehicles on the road. The signal was unnecessary. Just habit. Playing it safe.

As he turned the wheel and his sedan rolled onto the nondescript street in this nondescript part of the nondescript suburban town in Oklahoma, he thought about the cameras that were recording his entry. Secret cameras that no one else knew about except him and the security team who'd placed them—and they'd been paid to forget. The images would feed into the monitoring system's hub in John's study in the ugly house his family had called home the past few months.

Not just playing it safe, John thought. It went well beyond safe. Every move he'd made the past four years had been focused on security and invisibility, keeping his family from harm's way, from the risk of notice by the unseen boogeyman.

That threat was extinguished now.

What to do going forward?

As he drove past the homes of his neighbors—the staggered architectural relics of the 1970s and 80s that housed nice families who had never even met Sarah or John thanks to his insistence on playing it safe—he realized that the world was quite different today compared to when he last left this neighborhood.

When questioned by the FBI, he had provided them both his true identity and his current alias. They could contact him if necessary, and the agent to whom he had been speaking said that would almost assuredly be the case.

He had not shared with them any of his business operations. Eric knowing was fine. Trish, too. But no government hack needed to be privy to that sort of information. It wouldn't be pertinent to the case they were working anyway. When asked to fill in that particular blank, John informed them he was an accountant who had kept a low profile for obvious reasons. They accepted it at face value. He didn't think anyone would ever dig deeper.

And if they did? What then?

And if they didn't, what did the future look like anyway?

He really could settle down. Now that the Kane family no longer loomed over their lives, there was no harm in returning to the last name of Michaels. They could move back to Boston if they wanted. He could hang up a shingle and start his own consulting company. He and Sarah could reenter society. They could place DJ into a nice private school when she was old enough.

Then again, there was a certain freedom to living outside of society, particularly when you weren't worried about a madman recognizing your face if you happened to be in the wrong place at the wrong time. There was no wrong place now. They could travel. See the world. They had a healthy source of income. And John already had safe, clean identities for the whole family, ready to be assumed at a moment's notice.

After all, you never knew what the future held.

He angled into the driveway. He normally would have pulled into the garage and let the door close behind him before getting out of the vehicle, but that was then. Today he left the sedan in the driveway.

He stepped out of the car and stretched. It had been a long drive. Before he could take a step toward the house, the front door banged open and a little body dressed in yellow firefighter pajamas paired with green sneakers and a pink ballerina tutu came charging at him.

He dropped to one knee and opened his arms wide.

"Dad-deeeeeee!" DJ squealed as she plowed into his chest. He wrapped his arms around her and held her tight.

"Hey, baby girl," he whispered.

"I'm not a baby," she protested.

"My mistake, pumpkin." He held her at arms-length. "Definitely a mistake. In fact, you've grown. When did you get so big?"

"Yesterday."

John laughed and pulled her into his chest again. He looked up to see Sarah jogging from the front door in her yoga pants and t-shirt. It wasn't easy keeping up with a two-year-old tornado.

He stood, DJ still in his arms, and Sarah embraced them both.

"DJ-sam'wich!" his daughter cried from between them. Her hair smelled of baby shampoo. It was the best thing in the whole world.

"I'm glad you're home," Sarah said. She was crying. Just a little.

"So am I," he told her and kissed her over the top of DJ's head. He may have been crying just a little, too. He wanted to cling to the moment forever.

But that's not how life works.

He ended the kiss and said, "I have an idea. It was a long drive, and I need to stretch my legs. What if we walked to the park?"

"Really?" DJ asked.

Sarah looked skeptical. "You mean, walk, out in the open, exposed, walking together, like normal people?"

John smiled. "Yep."

"I think I like the sound of that." She kissed him once more.

He spun DJ so she was facing away from him, then lifted her up and over his head, settling her onto his shoulders as she issued a delighted "yay!" The ruffles of the tutu scratched against his ears.

No, you never can know what the future might hold, John mused to himself. *All that matters is how you live today. And who you live it with.*

He held DJ's feet and extended one elbow toward his wife. Sarah threaded her arm through it, and they set off for the park. Walking. Out in the open. Exposed. Enjoying the morning sun.

THE BOOK THAT STARTED IT ALL...

BOOK TWO OF THE THRILLOGY...

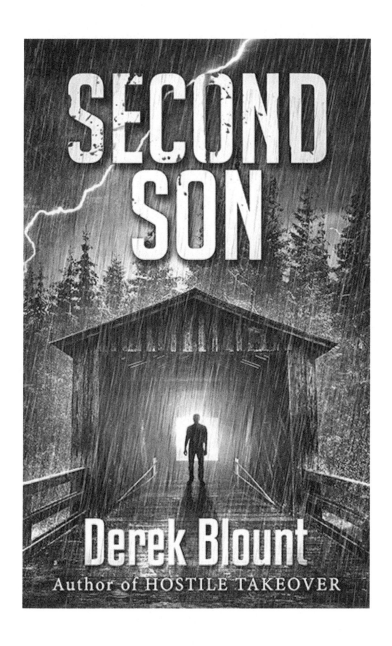

SECOND SON

Derek Blount

Author of HOSTILE TAKEOVER

ALSO AVAILABLE FROM DEREK BLOUNT

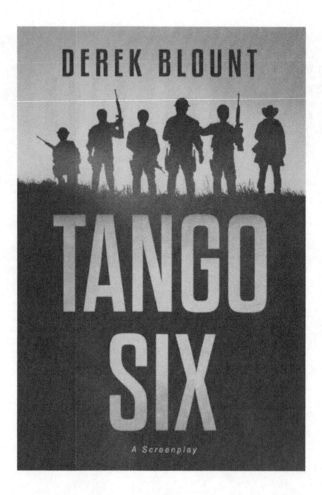

An advancing war.
          An impossible rescue mission.
                    One chance to save the world.

Brimming with unforgettable characters and imbued with the same brand of adventurous fun as the Indiana Jones film series, *Tango Six* will rivet you with suspense, laughter and fist-pumping action.

A Note from Derek Blount

Thank you for reading *Final Reckoning*. If you haven't yet read the first two books of the thrillogy – *Hostile Takeover* and *Second Son* – well, you're tackling them out of order. But that's okay. I think you'll still enjoy the first two novels. Please give them a try.

Also, please join our email list at *derekblount.com* for notifications about future work The Hostile Takeover Thrillogy may be complete, but there are other stories yet to tell.

Please note that *Final Reckoning* is a work of fiction. Texas State College and the town of Abramsville do not exist outside of our collective imaginations. They are fictional amalgamations of aspects of various towns and universities in the South.

One of those prominent southern institutions of higher learning is Texas A&M University, home to a storied tradition known as the Fightin' Texas Aggie Bonfire. What began with the burning of a scrap heap in 1907 eventually became an annual event attracting up to 70,000 attendees to watch the student-constructed tower of logs light the night sky.

On November 18, 1999, the Aggie Bonfire stack collapsed while in the final stages of construction. The collapse claimed the lives of 12 Aggies and injured 27 others. My heart aches for the loss of those lives and the impact on Aggieland. Please know the bonfire portrayed in *Final Reckoning* is not meant to be a representation of the Aggie Bonfire, and no disrespect is intended toward those affected by the 1999 tragedy.

Thank you for indulging that sad note.

In other "thank you" news...

Thank you to my wife, Bethany, who is not only an amazing wife, partner and forever best friend, but who is also a talented editor. She gets first crack at anything I write, and her red pen is smart, judicious and patient (knowing the writer is going to argue a case against each loving correction). I love you.

Thank you to my boys for helping me see the wonder in this world through your eyes. And thank you for having faith that your dad is the best writer in the world, even though you're both too young to have actually read any of these thrillers. Give it time. No need to grow up too quickly.

Thank you to my parents, whose examples taught me to be a husband, a dad and a man. When I was young, you told me I could achieve anything to which I set my mind. Still putting that to the test, but I'm pretty pleased with having a thriller trilogy under the ol' belt. Thank you for believing.

Thank you also to my in-laws for being lovingly supportive of the hopelessly optimistic writer with whom your daughter chose to make a life.

Thank you to my sister, Jessica, who has no idea how much she influenced me over the years.

Thank you to the Lord above for blessing me with so many extraordinary people in my life. And for all those special people...Ephesians 3:14-21.

Thank YOU, dear reader, for investing your time with me. I hope our journeys together are always worth your while. May there be many more.

Made in the USA
Coppell, TX
06 December 2020